SPARKS OF
BRIGHT MATTER

Leeanne O'Donnell started her storytelling career working in radio with RTE and BBC, and has made a number of award-winning radio documentaries. *Sparks of Bright Matter* is her first novel, which she wrote from her home on the foothills of a mountain in the remote south-west of Ireland.

SPARKS OF BRIGHT MATTER

LEEANNE O'DONNELL

eriu

First published by Eriu
An imprint of Black & White Publishing Group
A Bonnier Books UK company

4th Floor, Victoria House,
Bloomsbury Square,
London, WC1B 4DA

Owned by Bonnier Books
Sveavägen 56, Stockholm, Sweden

 @eriu_books

@eriubooks

Hardback – 978-1-80418-412-7
Trade Paperback – 978-1-80418-507-0
Ebook – 978-1-80418-583-4

A CIP catalogue of this book is available from the British Library.

Typeset by IDSUK (Data Connection) Ltd
Printed and bound by Clays Ltd, Elcograf S.p.A.

1 3 5 7 9 10 8 6 4 2

Every reasonable effort has been made to trace copyright holders of material reproduced in this book, but if any have been inadvertently overlooked the publishers would be glad to hear from them.

Eriu is an imprint of Bonnier Books UK
www.bonnierbooks.co.uk

For my parents Liam and Frances, without whom I would never have become a writer, and for Iseult without whom I would never have written this book

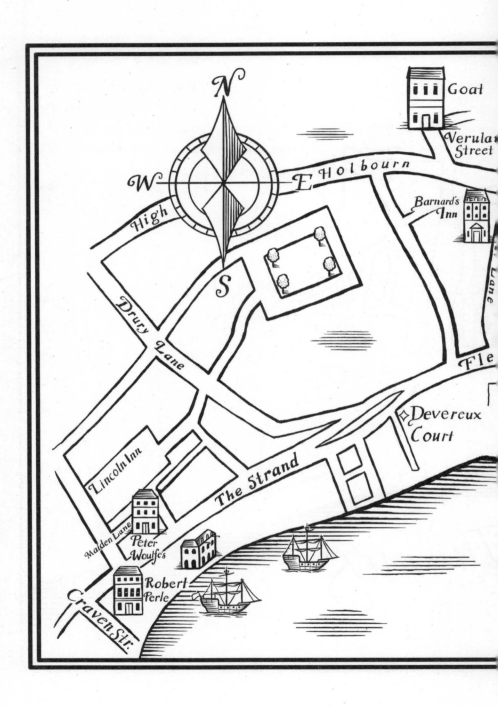

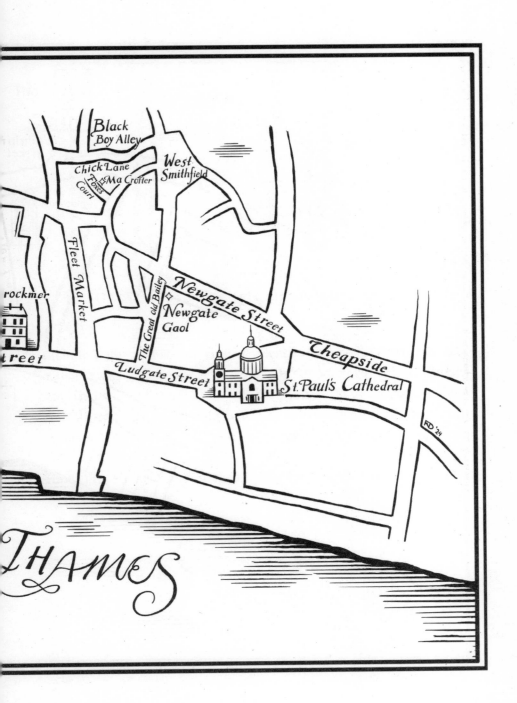

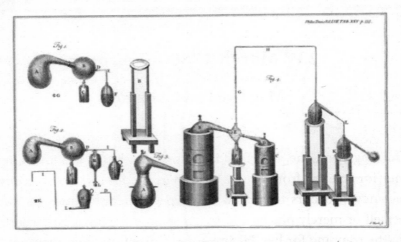

Chemistry apparatus designed by Peter Woulfe (1727–1803)

The last true believer in alchemy was Peter Woulfe, the eminent chemist and a fellow of the Royal Society, who made experiments to show the nature of mosaic gold. He had long vainly searched for the Elixir, and attributed his repeated failures to the want of due preparation by pious and charitable acts.

English Eccentrics and Eccentricities, *John Timbs (1866)*

Chapter One

23rd March 1780 – *Equinox*

Mag Pye Lane, London

On Mag Pye Lane, Mal Burkiss eats a thrush. He has just bought four for a penny from a dirty woman in a red shawl. In a rare flight of fancy, it occurs to him to wonder whether she traps the birds herself or merely plucks and roasts them – having a boy, a son, to do the trapping for her. He imagines himself catching thrushes for a woman in a shawl who is also his mother – bringing them to her, chirruping, so that she can wring their fresh necks. And then his fancy fails him; he cannot imagine how he would address her or she him, or whether she might give him a bird to eat for himself.

He turns his attention back to his own thrush and, running the slim bones through the clasp of his teeth, pulls the last of the stringy flesh into his mouth. He is aware already that the food has landed as light and inconsequential as a leaf on the vastness of his hunger – a hunger that attends him constantly. He drops the pale carcass, blinks his dull, brown eyes and resolves not to think of thrushes again until tomorrow. He is thick-boned, wide-hipped and could have made a big man with proper feeding – instead, he is somewhat squat, his legs too short for his trunk and his long arms. He is tired today; a spring fog has crept up from the river and Mal feels as if he is wading through something thicker than air as he returns to Barnard's Inn.

When he enters Peter Woulfe's rooms, Mal finds him alone and standing so still that he almost fails to spot him. Woulfe is standing by the bookcase, a large, bright piece of quartz in one hand and an open book in the other. The tall, thin form is perfectly motionless. That Peter Woulfe should be standing still and intent, his body alone present while his mind wanders far away, is not, in fact, unusual, but today Mal knows that something is amiss. It is not quite that he can smell it, some shift in the atmosphere of the room, it is that his intuition is as slight and unsettling as a scent half remembered.

He moves cautiously into the room, his head instinctively dipped, his feet moving quietly, looking about for some clue – and as he moves through the grey light admitted by the first window in the long room, his heart seizes in his chest. It is clear to him that the furnace at the back of the room – the furnace he has privately named Old Smoky – has gone out.

How he knows this for certain at this distance, with the door of the furnace shut fast, he cannot say, but he perceives a stillness, a dullness about the object, that is the very opposite of fire. He does not question this perception, has not the sophistication to think that perhaps his mind is shaping its very worst fear, but he does know that he must traverse the room and establish beyond doubt that there is no longer a fire in the belly of Old Smoky. That he must do this without his master's knowledge is evident. It is possible that, if he moves slowly enough, Woulfe, who has not even turned his head, will not notice him passing at the far side of the room. When he has felt with his own fingers the cool touch of a dormant furnace, when he has seen for himself the dark, lifeless embers on Old Smoky's grate, then Mal knows he must run as fast as his legs will carry him.

Mal Burkiss does not count well, but he does know that Old Smoky has been lighting continuously – all day and all night without fail – for many, many weeks. He recalls the day, as autumn was beginning to cede to the grip of winter, when Woulfe had placed, with utmost care, a crucible containing a most noxious mixture within Old Smoky's heat chamber and had instructed him, his eyes ablaze, to keep the fire burning, the heat constant, upon pain of death. He had watched Woulfe attach a piece of paper, with string, to the handle of the furnace door, had seen upon the paper a series of markings that he knew to represent words, had in fact listened as Peter Woulfe read out these words – a prayer, an invocation, addressed to God and his angels, words that Mal only half understood – in a tone of voice mixing solemnity and urgency with such an unusual degree of force that it had lodged a sharp edge in his mind. That night he had moved his sleeping mat from its place by the central hearth and had taken to sleeping beside Old Smoky, curled with his back to its heat, his body habituated to its rhythms with something akin to the attunement of a lover. At first, for one week, or perhaps two, Woulfe had checked the furnace anxiously, monitored its fuel consumption, issued strictures against the use of too much or too little, but as time wore on he began to leave Mal and Old Smoky to their own devices. And Mal, with no small degree of jealous pride, had seen this as an expression of trust. Peter Woulfe would have been surprised to realise that he trusted Mal Burkiss, relied upon him in any significant way at all, but in fact he did, and thus could turn his mind to a promising distillation amongst other pressing matters. And so, as he creeps along the room towards Old Smoky, pain spreading though his chest, Mal Burkiss experiences a high anxious ringing in his ears and a sense that his small world is about to crumble about him.

When Woulfe turns his head, there is a far-away look in his bright-blue eyes, so that, while he appears to be staring directly at Mal, who has just extended his hand to touch Old Smoky, he in fact sees nothing. Mal freezes, his hand resting on the furnace. The furnace is warm, but Mal can tell it is just the residual heat of a furnace that has recently gone out; there is no smell of smoke, and even in the short moment his hand has rested there, he believes he can feel the surface cooling further.

As Woulfe continues to stare, the objects at the end of the room – the furnace and Mal standing frozen beside it – begin to resolve themselves into identifiable shapes.

It takes a moment – a heart-stopping, agonising moment for Mal – before Peter Woulfe realises what has happened. That his experiment is ruined, that months of expectation have amounted to exactly nothing, is beyond doubt. That it is entirely the fault of Mal Burkiss is as clear as the look of pure, distilled guilt on the boy's face. The realisation that this one failure is symbolic of all his failures descends on Peter Woulfe at the same time as a truly enormous rage begins to build from the pit of his stomach.

As he steps forwards towards Mal, he is propelled by both despair and fury – and it is the despair as much as the fury that causes him to bring back his arm, his face quite twisted with the effort, and fling the lump of quartz he has been holding in the direction of Mal. Immediately, the movement itself provides a degree of release for him, and as the rock leaves his fingers, he begins to regret the impulse, thinking that some item of importance is bound to be broken. In the space of time it takes for this thought to form, the rock completes its journey and lands with a dull thump on the floor, but not before it has connected with the skull of Mal Burkiss, which emits a sickening crack as the temporal bone caves in.

It is Peter Woulfe's turn to stand frozen as Mal begins to sway gently. He watches as Mal's knees give way and he crumples slowly into an inert heap.

∽

Peter Woulfe possesses a number of human skulls, and amongst his collection is the skull of a young adult male. When he crouches to examine Mal, it is this smooth, clean skull he holds in his mind's eye and not the blood-clotted mass before him. He sees how the temporal bone, caught at a weak point, has yielded beyond repair.

He has, in his fifty-three years, seen countless broken bodies, considers himself to have a strong stomach, a cool, experienced head. But this time, something is different. He is all a-tremble, quite horrified by what he has done, quite unbalanced. He believes he can taste the metallic tang of blood in the air; he can certainly smell it, and he moves his hand to cover his nose.

His eyes move to Mal's thick, brown hair, and just above the ear, Peter Woulfe sees pale and greasy flakes of scalp – larger and greasier than he would have imagined. It is not that he deems Mal's scalp to be unclean as such, but the proximity of the boy's imperfect humanity turns his stomach as even the blood could not, and he moves his head abruptly and empties his belly upon the rug.

He is now assaulted, his senses excruciatingly alive, by the smell of blood, the stench of his own vomit and the particular scent of greasy, flaking scalp.

He wants more than anything to be elsewhere. He would like to leap up and walk swiftly, even run, across the room, out the door, down the stairs and thus into the outside world – where he could keep walking, running, moving quickly until he leaves the smells and the broken boy far behind him. His body in fact begins to move of its own volition – his legs start to straighten, and his head turns towards the door, before his mind catches up, and he pauses. And as he lets gravity pull him down again, a low animal moan escapes him.

It is, amongst other things, extremely inopportune timing. Peter Woulfe places the index finger of his right hand into his mouth and bites down on it. Just before the world came into focus not five minutes earlier, he saw something altogether new in the book he has been scrutinising for more than thirty years. Something extremely important, which he has now forgotten.

He puts his hand on the boy's wrist; he cannot detect a pulse. There will of course be questions. He knows he can prepare himself to provide satisfactory answers. But then there is the matter of time. He sees this day and probably the next one evaporate in a series of exchanges about this dead boy. His head begins to feel like a steam-kettle without an outlet, and each new thought surges with unwelcome pressure.

Into Peter Woulfe's head comes, fully formed and clear, the image of Robert Perle's smooth, capable face – and despite his efforts to review his options, his mind settles stubbornly on Robert Perle. It becomes clear to him that Perle alone has the competence to manage the situation, but there is also something unusually clean about Perle that serves as an antidote to his present feelings of disgust. He could write a note. He could say, *come at once*. It would be quite simple; then he could run down the stairs to the porter's desk and ask Jagoe, keeping his voice even to avoid suspicion, to have it sent to Perle with utmost haste. There are urchins everywhere waiting to run across London for a hapenny.

He reaches for his pen – the nub needs sharpening, but it suffices . . . and so he writes:

Perle,
Come at Once.
Woulfe

It is when Robert Perle enters the room twenty minutes later, bends to the boy and declares him dead, that Peter Woulfe begins to cry silently – thick, fat tears escaping down his cheeks.

Perle notes them with swiftly hidden astonishment and says, 'Yes, a most unfortunate accident,' gazing diplomatically down at his own feet. 'But never worry, Woulfe – we shall have him away in a trice.'

In fact, Perle knows that it will take more than a trice to remove the boy without exciting comment. His mind begins to whirr, and it seems to him that his own man, Gorridge, would be best placed to secure the services of two stout urchins who could carry the body out under cover of darkness. And Perle himself knows of a resurrection man down by the docks who will pay ready money for a fresh corpse.

He turns to Peter Woulfe, puts his hand upon his arm (something that Woulfe dislikes) and says firmly, 'I shall send for help, for assistance of the most discrete kind, and in the meantime, you will take yourself down to the Temple Coffee House and await me there.'

As this is what he wants to do more than anything, Peter Woulfe pauses and stares out the window. The question of whether he can trust Perle arises in his mind. He does not like to think of Perle alone in his rooms. He is beginning to shape a sentence suggesting that he, too, will stay and assist, when out of the corner of his eye, he perceives a slight movement on the ground. He moves his head and looks intently at Mal's body on the floor. There is no movement now, none at all, but he could not swear to it – not even now, with the inert body before him – that his eyes were merely tricked by his overwrought imagination.

This ghost of a flicker of possible movement is too much for him, and he knows now that he must leave immediately. He must be away, irrespective of the risks. He looks closely at Perle, prepared to be reassured, and is dismayed beyond all proportion to note that Perle is uncharacteristically imperfectly shaved – just above his jaw-line there lies a dark patch of growth that the barber has missed.

But Robert Perle – entirely unaware that he is anything other than perfectly presented – turns to hold Peter Woulfe's gaze, his bright – brown eyes alive with an air of confidence and certainty.

'It is much the best way, Woulfe.'

Peter Woulfe nods, but as he moves quickly towards the door, he is aware that he is doing so against his wiser judgement. His mind is filled with the image of Perle's jaw-line, the hairs sprouting defiantly along the smooth plane of his cheek. He does not look back at the heap on the floor, does not choose to risk it, but just as he reaches the door, he believes he detects a soft scraping noise, the kind of sound that fingernails might make if they were drawn across a wooden floor by the clenching and unclenching of a weakened hand. And so he increases his pace, his feet clattering, his face wet with tears, and gallops down the stairs of Barnard's Inn and out into Fetter Lane.

∽

Robert Perle decides at the last moment to accompany Gorridge and the body of Mal Burkiss to Greely, the resurrection man. It makes little sense for him to be out in the streets of London with a dead body – with evidence of a crime committed and a further one about to take place – but as he sees Gorridge's boys hoist the body, while Gorridge frowns competently and says, 'Handsomely now, hup hup,' Perle experiences a strong reluctance to let the body out of his sight.

Wrapped in Peter Woulfe's rug and bound around and around with thick twine, a pole running through the length of the rolled rug to take the weight, the bundled-up body looks to Perle's eye to be the very height of suspicion. The dark-browed boys themselves – so alike in height and countenance that they must be brothers – the shape of their burden, and Gorridge in incongruous attendance seem a picture that Perle imagines could fittingly be entitled *Murderers, Thieves and Vagabonds*, and so he wrestles for just a moment with the possibility of steering straight for the Temple.

He decides to follow Gorridge and the boys at a discreet distance. But he has reckoned without the fog, and when he emerges into Fetter Lane, a few heartbeats after Gorridge, it is only by knowing that they must have turned right to take the shortest route to Greely that he catches a glimpse of them and contrives to follow them at all. It is then as much as he can do to keep pace. Gorridge has chosen his stout urchins well, and they move swiftly and silently.

The night itself is still and oddly pale; moonshine somewhere behind the fog has set the world aglow.

Perle finds that he is excited – by the fog, by the body itself and by the impending encounter with Greely. Greely appears to live where he works, along with his cadavers and the river fog, which moves in for months at a time, in a creaking timber storehouse by the Thames.

Perle has met Greely three times before. He finds the resurrectionist quite repulsive – his bland, watery eyes, the dank wooden structure he inhabits, the smell all around of river water and rot.

And each time, the repulsion has mingled with an excitement that lingers long after the repulsion has dissipated.

Perle ducks his head and enters. It is cooler inside. Greely, he suspects, deals in more than one kind of illicit trade, and not all the befogged misshapen bundles on the floor are necessarily the bodies of the recently departed – but some certainly are, and Perle feels his pulse quicken.

Greely is standing in the pool of light cast by a lamp that he is holding steady. He is flat-lipped and clammy-skinned. His nostrils flare in the lamplight from below.

The boys have lowered their burden to the floor and are flanking Gorridge, who stands respectfully with his head slightly bowed, looking just as he might in the hall of Perle's house on a Sunday morning.

Greely sees Perle's shape by the door, raises his lamp, appears to recognise Perle in the gloom and nods at him, before crouching down beside the body and setting his lamp on the floor.

Perle sees a knife flash as Greely cuts the twine quickly, once, twice, and then a third time. Perle realises Greely means to save the twine and watches as he carefully unstrings the bundle. The resurrection man looks up at Perle as if he has tasted some of his impatience drifting across in the thick air and shows him his yellow teeth by way of a smile.

'What have we got here then, sir? Selling this time, are we? Going into business?'

'A prime specimen, Mr Greely.'

'I'm sure it is, sir.' Greely nods to the boys. 'Give us a hand.'

And between them, they reveal Mal lying on his front, his arms tight by his sides. Greely heaves at the boy's coat and turns the body with an expert movement.

'Not so very fresh. Half a day. And a bit of damage up top.' Greely sniffs and nods slightly in the direction of Mal's head.

'Do you receive many undamaged specimens, Mr Greely?'

'Oh, you'd be surprised, sir.'

Robert Perle has been calculating while he walked. Three months previously, he procured a human hand from Greely; it was severed neatly just below the wrist – rigor had set in – but the hand was splayed ready for dissection. This cost him six shillings.

Some weeks later, he bought a human heart and a brain for five.

His most recent purchase was a foot, and Greely held him to ten for it on the grounds that it was fresh and undamaged – an excellent example.

Greely stands and approaches Perle, the lamp swaying, light racing out to the far corners and up the dark timbered walls before settling around them.

Perle feels a ripple of disgust as Greely stands too close to him and peers up intently.

'You have a figure in mind, I'm sure, sir.'

If Perle were striking a deal with a respectable tradesman, this is where he would smile. As it is, his lips soften just perceptibly.

'Well, Mr Greely, given the price of a foot, a hand and a heart combined amount to twenty-one shillings, I'm sure we can start with a multiple of that.'

'And a brain, if I recall, sir.'

Perle wishes he had mentioned the brain, but he continues as if Greely has not spoken. 'A multiple of ten seems to me to represent excellent value.'

'Oh no, sir.' Greely rocks back slightly on his heels. 'That's not how it works at all. There is work to be done, you see, before achieving such prices for individual parts.'

Perle inclines abruptly towards Greely, sees his eyes widen slightly at the movement, knows he has unsettled him.

'Work, Mr Greely?'

'Yes, sir. Work. As you would surely appreciate, were you to observe it. And some might say not the most pleasant work, either.'

Perle thinks of knives plied with force and a joint of rare beef on his dining-room table. His stomach is unmoved, but he feels a flush spreading across his back and up his neck.

'Well, let us say four guineas. In consideration of your work.'

'No, no, sir. While I am not denying the freshness, fresh is not as hard come by as you might imagine these days. What with the sickness and the winter just gone.'

'That, Mr Greely, is not what you told me when selling me a stiff old claw from this very spot months ago.'

Greely holds his eye. 'It's a question of supply and demand, sir. In this trade.'

Perle realises that he has misstepped by not emphasising the wholeness of what he has to offer. He sees Mal's feet pale in the gloom and realises that the shoes he was undoubtedly wearing when Perle first arrived in Peter Woulfe's rooms are missing. One of Gorridge's urchins has helped himself.

'Fully clothed, fresh and in prime condition – come, Mr Greely, you are not the only man in London who could take him off my hands.'

Greely does not shift his unblinking gaze. 'But you're here now, ain't you, sir? And clothed he may be, that I don't deny, but he has no shoes.'

Perle's eyes narrow; he wonders if his very thoughts are floating across the sodden air to Greely.

'I am a busy man, Mr Greely. I have an item that is of undoubted value to you, but I will not stand here' – the word *here* cracks across the room – 'all night speaking of shoes and seasons. I would as well fling him in the river. It would be no great matter.'

Greely smiles. And Perle is now quite sure that he has unwittingly caught one of Greely's thoughts – he could throw the body in the river, but Greely would fish it out. Wherever it might go in – into that vast, ever moving body of water – Greely would be waiting when it came to shore. And Perle touches a sensation he cannot name – as if the river water itself runs through Greely's veins, whispering secrets in sibilant code.

But Greely is considering the damage that would be done to the undoubtedly prime specimen were Perle to carry out his threat. And Perle says, 'Just think of all that bloating, Mr Greely. All those fish nibbling. It is better we come to an agreement here and now.'

If Greely is surprised that Perle has read his thoughts, he does not show it.

'Two guineas. You can't say fairer.'

'Three.'

'Two and six.'

'Three, Mr Greely.'

'Two pounds ten and six.'

'Done.'

Greely pulls a leather pouch from the recesses of his dank clothing and carefully counts out the coins into Robert Perle's open palm.

Perle relishes the touch of the coins, the weight, the clink of one upon another.

When he steps out into the night, he feels the shift in temperature, the soft, warm kiss of the fog, damp and over-intimate, upon his cheeks. He feels quite completely alive. It has been a most exciting day. He thinks of Peter Woulfe sitting in the Temple Coffee House and wishes to be there with him – knows in his gut that Woulfe will be raw and receptive for a time after his distress, but that time will not be indefinite.

And so he steps out at pace, Greely's coins in one pocket and a much-marked sheet of paper from Woulfe's waste-paper basket in the other.

Chapter Two

Temple Coffee House, Devereux Court, London

When Peter Woulfe sees Danby Scott's bright head shining in the tobacco fog of the coffee-house, he is certain that the young man has been thrust into his path by a higher power intent on providing balm for his turbulent soul.

Danby is sitting with a crowd of other young men. A story is being related, and they are leaning in to get closer to the speaker – a thin, intelligent-looking man with wide, expressive eyes. Danby is utterly engrossed; his shapely mouth is slightly open and his hand, resting on the tablecloth, is stretched towards the speaker as if he were, moments ago, about to interrupt, were about to add to the narrative some morsel of his own that has now been lost in the keen flow of the speaker's story. All the men are ready to laugh; in fact, it is clear that there has been much laughter already and that the next explosion of mirth will be but part of a sequence of hilarity begun some time ago.

Peter Woulfe sees some part of this as he makes his way across the room. He sees that the men Danby Scott is sitting with are young and amused, but he notes this vaguely, with impatience and some degree of distaste. He, too, has been young, has sat in eager gatherings and laughed beyond all proportion at bawdy stories, but he has lived long enough to know that it matters not a whit. In fact, observing the gathering, their intentness, their evident belief that they are the most amusing fellows ever to have sat at a coffee-house table, causes a heaviness to form in his belly on top of the existing turmoil. It is as if the last fragments of an old dream have been swept aside, and he knows now for certain that his own youth and laughter were just as foolish and unoriginal as that displayed before him.

And so, when he arrives at the table occupied by Danby Scott and his friends, his distress and this new hint of sadness combine to give him a most imposing appearance. His blue eyes are overly bright, overly wide. His cheeks are flushed, and his voice, when he begins to speak, sounds harsh and urgent.

'Good day, Mr Scott – I would be glad of a moment with you.'

Peter Woulfe has paid no regard at all to the rhythm of the story, to the fact that Campbell, the young man who is speaking – who has skilfully held the reins of his friends' hilarity for the past five minutes and more – is about to reach his climax, and that all the young men are poised to explode with laughter at the very next sentence. In fact, Woulfe's older, deeper voice cuts straight across Campbell's as he addresses Danby Scott.

Six faces turn to him, and he is somewhat abashed by this – he unreasonably expected only Danby to hear him, has no interest whatsoever in the remaining five faces and wishes they would turn back to their foolish business or evaporate into thin air.

Danby takes a moment to readjust. His mind is filled with Campbell's story of a naval officer who kept not one, not two, but three married mistresses at the same time. That Campbell's story has one final flourish he does not doubt; it is clear that the situation Campbell has described, compromising as it is, leaves room for one last twist, one last plunge into delightful and arousing absurdity. And so Peter Woulfe speaks again before Danby has gathered himself sufficiently to reply.

'There are some matters I would like to discuss with you.'

He speaks faster than usual, eager to be away from these young faces, eager to be at a smaller table in a darker corner with a dish of hot coffee and Danby's undivided attention. He is sure than the young man's presence alone will soothe him, but some part of his secretive nature is also weighing the possibility of telling Danby about the events of the morning, of gathering up his story and pushing it across the table to him, as if it will help him to be rid of it.

Danby meets Peter Woulfe's gaze and, as if it has travelled down his spine, experiences a jolt in the pit of his stomach. His inner voice clearly frames the sentence: *why, the man is quite mad.*

But he stands to take leave of his friends with a natural courtesy, nodding to Campbell, who is quite put out, who knows that he will never again bring his story to such a perfect pitch, who would have liked to see Danby in particular explode with unrestrained laughter.

Danby walks with Woulfe across the room to where Bouchier, the head waiter, is standing. Bouchier has an unerring nose for human emotions and senses at once that a small, discreetly placed table is required for the gentlemen, and that they would do well to be contained in a dark corner where their own private drama can unfold in peace.

Once they are seated, Woulfe, with his back to the wall, feels flooding through him a wave of exhaustion that almost brings him to tears. Danby looks attentive and polite; he has swallowed his irritation right down in the course of their passage across the room and sits prepared to be respectful. He is, now that he has the space to remember the fact, quite intrigued by Woulfe, by his reputation as a chemist and by the aura of secrecy that surrounds him.

Walking along Fetter Lane with his cousin Perle just last week, Danby had met Woulfe for the first time – standing outside the entrance to Barnard's Inn with a cast-eyed youth by his side. Wild-looking, tall and severe, wearing a shabby cloak, Woulfe was supervising the delivery of a cart-load of firewood. The young fellow beside him, standing unusually still, drew Danby's attention for a moment. He was so still, so absent-looking that he must be slow-witted. A squat, stunted-looking fellow – on second glance, likely to be more or less the same age as himself, but different in every other way. So pale, so blank, he seemed to be barely animated at all. Danby wondered how the youth could be possessed of the same kind of animus as himself, and yet he knew, theologically speaking, that he must be. A soul is a soul. Just then, he heard the words, *bone dry, sir, cross my heart* from the cheerful carter, and he noticed Peter

Woulfe's bright eyes, his severity as he picked a log from the cart, tapped it, sniffed at it and tossed it in his hand. What his cousin and Woulfe spoke about during their brief exchange Danby cannot remember, but he remembers a surprising hint of deference in his cousin's manner and the swivel of Woulfe's gaze as he brought his attention to bear upon Danby.

Walking away, Perle muttered, 'He looks young does he not? Peter Woulfe? For a man of his age? He looks younger than he in fact is and *considerably* poorer than I suspect him to be.'

Danby Scott, to whom everyone over the age of thirty seems ripe to be measured for a coffin, simply shrugged as he stepped around a pregnant sow rootling in the filth of Fetter Lane. He had no idea whether Peter Woulfe was too young for his age or too rich for his clothes. Everything about London was still new to him – the press of people all around, the *smell* of them all, the dirt, the buildings above him drunkenly leaning towards each other, the ceaseless noise and the endless motion.

Perle continued, as they reunited in front of the sow, 'A vastly knowledgeable chemist, and skilled, too' – he put a finger to his lip in mock secrecy – 'in the arts of the ancients. A *most* lucrative business.'

But more than his cousin's words, Danby's senses, acute as they were to all the newness, to the sea of impressions presented to his eyes and ears and heart, told him that he had just had a significant encounter. This brief meeting with Peter Woulfe, his observation of the odd fellow at his side, stand out in his mind like something rare and shiny lying on the muddy foreshore of the Thames.

Danby has not, however, forgotten his strong feeling, just moments ago, that Woulfe is mad – and has in fact pulled some softer parts of himself in closer. His mind has taken a step back, to engage with Woulfe from a safer distance. Danby has done this unconsciously, speedily and thoroughly – and no one watching would know from his movements or his speech, from his open and friendly countenance, that anything had changed.

Peter Woulfe does not know it, and he looks at Danby as he would look at a dear old friend.

'This meeting is quite fortuitous.'

'Yes, sir, indeed.'

In the pause that follows, Danby waits for the older man to speak and looks neutrally at the wall.

Peter Woulfe wishes to say, *no, no, do not agree with me just yet; you cannot possibly know.*

He studies Danby – beholds the radiant clarity of his fresh cheeks, the shine in his green eyes, his evident goodness – and he believes that the young man's innocence and beauty is acting on him like a truth potion.

'My morning has been somewhat fraught with . . . difficulties.'

Danby moves his eyes to Woulfe's face and says with genuine concern, 'I'm sorry to hear that, sir – indeed, I am. I trust your work continues as you would wish?'

'No, no.' He waves his hand. 'It does not concern my work.'

Peter Woulfe is somewhat surprised that Danby has not silently understood the magnitude of his distress. Also, his mind goes to his workbench; he remembers that Perle is alone in his rooms, and he experiences a most uncomfortable sensation of violation – he imagines Perle touching the apparatus, sneering perhaps or, even worse, making some small adjustment. And that is not to speak of his notes, lying open on the table, encoded to be sure, but still there for all to see. He is within a whit of standing up and racing back to Barnard's Inn when he remembers the broken body, the sickening smell, the horrifying hint of movement on the floor.

'No, no, it is very much worse than that.' Peter Woulfe has not confided in anyone for many years, has forgotten, if he ever knew, just how to do it – and so his voice when he speaks is filled with what sounds like rage. His throat has tightened; his brows have drawn close together.

He appears to Danby to be the very picture of Fury. Instinctively, he begins to search his conscience, as if the older man's anger must be related to him, to some guilty behaviour of which he is not immediately conscious. He conducts a sweeping review, skips over the older sins tucked away in the recesses of his mind, arrives at his recent sins, considers the filthy thoughts that have plagued him since his arrival in London, where it seems the pleasures of the flesh are for sale on almost every street corner. He dismisses these as unlikely to have troubled Woulfe, troubling though they have been to him, and he looks with scarcely suppressed puzzlement at the older man, who has now, with nostrils flaring, put a tremulous hand to his jaw.

'There has been an accident. At my rooms. A most unfortunate accident.'

Danby thinks of fire, a glorious and comprehensive conflagration, broken glass, chemicals casting coloured flares upwards, windows bursting out into the busy courtyard below.

'It is my assistant – the fellow who keeps the fires.'

Danby has a startlingly clear memory of Mal Burkiss, standing as he did by the entrance to Barnard's Inn. Cast-eyed, lumpen, marked forever by misfortune. He has encountered hundreds of such folk during his few weeks in London but has had occasion to look at none of them as he looked at Mal on that strangely alive morning.

But he merely nods. He feels it is inappropriate to remember him.

As Woulfe goes silent, Danby prompts, 'An accident?'

Peter Woulfe wishes more than anything to communicate his feeling of distress to Danby, to convey the extreme difficulty and unpleasantness of the morning, but as he reviews the past hour and searches for the right words, he feels a heavy, old sadness weighing on his chest – and he cannot tell why, cannot ascribe it to a particular cause. He is afraid that he will cry openly, and if he begins to cry, he is not sure whether he will ever be able to stop.

He looks at Danby, who has now begun to examine his cuffs.

'There was a significant amount of blood' – Peter Woulfe raises his hand to his temple, his fingers gently circling the soft skin – 'on his head. And damage to the temporal bone, I believe.'

He looks at Danby and sees from his puzzled countenance that he has not conveyed a tenth of what he wishes to convey.

'It was most unpleasant. I believe death was instantaneous.'

'His head?' Danby touches his fingers to his own temple.

Peter Woulfe nods.

Danby exhales; some degree of the older man's distress has in fact communicated itself to him. 'I am sorry for it.'

He is not sure, beyond that, what he should say. He *is* sorry. He feels most uncomfortable about it. His kind heart is pained that this young man, at whom he looked so intently, should have come to such an abrupt end. He does not go so far as to frame in words the thought that hovers at the edge of his mind – the thought that, if matters were different, he, too, could be squat, cast-eyed, stupid-looking and dead before his time. He does not catch the thought in order to examine it, but it is the first time in his charmed life that he has entertained the ghost of a suspicion that his luck and his looks, his health, his very character, may not be as integral to him – to the man Danby Scott – as, say, his bones and his teeth and the heart that beats within him.

'A simple loss of footing – a most unfortunate accident.' Peter Woulfe cannot quite believe what he is saying, but as he speaks, he begins to feel immeasurably better. He turns both hands so that his large, pale palms face upwards, fingers splayed, and he looks at Danby with a small, sad smile.

Danby nods gently in sympathy. 'Most unfortunate, sir.' He continues hesitantly, 'I suppose one could say a prayer for his soul?'

Woulfe's eyes light up; he looks at Danby with relief. 'One could! One certainly could!'

And at the thought of such a prayer, his mind is suddenly filled by the shawled peasants of his Irish youth, the howl of the keen, the sound of grief cast skywards – the peasants losing themselves entirely in the singing, as if the song were in fact singing them – how it had seemed to him as a boy that they knew themselves to be but a blameless speck in the great world's turning of life and death.

And Peter is elated by this vision – he believes, for now, that he, too, is but a blameless speck, freed from the endless requirement to steer his course through a remorseless universe, and freed, more pertinently, from responsibility for the broken, oozing, nauseating events of the morning.

Danby's mind is beginning to wander. He can hear his friends laughing at the far side of the room. Another story no doubt, and a very funny one at that.

∽

Peter Woulfe sits rapt in contemplation of his dish of coffee. He has never noticed before the richness of the colour, how, as he moves the dish gently in front of him, the lamplight brings out new tones. It is also quite delicious in a way that surprises him. Coffee he has had aplenty in the past, but there is something about this particular dish on this particularly distressing day that brings him to near delight. He is thinking, too, about the beans, the particular compound within that appears to have specifically matched itself to mankind's refreshment needs.

As the bitter liquid hits the back of his throat, it strikes him that people are the most extraordinary creatures – to pick these beans, sail them quite halfway across the world, to brew them thus. His heart swells – it is quite a remarkable thing to be a man, to be part of this vast human endeavour. To be a living man, not just bone and flesh like that unfortunate boy. His mind so frequently dwells on the angels, the world beyond, that this thought surprises him, delights him.

And that fine fellow, the head waiter, just to see him there upright and alive, his spine holding up his skull, his heart a beat within. Woulfe thinks of all the men who laid stone upon stone to build this very coffee-house – he spares but a moment for the women who bore and suckled them – and Danby Scott is a prime example of the human creature, so young and fresh and full of promise, a brain and a body primed for a glorious life.

Danby is wondering how he can decently leave when he sees his cousin Perle approaching them from across the room. He intuits in an instant that, while Perle was expecting to encounter Peter Woulfe, he is displeased to find that he already has company. Danby suspects he is particularly displeased to see that the company is his young cousin. But this is not at all evident in the manner in which he greets the pair.

'Woulfe, Cousin Danby, what a pleasure.'

Peter Woulfe looks up with dismay. 'My dear fellow. I had forgot you entirely.' Woulfe's face begins to take on something of its earlier pallor.

If Perle is surprised by Woulfe's statement, he does not betray it. He merely nods and says, 'I shall take a dish of coffee with you gentlemen.'

Peter experiences an unpleasant slippery sensation – he cannot, in this moment, remember when he first met Perle, is at a loss to understand how he has remained acquainted with him. It seems strange to him that he should have established any kind of intimacy with this man – he is altogether too smooth, and surely only a fop would knot his neckcloth in such a manner.

Distracted as Peter Woulfe is by his own dismay, he misses what Perle says next and thus is not sure how, without any breech of etiquette, Perle has made it impossible for Danby to remain at the table. But, sure enough, the young man, having not even finished his coffee, is preparing to rise. Woulfe barely resists the temptation to grab him by the sleeve.

As he watches Danby's receding back, he decides he cannot remain for long in Perle's company. It is quite impossible that he should be sitting here with this man – there is his work to consider; this is just the sort of thing he cannot afford to let interfere with the work. It is at a critical stage, all so delicately balanced.

Perle leans forwards. His eyes are quite bright, and while his tone is even, Peter Woulfe receives the impression of barely suppressed excitement.

'That matter has been attended to.'

Peter blinks a number of times in quick succession in an attempt to erase the image rising in his mind, an image that combines the caved-in temporal bone of Mal Burkiss and a slowly congealing pile of vomit.

'There were no unanticipated difficulties.'

Peter Woulfe, lips pursed, eyebrows drawn together, merely nods. He imagines a body hastily concealed, an inert hand or leg emerging where it shouldn't. He thinks, too, of the unpleasant things that happen to a body in the hours after death.

A silence settles between the pair. Perle sees that he must wait it out.

A feeling of injustice begins to rise in Peter Woulfe. That he should be stuck here with this man when he could be attending to his work or discussing the nature of coffee with Danby Scott. Why, what is it the fellow wants? It occurs to him it is gratitude, and he wrestles for a moment before saying, as sincerely as he can, 'I am most grateful to you for your assistance, Mr Perle.'

'Not at all, Woulfe.' Perle speaks quickly, fluidly, and Peter sees immediately that more is required of him.

'A most unpleasant situation.'

Perle remains impassive.

Peter Woulfe tries again, but with a mounting sense of unease. 'Most grateful.'

'Not at all.' Perle moves his head sideways as if to indicate the trivial nature of the favour.

No, it is not gratitude that Perle wants at all.

Peter suddenly feels quite unwell. The coffee begins to seethe in his stomach. His mind fills with an image of his weighing table, his beloved scales, the minutely calibrated weights, and he wishes more than anything to be back in his rooms. And it is Perle who is keeping him from his work. It is quite intolerable.

'Mr Perle, I have a most important matter to attend to. A matter of some urgency.' Peter Woulfe stands up abruptly. 'I am, as I have said, most grateful to you for your assistance . . . in this most unpleasant matter.'

Perle conveys nothing but absolute courtesy as he bids him good day. If he had the inclination to speak honestly, he would acknowledge the other man's unease; he would say, *yes, you are quite right, I do want something from you, but I am not yet sure what it is.*

For Robert Perle has not yet assessed the value of the service he has rendered, how best to extract maximum value – it is as if he is still totting up a lengthy bill and, with his pencil hovering over the ledger, is inclined to round it up but may well round it down if he could thereby gain further advantage. While this is not quite as he imagined their meeting proceeding, he is not unduly perturbed – it gives him time to assess the other essential element in tailoring a bill: evaluating just what cost the customer can bear.

Perle feels sure that, while Peter Woulfe may look to be a volatile, irascible eccentric, he in fact partakes of a certain kind of greatness. Woulfe has a commitment to his work that verges on the insane and a mind that Perle has not seen equalled – he does not doubt the depth of his knowledge on chemical matters, the sharpness of his wit. He has seen him stand before the Royal Society and deliver a paper of the utmost obscurity to a receptive and respectful audience. He knows that Woulfe is deeply engaged in the quest to make gold from the base metals, that he is well resourced – having amassed something approaching a fortune in the course of his life's work – and that he has, in fact, invested a considerable amount of this money in his attempts thus far.

All in all, there is something about Woulfe that makes Perle, master-punter that he is, believe that he could well be the one to make the breakthrough. Yes, Robert Perle believes that Peter Woulfe may have, or be about to have, something of immense value, so as he watches Woulfe's tall form pass hurriedly through the lamplight outside the Temple, he resolves to be patient.

Chapter Three

In the Fog

Mal Burkiss, his naked skin never touched by the sun, is even paler than the milk-pale world through which he moves. He is not sure where he is going or why, but he knows he cannot stop.

He suspects he is dead, and he fears that this aimless movement, this alien world, will be his lot for all eternity. Cool, damp air sits on his back; his arms are wrapped tight to protect his chest. He cannot feel his feet or his hands, is not sure if they belong to him anymore. He sees his breath joining with the cloudy air around him and wonders if it is his own breath that has filled the sky. He cannot remember how long he has been moving and breathing, but he thinks perhaps it has already been forever.

He is acutely aware of his uncovered cock and his tight, cold balls; he thinks of the man in the Bible – how he was naked and unashamed, proud in the garden. And out of some dark corner of his mind, there comes a picture of a beautiful garden full of soft growth and delicate light. He sees it as if he has known it intimately, and he wishes to weep for the garden, because wherever it is, it is certainly not here in this lost world of the dead.

It is not his habit to weep when the urge comes upon him, but now he cannot stop the tears. His mouth hangs open; salt water and snot run down his face, and a gasp of loss rises in his chest. And the more he sobs, the more his want rises in him – until he thinks he may crack wide open with grief.

And then, first as a wisp, just out of reach, he catches a hint of birdsong.

He turns his head, sees only pale stillness surrounding him, no world for a bird, but the song mounts – the fluting, eager call of a small bird in spring, looping urgently now around his head. It is clearly trying to tell him something, and so he twists again and peers up – and it is just then that ground comes up to meet him, striking his head, pressing itself, colder, damper, harder than the air, along the length of his body.

His mouth and his nose fill with silty dirt; his world has gone dark – it feels softer, more familiar, easier to inhabit than the white, uncertain world of breath. And what is more, he can see the garden more clearly now.

The bird continues to sing, but more gently now, as if she knows how tired he is and how his whole body aches.

The garden has the look of morning, of newness quietly unfolding.

There is a nest – grass-woven, moss-lined, green and tender – held in the fork of a branch bursting with spring buds.

Mal curls himself up, knees against chest, arms clasping his ankles so that he can fit himself to its shape, and as he feels the nest closing softly, warmly around him, he realises that it has been made especially for him.

A pearl-bright drop of dew sits in the mossy mesh. It is the most beautiful thing he has ever seen, so bright and alive it might hurt his eyes. It is what he imagines the world's most precious jewel might look like, surely the thing for which Peter Woulfe has been searching. He knows he cannot touch it with his meaty paws, so he leans and extends his tongue delicately to take it in his mouth.

A soft, deep glow spreads through him, lighting up his mouth, his throat, his heart, his gut, spreading right down to his feet and his hands, which are now alive and tingling. His body feels light and delicate. His dirt-encased lips stretch to a smile; his whole being is filled with delight. He is as big as the world, as bright as the sun, as beautiful as the moon.

The streets of London abound with the particular gold sought by Sukie Bulmer. Using a flat, tarnished shovel, its handle long ago shaped to her thin, gnarled grip, she scrapes and scoops piles of dog shit into a canvas sack. Some days are better than others, but there are never really bad days – heavy rain is the worst, everything sloppy, no nice clean scoops, a sack half full of water – but taking it on the whole, as Sukie does, there is satisfaction in the task and always a ready market. Added to that, her old bones descend readily into a squat, so she hasn't got the bad back of some of her fellow bunters.

Every morning, as the streets begin to wake, Daggert the Pure Man comes with his cart, weighs, squints, haggles and gives her solid coin for her efforts. Sukie has made her enquiries, has a clear sense of the value of dog shit, knows that it goes to the tanneries, that it is somehow essential, and she holds Daggert's eye with confidence while the price is set. The great thing is to be early; she has her patch all right, claimed these last ten years – but leave it long enough, and it would be stripped bare regardless. So Sukie wakes well before first light, sets off with her sack.

This foggy morning feeds her worst fear: that her eyes will completely cloud over and she will have to give it up and sit somewhere and starve. But she has a voice – she could sing. Sing and starve, she thinks, and a laugh rises from her belly. She has been hungry often enough over the years to know how little her body needs; she knows in her bones that, having got this far, she will always find enough to get by, that it will be something other than the hunger that gets her in the end.

In the fog, she can barely see her own feet, so she crouches down and prepares to proceed along at ground level – a movement like a swan on land. One scoop – greenish fresh, definitely dog – and she sees Mal Burkiss.

She has seen all sorts laid out in the London morning. This month alone, Sukie's patch has yielded coins, three hats, one gentleman's cloak, a half-empty bottle of rum and two watches – one taken from the pocket of a drunk gentleman who snored but did not stir when she unhooked the clasp. And she has had her share of the dead: dead dogs, one dead sow and one girl, dead in the archway between Fairley's warehouse and Dobbs. Dead of the cold, Sukie had thought – so thin there was nothing on her. The girl was blue-tinged, yellowed around the eyes, inhuman in her colouring, her limbs askew – she could have been a doll but for the ragged clothes and the lack of prettiness. Sukie moved on that time with a mumbled blessing, knowing well that, forty years ago, it could have been her own young body slumped thin and useless against a wall.

This time, it is different. Mal Burkiss lies pale and smooth on the ground, curled up, fresh-hatched and oddly perfect. She can see the rope of his spine, his rounded shoulders – she can tell from the covering on his limbs that he is far from starving. She wishes to touch him and so moves closer, ignoring a pile of pure immediately to her left.

She lays her hand lightly on his shoulder, feels that he is colder even than her bone-cold hand, moves to clear his hair from his brow, sees that the skin on his face is not yellow nor blue but translucent white, a paper-thin layer between the outside world and the mysterious workings within. She sees the dirt on his mouth, the snot congealed around his nose, and wishes to scrub him clean – without thinking, she spits on the corner of her shawl and applies it gently to his face. But the dirt is ingrained, does not come away easily, and as she applies more force, his eyelids begin to flutter.

She pauses in her scrubbing, leans in and peers intently at his eyes, so that when the fluttering, jittering eyelids finally slide open, all that Mal sees is the weather-scrubbed face of Sukie Bulmer.

His lungs force a large, ragged breath, the shocked gulp of the submerged, and a howl of pain breaks from his throat. Every muscle, every bone screams. He closes his eyes, his mind frantically reaching for the last fragments of his garden, the mossy nest, the magical dew, but a thin, dry hand slaps his cheek – once gently, twice more firmly, and then a third time so that it positively hurts.

'Here, boy! Here!'

And his eyes open again.

His good eye locks onto her right eye – watery blue, red-rimmed – and he cannot look away.

He takes another painful breath.

Sukie, her hand resting on his cold shoulder, finds that she cannot look away either, his coffee-brown, hazel-flecked gaze seems shockingly familiar; and so they remain – Mal taking one breath after another, Sukie crouched and intent.

The pain in Mal's body has broken up; the right side of his head, crushed against the ground, threatens to overcome him altogether, such is the agony. He moves his head the slightest fraction, and his mouth opens wide in a circle of horror.

Sukie places her hand on his cheek, says *shush shush*, her lips stretching into the unfamiliar shape. She feels quite adrift, as she has not done for many years. There is not much that has bothered Sukie this long, long time; she has seen so much living and dying. But for some reason, Mal's pain is singing in her own bones; her heart is pounding in her chest. She wishes to do something to ease his pain – but is not sure what. She thinks he could do with a sup, a wet cloth across his face. She thinks of the old woman with the herbs out the back of Windmill Court. She would move him, but she cannot carry him. He is too big; she is certainly not strong enough. She strokes his cheek out of helplessness more than anything.

She has not touched another person like this for as long as she can remember. He is so soft and, to Sukie's eyes, so beautiful, that her heart stretches painfully in her chest. She feels sure that there is a desperate question in the brown eye staring so intently at her, and she wishes more than anything to find the right answer.

She says *shush shush shush* again, beginning to feel quite desperate herself. She knows she must move – she can no longer tolerate this painful stillness – so she pulls her gaze away and moves her hand to turn his head, revealing a blood-clotted mass of hair and skin. She inhales sharply, squints judiciously, thinks that it is not so bad. She can see that the blood has caked and made a small wound look big, decides that some hot water will do wonders.

And then, abruptly and with some fierceness, she says to him, 'Up with you, you great lump – up with you.'

Instinctively obedient, he begins to shift slightly, hesitantly stretches out his legs; his knees come away from his chest.

'Up, up with you!'

She watches as he slowly unfurls, casts an appraising eye at his hands, his feet, his cock and balls, notes with a mixture of relief and pleasure that he is complete, notices for the first time his wandering eye – her lips disappear; she makes a small sound in the back of her throat: *huh*. Thinks, *it could be worse*.

She takes him by the hand and pulls him to sitting. All the while, tears are coursing down his cheeks.

'Up with you – up up up!' And she stands herself with a surge of urgency, leans to take his hand again. Her mouth pursed with the effort, she begins to pull him up, leans her whole weight back so that his arm extends and his body begins to move.

She is not tall enough, not even nearly heavy enough, to shift him upright.

He seems not to have understood what she is doing, and she fears for a moment that his wits are astray.

She slaps him on his extended arm. 'Up up up!'

Mal, his eyes narrowing with comprehension, rises suddenly, and Sukie descends abruptly to the ground, the wind quite knocked out of her.

A smile lights up Mal's face.

He speaks for the first time. 'Up!'

Sukie begins to laugh – a dissonant crow caw of relief and breathlessness. He pulls at her hand, and she stands slowly. He is a head taller than her. She takes off her shawl and ties it around his waist. She knows that the world is beginning to wake and cannot bear the thought of the carter, the sweeper, the crier seeing him naked and bloodied, wearing an old shawl like a skirt.

He is still smiling, as if the pain has somehow receded, but she can see that his teeth are bouncing off each other and his whole body is a-quiver. Still holding his hand, she stoops for her sack and shovel.

'Come along then. Come along!'

And she sets off at pace, leading Mal along behind her.

⌒

Greely, waking alone in his riverside shed, oozes out of his damp bedding as the sun begins to rise. He runs his clammy hands across his clammy face, before reaching back for the tinder-box tucked beneath his pillow. He crouches to light the lamp waiting on the floor beside his narrow bed and, as he does every morning, moves slowly across towards the door to fill his lungs with the dank, river-laced air. His lamp fills the shed with light and shadow enough for him to notice that something has changed since he drifted off to sleep. There is something missing.

He looks at the covered shapes on the floor; he counts one, two, three, four, five – yes, there is something missing. He looks at the place on the ground where Mal lay – the sheet covering him has been cast aside; there are no marks on the floor, no blood, no sign of the liquids that sometimes leak from the dead. Greely scans the room. Sometimes they move after dark; it has happened before – you place one just where you want it, but then in the morning, it is over by the small, grimy window that looks out onto the river. But no – he turns slowly and sends the lamp-light flowing around the shed – there is no sign of his most recent purchase anywhere.

He moves, unruffled, to check the trunk where he placed the clothes he removed from the boy the night before – they are still there, folded with care. He crosses to the door, noticing now that it stands slightly ajar. Pushing it open, he steps into the morning mist and scans the narrow lane to the left and then to the right. There is no sign of his missing property – he could have been robbed; he would not put it past Perle . . . but all the same, it is unlikely ... He emits something between a soft grunt and a sigh.

The truth is, sometimes things slip away from you. The truth is, Greely knows it better than anyone, sometimes the dead walk at night.

Chapter Four

27 Craven Street, London

Robert Perle enjoys silence in the morning. Breakfasting alone, he muses on sugar, wishes he had got in on it before it was too late. Sugar or coffee – but even coffee is sewn up now. He is not in a position to buy shares and see a tidy sum accumulate. He must be in at the very beginning of something – the moment before it takes off, when a very modest amount at just the right time can produce untold riches. Something very large coming from something small, as if by magic – a spore mushrooming in the right conditions. He craves it. He can feel the desire in his belly. Some days, having seen all the materials in Peter Woulfe's rooms, he thinks Woulfe will find a new substance altogether, something more valuable than gold. In his most hopeful moments, he dreams of something beyond imagining – something beyond mortal measure.

He has all his life been surrounded by wealth; the very finest things have been within touching distance. And he likes to touch, believes that his fingertips partake of an exquisite sensitivity. He runs his thumb across the pad of his fingers as other men might test a tool. The stockings he wears today, for example, are high-grade silk in duck-egg blue. He knows them to be of excellent quality, but he knows, too, that there are better stockings available and that other men have them – Carew, for example, a man of no special ability, who has done nothing of note other than be born the first son of an enterprising father, is invariably clothed like an Arabian prince. Clothing aside, Perle snorts delicately, there is nothing princely about Carew.

And as he does every morning after breakfast, Robert Perle considers his finances. He sits quite still while Mrs Waites clears the table. She piles the plate, gathers the cutlery slowly and quietly.

He runs through his outgoings, starting as always with the greatest. There is the rent on this house. The cost of Gorridge and Mrs Waites. The girl, Annie, in the kitchen. Wages for them all – and then he considers how much they eat. He must ask Mrs Waites – how much does Annie eat? What is it exactly that she does? Which leads to the grocer's bill, the butcher's bill, the coal man. Candles – why, for he all knows, Gorridge burns candles 'til the small hours in his little chamber. But what to do without Gorridge? Or Mrs Waites, for that matter.

Then there is his workroom. His dissecting room. The equipment. His instruments.

There are the horses, the carriage. It is quite extraordinary how much it costs to keep a carriage these days in London. It may be that the carriage will have to go. He can hire hackneys, take chairs where necessary.

He decides he will pay Peter Woulfe a visit. He writes a note, calls out, 'Gorridge, Gorridge, have this sent immediately to Mr Woulfe at Barnard's Inn.'

He does not meet Gorridge's eye. Anything that happens at night is not to be mentioned in the daylight.

Chapter Five

Barnard's Inn, Fetter Lane, London

Peter Woulfe cannot rouse himself. He has risen at four without fail every morning for over thirty years, but this morning he wavers. He is accustomed to reaching inside himself and finding resolve, but this morning he is shocked to meet a weakness he has never encountered before, something fluttery and tentative that is entirely unfamiliar – as if someone has swapped his inner lion for an ailing butterfly.

Robert Perle is blackmailing him – smooth and certain, he comes on Saturday afternoons to collect three guineas. An embarrass-ing amount – large enough that it pains him to hand it over, small enough that he can sustain it almost indefinitely. Perle does not con-tent himself with the guineas – he touches his books; he peers at his apparatus. After four weeks of these odious visitations, Woulfe has begun to despair. He can see no end.

As he lies in his bed, he is sure he has never before felt such heaviness in his limbs. He does not try to move. In fact, within seconds, he is occupied by the possibility that he will never be able to move again. He is breathing slow and shallow into tired lungs so that his chest does not appear to shift at all. His mouth itself is rancid, but there is another distasteful flavour that belongs to the air, a dankness that goes beyond the usual dampness. Tomb air, he thinks – why, if air were to be sealed in stone, still as death for a thousand years, this is how it would taste. At this thought, his inner flutter rises into panic. How does he know he is still alive? Having not yet opened his eyes, how is he to confirm that he is not in fact dead and buried? That would certainly explain his inability to move.

He feels a sob rise; he is so weary, too weary to be dead on top of everything else. He considers the sob; would he feel one rise if he were a spirit? And then it comes to him – this has to do with Mal and whatever spirit he possessed. Peter now suspects he is not dead at all but haunted. The lad's spirit is around – and it is that which has stilled his own body, brought the smell of death, filled him with fear and weakness. He is sure that he can feel a presence about him – something that is not of him, something foreign. His mind fills with an image of Mal, his flat, broad face, dull, grey skin, one eye a-wander . . . and the other staring right at him with such deep reproach that he cannot bear it. The eye boring in on him, with no escape. It is intolerable. He cannot submit to it.

With one great heave, he sits up in his bed and opens his eyes.

His room is dark; a dim, grey light is creeping in around the curtains – moonlight filtered through mist. The air settling on his shoulders is damp. The fire has long gone out; the room lacks warmth or life – indeed, it is hard to imagine that there is warmth or life anywhere in the world this morning. But the room is empty. There is no etheric young man pinning him down with a reproachful gaze, no spirit hovering. He is quite clearly completely alone. Whatever was there has now gone.

His heart is thudding. His limbs are still weary, but he is alive, and he is alone. He resolves to swing his legs out of the bed. He will light a lamp and then light the fire. He will do these things that Mal would usually do. He will fulfil these tasks without excessive consideration, just as the lad might. Then he will attend to his prayers, and then he will dress. He reaches for his tinder-box, fumbles slightly, lights the candle by his bed.

He moves across the room and brings the candle to the wood shavings on the grate. They begin to glow and curl and flame. He is held rapt by the flickering light, is quite delighted when the sticks he gently lays upon the shavings begin to whicker, speaking to each other in a delicate language that seems deeply familiar. He piles on more wood, waits crouched by the grate for the sustained crackle to tell him that the fire is safely established. And now his room is lit by the soft glow of the candle, and the fire throwing dancing shadows on the walls.

He kneels to pray; he closes his eyes – the image of Mal rises again. He opens his eyes. He will pray this morning with his eyes open; he will pray with all his might. He will plunge down inside himself, past the fluttering butterfly and find his true, noble self. He will bring that self to the fore, to be held in the eye of the all-seeing, all-knowing, all-forgiving Divine. He will cast that other weak and frightened self aside.

He has prayed with fervour every day of his life, searched for the true path so long. He has read the works, listened to the preachers, participated in the most sacred of ceremonies – and what has it all come down to? He distils it this morning to one question: is there something in him so valuable that it can render all his failings moot? Something deep inside that is so good and light and true that it transcends all need for good works?

Chapter Six

June 1744 – *Midsummer*

Maiden Lane, London

Peter Woulfe at seventeen is tall and tightly wound. His height is accentuated by his long, thin body and his habit of taking great loping strides with his large, heavy feet. As he moves along Maiden Lane, his head dips and falls like a boat at sea. It is late evening, and he is carrying a book through the streets of London.

The sky is light with the particular vividness of midsummer, but he is only dimly aware of the time of day, of the season, of the book he is carrying – he has spent the last hour preparing a mixture of horse dung, sand and straw with the utmost care. Josiah Sweetnam, apothecary and erstwhile alchemist, his master and mentor for the summer, believes himself to be on the verge of a great discovery. Peter, in this, his first month in London, is consumed by the possibility that, after years of thankless toil, Sweetnam's work will come to glorious fruition while he is present. He believes that, by rigorous attendance to his duty in the matter of mixing dung, he may well provide the vital element of care and exactitude so necessary for great work to flourish. Perhaps four-fifths of his mind is occupied thus, leaving the remaining fifth to hold the book, a precious tome, wrapped several times in waxed linen, and to remember the directions that will bring him to the lodging house of the book's owner.

It is partly Peter's level of mental abstraction that will render what he is about to see so shocking. Certainly, it is as if his unguarded mind is particularly porous in the moment that he crosses onto Fleet Street and sees, standing not fifteen feet in front of him, a large naked man with his arms outstretched to the heavens.

The man's nakedness strikes him, as well it might – but more than that, the wild bright intensity of his eyes, the flecks of pale foamy spittle on his pink fleshy lips, the terrifying animation of the man's entire being, combine to impress upon his mind an image that he will be able to summon in vivid detail until the day he dies. What he perceives, aside from the nakedness, the semi-tumescent, entirely unexpected nakedness of the man, is that this man has somehow overflown his body – he is manifestly no longer contained by his flesh and blood. He has risen up out of himself, there on the side of Fleet Street in the bright evening light, and his essence is currently at play – at livid, uncontrollable play – in the space between his head and the sky above.

From the threshold of the house behind, a portly man is brandishing a cloak with increasing urgency and not a little distress.

'Please, sir, allow me . . . allow me . . .'

Peter notes an accent, perhaps Dutch, which appears to be thickening with the portly man's agitation.

'My good sir, you must cover yourself. Dear sir, I beg you.'

He comes forwards and moves delicately around the naked man, for all the world like a bullfighter, but the naked man moves as though burned from the touch of the cloth and skips, light-footed, out of reach into the middle of the road. He flings out his arm and points at the portly man with such force that he is brought up short, as if by the point of a sword. The naked man begins to speak, but the words that issue forth – with an agony of stop-start stuttering effort – are for the most part unintelligible to Peter. He hears the word *angel* and then the word *Jews*.

The portly man with the cloak appears to have tears in his eyes. 'Baron, I beg you! Your cloak!'

The naked man attempts to speak again, and Peter holds his breath. It is clear that what the man wishes to say is of the utmost importance to him, a matter perhaps of life or death.

Forcing his lips to take shape, the man begins to speak, and the first words come at a run: 'Kind sir! An angel of heaven speaks to me now . . . with a message for the Jews . . .' Then his mouth fails him once more and no further meaning can be wrenched from the sounds that follow.

A crowd has begun to gather. Peter becomes aware that his mouth is open. The exchange between the two men and the ribald laughter of crowd threaten to dissipate his feeling of having seen something truly remarkable, and he wishes to run with what is left of this sensation back to his room at Mr Sweetnam's – there to make some sense of it, to contain it in a specimen jar in the corner of his mind. And so he turns, and as he turns, he remembers the book, clapped tight to his chest, what he has been calling in his mind 'the baron's book', and just then the portly Dutchman appeals again.

'Dear Baron, dear sir, remember your illustrious name.'

And it becomes clear to Peter that the man he seeks, the owner of the precious book, Baron Swedenborg, currently residing at Brockmer's house off Fleet Street, and the naked man in the middle of the road are one and the same.

He cannot return to his master with his errand unaccomplished. It is not within his character at this point in time to allow such a simple task to overcome him, to shape the words that would explain why he could not deliver the book to the baron. He considers approaching the portly Dutchman and handing over the book with a quick word of explanation, but that would require a degree of gross insensitivity that he cannot imagine exhibiting – nor can he imagine skipping past the crowd and entering the house behind in order to find a suitably responsible pair of hands in which to place the book.

So, he stands where he has stopped, the book clasped against his chest.

෴

As though he were a large bell, struck recently with some force, Peter Woulfe's body is alive with a delicate tremor. The sun has dipped below the buildings on the Strand, and as he walks back towards Mr Sweetnam's house, the sheen of sweat along his back begins to cool, and he shivers.

He is still carrying the book, now tucked under his arm. It feels more awkward and much heavier than he could have imagined on his outward journey. He, on the other hand, feels quite light, quite unusually light, as if his feet have become buoyant and cannot be trusted to maintain their connection with the ground.

Also, something has happened to his eyes. At least, the appearance of the Strand startles him. It looks entirely different to how it did when he passed through not fifteen minutes earlier, now appearing to be unremittingly, melancholically grey. And every beast, every man, woman and child in sight looks grubby, tired and provincial. The movement of people – a man whips a horse; another man bawls with rage at a boy who darts in front of his cart – seems to Peter to represent all that is ugly and unharmonious in human existence.

And more than that, he questions now the very reality of the world he sees before him. It seems to partake of a slimmer, less convincing kind of reality than that which animated the naked man and his portly Dutch friend. It seems to Peter that the people on the Strand on this June evening – even the man whipping the horse, his mouth slightly askew with the effort – are not really there at all, or if they are, then they are as tentatively connected to their actions as the players he has seen on the stage at the Theatre Royal.

He turns down towards the river, feeling that perhaps sight of that great living mass will reorder his vision. Thinking that a route by the water cannot be much longer than the one he followed on his way from Sweetnam's house, he turns away from the busy, ugly spectacle of London at the close of day and into the nameless alleys leading to the river docks. The sun dips further and casts the evening towards night. As the darkness gathers, faster than he anticipated, he finds he is not at all sure that he knows where he is going and how he will find his way. The alley along which he walks appears devoid of all human life. He hesitates for a moment to consider turning right or heading forwards to where he feels the river must lie.

A hand takes hold of his left arm, and his feet leave the ground as the blood rushes painfully to his heart. As he regains the ground, he turns his head to see his attacker and finds he has flung his hand against his chest in the manner of a distressed lady. A small, pinched face smiles up at him.

Sukie Bulmer has recently reapplied bright-red paint to her lips, but that cannot hide her missing front tooth, the pockmarks on her forehead or the hungry look in her wide grey eyes.

'Startle you, did I?' Sukie sidles around until she is facing Peter and her small, thin body is pressed against his.

'No, no, thank you,' he stutters. He is well aware that sex is a sin, well used to wrestling his urges, incense and hellfire mingling in his mind to ward away temptation.

'Oh, come on, a lovely boy like you!'

Peter Woulfe begins to speak more clearly, more firmly: 'No, not tonight.'

And Sukie lifts her hand to touch his cheek, saying again, 'A lovely boy like you.'

Her fingers brush his face gently, and there is something in her touch that stalls Peter, a tenderness, a delicacy that for one absurd moment makes him feel he is about to cry. His throat tightens; his eyes glisten. He feels young and alone – feels as if this touch promises the only possible comfort in the world. He looks down at Sukie, and she in turn looks at him. Perceiving the dampness about his eyes and the slight wobble in his lower lip, she smiles her true smile and touches his cheek again.

'Come on, then – it'll make you feel better.'

With a simplicity that is rare in her complicated existence, Sukie yields to the pull of some untold human gravity and lies her head softly on Peter Woulfe's chest. He stands there, feeling the slight weight of her head against him, and an exquisite calm floods through him. It is as if his world is reordering itself around their two bodies, as if a charge of restless, rootless energy has been earthed. Then, as naturally as thirst on a hot day, he feels himself stiffen against her. She takes him by the hand and leads him into a smaller, darker alleyway, and he knows now that it cannot be a sin to feel like this, cannot be a sin to feel tender and whole and alive.

Sukie positions herself against the wall and pulls him towards her. His right arm is still occupied by the baron's book. He hesitates for just a moment before bending down and leaning it against the wall. She wraps her thin arms around his waist and pulls him closer. He dips his head and tentatively kisses her temple. As he inhales the unfamiliar scent, a flare discharges in his belly. Within seconds, he has buried his nose in Sukie's neck. He detects the smell of female perspiration, along with a scent more cloying and floral, perhaps powder – and something else, a smell he has no words for, a note tucked in behind the other smells that tugs at the furthest corner of his memory, as if he has found a hint of something precious that was lost long ago. And so, his nose leads him down around her bosom and back to the nape of her neck, his belly all the time flaring with exquisite pleasure. And there, at the nape of her neck, he wonders where the true source of this smell might lie, and if it might be possible for him to find that place and stay there forever.

Just then, Sukie opens his breeches and slips a practised hand inside. Peter Woulfe emits a low animal groan at her touch and begins to straighten up. Sukie arranges her skirts deftly with her other hand and guides him firmly towards her, stretching up on her toes, wrapping her right leg around his waist with the accustomed ease of a dancer – sliding back down, with the aid of gravity and taking Peter's unusually large cock inside her with surprising ease. Peter knows only that this is the most perfect moment of his life. His hips begin to move, pushing Sukie back against the rough brick wall. She wraps her other leg around his waist as he thrusts – his eyes closed tightly, his mouth agape. All of him racing to a point of impossible ecstasy.

He grazes his head on the wall with his final thrust.

'There now.' She pats him on the back. 'There, there.'

He is filled with an immense sense of gratitude.

'That'll be thruppence.'

He fumbles for his coins.

Chapter Seven

Foxes Court, London

Sukie Bulmer begins to wake. Her morning mouth is gin-tight and dry, her head twanging thin and taut as catgut. She lies alone in the bed she shares with Sal in their low-eaved garret room. The day is awake around her, and the June sun pushes insistently under the door. The air is filled with the hum of flies, and to Sukie's sleepy mind, the flies are the sound of the sunlight itself pulsing through the air.

Then she remembers the book, sees it clear in her mind, remembers the sound of the spine shifting, the cover pulling away with a suck as she opened it for the first time. Her mouth unwittingly opens to an *O*, and more than gin, more than anything that she has held in her mind for a long time, she thirsts for another look at the book. She carried it straight back, wondering as the journey ate into her night if it would be worth the missed tricks, but not wanting to trust it to Pad or Sal. Pocket-watches and coins they might pool and share, as fair is fair, but this was something different, something in the way of a personal bounty. Something, though she did not dare to articulate the hope even to herself, that might just change everything.

Now, she opens the book at the first plate. What she glimpsed in the night is alive before her now: two roses so delicately drawn they could be real, their long thorny stems curving to frame two trumpeting angels on a ladder; a man asleep or dead at the bottom of the ladder; stars and a crescent moon at the top. She has never seen anything like this in her life, cannot even begin to fathom how such a thing could be made. She feels immediately that the image contains a message of great importance. There is writing, to be sure, across the middle of the page, but her eye skips past this as it would past scratchings in the dust.

She peers closer, her tongue sitting limp on her lower lip – it is all about the angels, surely? Their trumpets pointing towards the inert man. Have they paused on the ladder to tell him something? To wake him? How long have they been there, their wings aloft, ready for flight? Her fingers trace the outline on the page, circling along the curve of the rose stems and down the ladder, running lightly over the angels and coming to a pause at the figure of the man. No, he is not dead, not lying like that with his fingers loose and his head half turned. He must be sleeping. And Sukie Bulmer would like to take him by his shoulders and shake him awake, because he is missing the angels, their message, their trumpeting. She feels it is poor luck indeed that such a thing should happen – that angels might come, trumpets and all, just when the man is asleep.

She would dearly love to know what they are trying to tell him, but it seems to Sukie that while the man sleeps, neither he nor she can hear what it is. It is some time before it occurs to her to turn the page to see if he awakens.

But the next plate appears to bear no relation to the first image. It is far more beautiful than the first one – highly coloured with yellows and reds. There is a bright sun with eyes, nose and a mouth. There are four figures this time. Two more angels – bigger, brighter and more detailed than the angels on the first page. She can see the feathers on their wings, their curling golden hair, their loose clothing, such as might be convenient when flying. Not much in the way of tits but beautiful all the same – young, maybe, but old at the same time. And, feeling that her head might burst, Sukie turns her gaze to the bottom half of the page, where two smaller figures kneel on either side of something that reminds her of a cooking furnace, like the ones she has seen down in the hot, smoky kitchens of the chop-house. She leans closer to see why the man is praying, why the woman is so serious with outstretched arms; she leans so near to the page that she could fall in there and land beside them.

Her tired eyes begin to close; she lies back against her pillow, the book resting on her chest. She is both weary and restless, heavy in body yet reluctant to be land-borne. Her mind fills with angels flying. And though they fly close and smile when she reaches out, she cannot quite touch them.

∽

Peter Woulfe flies in his dreams – as if his mind is skimming the surface of a vast sunlit lake, he can feel the kiss of the wind, is aware of the cool water beneath him and the light at play all around.

He awakes, his face deep in his pillow, his arms flung out to either side, and thinks immediately of Sukie Bulmer. That is to say, he thinks of the weight of her head against his chest, the smell of her neck, his own ecstasy as he entered her, but not her name – he does not know that she is called Sukie Bulmer, that one of her possible fathers was called Bulmer or Butler or Buller, and that her mother, in a flush of love for her tiny baby, liked the sound of Sukie, linked it with the puckered-up suck of the child at her breast. Said *Sukie Sue, Sukie Sue*, as she kissed the small creature's brow.

He clatters down the stairs from his attic room, his large feet awkwardly overhanging the narrow steps, his head dipped, and almost collides with Josiah Sweetnam, who appears this morning to be smaller and more hunched than Peter remembers.

Sweetnam looks up with suspicion at Peter Woulfe; he detects an unfamiliar ebullience in the young man, and his short pink nose twitches. He closes his mouth around his ungainly teeth, pursing his lips in disapproval. He does not know what it is that warrants his disapproval – he merely senses that young Woulfe is happier than is quite right. He notes the painful-looking graze on his head, which Peter has forgotten about, but does not mention it in case that could be construed as concern or interest in the young man's well-being.

'Come along – there is much to do,' Sweetnam says abruptly, and Peter follows him into the workroom.

Peter's buoyant mood is unaffected by Sweetnam, even though he is obscurely aware that Sweetnam will now make his day as unpleasant as possible, aware that he has made a mistake by coming down the stairs with a smile on his face. He sees now that a man of Sweetnam's character could not fail to consider it his duty to realign the balance of misery in the world by compensating for any unexpected happiness with a slew of onerous, thankless tasks.

Sweetnam believes that Woulfe has been cosseted and dislikes him for it. He knows that there are men of means behind him, while he, Josiah Sweetnam, has had to work for every item in this building. He has tried, in his own way, to convey this to Woulfe, has tried to make the young man understand that not everyone has a father and uncles whose influence can permit them to land here in the middle of this shop of delights, with sulphur, with antimony, with mercury, with dishes and jars, with a furnace and fuel for it . . . Woulfe has gained entry by the simple means of a letter from his uncle in Paris and a banker's draft for his bed and board. Sweetnam, the son of a bookbinder, has had to battle for his current modest station and feels all the time as if it might be taken from him, leaving him to scrabble at a different trade – one that might just feed his body but would starve his soul.

Peter Woulfe knows none of this and would not care if he did, but he once lifted the piece of black cloth covering the small bench at the back of the workroom and revealed a row of delightfully delicate chisels lined up in decreasing order of size, a thin, smooth blade that could fillet a fish, three pale pieces of baleen bone, and a spool of linen thread. It took him a moment to place them as the tools of a bookbinder and he had quickly pulled the cloth back, finding them both intriguing and also slightly womanish.

Peter, as he sets about rinsing and drying ten already clean and dry glass beakers, does not experience a diminishment of his happiness; he does, however, see Sweetnam with a new and startling clarity. He sees that Josiah Sweetnam is a small man and an unhappy one, and more than this, he sees that Sweetnam will never have the success he craves. Suddenly, everything about Sweetnam appears wrong – somehow crooked and lacking: his shoulders, one held higher than the other, his small, meaty hands, his watery blue eyes, the very way he stands at his bench. Peter detects uncertainty, a lack of potency about Sweetnam's posture, and he wonders how he ever believed that this man would make a great discovery.

Sweetnam looks across at him angrily as if he can read his thoughts. 'Did you deliver the book to the baron himself?'

Peter has forgotten all about the book. His last memory of it is the sight of it leaning against the rough brick wall in the alley. It is possible that he picked it up and brought it home, possible that he did not – he has forgotten his journey home, cannot remember a step of it, as if he were quite the worse for wine. He pretends not to hear, casts desperately around his mind for some clue.

'Woulfe! Did you deliver the book directly to the baron or not?'

Peter looks directly at Sweetnam and lies. 'I gave it to the Dutchman.'

His heart has begun to pound in his chest; his happiness is now somewhat diminished, but he sounds clear and sure.

'Your instructions were not unduly taxing, I trust? Merely to hand the book, the extremely valuable book, to its owner, Baron Swedenborg.'

'No, sir.'

Peter's head is flooded with the image of the naked baron in the evening sun. He forgot about the baron, about the book, about everything except Sukie, and now he revisits the image with a sense of astonishment. He dips his head quickly, appearing to scrutinise the interior of the glass beaker he is holding – his memory of the baron is so bright, so alive, that he fears Sweetnam might catch a glimpse of it.

But Sweetnam, who is now frowning fiercely at Peter, does not appear to be glimpsing the vivid image in his head. No – Peter, glancing up briefly, sees that Sweetnam looks very much like his usual dissatisfied, irritable self, but there is something else, too, a tightness around his eyes and mouth that looks very much like fear.

'It is a very, very important book, Woulfe. I told you, did I not, how vital it was that it was delivered safely to the baron?'

'Yes, sir – do not worry, sir. The landlord assured me he would give it to the baron directly.'

A flush rises in Sweetnam's face; his voice shakes a little as he speaks. 'There will be hell to pay if he did not.'

Peter nods and looks quickly down again at the beaker in his hand.

Sweetnam looks at the top of Peter Woulfe's bowed head. For a moment, he can barely breathe. It is possible that, by entrusting this cosseted dolt with delivering the book, he has made the biggest mistake of his life. He clenches and unclenches his fists. He will find out soon enough one way or the other. And if his worst fear comes to pass, he will have to run for it. It is as simple as that.

As his heartbeat steadies, Peter thinks to himself that this morning is just another in a long line of mornings to Sweetnam, thinks that this small, frightened man could not possibly understand the transcendent events of the previous night. It is just like him to get into a fearful flap over a book.

Calming himself, using his long index finger to pick a minute piece of white fluff from the base of the beaker, Peter brings his mind back to the immediate problem – he cannot remember when he last saw the book, but it is clear that whatever else happens, he must find it and deliver it to the baron without delay. He will resolve the problem calmly and competently, and then he can move onto more important matters like making love to Sukie and learning how to attune his hearing to the voices of the angels.

In three hours, when Sweetnam leaves to dine, as he always does at the chop-house on the corner, Peter will race to his room and search for the book. Maybe it is simply under his mattress? One way or the other, he will be out walking in the streets of London in the dark tonight – with the book or searching for it. And his mind returns with pleasure to Sukie – who will be beside him as he walks, her head just reaching to his shoulder, her small, light hand in his, until they stop walking, as they inevitably will, and she pulls him towards her again.

Peter's mouth opens, and his eyes haze over; he suppresses the small gasp of pleasure tugging at his chest. He moves to pick up another beaker, knows he must take himself back again to merely walking by her side . . . back further to when they will meet, and she will smile a thin-lipped little smile, and he will touch her cheek gently as he looks into her wide grey eyes.

⟳

The long summer day is ceding to night, and Peter stands alone in an alley between Fleet Street and the Thames. He has been walking about for some time now, and he feels he must pause, because his aimless movement is beginning to feel foolish.

The book was not under his mattress – an inconvenience to be sure, but as he thought about it, it became clear to him that the first and most important thing is to find Sukie. Then he can make love to her *and* ask her, respectfully, carefully, about the whereabouts of the baron's book.

But it simply did not occur to him that she would not be there. He has been approached a number of times, once by a girl with round cheeks and tight blue eyes – he felt a jolt of repulsion at the sheer wrongness of this girl. His limbs are heavy, and his mind has begun to sink from the height of delightful expectation that sustained him through the day. He can feel sweat beading along his upper lip. He resolves to stay all night in the alleys if need be. His left shoulder tightens up against his neck. All night, if it should take that long, and the following night, too.

He has not fully accounted for the dark. The moonless dark, which seems to have arrived with great suddenness, is as absolute and unsettling as soft palms pressed across his eyes. He is now acutely aware of the smell of urine, the particular tang of piss in summer. His ears fill with sounds – scratchings and rustlings and a muffled shout from somewhere above him and to the right. And then what could well be footfall farther along the alley.

He feels the clench of fear in his belly. He begins to move; it is too hard to stay still. He will walk up this alley and down the next one.

And it is just as he propels himself around the corner that he collides with some force into Sukie. Some sharp part of her, perhaps her angular shoulder, connects painfully with his chest. He is instantly sure it is her, can tell from the thrum in his belly, but he is unable to speak. He begins to rub his chest.

She recovers more quickly and makes a playful grab at him. 'All right, handsome, where you off to, then?'

In the pause that follows, Peter realises that she has not recognised him.

'Come on, now.' Her pale face tilts up. 'A lovely boy like you.'

'I . . . I . . .?'

At the sound of his voice, Sukie pauses. She has an excellent ear for voices. Living mostly by night, she has grown to distrust faces, knows how lamplight can soften a cruel mouth – but she has yet to meet a clinker who can mask his voice. Even the stuttering syllable uttered by him tells her that she has met this fellow before – recently, she feels.

'You haven't forgotten Sukie now, have you?' Her arms slip around his waist.

He feels a rush of relief at knowing her name, of having it handed to him without the awkwardness of having to ask. 'Sukie.'

The additional speech confirms what she suspected – that he is as he sounds: a soft eager fellow, who will please easy.

'Come on then, handsome. You know Sukie. Always worth a twist. Thrupenny special for you.'

It seems to Peter that it would be better to take Sukie first before enquiring about the book. Given that he must do both, it is clear that the order of events will matter. To enquire first may well set her to flight – or, if not to flight as such, the enquiry could reasonably be expected to impair the experience.

When Peter takes Sukie for the second time, he fears initially that his pleasure is not as exquisite as it was the first time – he is not quite so comfortable; and as he thrusts, he is conscious of a slight disappointment. But Sukie shifts; he feels her breath in his ear – and he is flooded with such delight that he immediately forgets his disappointment.

It is as he counts three pence onto her open palm that he decides to mention the book.

'Sukie.' He says her name with what feels like tenderness. His throat is dry, and his breath has not reclaimed its rhythm, so in fact he sounds strangled, young, uncertain.

She says nothing.

He does not wish with his first enquiry to impugn her honour, does not wish to accuse her of theft or to threaten her, and so he becomes quite formal, quite respectful.

'There is a matter I would very much like your assistance with.'

Sukie, for her part, has remembered him: the size of his cock, the particular eagerness of his appetite – and she has connected him immediately with the book. The precious book that lies hidden under her blanket at Ma Crofter's. She suspects from the shift in tone that he is going to mention it, so she dips her hand into his breeches, squeezes him gently. She hears the air rush from his lungs in a grunt, and she moves sleekly away, off into the dark – quick and sure as a cat, so that he finds himself stumbling, calling her name into the night.

∽

Half an hour later, Sukie stumbles into The Goat. She has already stopped for gin. The tallow-lit room is full of hot bodies, the smells of summer sweat, tobacco, gin and beer. Where there is a flame of a candle, Sukie sees spheres of light dancing, a soft sea of colour swimming around her. Tonight, it seems that Dick Pointer is possessed – the sound from his fiddle racing out into the hot air like a living thing. There is no room at all, and yet people are dancing, their movement clearing space enough.

And suddenly, up close, there is Sal, embracing her with a shriek of delight.

'Where you beeeen? Where you beeeen?'

Sal's face is red from the sun, her eyes bloodshot, nose and cheeks raw and sore-looking. She has been drinking all day on the hill, forgetting about her complexion, forgetting about everything.

She thumps Sukie's upper arm with pleasure. 'I'm that pleased to see you!'

Sal pulls Sukie into a reel, and they swing so fast and fierce, with no care at all, so caught up are they in the whirling motion, that they crash against a table and spill beer – causing folk to rise up and roar at them. But they spin on, for Dick has not paused in his playing, and they turn so furiously, hands clasped, their weight leaning out, that Sukie wonders what would happen if she were to let go. She sees herself for a moment – let loose, flying out through the press of bodies, out through the wall and up into the sky.

But Sal is holding tight as tight, and in time, in a turn and a turn and a turn more, the reel spins out, and they run out of breath and collapse, laughing, into a corner.

Sukie and Sal make their way home; the moon is bright, the night still warm. The house is darker than the street and thick with the smell of many sleeping bodies. There are forty-six people living here – packed tight, head to toe, babies to bosoms – from the noisome basement up as far as the garret room that Sukie and Sal luxuriate in. Dreams fill the heavy air. They place their feet quietly on the stairs. Once across the threshold, as if entering the room has changed her, Sal takes Sukie's wrist firmly in her hand and leads her to the bed. Sukie leans her weight back so that Sal must pull her, but she follows all the same.

There is a directness in Sal that Sukie trusts, a matter-of-fact seeking after pleasure – like a person might clear out a room in search of something precious. She feels as light as a bird beneath her, marvels at the strength of bone – that the cage for her heart and her breath holds fast against Sal's weight and movement. It seems to her now that Sal seeks a secret; it is at the tip of her tongue, a secret that has everything to do with Sukie. A secret that is caught up with the sob buried deep inside her. And she might just find it this time.

And then there is stillness and Sal's breath, heavy in the nape of her neck – and Sukie's thoughts turning slowly . . . to the hot night to come, to the angels flying through her book . . . and the red ribbon she would like for her grey bonnet. Until Sal's strong fingers begin to move again, her wet mouth opening, a tongue flick, and then it is just the angels flying fast and furious into the sun.

Chapter Eight

St Paul's, London

Sukie dislikes the bookseller straight away. Up close, leaning into his high, burnished counter, she sees his jowls and his florid cheeks and thinks he could as well be a pig buyer. Not at all what she had hoped. She imagined a thinner, more soulful man. She has walked the length of Fleet Street, passing many booksellers' on the way, to the arcing churchyard under the shadow of St Paul's, thinking that the book, her precious book, must be placed in the right hands.

The bookseller knows exactly what Sukie is the moment the door opens. The bonnet and ribbons with which she has armoured herself would have revealed her calling on their own, but her slight frame and her small, pinched face, marked by childhood hunger and ill health, are further confirmation. He thinks of himself as a kind man, and so he greets her a shade more jovially than he would ordinarily.

'Good day, miss – may I be of assistance?'

Sukie's eyes narrow. She would like to turn around and walk back out the door. She holds the book awkwardly under her arm. At times, since she found it, she has been sure she would keep it – keep it forever, merely to look at. At other times, she has known that the only right-minded thing to do is to sell it. It is undoubtedly valuable. The weight alone, the rich colour of the plates, tell her that much – but she suspects it also has a deeper value, a value that would be clear to a more knowledgeable person. She thinks of various enormous sums, imagines enough to take airy rooms in a seaside town. But now that she is there, facing the bookseller, she begins to doubt her decision.

'What have you got there, miss? Lay it up here, and I'll take a look.'

She sees his plump pink hands waiting on the glossy wooden counter and thinks of a pig's trotters.

'No need to be afraid.'

'I ain't afraid,' Sukie responds scornfully. But in truth, once she says it, she realises she is afraid. Not of the man himself but of what might happen when her beautiful book is exposed to his gaze.

But all the same, she places it on the counter. The bookseller begins to unwrap the waxed cloth; he can tell that the book within is not a natural match with the girl in front of him. As he reveals the cover, his bushy eyebrows rise up his brow.

'Very nice,' he says, in a tone that Sukie does not appreciate. 'Very nice indeed.' He opens the book. 'And where' – he raises his head and looks at Sukie – 'did miss come across this?'

She tilts her head to the side, meets his gaze and says, 'Know a lot about books, do you, mister? Know enough to tell me what it's worth?'

The bookseller does not respond but turns another page, turns swiftly back to the beginning, moves to the back of the book and leans right over to peer at the inside of the back cover. Then he closes the book, lays his two hands upon it and says to Sukie, 'This is certainly an unusual book. And when we speak of worth, it is not of worth to a great many people but may indeed be of great worth to a select few.' He is pleased with his sentence and smiles slightly, as he waits for Sukie to speak.

Sukie is suddenly overcome with anger. This exchange is far from what she envisaged. She knows that the bookseller is playing her, showing that he has more words and more knowledge than she does, and that there is very little she can do to redress the balance – very little, that is, but take her book elsewhere. And so she reaches over and pulls the book quickly towards her. The bookseller's hands make a small dull sound as they connect with the counter, and his eyes widen in surprise.

'Maybe you ain't select enough, mister – maybe your shop ain't big enough for a book like this?'

Sukie does not see well into the distance. When she looks down, the ground beneath her is shrouded in a soft mist that begins somewhere below her knees. Details merge; everything blurs. But she can tell a person at a hundred yards by their walk. The drag of a left foot, the tilt of a head, the tightness of a shoulder. These movements are as clear to Sukie as a face in daylight is to others. And up close, a hand's breath from her face – why, she can see better than anyone, and having seen a person once at this distance, she will never forget the curve of the lip, the line of hair on the forehead.

But it is not seeing that she attends to most as she makes her way from place to place. No, when she walks the city, she does not look so much as feel her way around. Smells and sounds guide her, and something else that is more than a combination of both. It is as if she has a footstep map in her mind and her feet themselves can tell one place from another.

And sure enough, the city is criss-crossed by pathways that are all misshapen in their own distinct way. Everywhere is puddled in the rain, fully swampy at times – or, when it is dry, then it is gritty, stony, hard on her shoes. There are cobbles by The Goat, a layer of grit down by the docks, and along Fleet Street, there is a flat grey stone that is easy to walk on but makes her feel oddly dismal. And even these finely laid paths break here and there into the slush of roads, and sometimes into nothing at all – why, once she heard of a boy who fell right through a grating into never-no-more. As if the city had swallowed him whole.

And of course, Sukie knows her patch: the corner by the almshouse that floods quite half across the road at the least bit of rain, the stinking sludge that seeps into the alley beside The Goat – as if a peculiar kind of filth has been brewing there beneath the surface. She does not venture far beyond the half mile encompassing Ma Crofter's, The Goat, and the warren of alleys between Holbourn and the river, especially not in the daylight with the noise and the light and the shove of people.

In the dark, she can pick up a scent: the drift of breath from another person's mouth, tinged with gin or beer or tobacco, the stagnant green snot of winter, the smells of sickness and health, the tang of armpits and crotches. Oh, what she can tell from a scent. The goaty old men, the fresh sweaty boys, some men quite stinking with want. And that is not to speak of the dog shit, horse shit, pig shit, human shit. By night, these smells are one thing, as if they, too, are slumbering, but by day, it is all alive and stirred up, all wafting into the air around her – which is already filled with noise: the criers crying, the traders casting their voices into the crowded air, all vying to be heard with their pamphlets and their eels to sell and their rabbits and their old clothes. No, it is altogether too much during the daytime, like a rasp against the skin of her mind.

And so, she inhabits the night, sleeps much of the day, darts out at midday to buy a pie, darts back again to her room, slumbers a bit and begins to come alive by the late afternoon. She is not really alert, not really herself until the first gin burns its way down her throat. And she is in the habit of waiting until she is near dead with the thirst before she has her second gin. She has learned this the hard way – having drunk too much too soon, felt it plunge through her stomach, course too quickly through her veins, found herself waking on sickly straw and the night half gone with no tricks, no pennies in her pocket, just a crashing head and a fit of the weeps. No, it is better to wait, and she waits, too, between the second and the third gin. After that, well . . . it depends on the night, on the company and the contents of her pocket.

She likes company well enough. But she likes to be alone, too. When she and Sal push off in different directions to walk the streets, she feels a lightness that is quite the opposite of loneliness. She suspects that Sal would stay arm in arm, working the clinkers in pairs, if she had a choice – even for half the pennies. But Sukie herself has never felt lonely, has never in fact felt quite alone. And this, despite having no family to speak of. None that she can remember. She recalls old Kitty in the market telling her when she was very young that she once had a mother but that she was dead, and the word *dead* coming out of Kitty's mouth was like a hole suddenly opening in the ground in front of her.

And without an aunt or a cousin or even an uncle to tell her, she does not know how her mother died – or, as her younger self wanted to ask, why?

She does not know where she is buried, who buried her – if she was buried at all or simply discarded. She does not know, having no one to tell her, that her mother was the last to die of three sisters who made their way to London from a far-away village tucked between the sea and a sparse mountain called Mount Gabriel on the south-west coast of Ireland. Three sisters with the same russet hair that she has, the same slight, nimble body. Annie and Aggie and Maura. Three strong resourceful girls. It had seemed like good odds to their father, putting them on the cart and watching their bright heads recede from him.

With their mother dead, Cornelius Leary believed he was doing his best – sending them all off, at the same time, by cart and then by boat, to a place he could only barely imagine. His three girls, terrified and elated, as if they were jumping off a cliff and trusting their wings to grow on the way down. He turned away and said to himself that at least they were together, the three of them – and that just a bit of luck might do to keep them all aloft.

For a moment after they left, he had a bone-shivering sense of himself alone, sinking into the bog – slipping slowly, surely, under, taking with him his cabin and the scrap of land around it. And then he remembered that he had not left himself alone at all, and he slipped his hand into the crook of his eldest daughter's arm. The one he had kept behind. Because he loved Bridey the most, and he hated her the most. Because it was he who had scraped and saved for the tickets, and so it was he who could decide who stayed and who left.

Chapter Nine

December 1739 – *The Great Frost*

Mount Gabriel, Cork, Ireland

After a motion-filled fury of wind and rain through the night, the world has gone still and white – a change as complete and sudden as a wrathful spell. Peter Woulfe wonders about the blood in his own body, feels it getting thicker, more sluggish as he walks away from the warmth of his big, square house. Looking back, he sees that even the hearth smoke is slow in the air. There is no birdsong, no flight. The fish are stilled in the frozen water of the pond; he can see three of them caught fast. Whether they are alive or dead, he cannot tell. He imagines that he, too, could pause for a moment too long and be held by this pressing cold, frozen to this very spot – and so he wills himself forwards, away from the fish and up the lane towards Bridey's cabin, towards the snow-covered summit of Mount Gabriel gleaming above it.

At thirteen, Peter is slight and delicate looking. His blue eyes are big in his narrow face; his fine new winter coat, generously cut for longer wear, makes him look younger than he is – the sleeves almost cover his hanging hands; his face is winter-pale against the dark-green wool of the upturned collar.

Bridey's cabin is less a cabin and more an extrusion of mud and stones emerging from the top field. Today, the frost-coated thatch of the cabin is fiercely bright above the greying lime of the walls. He has known it all his life, but in this new white world, it looks different: uglier, meaner and somewhat misplaced. On this coldest of cold days, it seems to him that the very worst of the frost has gathered at the top of the field, is in fact sitting on Bridey's place.

He wonders for the first time why that particular spot was chosen and by whom. It is ill-drained, so that the walls must surely suck moisture from the soil on all but the driest days, the scraggy ditch of hawthorns offering scant shelter from the winds of the north. Her two tiny windows glint at him as he approaches from the east. And, now that he looks at it, surely Bridey's thatch sits lower than most? Pushing down right onto the windows, which in turn are barely off the ground, so that if any light at all creeps inside, it must be by accident. It seems to him, too, that Bridey's place is smaller than the other cottages down the lane. The full stretch of it barely contains the door with a window squeezed on either side.

Peter shivers. The cold is pushing up through the soles of his boots, but it is not the cold alone that makes him shiver. Was it his father or his father's father who had the place built? Was it for Bridey herself or someone else? Why, if you wished for someone to live in the cold, damp dark, there would be no better place for it. He thinks of his own square house, the long windows, the high ceilings. He experiences an urge to reach up, as a giant might, and shift Bridey's place around so that at least it might benefit from the southerly light. But then he imagines the whole thing crumbling in his giant hand, stones coming asunder, the thatch caving in on Bridey.

He knocks quickly and, without waiting for a reply, opens the door and ducks inside, closing it before any heat can escape. His thoughts have unsettled him, and he is almost expecting to see Bridey still and waxen on her stool by the fire. She is on her stool, to be sure, sitting right in on top of the hearth, but her fire-flushed cheeks are ruddy, and her eyes are bright in the dark cowl of her shawl. She looks up as he enters.

'Petey-boy.' It is a statement. She names him as she might say, *there is the cat.*

He nods and experiences his usual flush of excitement. No one knows where he is. They are all huddled up in the house against the cold. He has not been forbidden to visit Bridey, because no one would think to forbid it, but all the same, these visits have the feeling of transgression.

He sits on a three-legged stool across from her and stretches towards the fire. His back feels the cold pushing in behind him, and the earthen floor chills the soles of his feet, but the turf fire is burning strong, casting a small, smoky circle of warmth.

'The cold is fierce.' He slips out of English and into the Irish he always uses when he is here. '*Tá an fuacht fíochmhar.*'

Bridey nods.

'The father says he has never known the like.' Peter looks to Bridey for confirmation. 'He says the water in that well has never before frozen, not in his father's father's time.'

'No.' She shakes her head. 'Never in my time or any time that I have heard of.'

Peter is quite sure he hears a note of satisfaction in her voice. He leans closer, to see her better. 'Colder than ever before?'

She inclines her head with a small, suppressed smile.

He says carefully, 'It is fierce cold.'

'It is indeed.'

Peter feels his heart leap against his chest. 'Bridey, what did you do?'

'What did I do? What did poor Bridey do?'

'Aah, Bridey, tell me – please tell me.'

'Sure, what could an old wan like me do?'

Peter sees that Bridey is trying not to smile, that she is quite delighted by this exchange.

'Aah, Bridey, tell me . . . do!'

'I'm telling you, Petey – what could an old wan like me have to do with anything?'

He sits back and says nothing. He is quite wild to know, but he sees that his eagerness is getting him no closer. He will wait now for her to speak. He will look at the fire. Out of the corner of his eye, he sees Bridey stretch her dirty bare feet out from under her cloak and closer to the fire. She wriggles her long, straight toes. Peter squeezes his eyes shut, but he can still see her toes moving in his mind's eye. The thatch above them creaks under the weight of the frost.

He opens his eyes and steals a look at her face – she is looking at her feet with satisfaction; she appears to be quite absorbed, as if she has forgotten he ever existed. He understands now that he cannot possibly out-wait her, she who has made an art of sitting still and silent on this very stool.

And so he prompts her. 'Is it like last summer and the rain?'

She says nothing.

He leans back in to catch her eye, sees a glint of what he takes to be assent. 'It is!' He claps his hands together. 'But, Bridey, how? This is more than a bit of rain.' He squirms uncomfortably. 'The father says there'll be plenty of people frozen to death. Frozen quite still in their steps.'

'He says that, does he?'

Peter Woulfe nods.

'Well, I'm sure he's right so.'

Peter takes a roll of bread from his pocket and a short stubby cylinder of butter wrapped in paper. He hands them over to Bridey.

All of her attention falls with pleasure on the food. Her lips purse as she cracks open the roll with her thumb, burying her nose in it for a moment, before lovingly uncovering the rich yellow butter, which she finds to be as hard as stone. 'Cush cush cush,' she says affectionately and rubs it gently between her palms, leaning in even closer to the fire, coaxing it like an unsettled child until it is just soft enough for her to take a scraping with the back of her long thumbnail.

She brings her thumb towards her already-open mouth before she appears to think the better of it and pushes the butter instead into the soft belly of the bread roll. She scrapes at the cylinder again and again until she has enough to cover one side of the roll with a thin layer. And then she pauses, looks critically down at the roll and speaks: 'I'll say for Maggie Donnell that she makes a fine bright butter.'

She is missing one of her top front teeth and two of the bottom, so she bites sideways at the roll, clamping down and pulling away with her hand to break the bread. And as she chews, small noises of pleasure escape her, such as Peter remembers hearing from his brother, years ago, as their mother spooned mash into his avid mouth.

Feeling that he's watching something quite private, Peter turns his attention to the fire while Bridey takes another mouthful. He thinks again of the cold and the stillness that comes with it, begins to dread his walk back to the house when he himself might be frozen in his steps.

When Bridey's voice breaks in upon the silence, he startles.

'I suppose I could tell you a small bit if you swore on your mother's life not to tell a soul.'

Peter loves his mother, so as he nods, he crosses his fingers surreptitiously.

'Swear it!' Bridey's voice is still claggy with food.

'I swear it.'

She nods, satisfied, swallows twice and looks down at her bread. There are two bites left. 'It's a sup I need. There.' She indicates the kettle suspended by the fire. 'Pour me a drop, Petey.' And she proffers a can, which has been sitting on a small shelf by her shoulder along with a pipe.

He lifts the heavy kettle and pours a stream of dark liquid into her can. She takes a draught and sighs with pleasure. She begins to speak in a low, urgent voice, so that he has to lean forwards to hear her.

'So, when it's the right day that's in it, I have no bite, no sup all day, and the belly is gnawing, and the lips are dry as straw, but the old body is as light as a leaf. And just as the dark is coming down – no sooner, mind you – when the last bit of light is colouring the sky, it's then that I go off.'

Peter imagines Bridey – dark and feathered, going right up into the air.

She stretches out her arms under her cloak, and indeed, they look like wings.

'That's when the wind gets into me and the dark and the fierce force of the night.'

He can see her: flying round about the cottage and then getting higher and faster, over the pines, across the bottom field, along up to his house. Swooping round close into the roof so that if he looked up, he'd see only a shadow that he might mistake for a crow. A flapping sound, a shift in the wind.

She begins to speak rhythmically, her head swaying. 'And I say to that last bit of sun – I say, it's me, Bridey Leary.' She raises her hand and jabs the air between them for emphasis as she says slowly, 'And I know you.'

It feels to Peter Woulfe that her sharp finger has landed on his chest.

Then she turns her finger back upon herself and says fiercely, as she taps her own breastbone, 'And you know me.

'And then I say to the wind – I say it is me, Bridey Leary, and I know you.' Again, she points her finger fiercely at Peter before turning it back on herself. 'And you know me.'

It seems to Peter that nothing in this world could pull his eyes away from the movement of Bridey's hand.

'And I say to the water there in that stream' – she points out the door, before her finger swivels back to Peter – 'I say, I know you, and you know me.

'And then I say to the wide dark night' – she raises her hand above her head – 'I say, it is me, Bridey Leary, and I know you, and you know me.

'And then I say to the mountain herself' – here she points down to the ground, her voice getting slower – 'it is me, Bridey Leary. And I know you best of all, because I came out of you, and I'm going back to you soon.'

Her hand drops back to her lap, and she breaks off to ask him sharply, 'Do you see?'

He must clear his throat before he says, 'I do,' in a small, strangled voice.

'And then, when I know it all, and it knows me, when we are gone through each other through and through . . .' Here she laughs, a surprisingly light and girlish sound. 'Then I forget it all!

'I forget about the sun gone down over the hill and the wind blowing and the water and the wind and the earth and the wide dark night. I forget it all! And then there is no sun or wind or water or earth – there's no night to hold them . . . sure, there's nothing but nothing. Not even the dark.'

She stops for a moment, still as stone.

And Peter is quite terrified, feels that he is falling backwards into a wide, endless hole that is not even dark.

'Do you see? Petey, do you see?'

He manages to nod.

'And when there is nothing at all' – there is a softness now, a warmth, to the old voice – 'that's when it all begins. Begins to begin. A smalleen wind stirs up a smalleen bit of nothing . . . and the bit of nothing stirs some small biteen of light . . . and the light stirs the wind, and the dark comes in around the light.' Bridey's hand rises from her lap and makes a gentle swirling motion through the air.

'And then we shape up the earth, like flesh on bones.' She gives a small, satisfied nod. 'And then we call back the water to flow through her.'

She pauses here for a moment, as if she is lost far, far away, before looking directly at him. 'And then Petey, sure, 'tis a small thing to call in the cold, to ask it to come creeping pale along the ground, to ask the water to fall still as still . . . and the ground to go hard as stone. 'Tis a small, small thing altogether.'

And Peter does not doubt her, not for one minute.

She brings the cup to her lips and takes another pull.

Peter would now like to be away from her. He stands and, as he does so, remembers that he has another piece of bread in the other pocket of his coat. He was planning to nibble it as he walked home, but instead he pulls it out and hands it to Bridey.

She takes it as her due, producing from the fold of her cloak a surprisingly clean bright handkerchief in which to wrap it.

'You're looking at my fine bit of cloth, Petey, are you?'

'No.'

'Your blessed mother gave me this.' She smooths it out lovingly on her lap and places the bread in the middle. 'So she did.'

'My mother gave it to you?'

'She did.' Bridey nods. 'She's a fine woman all the same, your mother.'

'But when?' he asks.

He cannot imagine Bridey and his mother meeting without his knowledge, conversing like this. Cannot imagine what might be involved in the transfer of a handkerchief from his mother's hand to Bridey's – what words might accompany such an action.

He knows, of course, that they know each other, that they greet each other across the field, that his mother sends down turf in the autumn, references Bridey in conversation as she might any other piece of landscape – but he feels quite thrown, quite confused by the new images crowding into his mind. He did not suppose that other people, especially his own family, could possibly know Bridey as he knows her – not just as a shape in the middle distance, as familiar and necessary as the cottage itself or the bank of hawthorns, but a Bridey who talks and drinks and eats the bread that he sneaks from under Maggie's nose. This Bridey, who becomes the wind and the sun and the night, and shrinks them all to nothing.

He would have been less shocked to discover that Bridey didn't exist at all – that he had invented her himself – than he is to realise she has a foothold in the outside world, connections with his own mother that he knows nothing of.

'Do you not believe me, Petey?'

'Oh, I do, I do, Bridey. I do, of course . . .' he protests.

'And you're asking yourself why a fine woman like your mother would give old Bridey a bright bit of cloth.'

He has not got so far as to wonder this, so he shakes his head helplessly. 'No, no. I'm not.'

'Aah, you are! You're wondering why, all right, and let me tell you, it's not from me you'll find out!'

'No, Bridey, I'm not . . .'

'Let me tell you just this – she gave it to me, and she was happy to give it! And I tell you, I was happy to take it! But' – she pins Peter with her finger – 'you won't tell a soul, Petey. Not on your life and your mother's. You won't speak of it to a soul.'

'No, I won't – of course, Bridey.'

'Go on away now so.' She indicates towards the door with her hand. 'Go on away, and don't forget what I told you today.'

He begins to move towards the door, away from the heat of the fire. 'I'll come back tomorrow . . . with a bit of something.'

She nods. 'Go on away now.'

He closes the door as quickly as he can behind him and turns into a cold that takes his breath away. He begins to walk as fast as he can, towards the solid square presence of his house. He feels sure that if he doesn't keep moving, he will certainly die.

He walks on, aware all the time of Bridey behind him and the snow-covered mountain rising up behind her.

When he stumbles into the warm kitchen, feeling that he has crossed a continent, no one looks up. His brother, Maurice, is sharpening his knife; Maggie is pounding something at the bench. Her broad cheeks are flushed, and some of her greying hair has escaped from its bun.

His mother, half in, half out of the larder, calls back at Maggie with exasperation. 'There's a whole jar there, as I believe I told you.'

'It's fierce cold,' he stutters as his lips begin to defrost.

Maurice says to him, 'Jack Scally says we can skate on the lake.'

Peter shivers, and his mother looks over at him sharply. 'Go on over there to the fire, Peter, and take off your coat. You're not getting ill now, are you?'

He shakes he head.

'You're as pale as a ghost. Swing your arms there. Clap your hands together.'

He wants someone, ideally his mother, to ask him where he has been.

He says again, 'It's fierce cold out there.'

But his mother turns back to Maggie. She has not finished her point about the jar, and Maggie knows it. She pauses in her pounding and assumes a familiar, patient expression, as Peter's mother speaks with carefully controlled indignation: 'A whole jar there with the seal still on, and I nearly sent to Cork!'

'And where was it, I ask you? Was it on the shelf with all the other blessed berries? It was not!'

Peter's mother replies with an exaggerated version of her refined intonation. 'Cherries, Maggie, are not quite berries. They fall into a different category and were accordingly to be found with the preserved fruits on the lowest shelf. Maurice' – she turns in exasperation and shoos him with her left hand, while holding the jar in her right – 'go and do that somewhere else; you're slap-bang in the middle of the way there.' She turns back to Maggie and reads from the label on the jar: 'Finest quality sour cherries, from Kent, England no less.'

Peter watches them as if from a great distance, the familiar interplay now looking absurd and alien to him. Can it be real at all, the warm kitchen, the smell of stew, his mother and Maggie, his brother frowning at his whetstone?

He says, louder than he means to, 'It was Bridey Leary I saw.'

His mother turns from Maggie and says, 'Oh?'

'Yes, down at her cabin.'

Now that he has started, he is not sure what it is he wants to say, so he mumbles, ''Twas fierce cold.'

'And how is Bridey Leary in this fierce cold?'

Peter believes he detects an unusual note in his mother's voice, and he looks attentively at her as he says, 'She has the fire going strong, all right.'

His mother nods. 'And what were you doing down there at Bridey Leary's cabin?'

Peter shrugs. 'I was just out looking at the cold.'

On an ordinary day, he would tell his mother about the stillness, about how he is sure there is a stillness inside of things that is brought out by the cold, that there must be a relation between warmth and movement – a relation down at the deepest level of existence. He would begin to work out his theory in a flow of words directed at her, and she would listen attentively and appreciatively.

But just now, he barely recognises her, for that all he knows the contours of her face better than his own.

Peter's mother says carefully, 'Bridey Leary. Well, I suppose it would be a fine thing to bring her a bite every now and again in this weather.' She looks to Maggie, who nods almost imperceptibly and indicates the oat barrel.

'A bucket of oats might be the thing.'

'And maybe a bit of butter,' Peter's mother adds as she turns back to him and holds his eye firmly.

'You will see to it, Peter, that Bridey gets a bucket of oats and a pat of butter every week while this weather lasts.'

His heart sinks. He does not know what he wanted when he mentioned Bridey, but he now feels quite unbearably adrift, as if the warmth of the kitchen, of his family, of his mother – who is undeniably beautiful when she laughs – is not enough to hold against what he has just encountered. And, rather than feeling comforted by the sanction of Maggie and his mother, he wishes he had said nothing at all and could continue to sneak food for Bridey and go there only when he wanted to – without anyone knowing. Now, everything is different.

And as his mother turns back towards the larder, he feels a pricking of something like suspicion. First the handkerchief, now the oats. What does his mother know about Bridey? And why is she sending him back?

∽

The incessant rain has been colder and fiercer than anyone can remember. The seasons have disappeared; a slight push of growth in late spring was immediately coated over with frost. And then, just when they thought they must be through the worst of it, a thick snow fell in May. So now, with what should be summer on the way, the cattle are still squeezed, bellowing, in the big barn, and having churned up a thick layer of mud, they are caked in it up to their hocks. They peer suspiciously through the clouds of their breath. Their legs glint with frost. They bellow ferociously when Padeen and Mike haul down the hay.

.Everyone has taken to wearing their coats inside the house. Peter is tempted to wear his to bed. There is a new hunched darkness to his family. The adults have become drawn and pale. His mother's face now habitually wears the distracted expression it assumes when she is working with figures. Her eyes slide off to the side, and her mouth gently moves as she sums and subtracts. She stands with Maggie in the kitchen and in the barn, counting sacks of grain, measuring, writing figures in the small notebook she carries everywhere. His father's jaw has set firm – he has put big black locks on all three barns, and every night he slides heavy bolts across the front door, the kitchen door and the side door. Padeen, six foot three and built like a bull, known as Small Paddy on account of his great size, shadows his master, worries with him, monitors the woodpile and the turf stack. To be sure, there are vast piles of firing set up against the barn – enough, you would think, for a lifetime – but all the same, Peter notices that they are beginning to diminish now there is only taking away and no adding.

Everyone has slowed their movements. Except when they must attend to the cattle or check the sheep fence, Peter and his brothers slouch around the house, morose and inert. And all the time, there is an unspoken fear that is not to do with the weather but to do with the barn full of grain, the barrels of potatoes, the woodpile, the fat pigs smoking in the chimney. To do with the large box of coins he knows his father has hidden under a floorboard in his bedroom, to do with the constant awareness of the folk around, all of whom began this never-ending winter with smaller woodpiles, fewer sacks of grain. People like the Connors and the Learys and the Keadys.

And his mother and Maggie have them into the kitchen, all right – there is a steady flow of people, and to be sure, they give each and every one a sup and bowl of porridge. Maggie is never still. The big black pot is perpetually astir. But he sees something in their faces when they rise to leave – especially Annie Keady, who has the baby mewling under her shawl, Annie who he does not like, has never liked, Annie who once delighted in pinching him black and blue because she found him at the apples. When she casts her eye around the kitchen before she leaves, he feels a prickle of fear up his spine as she looks at the fat hams smoking in the hearth. And he notices the next day that his mother has quietly moved them further along the chimney, so they do not catch the eye in quite the same way.

All this time, through the cold and the rain and the snow, he goes once a week with oats to Bridey. These days, she barely nods as he sets the bucket on the floor and the handle clangs against the rim. Says not a word to him about the sun or the wind, the water or the earth. The cold, bare mountain rising behind her cabin has become linked in Peter's mind with Bridey herself. He finds he cannot look directly at either Bridey or her cabin or the mountain anymore, and he has now developed a habit of squinting shyly sideways at everyone.

Every time he trudges up the lane, swinging the bucket in his gloved hand, he is sure he can feel his mother's eyes on his back. He knows her watchfulness means something important – he cannot tell if it is that she is proud or worried. Proud of him walking out, putting one foot in front of the other in the cold? Or worried that the fever will catch him on these short journeys up the lane – this fever that thrives in the cold? Though, to be sure, the fever prefers the poor folk from the small dim cabins clustered near the commonage. That much is clear. It has an unseemly appetite for the innumerable mud-coloured children that once spilled out of each cabin in the mornings – taking one or two children from some families but five, six, seven, eight, and the parents, too, from others. The cold, hard ground will barely yield to take the bodies.

And all the while, Bridey remains untouched.

His dreams in this cold, cold, sickness-ridden time have become strangely hot and full of fire. They are vivid and distressing, coloured by bright flashes, more real than daytime. He dreams of Bridey flying around his house, of the mountain behind her overflowing with liquid fire and engulfing them all – of bright beautiful beings with enormous wings singing out into the night. He tells no one.

He grows three inches in two months, becomes lean, gangly, almost transparently pale.

During his waking hours, he becomes obsessed by the rock samples he has always collected. He goes out in the cold to bring home wonderful chunks of quartz streaked with copper and strange shiny lumps of green stone that glisten. He wants to know how these specimens are formed, wonders what could possibly have happened in the belly of the mountain to make such bright matter out of all this dullness. What could have conjured it? From the shore, he carries back huge, flat pieces of old red sandstone. He looks so long at the textured surfaces that he begins to see images in the intricate shapes – he keeps one large piece by his bed in which he clearly sees the face of a beautiful woman singing.

There are not enough books in his house – not enough books anywhere in the village or even in the entire county of Cork – to answer his questions about rocks and crystals and the insides of mountains. He knows there are men somewhere who know these things, and he longs to meet them. His endlessly distracted father is nothing short of useless, muttering always about sheep and wool and cattle and the price of butter and sometimes about cloth and import tax.

Instead, whenever he can, Peter watches O'Mahony, the blacksmith, and delights in the flare of the forge fire, the way everything glows in the fierce heat, the way what is solid becomes fluid and then solid again, the way all the hammering shapes something out of nothing.

His watchful mother is thinking many things but mostly of the day that will inevitably come when this ferocious winter eventually retreats, when she will stand by the shore at Canty's Cove and watch Peter clamber into a boat, just as she has watched his brothers before him. Her well-reared Catholic sons, schooled in Latin, fluent in Spanish and French – boys who have been sent off to the vast network of cousins and uncles who are prospering in Catholic France and Catholic Austria and Catholic Spain. James is already at sea, Daniel and Thaddeus are banking in Madrid, Stephen is soldiering in France, and Maurice is destined for the farm. They are better off not all in the same basket.

These are the thoughts she is permitting herself as she watches her youngest son during his last few months at home. She allows herself to run down the list of her sons as if they were yearlings to be broken-in and sold. But sometimes, her heart beats fiercely in her chest, because they are not yearlings. They are her well-reared sons, boys she has fed up with beef and butter, sinewy handsome lads – each one took her twelve or thirteen years to grow. And soon, Peter – gangly, half formed, particularly sweet and innocent – will be gone from her, too.

This is what it comes down to: boys must prosper; families must prosper; there is nothing here for him. It does not matter that she loves him the most and would like to keep him nearby. He will go to Paris, to his godfather Stephen.

He will have the best start of the lot of them with his father's youngest brother. Stephen Woulfe has married well and is the cock of the walk these days, in his fine house in Paris, with his bank prospering and a growing reputation amongst the network of influential Catholic emigrants stretching across northern Europe.

It has been decided that Peter will be allowed to follow his interests – to the extent that a fascination with rocks and crystals, how birds fly and what starlight might be made of can be in any way compatible with having a profession. He will train as a physician at the Faculté des Arts de Paris. And Stephen will keep him on the straight and narrow. She will cease to find shells, rocks, crystals and all manner of bones laid out on her dining-room table. Her house will cease to smell of the concoctions he brews. Peter will come to understand the human body and its ailments through his studies. She wonders if he has the stomach for sickness really but knows it will occupy his curious mind. It is her fervent hope that his own peculiar genius will be recognised – that he will be valued.

Peter will go to off to this alien world she does not know, where he will speak a language she doesn't understand. He will train in Paris, spend summers in London. He may not be home again for three or even four years. He will take with him two plain shifts, two ruffled shirts, two books, a spare pair of boots, a second suit of clothes and his winter coat. He will carry a purse of coins to buy what he needs when he arrives in Paris. He will be well equipped. She reassures herself, but she does not feel reassured.

The only thing that she finds remotely reassuring is the thought that at least once he is gone, he will be far away from Bridey Leary and her stories.

Chapter Ten

June 1744 – *Midsummer*

Maiden Lane, London

In the short, hot nights of summer in London, Peter Woulfe's dreams are filled with Sukie. The taste of her, the smell of her, the sharp edge of her hips against him. But he cannot see her face, and she is always leaving him, so he peers anxiously and chases shadows for what seems like eternity before waking exhausted. As the clatter of the house drags him into wakefulness and he learns again that she is nowhere near, he experiences a sense of loss so acute he can only barely restrain himself from curling into a ball and howling at the ceiling.

He is both utterly convinced of the reality of his feelings and completely mystified. On the one hand, he cannot understand the mechanism by which copulating with this girl has quite destroyed his life – his mind, previously adept and focused, has become a mere quagmire of desire and carnal filth. His heart, too, is activated in a way that confounds him utterly. He has an ache in his chest that is no mere phantom; indeed, he has gone so far as to look at himself for signs of injury. For a moment, he was quite expecting to see a bruise swelling across his pale flesh, taking in a region spreading from his lower left ribcage to his breastbone. But no – of course, there is no outward sign. He rebukes himself sharply; this is further evidence, if more were required, that his brain has gone quite soft. But all the same, which is the more ridiculous – that love might bruise his flesh or that his entire being should somehow be crumbling from within?

He lists his symptoms. He cannot eat – not that there is anyone to notice. His face is grey. His eyes, red and raw, are set in sockets so deeply purpled that he looks quite ill. Loud noises and sudden movements cause him to leap on the spot. All in all, he feels so utterly wretched, so completely unbound, that he begins to suspect he is going mad.

As he pulls on his breeches, he consoles himself with the thought of taking to the streets again tonight and finding her. This time, he will manage the matter differently. It is quite intolerable to have this uncertainty.

∽

Peter Woulfe is walking slowly past the chapel on Fetter Lane, thinking of Sukie Bulmer, when he recognises Baron Swedenborg. Some change that has come over the older man's face gives him pause – there is something in the blue eyes that suggests a chastened child. His mouth is thin-lipped, and just now these lips are held tight like unruly horses on a rein – and the tightness, the almost fearful restraint, seems intimately linked to the man's chastened air.

Peter absorbs this impression in a matter of moments and shifts his gaze, but not before Swedenborg becomes aware that he has been scrutinised and looks around. Peter glances back at the baron's face for one last look, and their eyes meet. He feels a flush rising; the image of the respectable gentleman in front of him naked in the evening sun, along with the painful matter of the baron's precious book, combine to make this a most inopportune meeting. He resolves, now that their eyes have met, to say *good day* and continue walking. These circumstances are too far from ideal.

And so, as he draws level with the baron, he says, 'Good day, sir,' meaning to convey just the merest civility.

But the baron, with an almost childlike candour, an unsettling openness, leans slightly forwards, his head at a tilt, as if to ask, *are we acquainted?*

Peter Woulfe sees that this man has recently shed a skin and that whatever layers have been left to him are quite insufficient. It is clear that he is altogether too raw to be out and about. And so Peter pauses, if only to reassure the older man – but once he has stopped, he cannot quite find the means to say, as he would like, *no, we are not acquainted, not as such. I have seen you naked, in communion with the angelic orders, and I have lost a valuable book belonging to you.*

So, he says nothing but continues to flush and raises his hat respectfully.

Swedenborg raises his own hat politely, and in the pause that follows, Peter Woulfe is excruciatingly aware of the rash of pimples festooning his forehead and the fact that his arms are too long for his summer coat.

It is now impossible to move on without saying something.

His mouth is unaccountably dry; he clears his throat. 'Peter Woulfe, sir, at your service.'

'Volfe?'

'Wu-oulfe.'

'I know your father?' Swedenborg is puzzled, his mind stretching for a lost connection.

'No, sir – I do not believe so.' His mind lands on an unhappy image of his father in Cork, stacking coins on a counting desk, muttering about the price of butter, the duty charged on cloth. 'That is . . . no. Though, perhaps my uncle in Paris?'

'Volfe?'

'Wu-oulfe.'

The thin lips, circling with effort, repeat the sound. 'Wolf.'

'Yes, exactly, sir.'

'But no – I know no Wolf in Paris'

'No, sir?

'No, alas.'

'Perhaps my brothers in Madrid?'

Swedenborg pauses, looks up, as though to scan an inner inventory. 'No Volfes in Madrid either. In fact, I fear my acquaintance may be entirely devoid of Volfes!' The baron's face softens into a tentative smile, and Peter, finding that he likes this man, smiles back.

'Not entirely, sir, if I may be so bold.'

'Quite correct, young sir – not entirely.'

'Excuse me, sir, but I have the pleasure of addressing Baron Swedenborg, do I not?'

'You are familiar with my work, Mr Volfe?' Swedenborg expands visibly before Peter Woulfe's eyes.

'Yes, sir – no, sir – to some degree, sir. That is, I have consulted your *Philosophical and Metallurgical Works*.'

'Excellent, young sir – an excellent beginning. A young scholar!'

Peter does not know how to contain the discomfort he is feeling about the baron's book, and so he decides that it would be better were he to erase knowledge of the book entirely from his mind for the time being. It seems to him now that there is something wrong about the book – that there has in fact been something wrong about the book since it was first handed to him. Yet Peter Woulfe feels that there is something quite right about this meeting with the baron. He would like nothing more in this moment than to discuss metallurgy with Baron Swedenborg.

Once he suspends the matter of the book, he finds he is as keen to peer into the man's esteemed brain as he is to convey his own brilliance to Swedenborg.

There is something aflicker around the baron that attracts Peter, some remnant – out of focus, to be sure, and hiding just out of his immediate vision – of the brilliantly coloured evening on Fleet Street.

He is not sure whether to begin with reference to his own efforts to assay cassiterite or to remark upon Swedenborg's work on copper.

And so he stutters, 'I have found your work most helpful – that is to say, in my work with the grosser metals, the action of the . . .' And as he speaks, he realises that what he wishes to know more than anything is what it is like to speak to the angels – what it is like and how he, Peter Woulfe, could do it, too.

The baron appears to listen intently; he is leaning towards him, but when he speaks, bringing his bright-blue eyes to bear upon him, it is as if he has not heard him speak at all. 'Are you a godly man, young sir?'

And Peter knows immediately that the baron can see right into his sullied soul. He eyes widen, and his lip begins to tremble. 'Why . . . yes, sir.'

The older man takes hold of his arm with an urgent grip that sends a jolt right through him. 'If I speak, will you understand? Will you?' the baron repeats, urgently, his grip tightening and his eyes boring into Peter Woulfe, who is desperately trawling through his mind for a sentence that will convey his singular truth. He is both terrified and desperately curious.

Faltering and stuttering, what he says is: 'The angels . . . sir . . . what is it they have said to you?'

Immediately, the baron's bright eyes begin to glisten. 'The speech of angels . . . there is no beauty like it on this earth. I would call it the sound of love itself, but you have not known love like it.'

And Peter thinks of his mother and Sukie conflated in one confusing image.

'No, you have not known love like it, boy.' His eyes bore deeper into Peter Woulfe. 'You are seeking, but do you see?'

And Peter speaks urgently, roughly. 'I wish to see, sir. I wish to see what you see.'

The baron's eyes shift, as if he is now looking through him. His lips soften, begin to tremble delicately. He speaks slowly. 'They are speaking now, young Mr Volfe – an exquisite sound fills my ears.' The baron's face suddenly lights up. 'There is something they wish to say to you.'

The blood drains from Peter face; even his lips are pallid, so that he almost appears to glow.

He pulls his arm free of the baron's grasp. It is clear to him that the angels know about Sukie, know about the book – have seen him thrusting against the alley wall as clear as if it were daylight.

'Perhaps you are to help me with my new labours?' The baron's voice shifts to a more urgent tone.

Peter has taken a step back from the baron. 'I must leave you now, sir. I fear I have an urgent appointment . . .'

The baron appears not to hear him, and as he runs away without looking back, Peter Woulfe begins to cry – he has hoped all his life to converse with an angel, and his heart is sick with the thought that there may never be a better chance.

⸻

Night has barely fallen before Peter creeps down the stairs of Sweetnam's house, shoes in hand, his face bunched in concentration as he carefully avoids the third step, the seventh step and the second from last step – all of which creak outrageously.

The night is fresher; the air itself feels lighter than it has been as he walks briskly towards the river, and to his great relief he finds Sukie almost at once down by the docks. But he is surprised when he is facing her – the flesh-and-blood Sukie – to be quite thrown. There is something in her presence that is altogether different to his imaginings, something he had not considered – he cannot put his finger on it.

As she says, 'You again, is it? The lovely boy?' he detects something in her voice, a subtle lilt towards the end of the sentences, a softness around the *s*, that reminds him of the girls from home.

Though she is standing not a foot from him, he perceives the distance between them to be immense, greater by far than he had accounted for. He is acutely aware of where she begins and he ends. He is not sure at all how he will go about getting his thoughts into her mind. What had seemed a simple matter earlier in the day – a matter of words coming out of his mouth and floating into her ear – now seems so difficult as to be almost ludicrous. Were he to shout across this impossible chasm, what chance would there be of being heard? He now doubts himself entirely, is no longer even certain what it is he should shout.

And so he says nothing, and as she closes the gap and her arms snake around his waist, he feels young and very foolish.

She presses her body against his, and he is quite ill with self-disgust.

'Sukie.'

'Mmm.'

'Wait . . . if you please.'

She makes a gentle thrusting motion against him.

'No, no!' He attempts to disentangle himself from her grip. 'Sukie, there is something I wish to say, something I wish to ask you about.'

He feels her body tighten; she falls still like an animal about to flee, and so he takes hold of her arm, his long, strong fingers encircling it with ease.

'No, don't go.'

He stretches, moves surprisingly quickly and accurately, to grab her other arm. He sees her eyes widen in the moonlight. She is quite caught. He feels a calmness settling upon him, as if a space has opened up beneath his ribcage. He wonders for a wild moment if this may not be the answer – to dispense with words altogether, to bring her by force alone back to his rooms, to hold her there forever, to use ropes or chains, something anchored deep into the wall. Anything at all to remove the possibility of her leaving.

But while he can hold fast to her here in the moonlight, he cannot quite imagine the next step – the bundling, the hauling of her. To be sure, she is not struggling now; she has gone quite still. He can hear her breath, soft and shallow, and his own breaths, deeper and more ragged alongside hers. He thinks perhaps they could just stay here, like this, forever.

But her arms have gone limp in his grasp; it is as if he is now holding a dead weight, as if the living part of her has detached itself from her taut young body and left something else in its wake. And in the complete absence of resistance, he cannot judge the tension he should be applying to his grip. It is suddenly most unpleasant, and so he shakes her arms gently, as if to wake her, and says, 'Sukie, I wish only to speak to you, not to harm you in any way.'

Sukie remains mute and still. Her mind is filled with the book. She knows he wants it back, knows he could have her hauled up before the magistrate . . . have her branded, have her hanged. She thinks of thief-taker Dunbar – the way he dragged Lizzie Egan off screaming and spitting.

'Sukie.' Peter shakes her again, feeling quite desperate. 'Sukie, I will let you go if you undertake not to run. I wish only to speak to you.'

Still, the inert silence.

He leans closer, as if to peer into her eyes, to find her there hiding. 'Sukie, please. It is an offer I wish to make you. An excellent offer.'

'Let me go, and I'll hear your offer.'

'Do not run. Do not. It is an excellent offer.'

His fingers loosen; he moves his hands away slowly.

She stands there, her chin jutting, her whole body reanimating as he withdraws.

The only word he can think of is *guineas*.

'Guineas . . . Sukie . . . Guineas . . . that is what I wish to offer you. Guineas . . . I mean to say . . . two guineas.'

Sukie's face remains impassive. She has never owned a whole guinea. Merely pennies and shillings. She imagines the weight of two guineas in her hand . . . and the book gone.

'Or three, three guineas, Sukie . . .'

She experiences a moment's pity – why, he is like a baby out to be robbed.

But all the same, she says, 'Three guineas? Three guineas is easy come by, mister. You know that.'

It occurs to her that he is so green she could come out with both the money and the book if only she plays it right.

'Yes . . . but there will be food, too – good food and in plentiful supply . . . and wine if you wish it . . . on the occasions . . . the occasions that you might wish for wine . . .'

Sukie frowns, narrows her eyes and looks up at Peter Woulfe's face. Maybe his wits are astray. Maybe the poor lad has no wits. But she resolves to say nothing, that being the best course of action in most instances.

He says, 'It is not uncomfortable . . . that is to say . . . you could be quite comfortable . . . and there would be the three guineas.' He gets into his stride. '. . . And the food . . . and the wine . . . and perhaps you would like some . . .' His hand rises up in the air; he mimes rubbing silk between his fingers and his thumb. '. . . some ribbon?'

'Look, mister . . .'

It is quite a dagger in his heart to hear her address him thus.

'No, no, my name is Woulfe – Peter Woulfe.'

'Look, Mister Wolf . . .'

'There is the matter of silence . . . or at least . . . it would be quite disastrous for there to be any undue noise . . . but that aside . . . the matter of maintaining silence aside, I do believe you would be quite comfortable . . . and safe . . .' His speech is quick and urgent, his heart loud in his ears, his shoulders rising up.

Without thinking, she lays a hand on his arm, speaks quietly as if to soothe him. 'Look, Mister Peter Wolf . . . if it's guineas you're about, that's one thing . . . guineas, I understand . . . and the question is how many . . .'

'And how often. That is the other matter, Sukie. Or should I say how long?' He smacks his hand on his forehead. 'I have not made myself clear . . . The three guineas must relate to a period of time or a number of . . . occasions . . . and therein lies the confusion. If I were to say three guineas for one week, what say you to that?' He breathes out, feels he has got to the nub of the issue, laid it out fair and square for her. 'And we could start tonight, this very moment, unless of course you have . . . items . . . clothing and such that you would wish to bring with you . . . from your own rooms . . .?'

'Rooms?'

'My rooms are but a quarter-mile away. We could walk there . . . together.'

Sukie sees that she has failed to grasp something, sees, too, that he is nervy, uncertain, desperate – she can still feel the echo of his fingers on her arms, wonders if he might be dangerous, is quite taken aback that he has made no mention of the book. It could be a trick. Or he could in fact be stark mad. She thinks she could run now, just run – but there is the matter of the guineas, so instead she asks warily, 'You want me to come to your rooms?'

'Yes! Yes, exactly . . . for the duration of a week. You.'

'Me?' *Not the book,* she thinks. *Just me.*

'Yes, for a week. And in return, the sum of three guineas.'

'And how do I know you'll give it me?'

'I'll give you one now, and two next week.' He thinks for a moment. 'Tonight will count as one night and then six more. A week of seven nights. And days.'

'Well, I can't come just like that.' She puts a hand on her hip and leans away from him, clicks her fingers together and says 'Puff!'

'No, no, you must have . . . items . . . that you might require . . . for a week.'

'And' – she glares at him suspiciously – 'folk to tell. Folk as will miss me if I just disappear.'

'Of course.'

And, she thinks, a precious book to hide – somewhere where Sal won't see it and flog it for near nothing before she gets back. She thinks she would be better off really to run now, to run fast and to stay away from these alleys awhile until this fellow forgets all about her – to keep her book safe and get a good price for it. But three guineas is three guineas, and more than that, there is something about him, his eagerness, his appetite for her, that appeals to her in some way. She thinks of a week in his rooms, away from Sal and Pad, drinking wine instead of gin. It might not be the worst. Unless he has some filthy stuff in mind. But then, there might be a window she could get out. And there is the matter of the book – they are entwined in her mind, this Wolf and the book.

And how she makes decisions, big ones like this, is never really a matter of weighing the ups and the downs, the ins and outs. She simply knows somehow what she will do before she has thought it through – often she doesn't bother to think it right through, but sometimes, like this time, she plays awhile as if she hasn't already decided, plays it out to let her mind catch up with what some other part of her already knows. And so she pauses, squints, appears to think, and the pause seems interminable to Peter.

When she says, 'All right then. One week. Three guineas. And food . . . and wine . . .' he expands before her, and words tumble out of his mouth.

'I do assure you, you will be quite safe . . . and comfortable.'

Chapter Eleven

Maiden Lane, London

Sukie's sleepy mind stretches out and finds it is not at home. She has a lofty sense that there is space above her head, not the looming ceiling of her garret room. And it is not Sal beside her. No, a bigger, more angular presence is breathing slow and deep. Peter the hungry Wolf. Call him starving more like.

She opens her eyes. His face is not a hand's width away. The morning sun is creeping round the curtains, and his skin glows pale in the dim light. She can see the thin blue veins on his eyelids, examines the purpling hollows under his eyes – thinks you could have a cloak that colour, in velvet to catch the shades. She is quite beautifully comfortable, the pillows so soft, the temperature just right. She would not like to move or make a sound and rouse him. No, once he awakens, she will no longer be able to lie just like this. So she closes her eyes lest even the fall of her gaze might disturb him. She thinks she will just pause like this on the brink of sleep and consider the comfort of her limbs, but in fact she tips over into sleep, and when she wakes again, it is to find Peter the Wolf's eager eyes upon her as if he has been waiting. And when he groans his way inside her, she is aware of his motion, his breath, his pleasure, but is quite indifferent herself. She is not really there at all.

Working nights, the gin helps to cloud her mind, and it is as easy as anything to drift away, but this morning, even without it, she finds she can manage quite well. Just as she has for years and years, taking herself away when necessary, coming back just after. Just as she does this time, coming back to pat him gently on the back, feeling something approaching fondness for the smooth angularity of his shoulder blades.

Peter feels his body as a new and powerful thing. There is something in the matter of his weight on Sukie, the length of him stretched out, and the contact of skin on skin that makes him feel that he could sprout wings and fly up over the city – fly, at the very least; why, he might also lift the bed with one hand, or even the entire building.

The pain in his chest has been quite transformed; it still aches, to be sure, but now with an exquisite sense of expansion. As he lies on top of Sukie, he can feel the thud of his heart, the thud of her heart – connected, as if for this moment the same blood is moving through them both. He moves his weight to his elbows, suddenly concerned that he might quite squeeze the life out of her, and she shifts and wriggles until she is curled with her back to him, and he has his arm around her waist, his chin resting on her head. He cannot believe his immense luck, to have found somebody who fits so well into the curve of his body.

As Peter the Wolf encircles her tenderly, Sukie thinks of the book. It is there beside the bed in the lumpen canvas bag, as close as she could leave it without having it in the bed with her. But all the same, far too close to Peter the Wolf, who could at any moment smell it out. She thinks now that she was stone mad to bring it with her. It is only a matter of time before he pries.

Peter rises from the bed and begins to dress; he hunches in upon himself and pulls on his breeches awkwardly, standing at an angle to the bed so that Sukie cannot see him in his drawers. And as he ties his breeches, he thinks very briefly, as he always does, of his father, left-handed, fluidly looping his own breeches in a way that seemed to his infant son to be impenetrably beautiful – a mysterious inversion of his own laboured childhood efforts.

Peter kneels abruptly. Sukie, watching him fold his height in half and rest his elbows on the bed, does not at first know what he's doing; it is only as he begins to mumble that she recognises the rhythm of prayer.

As he prays this buoyant morning, the familiar words have developed a new lightness, as if they have detached themselves from their meaning and now flow through him as pure sound, with nothing to snag on the thorns of his mind.

Most of his bedchamber has been sectioned off by two benches. It is a workroom into which a bed has intruded. The benches are cluttered with glass vessels, crucibles, magnifying glasses, and hanging on the wall behind the benches are pincers, pokers, bellows. There are limitations to be sure, but in a small space and without Sweetnam's knowledge, he has succeeded in creating a miniature lab, amply equipped. No furnace, but he has the fire and an old iron tripod that straddles the flames.

He holds the image of Sukie's body clear in his mind as he crosses the room to his cluttered workbench. He reaches for a shallow earthen bowl, runs his thumb around the rim and wonders at the beauty of its curve. It could almost be a cast of one of Sukie's breasts. That there is some significance to this correspondence he does not doubt.

As he clears a space for the bowl and picks up a glass jar containing white ashes, he realises that there must be significance to everything on such a morning. His fingers tilting the jar, the ashes spilling out into the earthen dish – why, every movement seems imbued with the deepest meaning. It is the rarest feeling, to be right there at the heart of himself – moving, breathing, transferring ashes – and all the time feeling as if the intent that animates him is flowing through him but not entirely of him. He has done this many a time before but never after such a night and never with Sukie here in this very room.

And so he knows that, when he mixes in the antimony and stokes the fire to life, everything will be different this time. Because of what has happened to him, his new strength, his new lightness, and because Sukie is there in his bed, her soul commingling with his, her energies radiating out around the room.

He crosses to the hearth clears the charred wood and places some wood shavings on the barely glowing embers. Then, rather than reaching for the bellows, he takes a deep breath and blows gently until the embers glow and the shavings begin to curl and flame.

Sukie lies in the bed; she is both watching him and not watching him at all. She wonders for barely a moment about the fire, so early and on this warm morning.

⁓

Peter's body is soft and loose; he stands at Sweetnam's workbench with the sense that he could as well be lying down. He wonders idly what force is keeping him upright. Sweetnam's abrupt instructions land upon him with a soft and muffled thud. He is indeed doing what he thinks Sweetnam has asked him to do – it seems to be a matter of measuring this greyish powder by weight – but he cannot for the life of him imagine why it matters. Even Sweetnam himself, while evidently in the same room, appears to be a vast distance away. He feels as if he has been wrapped round and round again in layers of sheep's wool.

And with everything so soft, he sees immediately that the man at the door does not belong. His brown coat and grey wig are quite inoffensive, but his stance suggests a pugilist about to swing.

The man's eyes seek out Sweetnam, who starts and says, 'May I help you, sir?'

The man in the brown coat advances quickly towards Sweetnam. 'Josiah Sweetnam?' His accent is notably neutral, hard to place.

Sweetnam nods and begins to speak, but before he gets a word out, the man in the brown coat takes him by his neckcloth, leans back and drives his head forwards into Sweetnam's face, breaking his nose with an audible crunch. He waits a practised moment while Sweetnam's first shocked howl of pain fills the room.

'Where is the book?'

Before Sweetnam can reply, he tightens his grip on his neckcloth, cutting off almost all the air to his lungs.

'Where is the book?'

Sweetnam's eyes are starting out of his head; blood is streaming from his nose. He has brought both of his hands up and is desperately pulling at the man's fingers.

'Where is the book?'

The man in the brown coat throws Sweetnam flat on the floor and kneels on his chest. 'It's a very important book, Mr Sweetnam – very important – and it is not where it's supposed to be.' He leans right in on top of Sweetnam's face. 'So, where is it?'

His fingers loosen slightly on Sweetnam's neckcloth.

Sweetnam speaks with what little breath has been left to him, the words issuing wetly through the blood in his mouth. 'I sent it to him . . . I sent it to . . . the baron.'

'Well, the baron does not have it, Mr Sweetnam.' The man's hand creeps back around Sweetnam's neck.

'I sent it.'

'I'm afraid that is impossible for me to believe. On account of the fact . . .' He pauses and begins to knock Sweetnam's head against the floor in time with his words. '. . . that . . . the . . . baron . . . does . . . not . . . have . . . it. Said you'd do it, did you? Pass it along to the baron, no questions asked? Changed your mind then, did you? Keep it, did you? Flog it, did you?'

Sweetnam's eyes are beginning to go misty.

The man in the brown coat looks piqued. 'No, you don't.' He slaps him lightly on the cheek 'Keep your wits about you.' He peers down at Sweetnam and shakes him by the shoulder.

Peter has gone so still he suspects his heart may have stopped. He is not sure whether the man in the brown coat has forgotten about him, whether he should dart for the door or stay just as he is.

A sound between a sigh and a grunt of exasperation issues from the man. He moves off Sweetnam's chest, turns to Peter, as if they were old friends, and says with disgust, 'He has fainted quite away.'

Peter blinks and says automatically, 'Yes, sir.'

'Can you wake him? With some' – he indicates the shelves filled with apothecaries' jars – 'preparation?'

Peter pauses, considers the question. 'No, sir.'

'I dearly hope he is not killed.' He looks to Peter. 'Then the fat really will be on fire.' He looks suddenly forlorn.

Peter finds he has unwittingly taken on a sympathetic expression in response to the man's tone.

'No, I think not. No . . . what is your opinion?' His eyes bore into Peter.

'No, sir.'

'Come and look at him, boy!' He beckons impatiently. 'His colour is good, is it not? Too good for a dead man.'

Peter steps across the floor, surprised that his legs work at all. He crouches beside Sweetnam. At the same instant he sees that Sweetnam is not dead, he realises it may well have been better for him if he were.

'No. He is not dead, sir.'

'Quite so, quite so!' The man exhales with relief. 'I didn't think he was. But you never know with these clever types.' He stands and brushes down his coat. 'Well! Well, now. What to do? Do you think he will come round sharpish?'

Peter has quite enough of his wits regained to hold the man's eye and say firmly, 'No. I do not. He has experienced a serious cerebral trauma.'

The man in the brown coat appears to consider this.

Peter continues, 'He may never fully recover.'

'Pshaw! He most certainly will! I will come back in a quarter of an hour to continue my business. Mind you tell him, if he wakes, that I am not far to seek and will be back before he knows it.' He begins to walk towards the door. 'He has no place in the country?'

'No, sir.'

'But you might tell him from me that, were he to visit a sister or an aunt in the country before I return, I should have little difficulty in locating him. And that the additional journey could well have soured my mood.'

'Yes, sir.'

Peter looks down at Sweetnam's closed eyes. He believes he detects a suspicious tightness around the brow, and it occurs to him that the man is pretending to be unconscious. There are a number of variables to consider and very little time in which to do so. Sweetnam's eyes may open at any moment.

Before Peter has considered much at all, he finds he is moving swiftly and silently across the room – backwards, his eyes locked on Sweetnam until he reaches the door and turns. Then he is leaping up the stairs to his room, to Sukie. It is clear that they should leave Sweetnam's house immediately. His first thought is that they should go to Paris together. He could pay the passage, though he may have to renegotiate Sukie's three guineas, depending on the fare. Surely Paris would be quite far enough away from the man in the brown coat and from Sweetnam's inevitable realisation that he did not deliver the book.

He fumbles with the key, flings the door open. He expects to see her sitting in the bed where he left her. But Sukie is not in the bed – not anywhere to be seen in the room, though he throws the covers off the bed and ducks down to check beneath it.

She is on the roof. Doors and windows being all one to her, she slipped out barefoot, her bag over her shoulder, when she heard the rhythmical sound of Sweetnam's head against the floor following his yowl of pain. She would as likely step under a carriage as wait for trouble to come up the stairs and find her. She has scaled many a wall, climbed higher and with less purchase, jimmied windows with just one hand free. She is quite at home in the air, weighs but a little and has strong wiry arms and resourceful feet. So, stretching with ease from the window ledge to the gutter, she has hauled herself aloft, her strong little hands finding purchase, her toes burrowing into the gaps between bricks.

The smooth grey slate is warm from the sun, and she feels a surge of pleasure – wonders for a moment why anyone would stay in a room when they could be on a roof. If she were as rich as Peter the Wolf, she would sit every sunny day on a roof of her own, coming down at night to curl up in the exquisite comfort of the bed. She knows well that this roof, Peter the Wolf's roof, runs straight to the next roof and thus the next and so on and on; she is quite sure she could be half a mile away in no time without touching the ground. But she waits all the same, perches on the ridge, head against the chimney stack, for the trouble below to subside.

Below her, Peter is beginning to call her name. He cannot shout as he would like, must keep her presence from the rest of the household, so his voice is clogged, urgent and secretive at the same time.

He has found her black boots, holds them in his hands, is startled into stillness by how small they are. Once fine, they are scuffed and worn soft with use; the leather is beginning to pull away from the sole, like an ugly creature's mouth about to open. They were surely made for a wealthy man's wife or, more likely – Peter notes that his extended hands are longer than the boots – for his child.

Why this should stop his heart, he does not know, but it does. It is as he puts them gently back on the floor that he realises Sukie has gone out the open window. He is quite certain.

He leans out, twists around, calls upwards softly, 'Sukie, Sukie?'

Sukie hears his voice; a small sigh escapes her. She considers for a moment the possibility of setting off away from Peter the Wolf across the hot slate and onto the next roof. Instead, she swivels on the spot delicately and slides part-way down the pitch towards the open window.

'Psst. Here!'

Peter Woulfe hears her voice with a relief that almost blinds him. His long torso is contorted, his neck straining up. 'Sukie.'

'Yes.'

'Sukie, come down. I cannot see you.'

'I'm here.'

'Sukie, can you hear me? Sukie?'

'What?'

'Please come down this instant – it is a matter of great urgency.'

She slides along the slate, pauses and slides again to the edge of the roof, where his anxious face looms into focus.

'Take care!'

'Give way,' she says authoritatively. 'Move over.'

Peter reluctantly withdraws into the room, and within moments, Sukie eases herself through the window.

'We must leave immediately. There is a man . . . who will . . . kill me . . .'

He decides not to mention the matter of the man in the brown coat trying to kill Sweetnam, the uncertainty as to whether Sweetnam would hand him over to this man or kill him himself. He decides not to mention the matter of the book leaning against the wall of the alley that first night with her. All these matters must be discussed, but not at this moment. No – better to get straight to the nub of the issue: he is in grave danger.

'I am in grave danger.'

Sukie merely nods, moves quickly to sit on the bed and puts on her boots. Then, standing, with her bag slung over her shoulder, she waits for Peter Woulfe to move.

Peter looks at the cluttered room, decides that he will have his belongings sent on. A risk, to be sure, but it is the preservation of his mind and body that dominates his thoughts. This axis of self has always seemed valuable to him, but even more so now after his night with Sukie. The mind that holds the thoughts, the body that savours Sukie, and now Sukie herself – these are the irreplaceable elements. He will take only what he can carry – and as he dashes around the room, he first seizes the jar containing the ashes, and then hesitates over two further jars before checking the stoppers and thrusting them into his leather bag. He rapidly adds a sheaf of notes, two books, his small scales, a wooden box. He finds he cannot fasten the clasp, fumbles, swears, takes the scales out and forces the satchel closed, throws the bag over his right shoulder, takes Sukie's hand and pulls her towards the door.

He fills her view as she follows him down the stairs, and so she stumbles into his back when he stops abruptly on the first-floor landing.

Josiah Sweetnam, pale and ominous, blood streaming from his broken nose, stands in Peter's path.

'Woulfe!' The word comes out as a shriek. 'What have you done with Baron Swedenborg's book?'

Peter decides at once to knock the older, smaller man to the floor, but he pauses for just a moment – and it is in this fraction of time that Sukie slips past him, past Sweetnam, and disappears down the stairs.

Peter immediately moves to pursue her, but Sweetnam blocks him, and as their bodies connect, Peter finds that there is altogether more to Sweetnam than he has ever suspected. He is tight, fierce and furious. What is more, he is holding the long, weighty poker that usually hangs beside the furnace, and as Peter steadies himself to fight, Sweetnam swings the poker with great force into his right arm.

He clutches himself, and Sweetnam swings again, this time hitting his fingers. And now Peter, altered by the throbbing pain and the thought that the distance between him and Sukie is stretching with every moment, lurches forwards to engage with Sweetnam – but Sweetnam, as if he has done this many times before, trips him to the floor in one easy movement and pushes the point of the poker into the back of his neck.

He speaks in a new claggy voice, and drops of blood fall from his chin. 'You will not move, Woulfe – not move at all until you have told me what you have done with Baron Swedenborg's book. Or so help me, I will bash your brains out.'

And now, with Sweetnam forcing his poker painfully into his neck and his face pushing into the floor, Peter knows for certain that Sukie is well beyond catching.

Sweetnam leans on the poker. Peter feels it pushing deep into his neck and fears for his spine.

'So, you had a little tart up there all along, did you?' He twists the poker. 'Did you? Well, there is no time for your foulness now. That man will kill me, or he will kill you. Perhaps both of us. Where is that book?'

Peter begins to speak. His teeth are pressing into the floor; the sounds that emerge are impossibly muffled.

Sweetnam eases the pressure on the poker.

Peter turns his head, speaks frantically. 'The baron . . . I gave it to him . . .'

'You are lying – you said you gave it to the Dutchman.'

'To give to the baron . . . on my life. But the baron . . . his wits are astray . . . He is quite mad . . . standing without clothing, naked entirely, in the street . . . On my life, he is mad. The old man is mad.'

'Naked?' Sweetnam pauses. 'In the street?'

'Yes. Quite naked. Crying like a babe.' Peter wrestles for a moment with the feeling that he is casting something of great value into a sewer. 'He was weeping for the angels . . . His wits are all but gone . . . I gave the book to the Dutchman, his friend, to give to him . . . but the baron . . . why, he may have kicked it under his bed and forgotten all about it . . .' He feels a slight slackening of Sweetnam's intent and slowly turns around until he can push the poker aside. He continues to speak, surprised by his calm, firm tone. 'A man in his state could have done anything . . . and then forgotten it entirely.'

Sweetnam allows him to sit up. Peter sees that Sweetnam is terribly afraid, that he would indeed bash his brains out if that were to assure his own safety.

And so he speaks again with confidence. 'We must go to the baron – we must find him and kindly and firmly question him as to the whereabouts of the book. Kindness and firmness are of the utmost importance in these instances. That man' – he jerks his head to refer to the man in the brown coat – 'is quite the wrong man to send to someone such as the baron. No doubt he frightened him out of whatever wits remain.'

Sweetnam nods slowly.

Peter knows that, at all costs, they must leave the house. The house where Sukie is no longer. And so he presses Sweetnam. 'That man, he asked me to convey to you his firm intention to return . . .'

Sweetnam nods slowly, appears to think, and then swiftly cracks the poker across Peter's left ear.

Peter puts both hands to his ear and gasps in pain.

'You may think me of little consequence, Woulfe, but I swear to you that I will ruin you before you begin. You will help me find this book, or I will set that man on you until he beats the truth out of you. And if you run, no matter how far you go, there will not be an apothecary or surgeon in the kingdom who will so much as look at you when I have done. I will make it my duty to ensure that you are without friends and without any prospect of a guild.' He repeats slowly one word after the other: 'I. Will. Ruin. You. Do you understand?'

Peter looks at Sweetnam with barely concealed distaste. He wishes to say, *that damned book.* It is clear that a man like Sweetnam could never understand that the book – whether inlaid with gold or studded with rubies – is of no consequence set beside his association with Sukie, no consequence at all when compared to the feeling in his chest when they unite. Or to his work, which has just this very morning taken on new life, a whole new potency fired by the great release of energies. He knows himself to be on the brink of something truly great, and without Sukie, progress is unimaginable.

He realises with a start that Sukie and the book are entwined, and that he must pull them apart – for he has no use for the book, and Sukie is now essential to him. He must find both Sukie and the book – and then the work of separation must begin, for while Sukie is entwined with the book, and while these brutes – he includes Sweetnam in this thought – seek the book, nothing can be accomplished.

He does not doubt that he will find Sukie, if he has to turn every stone in London and peer beneath it, but this time, he will ask her about the book before anything else. He will explain to her. He will reimburse her accordingly, perhaps place a value on the item and pay her in coin.

That is what he will do. It could be quite straightforward, simply a matter of careful searching. But then he remembers his earlier feeling that there is something very wrong with the book itself, something he doesn't understand. Here, looming above him, is Sweetnam, a respectable man, no street thug, with his nose quite

pulped – and the baron is involved, a man of considerable standing. The scale is amiss – a valuable book no doubt, but only a book.
It seems to Peter now that the book does not match well with the
man in the brown coat . . . or with Sweetnam's fear. No, it is all quite
wrong . . . He has missed something, something essential.

⌒

Sukie runs, bag bumping, head down, through the press of well-
dressed fleshy bodies on Half Moon Street. All these people, all this
light – why, anyone at all could put a hand out and grab her. She
thinks about slowing to a walk – she would look less suspicious –
but her legs keep moving; her body cannot slow until she has found
some darker, quieter place.

Her bag is heavier now – the addition of a leather case containing three tortoiseshell magnifying glasses was a last-minute
decision as she followed Peter out the door. The book is thudding
hard against her back . . . the book . . . the book . . . the baron's
book . . . She heard that man say it – *the baron's book* – and, not
knowing exactly what a baron is, she knows only that his blood-
soaked fury along with the rich-sounding word *baron* proves the
enormous value of her book. So, she must run fast and run far,
despite the weight.

It is hot and lividly bright. Her eyes are watering; her dress is
unbearably tight. Her breath is beginning to burn in her chest
when she realises that she does not know where she is. She cannot even remember which way she turned out of Peter the Wolf's
house – and whether she has turned once or twice since. She could
as well be upside down or inside out for all she knows. She cannot
smell the river, the pit, the hounds ditch – has no sense of where
she has come from or where she is going.

The cobbled path she has been running on abruptly disappears,
becomes brittle, caked mud, and she is thrust back by the surge
of a busy, noisy street. Horses, carriages, carts, a pair of sweating

chairmen bellowing 'Give way!' pass within a whisker and almost knock her flat.

And oh, the noise – every sound travelling sharp on the bright hot air. The whine of carriage wheels, the incessant rattling, the dull roar of a hundred voices all at once. And when one carriage passes, there is another to replace it and another and another, as if everyone in the city is on the move . . . And now another carriage, two more chairmen, equally urgent, and this time so close that, even squeezed in against the wall as she is, the first chairman's elbow clips her head, and she flings a curse after him. Where is it that they are all going with such urgency?

It is not Holbourn, not Fleet Street. Those streets she knows and can cross at just the right place. No, she would recognise the motion, recognise the sounds – this place is utterly alien.

She clings to the wall and inches along, makes out the bent form of a sweeper clearing a crossing for a gent just to her left. She cannot remember if she and Peter the Wolf crossed this street in the dark, but fears they did and that it now lies between her and home. That, or she is wrong altogether and the crossing would take her even farther away.

If she were an angel now, like one of the ones in the book, she would fly straight over the road and all its noisy rushing, fly up into the air, and she'd be wearing a light, flowing gown that would be cool in the breeze, and from the air, she would see the way back to Ma Crofter's, without the need to press through all the fierce motion on the ground. That or, being an angel, she might know the way in her heart without having to find it as such.

And it is just then that the sweeper beckons kindly to her – 'Oy! Luv! 'Ere, come with me.' And, grabbing her wrist, he pulls her across the road. It is not at all like flying, this swift scurry, her arm outstretched, the rest of her following along behind – but all the same, before she knows it, she is on the other side. And then, as she begins to doubt entirely her wisdom in crossing, she smells the river in front of her, straight ahead and not far away – and knows that once she finds its banks she can make her way home.

Sukie thinks then of Sal and Ma Crofter and her book, but not of Peter Woulfe, who has gone right out of her mind.

Chapter Twelve

Chick Lane, London

Shapsel Nicodemus Stein is a tall, dark Jewish man with verdant eyes and long, delicate hands. He stoops in his low-ceilinged shop as if he were born for taller, freer places but must make do. In fact, there is an air of gentle surprise about him – as if he does not know how he came to be here in this shop at all, brokering coin and trinkets for the poor of Chick Lane. Of all the unfortunate people who inhabit these pitiful streets, who live and die, fail to prosper, scrape along – people of all shapes and sizes – he stands out as a man out of place, out of time. Were he to be found standing with a camel by a rich oasis, proffering dates, his physique and general demeanour would be entirely fitting. In fact, his puzzled warmth, his general air of kindliness is so incongruent that, rather than making him popular, it has only ever aroused suspicion – being so far outside the realm of the familiar as to be impossible and therefore highly suspect.

And demeanour not being everything, there is also the matter of his trade. He might indeed be best fit for proffering dates in the dry heat, but in fact every day he takes in the pitiful possessions of the desperate and exchanges them for coin. This he does fairly, scrupulously, under the terms agreed, but it does not endear him to his clients, who may trust him as far as that goes but will never love him for it. He appears to be inhabiting a timeless middle age. He could be a little older than thirty, a little younger than fifty. His beard is not flecked with grey; his movements are slow and considered.

Sukie is one of Nico's regulars. Being well versed in the art of the credible, she is the one appointed by Sal and Pad to dispense with their accumulated takings. They operate together in a small way, gathering little things, light things that can be carried easily and concealed. Watches, hats, purses, the odd bit of jewellery. Nico is known to hold himself above the brokers like Danieli and Golders down by the hill – brokers who are little more than fences and will turn a blind eye to anything, accepting even the most suspicious quantities of cloth, buckles, necklaces in plush velvet cases and silver plate with crests. So Sukie divides her custom between them – bringing Nico certain things, things that aren't too suspicious, things she decides have a feeling of quality about them.

Thieving is not Sukie's main calling; she has no passion for it. She picks pockets – and occasionally ventures through the upper windows of the relatively wealthy – just as she might pick fruit from a tree or berries from a bush, as if the seething city were a vast orchard and failing to reach out and take what is offered would be outright foolish. But as for the rights and wrongs of it – why, she has a loose enough feeling about owning, which extends to her own property. For sure enough, she has had things pinched, things she liked . . . a hat once, some shiny red ribbon, and another time her whole purse. And while she was put out about it, she did not experience any real sense of being wronged, feeling the circulating ownership of ribbons, hats, coins to be part of a vast impersonal flow, as if her ownership of a particular hat or ribbon or coin was no more necessary, no more right nor wrong than anybody else's. Having something nicked is no worse really than losing it on the street.

She sees how others thieve with careful planning and intent, sees the risks and the gain, has seen plenty of folk dragged off by thief-takers – seen brandings, hangings, the lot. She has also seen folk in the flush of success, red-faced, all a-tremble, with coins to scatter. She has seen Ma Crofter get steadily richer and plumper.

But when it comes to it, she feels it is easier just to sell herself.

The last time she was at Nico's, it wasn't to sell. It was to find a present for Sal, and she left with a pewter-backed hairbrush that Nico ran his fingers gently over as he told her the price. And Sukie, having sold him one similar the year before, was outraged by the figure, four times what he had offered her for her brush. She cursed him fiercely, haggled with him – looked at him with such distaste that he was quite taken aback – and she left with the brush, having paid just under half the original figure.

But all the same, it is Nico she thinks of when she decides she must sell her book. She cannot imagine bringing it to Danieli or Golders. She will not return to the bookseller's by St Paul's – she now sees that she could only ever be cheated in a shop like that.

But she is not – her lips thin at the thought – going to hand her book to Nico for any old price. She may not hand it to him at all – just let him see it for a moment, maybe without touching. It won't be like showing him a watch and letting him flick the cover and wind it, before leaving without it and with a few coins in her purse instead. No, not at all. And so, her chin is defiantly in the air as she pushes Nico's door open.

Despite the brightness of the day, it is dark inside.

Sukie makes out the tall, stooped shape of Shapsel Nicodemus standing by his bench, his figure lit by one candle.

He is quite still, as if he has simply been waiting for the door to open.

'Good day, Miss Sukie.'

'Morning, Nico.'

'I hope you are well, Miss Sukie?'

'Over the moon, and how's – your – father, Nico – what else?'

Sukie comes right up close so that she can see him clearly. His rich, brown beard comes part-way down his chest and obscures his face but for the occasional flash of white teeth when he speaks.

'I am glad to hear it.' He bows his head courteously.

All the same, thinks Sukie – he may be as odd as odd, but there is a nice clean smell off him, and his shop is quiet and peaceful, with everything where it should be, and no rush and push – like he has all the time in the world.

'How can I help you today?'

Her head is tilted up, his down, and there is still a considerable distance between them. Her chin reaches to the third shiny button on his long, dark coat.

'Well, that's just it, Nico – maybe I can help you.'

And she is aware as she speaks of something familiar altogether missing. He is there, within a foot of her, his male body pulsing under his clothing, and her sex is not in play at all. He is quite outside of that, quite unconscious of it.

'Oh, yes?' A small smile warms his face.

And despite her intention to be firm, to play it sharp, she leans even closer and speaks quickly, 'Nico, can you keep a secret?'

'A secret? Why, Miss Sukie, this head' – he taps a long finger against his brow – 'holds more secrets than there are days in the year.'

If he meant to reassure her, rather than simply state a fact, his statement does not succeed, because she thinks now of all the secrets he holds and is quite sure they are trifling when compared with the book – valuable to other people, she does not doubt, but not special like the book. And so she looks suspiciously at Shapsel Nicodemus.

But his hand has moved down away from his forehead, has come to rest again on the surface of his bench, and seeing his long brown fingers, shiny half-moon nails carefully trimmed, she decides on the instant to show him the book.

She puts her bag gently on the floor and squats down to remove it – rushing a little, aware that anyone at all could come in the door. When she rises with the book, Shapsel Nicodemus has moved slightly and taken a pair of spectacles in his hand. She lays the book on the bench and unpeels the waxed linen wrapping.

'Aah. It is a book.'

'Sharp one, ain't you, Nico?'

He peers down at it. Moves the candle closer. 'It is an unusual book.' His hands move towards the cover. 'I may?'

Sukie nods, and he turns it around to face him and opens the cover.

He is accustomed to the vagaries of his clients, has long learned not to question the origins of even the most surprising items, and so he merely leans lower to examine the frontispiece.

'*Mutus Liber*.'

'What?'

'*Mutus Liber* – that is the title.'

For all her ruminating, it never occurred to her that Nico would simply be able to read the book, to call out its name just like that.

'What kind of a name is that?' She is quite taken aback by the foreign-sounding words uttered in Nico's deep Slavic voice, is tempted to pull the book back to her, as if this matter of naming it in an unknown tongue is taking it further away from her.

'It is Latin.'

'Latin.'

'Yes.' He looks up from the book at Sukie, and she sees his green eyes are flecked with gold. 'I am no scholar of Latin, but Latin it is.'

'And . . .' Sukie trails off for a moment. 'Where is Latin from?'

'From?'

'Yes, where does it come from?'

'From a long time ago.' And seeing the flat, lost look on Sukie's face, he continues softly, 'It comes from the Romans – from what is now Italy, so you could say it is old Italian. But it is the language of scholars the world over.'

'So the book is from Italy?'

'No, indeed not.' He bends back down. 'This was printed in France in the year 1677.'

'Oh.'

'Yes.' He bends down again with his spectacles on his nose.

'1677,' Sukie repeats slowly. 'So it's old then?' She has forgotten what year it is now, has heard the number once or twice but had no call to remember.

'It is sixty-seven years old.' Nico produces the figure without hesitation, could in fact have calculated the interest at three and half

percent over the sixty-seven years at an original value of, say ...
three shillings, in the same beat of time.

'Sixty-seven.' Sukie adds the number to the small store of information she has about the book. Printed in France. The title is *Mutus Liber*.

Both heads are dipped over the open book, and they fall into an
easy silence, until Nico speaks. 'Well, Miss Sukie?'

'Well, Nico?'

'What is it you would like to do with your book?'

Sukie looks up at Nico. 'Do you know what it's worth? In coin?'

'No. In honesty, I do not.' Nico gestures around his small shop. 'I
do not trade in books. I know what I could give you for it, but that
may not be its worth.'

'That's just it, Nico. It's how much a thing is wanted, isn't it?' Sukie
begins to speak quickly. 'That's what gives you the price in coin. So,
how about this? There's a man as would kill for this book. Just like
that.' Sukie snaps her fingers. 'Easy as one, two, three.'

She leans in closer. 'And there's a rich man. A baron' – she
pronounces the word carefully – 'as wants it badly, too. And then,
there's another man, who's been near killed for it, as would give his
whole house and all his money, just to get free of the man as wants
it so badly he will kill him for it.'

Sukie holds Nico's green eyes firmly, to see if he understands, to
see if he's taken it all in – and sure enough, she sees that he has.

He straightens up slightly. 'It sounds like a dangerous book, Miss
Sukie.'

She continues speaking faster now, as if she has not heard him
at all. 'The thing is' – the thoughts are forming as she speaks – 'the
thing is to find that baron. That's what I think.'

Something about the word *baron* makes her sure that this is the
right course of action; she does not want to bargain with the angry,
violent men in Peter the Wolf's house; but surely a baron would be
a better sort of person, the kind as would strike a fair deal and not
swing fists or pokers at her and have her dragged off by a thief-taker
or flung in the river.

As she speaks, she becomes more sure – entirely sure, and aware that it is now Nico she must convince.

'A reward, Nico, from the baron. For returning his book. No funny stuff. Nothing dangerous. Just a fair reward.'

Nico is looking down at the book, turning the pages slowly. He is not sure if the book is something very sacred or very profane. There is nudity. He reflects on this calmly without his blood stirring. There are a host of characters displayed . . . angels, gods of the old world, cherubs – but more interesting to him than that is the activity of the mortals throughout the book: they are at work and deeply engaged in their labour. He recognises the particular quality of attention to craft.

He pauses on a plate divided into five scenes. A man and a woman work together, their activity progressing down the page. They are both calm and intent; they are mixing liquids then decanting them from big-bellied, slim-necked vessels. Then they attend to a furnace, a smile beginning to creep into the face of the woman. And then the final scene, which occupies the bottom third of the page and displays her naked: her smile is wide, as she stands hand in hand with the man, beside the glowing furnace. It is quite striking to Nico, this joint progression of the man and the woman down the page. It reminds him of something he cannot put his finger on, a cloudy memory from long ago – two people who may have been his parents, an activity he cannot quite see, a sense of togetherness.

Sukie is looking intently at him. 'Do you know? Do you? How to find a baron?'

Nico considers the question. Figures delight him, and he has heard it said that there are more than half a million souls in the great city of London. He would like to know the precise number – wonders indeed how any man could make a reasonable tot. Why, he knows of many crooked streets, the houses leaning drunkenly towards each other, where there are six or seven families in each room of each house – indistinguishable wraiths, somewhere between this world and the next, sharing filthy bedding, sleeping in turns. And that is not to speak of those who never seem to settle at all – even in a shared, squalid corner – but wander ceaselessly from place to place. How would one find an individual in this seething throng? One, he suspects, would be unlikely to find an ordinary individual, but a baron – now, that would be a different matter.

'Do you?' Sukie's question intrudes into his thoughts.

'Know how to find a baron? Why, Miss Sukie, that would very much depend.' He pauses, with a sense that he is at the edge of something, wonders if he might not be better advised now to pull back altogether.

'I know the name . . .' She screws up her eyes, purses her lips effortfully, trying to force the half-formed memory into certainty. 'I think . . .'

'The baron's name?'

'Yes.' Her eyes snap open. 'But I ain't going to tell you it just like that.'

'With a name, Miss Sukie, perhaps you could find him yourself.' Shapsel Nicodemus surprises himself with this suggestion. Partly he wishes to help, and partly he wishes to see his shop door close softly behind Sukie and her strange book.

'Na,' she says firmly with a small shake of her head. 'Na,' she says again. 'I need someone . . . someone . . .' She gestures vaguely in Nico's direction, indicating his size, his maleness, what she considers to be the respectability of his sombre clothing . . . and finishes firmly: 'Someone like you as can talk to barons and not be cheated.'

Shapsel Nicodemus has never yet spoken to a baron and doubts very much whether, as a Jewish pawnbroker with an accent formed on the western steppes, he has any of the great advantages Sukie appears to discern. But all the same, whatever his limitations, they pale beside Sukie's – her tiny pale face, her gap-toothed lisp.

'And so' – he bows his head slightly – 'if I am to find this man, I would require his name.'

'But if I tell you, Nico, if I tell you, then I keep the book until the deal is done. And if you bugger me over . . . I swear . . .'

Nico nods calmly. 'And we will agree on half. One half for you. One half for me. A fair split.' His long right hand mimes a clean chopping motion.

'Half! You bugger! It's my fuckin' book!'

And Sukie settles into a familiar stance, head thrust forwards, hand on hip. She knows this game. Nico, too, knows what is required of him.

Though neither of them enjoys the process as others might, they set about agreeing the deal with great vigour. Sukie might well be a terrier, disputing a rat with a much larger dog, and all but snarls at him as he suggests a share of four and a half in ten.

Nico holds his ground as Sukie offers two in ten, and he courteously counters with four in ten, Sukie laughs at him derisively and moves to take her book and walk away.

She is playing her part well, but in truth, her mind is far away, her thoughts almost equally divided between coins and angels. In fact, coins and angels are beginning to seem linked in her mind – the one connected to the other in a way she has never before imagined. Both being golden. Coins, though, are hard to the tooth, things of weight and consequence. And these angels are surely soft and flowing, weightless. Angels she can almost touch, they have become so real to her – smooth skin, soft hair, luminous eyes, and their movement like a gentle wind on a hot day. Why, she could swear she could smell them, too, all warm and milky, with something flowery underneath.

Nico, similarly, is holding the matter of the bargain that must be struck in one part of his mind while the tug of indistinct memory aroused by the book occupies the greater part of his attention. It is a feeling more than anything. It is somehow connected to this sense of worthwhile activity that came to him as he looked at the couple in the book. It has reminded him of a possibility that he has tucked far away in the recesses of his mind: that a person might labour, with skill and care, at a worthwhile task and produce something good at the end . . . and that this labour could be shared – a joint venture. It is quite the opposite feeling to the feeling he has for his day-to-day activity – standing alone in his shop, exchanging coins for watches, shirts, spoons, hats of indeterminate origin. Quite the opposite of the feeling he has for Katia, whom he knows is rustling about upstairs in their two-roomed flat.

But these thoughts do not sadden him. He had forgotten altogether that there could be anything more, and it is enough just now for him to remember the possibility.

And distracted as he and Sukie are, it is Sukie who appears to have won the day. He can tell this by the way she extends her hand to take his, saying, 'Two in ten it is, Nico. Agreed?'

Two in ten. He takes Sukie's hand. Of what, he wonders. What could this slim book be worth? And more to the point, what, if he can find him, might this baron pay to have it back? Nico feels a flutter of excitement, which may have communicated itself to him through the thin dry hand in his. Perhaps it will be an enormous sum – perhaps so big that two-tenths of it could be enough to . . . He casts around wildly for what he would do with an enormous sum – buy in stock? Take the lease on a loftier shop in a less desperate place?

'And the name, Miss Sukie?'

She removes her hand from his and begins to wrap the book in its waxen cloth. 'Well, it's Baron to begin with, all right, and then something foreign sounding like . . .' She pauses and says carefully, with a slight flush, 'Sweding-borg.'

'Sweding-borg,' he repeats, and the deep tone of his voice, the guttural echoes of the steppes, translate it from the sound that was in Sukie's head to something quite unrecognisable.

'No, more like Sweee-din-burg.'

'Sweeding-burg,' he repeats.

'Swee-*DIN*-burg'

'Sweeding-burg'

She looks at him with irritation. He, too, feels uncharacteristically irritated – this matter of pronunciation, this detail, seems entirely contrary to the expansive thoughts that filled his mind not ten seconds ago.

And so he straightens up and responds with a forced courtesy, with a formal, deliberate expression, 'I suspect the baron speaks in a different manner entirely, not as you might, nor I.'

'Maybe.' Sukie takes his point. 'But how're you going to find him if you can't say his name?'

'Miss Sukie, I will make enquiries.' Already, at the back of his mind, something is tickling . . . A book dealer he met at Synagogue.

'Well, I'll be back. Back tomorrow to see.'

And Sukie turns round abruptly and has gone out the door before Nico can reply, the bright hot street flashing briefly in his vision before she disappears.

Chapter Thirteen

Fleet Street, London

Peter Woulfe is perspiring. His damaged fingers are stiffening and swelling. His ear is throbbing. But most of all, he is furiously impatient. He is in a shabby hackney carriage with Sweetnam, jostling through the hot, noisy streets of London. If he could draw a line through the next hour of his life, he would.

He closes his eyes to the worn leather interior, shuts off the distinct smell of must. The damp, florid hackney driver and his false bonhomie Peter blames entirely on the weather. Though it is not yet ten o'clock, it is clear it will be one of those scorching London days – when the city appears to forget its northern latitude and seethes with an exotic heat. There is a rare old stink rising from the streets and the sewers – and the populace themselves.

He thinks of Sukie and his ruined experiment. The sense of possibility that was so alive in the early morning now seems unimaginably long ago. He knows little other than that he must recreate the morning's conditions at all costs. He must have Sukie – he cannot possibly lose her now that he has found her. And he must reclaim that joyous clarity he felt at his workbench, he must continue his work – and he must have Sukie by his side in order to do so. The two are one and the same. He must get free of Sweetnam and in a manner that does not tempt him to bring all his worst threats to bear. How he will manage the meeting with the baron, the question of the damned book, is not clear to him. But he suspects that his best bet may have to do with the baron's angels – some mention of them . . . or perhaps some appeal to them.

The baron is sitting in an easy chair in the bedchamber. He is dressed as an invalid might be: shirt open at the neck, a waistcoat, no jacket – respectable, but giving the impression of being in a delicate state. When he turns his head and brings his eyes to bear on Sweetnam and Peter, Peter is surprised to see that he looks quite well – neither as unbound as he appeared that first evening on Fleet Street nor as hang-dog and vulnerable as he looked on Fetter Lane. In fact, when he speaks, says 'Good morning, gentlemen,' Peter is quite taken aback by his measured tone.

Sweetnam bows slightly.

'Good morning, Baron Swedenborg, I am most grateful to you for receiving me. My name is Josiah Sweetnam, and this is my apprentice, Mr Woulfe.'

Peter feels a surge of distaste at Sweetnam's scraping manner.

The baron nods and opens his mouth as if to speak – but Sweetnam, nervy and anxious, speaks again quickly. 'We have come with regard to a most urgent matter. My young friend here was given a commission – that is, he was instructed to bring you a book. A most . . . interesting and important book . . .' Here, Sweetnam appears to falter. 'It was directed to you by a most influential French gentleman – a friend of Rouelle.' It appears to Peter that Sweetnam has put an unusual degree of emphasis on the name.

The baron nods, beckons with his hand and says calmly, 'Come in – come into the light. You have suffered an injury, sir? Quite recently, I detect?'

'Yes, an unfortunate fall.'

'My dear sir, I think you should sit down. Young man, pull over that chair.'

Peter heaves the chair in the direction indicated by the baron.

Sweetnam has blotted the worst of the blood on his face and applied a dark, sticky unguent to his nose – but looking at him as the baron must, Peter sees that he looks quite horrifyingly maimed.

Sweetnam lowers himself into the chair.

The baron leans forwards with real concern. 'May I offer you some refreshment? Perhaps a small glass of wine?'

Peter sees that the taut fury stoked by Sweetnam's fear is beginning to slacken – in fact, he looks weak and lost. Peter quite expects him to assent to the wine and the sympathy, but instead Sweetnam stirs himself and sits up.

'You are very kind, but I fear my task is an urgent one. The book, you see, was a very . . . valuable . . . one. As I mentioned, it came from a friend of Rouelle – a gentleman who was most insistent that you receive it without delay.'

'And you say this young man was charged with delivering it to me?' The baron looks at Peter, who is now standing in the light from the window. 'Why, we have met! Young Mr Volfe, the scholar and metallurgist.'

Peter nods. He cannot help a small smile forming in response to the warmth in the baron's voice before he remembers his compromised position and his face deflates abruptly.

'You remember Mr Woulfe?'

'Why, yes, I do. A most interesting encounter.' The baron frowns slightly, as if he is trying to remember something.

Sweetnam's eyes dart from Peter Woulfe to the baron and back.

'The book, dear Baron – I must ask you to consider the book.'

'There was no book.' Swedenborg looks directly at Peter Woulfe. 'There was no book that day? We spoke of my book – *Philosophical and Metallurgical Works* – but no other.'

Peter stands frozen. He says, 'Angels. We spoke of angels.' And then, with a glance at Sweetnam, he adds, 'If you recall?'

'I do recall, yes, quite clearly. We spoke of angels, and what better subject?'

The baron stares quite openly at Peter, as if he would like to peer right into his mind and extract something.

Sweetnam speaks into the silence. 'If I understand correctly, you recall the angels, but not the book?'

The baron turns his attention to Sweetnam, says firmly, 'There was no book, sir, making it most unlikely that I would recall it. The angels, on the other hand, were most memorable.'

Sweetnam, sounding superficially polite but irked, replies, 'Indeed. There was no book, but there were angels?'

Peter begins to hope that Sweetnam and the baron will bounce back and forth and forget all about him.

But just as the thought rises in his mind, the baron turns straight to him again. 'That is correct, is it not, Mr Volfe?'

'I . . . I did not see the angels.'

The baron sits forwards, interested now. 'It is not so much a question of seeing. There is some activation of the aural – in the sense of sounds filling the mind – but *seeing* . . . no, that is not an accurate description – not in the street, not in the light of day . . . as we were.' It is clear he is addressing Peter, as though Sweetnam were not present.

Peter stares beyond the baron at the strong morning light coming in the window, sees how it catches and twists in the glass.

Sweetnam persists. 'I can see that you are very much interested in angels, Baron, but I must beg you to expand on the matter of the book.'

The baron applies his gaze to Sweetnam. 'Rouelle, you say? A friend of Rouelle?'

Sweetnam nods.

And the baron continues, 'It is surely an extremely interesting book in that case. Monsieur Rouelle is a most skilled practitioner.'

Peter is still staring at the window; he is not quite able to pull his eyes away from the glare.

Baron Swedenborg pauses. He sits back in his seat. Peter has a sense of real weight coming into play, as if by intention alone the baron has shifted the balance in the room, has subtly reaffirmed his greater social and moral authority. In fact, if scales could weigh the elements active in the room, Peter imagines Sweetnam and himself flying up into the air when set against the baron.

'Well, I assure you I have not received it. It is unfortunate if it has gone astray. And now, gentlemen, I must rest – I have not been entirely well of late.'

Sweetnam rises slowly. 'I am most grateful to you for seeing us this morning. I would not have inconvenienced you for anything other than such an urgent matter.'

'I am sorry I cannot help.'

'You would not care for me to describe the book in question – lest it has slipped your mind?'

'Slipped? Like a fish out of a net?'

'Sir?'

'You might speak of a fish thus, but not I fear a book, Mr Sweetnam.'

Peter turns his gaze to Swedenborg, his vision now swimming from the glass-fractured sun, and the baron's face appears only in part, as though he has just one eye and a liquid nose, as though he is both there and not there. And Peter feels ill to his stomach, unsettled in the extreme.

The baron, looking directly at him, says, 'Don't you agree, Mr Volfe?' with what Peter feels is a significant degree of emphasis.

'Yes, sir.'

Peter finds he does not want to leave the baron. There are so many things he would like to speak about with him. The smelting of copper, the extraction of azure . . . the sounds of the angels. He would like to tell him about the work he is doing and how he believes it to have been affected by Sukie's presence. He is deeply drawn to the man. He must search for Sukie and the book; he must resolve the matter and return as a supplicant might and learn from the baron.

'Good day, gentlemen.'

'Good day, sir.'

'You may call again, Mr Volfe. We have much to discuss – the action of sulphur on copper, for example. Yes, Mr Volfe, that is one matter we could explore. There are other matters, too – perhaps of even greater interest to us both. You may call tomorrow. Early in the morning. We can breakfast together.'

Peter flushes with confusion. 'Yes, sir – thank you, sir.'

⁓

Sweetnam and Peter Woulfe stand on the street outside Swedenborg's rooms. Peter keeps his embarrassed gaze away from Sweetnam. It has been a monumental failure. Sweetnam has been dismissed, and he knows no more about the whereabouts of the book that he did an hour ago. And now, what to do?

Sweetnam furiously beckons him into the carriage. Peter has no sooner sat down than he experiences a sliding sensation in his gut: confined now in the small space with him, he realises he cannot possibly stay with Sweetnam. If he sits here, he must endure the questions without answer; he must rebuff Sweetnam's fury; he must wait in this quagmire of rage and incomprehension with no possible way out – knowing all the while that the only way to get the book is to find Sukie. It is quite clear that he must run, but if he runs, he knows he will risk everything.

Peter believes all of Sweetnam's threats – the older man will certainly ruin him. He thinks of his mother, his brothers, his father. His stomach slides further. He considers the store of coins in his purse, the draft on his uncle's bank that he carries concealed in the inner pocket of his coat. His hand moves towards his satchel.

Sweetnam has leaned forwards and begun to roar at him – but Peter does not hear what he is saying. He can see the contorted, angry face, the spittle flying, the ugly colour mounting as the eyes narrow. And, feeling as if he is casting himself off a cliff, he pushes Sweetnam back against the seat with all his might and leaps for the door of the carriage. He cracks his head on the door-frame, stumbles onto the uneven pavement, arms and lengthy legs all akimbo; his coat catches on the inside handle until, with a mighty wrench, he tears through the fabric, leaving the carriage itself rocking from the force.

And then he runs – runs as fast as he can, his satchel under his arm, dipping and swerving through the crowed pavement. He is sworn at, shouted after; one burly fellow's indignant 'Hey!' cracks about his ears like a whip. Feeling the sweat begin to bead on his forehead, his coat growing tighter, Peter looks back just once and sees Sweetnam's arms flailing in the air, sees the shape of his mouth open in anger, but cannot connect the movement with any individual sound amongst the cacophony.

He runs on, a grin beginning to split his reddening face, his feet beginning to enjoy the dance between the obstacles in front of him. Finding a rhythm in his movement, he begins to feel young and strong and free – free as he has not done since he came to London . . . He dodges a pamphlet seller, leaps over an old woman's barrow, jumps up to touch a high flap of awning, just for the fun of it – and so runs much farther than he would need to outpace even the most fleet-footed version of Sweetnam imaginable.

But soon, his breath begins to burn, his feet begin to weigh, and he slows to a walk and then a standstill. He has no idea where he is. He has certainly never been in this place before. To his left, a poor-looking sort of a shop, dark windows and tattered old awning. To his right, a decrepit house. On the corner, an alehouse. The buildings lean in close together. He becomes aware of being watched; a group of young men are clustered not ten yards away at the corner where the road fractures into a narrow alley. They appear to be laughing at him.

No one knows where he is. Not Sweetnam, not his brothers, not his uncle, not his father. He looks down to avoid their gaze, to gather his wits. The path is uneven, partially cobbled; there is a long, dry crack just in front of him – he feels slight enough that he could slip right through the crack into whatever lies beneath and never be seen again.

The young men begin to move towards him – all shorter than him by a good head, all dressed in the dull tones that merge with the tired brick buildings behind. The arms and legs are all a jumble. There are more than five of them, less than ten, he thinks – he cannot make out one from the other, moving as they are like a many-headed crab. And just as his feet awaken, just as he considers he might run for it, he discovers he is surrounded – the crab having split and encircled him as fast as the thought formed.

And one fellow, the burliest, gives Peter a little shove. 'No need to be afeared. No need to be afeared at all, cully.'

An unseen hand pushes from behind so that he finds himself even closer to the burly fellow, the ring closing in all the time.

'Oh no, no! No need to be afeared at all.'

But Peter is afraid, quite flatly afraid – of this huddle of impoverished beings who quite simply want whatever he may have, who will swarm over him, he is sure, and pick him clean. Whether they will leave him his life or not, he cannot imagine. He thinks of his mother – how he has not yet written to her this week, how he must write if it all possible, as she will be waiting for his letter. He wonders how it will happen – they would like his coat to be sure, his satchel, his buckled shoes – why, even his breeches. Will they knock him on the head first? Peter imagines himself stripped bare and motionless, sprawled out on this dusty, unfamiliar earth – and in the shock of self-pity aroused by the image, he finds he has opened his mouth to speak.

'Look, look, lads, there's no need for trouble.' He can hear that he sounds more Irish than usual. 'It's too hot for trouble.'

'It's very 'ot, all right.' The boy closest speaks as though the teeth are all loose in his head.

Peter casts around wildly, and his eye falls on the alehouse on the corner. A large man with arms folded over a grubby apron stands in the doorway.

'Sir! Sir!' Peter shouts over the heads of the boys in front of him. 'I would like to stand these gentlemen a drink of your finest ale.'

The man does not move.

'Sir, sir – an ale for each of these gentlemen and for you yourself, of course.'

The boy has moved closer, so close Peter can smell him – the rank odour of young male in the heat.

He shouts again, louder, more urgently. 'Sir, sir! Two pots of ale a head . . .! Including your good self. Your finest ale!'

And something passes between the man in the doorway and the many-headed crab surrounding Peter Woulfe, some barely perceptible exchange whereby the man shifts his position, turns his head a little in their direction, and the circle around Peter slackens slightly. He finds that he is moving now, crossing the narrow, uneven street, sidestepping, shuffling, still surrounded, towards the doorway of the alehouse.

⁓

By six o'clock – marked by the tolling of the Christ Church bells – Peter Woulfe is quite staggeringly drunk. He has by some miracle held on to his satchel; it stands between his feet like a wobbly calf. And his purse, though much, much lighter, is still hanging on its leather thong around his neck.

Some of the boys around him have names, and he has managed to connect one with the right face: the loose-toothed boy whose face leered up close is called Christian.

Peter now sees that Christian is, in fact, the head of the crab – for Christian has managed the conveyance of his money to the landlord, has carefully monitored and controlled the supply of ale. Peter now knows there are six boys as well as Christian – knows, too, that he has paid not just for nine pots of ale but for the subsequent refilling of those nine pots five times. His drinking mates are vocally insistent that he drinks pot for pot with them, so united in their clamour that it could almost be taken for good-will.

They speak in a manner and at a pace that makes almost all of what they say totally unintelligible to him. One boy has managed to convey his great luck in falling in with them.

'Was you to have been just one street down' – he nods out the door – 'you'd have come on the Goat Boys. Oh, they'd have had you, all right,' he says companionably. 'Had you well and good by now, and no ale or nothing.'

Peter has handed over coin; Christian has been punctilious about murmuring figures, calculating aloud, counting on his fingers and returning to Peter's damp palm a selection of small coins at the end of each transaction. The room is dark, warm, pungent – smelling of beer and farts. But he has not, in truth, paid much attention to his surroundings, being more concerned to keep Christian and his friends tight in the circle of his diminishing attention. He is aware of the pale large figure of the landlord looming just beyond his vision. He noted as his eyes adjusted to the dark that the place was almost empty, save for a fat man sitting alone and two other men standing at the far end of the room. He is aware of the rough wooden bench on which they sit, sees how it has been worn to a smooth tarry black by long use.

The first mouthfuls of ale were a delight – wet, sharp, refreshing and calming beyond all reasonable measure – and quite quickly, on his perilously empty stomach and his hot, overwrought head, the ale has turned his mood to barely suppressed elation.

He is alive; he is free. Christian is not such a bad sort, stepping across the room like a young king to place the brown liquid carefully on the table in front of him as if sharing a rare bounty. This is pot number six, or perhaps he has missed one or two – he counts back in his head and gets as far as two, employs his fingers, marks the third last pot as the one he drank with a pressing pain in his bladder before heading out, accompanied by Christian and three of the other boys, to piss collectively against a dark, damp wall, the sky a line of bright blue a million miles above them. As they pissed together, Peter could almost imagine the boys to be amiable if unusual drinking companions, but the manner in which they escorted him back inside clarified his status as near-prisoner – Christian stalking wiry and lithe in front, a boy on either side of him holding Peter's arms and another boy behind with a sharp little paw firm on his back.

But now that he is drinking his sixth or perhaps his seventh or eighth ale, he feels he is exactly where he ought to be. True, he has not spoken much above five words since he first sat down. True, the boys are laughing and shoving and spitting around him as if he were made of stone. Not that he minds the lack of conversation – he would prefer not to be distracted from the urgent matter of considering his situation, considering how to extract himself from his present company. Indeed, he resolved after the first ale to merely nod at his companions in such a way as to maintain this good-natured entente, but privately to direct all his mental powers to the near-impossible quandary in which he finds himself.

The trouble is he cannot focus his mind – cannot get beyond one, two, three . . . cannot, as the ales come faster and faster, clamber over even the first obstacle of how to leave this place. He can consider Sukie, and the urgency of finding her – yes, that is the first matter to consider . . . or the second . . . He finds that even his desire for her body has altered from the knife-like clarity of the morning, as if there is now a foggy gap between his mind and the undeniable fire in his loins. All the same, as her face swims into his thoughts, he feels a sob rise in his chest. He cannot lose her. And if he is not to lose her, he must find her, and if he is to find her, he must leave this place—

It is at this point in his considerations that one of the boys, a fair-browed boy with a runny nose and red eyes, nods derisively in Peter Woulfe's direction and says, 'Milaawd.'

His companions enjoy this so much that one of them punches Peter hard in the upper arm as he snorts with laughter.

And so the boy says it again – 'Milaawd, Milaawd, Milaawd' – his lips pursed in a strangely contrived manner.

Peter cannot at first make out the sound – knows well that whatever it is, it is designed to demean, and it is as the boy stands up, bucks his hips back and forth with an obscene leer and cries loudly, 'Oh yes, yes, yes, Milaawd!' that he realises he is saying *My Lord.*

One of the more vacant-looking boys takes the general hilarity further by reaching over to pat his head – but Peter grabs the offending arm and rises to his feet. Now, regardless of his eight or nine pots of ale, something is beginning to push through the fog – it is simply not tolerable that this creature should lay a hand on his head. He could fling him clear across the room. In fact, now that he stands up, now that he towers a clear head and shoulders above even the tallest of the gang, he feels he could fling them all across the room – one by one, if possible, but two or three at a time if necessary. He has recovered himself; he has had time enough to consider, enough ale in this dark, unfamiliar place – he is no longer to be jostled and shoved and spat around. He holds the offending arm firm in his grip.

Christian rises, too – with a smooth easy movement. His eyes have brightened and hardened; his lips have parted so that Peter can see the wet, animal pink of tongue in his eager, open mouth. Christian withdraws a wide knife from his jacket. It is a glinting brute of a blade, sharp without doubt – weighty and surprisingly large, surely too large to have been concealed in Christian's scanty, mud-coloured jacket. But there it was. It is the brightest thing in the room, and everyone is watching it.

Christian is certainly bigger now that he is holding the outsized blade. Peter is no longer so sure he can simply fling him across the room.

He sees now that Christian is the head of the crab because all along he has had the blade. That, or Christian has the blade because he is the head of the crab . . . No, no, no – it comes as a flash: Christian has the blade and is thereby the head of the crab because he is the one who will use it to greatest effect. He is not a young king; he is a butcher. And Peter Woulfe is conscious of himself as piece of meat to be jointed, cut apart, divvied up. Shin, hock, ham – boned and rolled. Heart, liver, kidneys – bloody on a slab. His clothes and belongings aside, it seems to Peter now that Christian would put his very flesh in a pie.

There are the thinnest shavings of time now between Peter Woulfe the person – the living, sentient being who can possess Sukie, can understand intricate alchemical processes, can love his mother, can piss against a wall – and Peter Woulfe the piece of clothed meat, blood-soaked on this dirty floor.

He has in his bag a small surgeon's scalpel, a neat hammer with a chiselled end, which he uses for rock samples, and a pestle for crushing minerals ... were he able to reach any of these, they would be damn all use to him – and this, after Sweetnam's poker this morning. It is now that Peter resolves, if he is to emerge alive, that he will never be unarmed again.

He loosens his grip on the boy's arm.

'Well now ... well now.' Christian speaks quietly, soothingly. 'Well now, Milaawd.' His eyes bore into Peter's, and Peter's world narrows to the dark points of Christian's pupils.

A door opens behind him, and he can feel as much as see the light change in a shifting rectangle across the floor. A wave of high, girlish voices crashes across them. And then they are surrounded, not by the voices alone but by the warm, pulsing bodies of an improbably large number of girls – girls who know the boys, call them by name, swarm in amongst them, paying little heed at all to Christian's blade.

One of the girls stands right up close to Christian, and Peter sees a change run through him – sees that the edge of his intent has slackened. The girl smiles at Christian, her breasts high and swollen, her lips moist, her cheeks flushed, and Christian frowns back at her and looks away across the room, as if something of great interest were happening by the window. The cleaver now looks like an outsized, ungainly attachment to Christian's small, tight body. She moves a little closer to him, seems oblivious to the blade, murmurs something indistinct to which Christian appears to assent by cocking his shoulder and jerking his head ceiling-wards. She runs her fingers down the sleeve of his jacket tenderly. Christian absently nods in Peter's direction, replaces the blade in his jacket and, turning away from the girl, walks across the room as she follows close behind him.

Addressing the back of his head, the girl whinnies, 'What about a drop of something, Chrissy?'

Christian spins on his heel, calls over to the landlord, 'This 'ere gentleman here would like to stand ye ladies a drink.'

And now, Peter is surrounded by innumerable bodies, sharp-elbowed boys and the soft breasts and rustling skirts of the high-pitched girls. He fears he might drown in the pungent press of flesh. He finds he has handed over coin enough to drain the pub dry and received another pot of ale before he knows quite how it has happened.

Christian and his girl have retreated to a dark corner, and Peter sees the girl leaning back against the wall, taking a deep draught of ale while Christian's head nuzzles hungrily into her bosom. As he watches, the dark-brown aureole of her nipple disappears into Christian's mouth, and her face distorts with what could be pleasure or pain.

Just then, the landlord shouts, ''Ere, into the back, you lot – c'mon, c'mon, none of that out 'ere.'

Peter finds himself jostled along through a narrow door up three uneven steps and into a foul-smelling, ill-lit room with three wall lanterns and sticky, beer-stained tables. It is here, within minutes, that he observes Christian's girl hoick her skirts above her hips with a practised flourish and present her rump to his grinding hips. The noise generated by Christian's gang and their girls is such that Christian's grunts as he enters the girl are barely audible, though he is little more than ten yards away from Peter Woulfe.

In fact, the noise and general melee is such that Peter believes he is the only one to notice, until he sees one of the boys standing in the corner, his eyes locked on Christian's girl, slip his hand into his breeches and begin to tug rhythmically. And just then, as if she has been waiting, a dark-haired girl with wide, flat cheeks detaches herself from the bigger group and comes to sit on Peter's lap. His evident tumescence appears to delight her, and she begins to laugh a high, thin laugh as she shifts slowly around on his lap. Within moments, she has one hand on his cock and the other on his leather purse.

'Bit light tonight, ain't we?' she says, weighing the purse in her palm. 'But I tell you' – and she leans right into Peter's ear so that he can feel her hot, beery breath on his skin – 'you look after me and I'll look after you, eh?'

And he would like to say, *no, no*; he would like to explain that he already has a girl, a girl he would like to marry – for he realises now, in a flash, that this is the solution: he must marry Sukie . . . He would like to explain this to the girl who is twirling her fingers so expertly around his balls . . . but he finds he has no words any-more, finds he cannot move, can do nothing but throw his head back against the wall and let his mouth fall slack.

Later on – and he knows it is later only because it cannot be earlier, for the light in the dim room has not changed, and Peter has entirely lost any sense of time – there is another girl astride him . . . a different girl, who smells of onions and has red unfo-cused eyes and surprisingly white, even, little teeth, teeth that flash as she smiles absently down at him.

It is just as he realises that this is not the same girl as the first girl, that he remembers that there was an altogether different woman straddling him a moment ago – a larger, fatter, older woman, whose breasts swung from side to side as she moved . . . Three women . . . Three distinct faces . . . Three . . . The number disgusts him, lands like a fist in his gut, and his stomach begins to turn with a twist of nauseating sobriety. What has he done? What has become of him?

He begins to heave and vomits a stream of dark-brown, partially digested ale all over the floor.

The white-toothed girl grimaces with disgust, stands up and moves away into the shadows.

Peter stumbles – one hand clutching for his breeches, the other hand clapped over his mouth, dark fizzing liquid coming out of his nose – down the steps through the now-crowded front room and out into the dark, cool street, landing on his knees on the uneven cobbles. He heaves and strains until he feels his stomach itself must be on the ground in front of him. The contents of his long-distant breakfast mingle with the fermenting beer swilling between the cobbles, and in horror, Peter drags himself away from his own mess, moving on his hands and knees, going farther into the darkness, feeling that, if he can get away from the mess and the noise of the alehouse and the light spilling out from the lamp above the door, then he can die in peace in the relative calm of the shadows.

But he does not reckon with what is already in the shadows. He lays his hot head on the cool, cobbled ground with relief before he notices the putrefying dog not six inches from his nose – ribs swollen, the skin a-swarm with maggots, one open amber eye glinting in the remnants of the alehouse lamplight. And his nose, suddenly more sensitive than it has ever been, registers the unholy stink of rotting flesh.

He gets to his feet in horror and stumbles away, pauses to vomit, begins to weep, wonders if anyone has ever suffered quite so much. Staggers farther away. Begins to shiver and realises that he no longer has his coat or his satchel – he reaches for his purse and finds that it is gone, too. He is lost and utterly without resources. His shoes flap open, the buckles missing.

He begins to whimper as he stumbles, and a prayer begins to form on his dry, quivering lips: 'Dear God in heaven, save me . . . dear God in heaven . . . I beseech thee, take pity on this miserable sinner.'

He knows that it is at times like this, when things can get no worse, that God steps in. He looks around desperately – it is now that he needs an angel; it is surely now that God will send an emissary.

He falls to his knees, closes his eyes and prays aloud again, from the very depths of his soul.

But there is no angel. He is quite alone. He has never felt so far from home.

He closes his eyes and begins to pray again, and this time he knows he must address his prayers to a higher power than God – and the image that comes to him is of a bright-eyed being singing out into the night sky, a being that looks like a bit like his mother and sounds a bit like old Bridey Leary.

Chapter Fourteen

October 1726 – *Samhain*

Mount Gabriel, Cork, Ireland

Mary Woulfe's sixth son is a doubtful scrap of a thing. Three months old and small, come too soon after his elder brother to thrive with any ease. He has displayed a lack of vigour, a delicacy from his very first cry – mewling, rather than roaring like his ravenous brothers. The house is busy. Peter's father, James Woulfe, has paid him little heed; his brothers are more interested in the litter of pups in the barn. Even Mary's mother welcomed her twenty-first grandchild with clearly feigned enthusiasm. Whether he stays or goes seems to be of little consequence to anyone except his mother. For her, his survival is a drum she must keep beating night and day without missing a stroke.

Mary Woulfe, wife of James Woulfe, is more pretty than beautiful – and all the better for that as a match for James, who, tall, ungainly and forceful, finds beauty alluring but too unsettling to wed. Mary's large blue eyes, creamy skin and curving figure combine to speak of a yielding softness that will accommodate a man's needs – be that his carnal desires or the cushioning of his weary head at the end of a long day. James knows better than anyone how her inclination to softness extends to her thoughts, which are to his mind fumbling and inaccurate, unreliable and somewhat erratic. But oh, she is soft and kind – her warm silken skin, her fine dark hair, her lips softest of all, and her neck smelling like a damp new loaf. He can forgive her any silliness for these moments of soft refuge in the night. And she has a wit that often surprises her husband – he finds himself smiling at her light darts of humour that hit the mark as if by accident. For her part, she desires James Woulfe's stability, his wealth, this fine house, this extensive farm inherited from his bachelor uncle, the lucrative partnership in his father's profitable cloth-importing business in Cork.

Mary wakes her infant son to feed him in the night, coaxes, cajoles, nurses him herself and brings in Peg Dooley, whose plump brown breasts promise rich, buttery milk, to give him an extra feed every morning and evening.

She has loved him excessively since the moment she saw him, long and lean, pale and serious, his huge blue eyes seeming to peer right into her soul. And it is not just that she loves him, for surely she loves Maurice and James and Stephen; she loves Thaddeus and Daniel – it is that if he were to die, she knows she would die herself.

She would leave her sturdy sons, her husband, her mother and her sisters without a second thought and fling herself into the sea at Jension Hill. That much is certain. It is her secret, this plan, this certainty – it is the only thing that gives her any relief at all from the constant dread that he will die. And all the while, in the three months since he was born, she has continued in her daily affection for the rest of her family, at times quite offhand about Peter, lest anyone suspects.

Her old father, visiting for the week, seeing his daughter cradling her youngest son, asks in a kindly, curious way, 'You're fond of him, are you?'

Mary Woulfe has always understood that she loves her father, a gentle and generous man, but as she looks up in surprise, his age-reddened face swimming into focus, she knows she would kill him as soon as look at him if it would help Peter grow stronger.

Indeed, in that moment, she wonders why the old man is still alive breathing air that Peter might need, eating food that could go to nourish him, taking up space and time that should by rights be Peter's – taking even this moment of her attention, which could be directed towards him.

And the vast gap between what she is thinking and what she can say in response causes her to laugh and say merely, 'Yes, quite fond, quite fond . . .' with a touch of sympathy for the poor, foolish man.

In the early afternoon of the 31st of October, it becomes clear that the child is very ill. His breathing is laboured, his forehead hot, his skin pale and damp; he struggles to feed. He has become floppy and inert in her arms.

She has rubbed his chest and his feet with embrocation, has had the steam-kettle going these last three hours, has put cool flannels on his brow, all to no avail – he is clearly worsening.

James sends for Dr Nelligan, who swaggers in flushed from his ride, his grey cloak splattered with mud, and hums and haws over the infant until Mary would like to run shrieking through the house, calling for someone else to come and help. Anyone at all.

But she bites her lip and begins to pace back and forth along the length of the first-floor bedroom, from the first window to the third window, creaking on the familiar floorboard by the wardrobe, pausing without thinking to look out.

She makes out a dark, still figure standing in the lane. Hunched and crow-like, it is a shawled female form. For a terrible moment, Mary thinks it is the banshee herself, not even waiting until dark, taunting her in the very light of day. And in that beat of time, she prepares to go right out and chase the creature off, howling and snarling, biting and thrashing, damning her own soul to hell, if damn it she must, to keep the banshee from her son.

But it is not the banshee; it is only Bridey Leary, standing out in the grey, lifeless October day. It is not quite raining and not quite dry; the air is heavy, the tired brown trees giving the occasional resigned sigh. The cattle huddled together in the near field are too morose to shift at all. Bridey's figure is the only spark of force in the dismal landscape; she is as still as her surroundings but different entirely, like something wound but not yet loosed.

Leaving the child to Nelligan and his father, Mary is down the stairs before she can think, slipping out past Maggie in the kitchen, pulling the back door behind her and calling out to Bridey.

'Bridey Leary, Bridey Leary, come with me this instant to the small barn, will you?' Mary waves her arm towards the smallest of the three thatched barns framing the muddy cobbled courtyard before rushing on ahead herself.

And when Bridey Leary pushes open the door of the barn, the smell of nutty hay and hen shit all around, Mary takes her arm and pulls her forwards into the soft murk.

She shakes Bridey's arm, shrouded in the damp, greasy cloth of her heavy cloak, and unleashes a stream of questions.

'Why are you here, Bridey Leary? Why were you standing out there like an auld crow? What is it you came to see? What did you come to do?'

'Oh, me, missus? Sure, I came to do nothing, not a thing but have a breath of air.'

'Don't give me your blethering ráiméis this day, Bridey Leary. I want none of your auld stories today . . . Tell me, for once and for all' – her grip tightens, and her gaze burrows into Bridey's bright eyes – 'tell me the whole truth and tell it to me now, this very instant, or it'll be that much the worse for you that you'll wish you were safely over the hill in your grave.'

'Ah now, Mrs Woulfe, there's no need to speak to Bridey like that, and me only a poor harmless woman . . . now, hush hush,' she protests as Mary opens her mouth in fury. 'Hush yourself, and I'll tell you – I'll tell you everything, and you'll be lucky to hear it.'

She sits down on a small bale of hay behind her and produces from the folds of her cloak a still-smouldering pipe, taking a long slow suck at it and exhaling before beginning to speak. 'The truth of it is I came to help you, girl. It is help that you need and no mistake.'

And Mary wants to say, *I'll give you anything, do anything at all, if you help him* – but she bites her lip.

And in the stillness of the moment, she fights the desire to rush back to Peter. It is intolerable to be this far away from him when he is so ill. For one dreadful moment, she thinks he will be dead before she gets back.

'Tell me.'

Bridey shifts her shoulders, flicks her cloak around her ankles – settles herself. 'Take your ease – there's time and more.'

She has come drawn by the scent of distress, unerring as a cat. Indeed, she saw Nelligan go by at a clip, but even before that, she knew something was wrong up at the house. She could smell it in the air. She knows, too, some part of Mary Woulfe's secret passion for her youngest child, knows that she has made a pet of him; Bridey has made out, through gossip and habitual watchfulness, that the poorly mite is of immense value to his mother. There's no saying what she might do for him – this powerful young woman with her house and her clothes and her pigs and her carriage and her big, strong husband and her five strong boys. No saying what Bridey Leary might get in the way of thanks if she can help her.

And if you asked Mary Woulfe why she believes Bridey can help her, she would not be able to answer you with words. She knows it's to do with a dark, ancient force she dimly remembers from her most powerful childhood dreams. To do with Bridey herself, to do with secrets and magic, things hidden and sometimes found. She barely hears the words issuing slowly from Bridey's mouth in her desperation to assent to whatever she proposes, says, 'Yes, yes,' and again, 'Yes.'

She races out of the barn, straight through the mud and the puddling water in her light house shoes, runs to the kitchen door, her eyes blurred with anxiety. She can still feel the shock of Bridey's spit-slick palm in her hand. They have agreed: Bridey will help Peter, and she will give Bridey what she wants, and even now, as she pushes the door open, she wishes she knew what exactly it is that Bridey wants – what exactly the price will be in shillings and pence.

She is aware already that it may not be as simple as shillings and pence.

⟿

Back in her cabin, Bridey feeds the fire and waits for Mary Woulfe to come with her son.

She alone knows of the small, soft bones buried on the threshold of this cabin – bones so soft that they would have dissolved into the earth like a bird's bones if she hadn't wrapped them with care in a bit of sacking. This is her secret. Her first and only babe. Borne in secret and brought forth alone.

She alone knows how she wrapped the lifeless child and buried her, first in the hazel wood, in the soft mulch of damp earth, with big flat stones laid all around to keep the animals off, and later – when James Woulfe finally had the cabin built for her and she'd dug the bundle out – how she dug the bundle out and tucked it in beneath the slab at the front door – scraping out a space when the men weren't watching and tucking the child in. And how, on the morning that she stepped in through the door and took possession of the small dark cabin, it was as if they had come home together at last, quieting a sick, anxious cry that had been singing in her belly for years.

Bridey does not think of the child much anymore – of her birth, her death or her burial, but she holds a constant awareness of the soft, powerful presence, and of what she learned that night about life and death and blood and earth and the pulse of sorrow running through it all.

When Mary Woulfe arrives, with Peter pale and drooping in her arms, Bridey is sitting fiercely still, balancing between the present and the past, the known and the unknown, the living and the dead. And long after Mary has allowed herself to forget exactly what happened to her son in Bridey's dim cabin, she remembers the cockerel's splitting shriek, her fingers in his warm blood, the thin skein of dark hair around her baby's neck, the cut of the wind as she stumbles through the dark, the jug heavy with water from the three streams in her bone-cold hands, the six flame-lit stones in a circle on the earthen floor, the stench of the brew on the fire, the pierce of the lance on Peter's feet, his cry of rage, and, all the while, the murmur of Bridey's strange, unintelligible words.

∽

And she remembers Bridey's hot, fierce eyes holding her own when silence finally falls and the child sleeps serenely. She remembers the harsh, sure rhythm of her speech.

'I went out, missus. I went out – I went out past the ends of the earth, and I got your blessed boy back. On my bended knee, I begged for him' – Mary remembers the slap of Bridey's open palm flat onto her chest – 'and I am sore tired now.'

Mary Woulfe remembers the glint of Bridey's eyes, how she had looked more awake, more alive than anyone Mary had ever seen. How at the word *tired*, a tiredness had come over her like a hot, heavy blanket, so that she could barely carry Peter home to the house, where she fell on the bed with him in the crook of her arm and they both slept right through until morning.

Chapter Fifteen

June 1744 – *Midsummer*

London

On this hot, hot morning in London, three men wake and think immediately, urgently of the missing book – all three wondering where it is and how they will find it.

Peter Woulfe, Josiah Sweetnam and a man named Sealy Hallom – for the man in the brown coat was but a terrier loosed, and Sealy Hallom, the man behind him, is much more dangerous. He is thin-lipped and hawk-nosed, consumed by the seriousness of his task – which is nothing less than putting the true heir on the British throne. He is certain that the future of mankind itself is in the balance – and that the blue blood he believes to be pulsing through his veins has determined the role he has to play at this most critical moment in human history.

Sealy Hallom has gathered a list containing the names of some of the most influential men in Britain. Assurances, words, the shake of a hand, all mean nothing when it comes to knowing who can be relied upon. And so these are witnessed signatures, authenticated by an impressive seal. The six signatories are pledging themselves to the Jacobite cause, offering men and arms to support Charles Edward Stuart in his efforts to reclaim the crown.

This single sheet of thinnest paper is intended to reassure its recipient of the unwavering commitment of its signatories, but as such, it is evidence of treason and would have them all hanged if it fell into the wrong hands.

Hallom has had this list concealed in the spine of a copy of the *Mutus Liber*. Josiah Sweetnam, apothecary, Jacobite sympathiser and bookbinder's son, has the necessary skills, is lowly enough to go unnoticed, and so was chosen to provide one of the links in a delicate, secretive chain that will lead all the way to Charles Stuart himself.

The book – a book with no text and fifteen colour plates, bound in cardboard and measuring twelve inches by twenty, a pretty book and a relatively valuable one – is just the sort of book a learned man might send across the channel to another learned man. And so, Emanuel Swedenborg, oblivious to its hidden contents, has been asked to include it, along with two other quite innocent books on natural history, in a consignment being sent to his friend Rouelle in Paris, and thus to Stuart. A small favour for his acquaintance Hallom.

But now the book is missing – and it must be found. At any cost.

❧

Peter Woulfe wakes curled in a foetal ball on the cobbles. The contents of his head have swollen and are pushing with excruciating intensity against his skull; his throat is dry, his tongue a dead creature slowly rotting in his mouth. It is dark; he is alone. He has no idea where he is.

He rises to his knees, closes his eyes and prays aloud, but when he opens his eyes again, all he sees is the dark. He staggers to his feet, his head swimming so that he nearly falls straight back down. He has not walked three paces when a figure appears before him.

'Did you think you could simply run? Run away? Like a little boy?'

Sweetnam's voice has altered beyond recognition, perhaps due to the crusting scab on his pulped nose, perhaps due to the caustic fear that has been eating through his guts for the past twenty-four hours – whatever the cause, there is a cold, fierce intent immediately evident, and Peter backs against the wall without thinking.

'Run down a lane or two, hide behind a wall? Tuck your head safe under your hat? You're quite the little sewer rat, Woulfe.' Sweetnam pulls a pistol out from under his cloak. 'I could finish you off just like that.' He mimes a pop. 'I wouldn't mind doing it one bit, but there's a gentleman who wishes to see you. A very serious gentleman who no doubt has his own pistol and can pull his own trigger when he wishes.'

～

Sweetnam's house now reeks of fear; Peter Woulfe smells it at once as the muzzle of Sweetnam's pistol pushes him in the door, an unmistakable stench underneath the familiar stink of bitter herbs.

His own fear now swamps everything else – including the sickening horror of being right back where he started yesterday but in a very much worsened state. Sweetnam bundles Peter along the narrow corridor and down the step into the furnace room – jabbing him in the spine with his pistol for good measure, so that he winces and stumbles into the sweltering room.

Sealy Hallom and the man in the brown coat are waiting; Hallom is leaning against the workbench, and the man in the brown coat is standing beside him. His face is flushed and damp; he mutters indignantly, 'It is as 'ot as hell in here – as 'ot as hell itself.'

Peter has never seen Sealy Hallom before and receives a first impression of him that is heightened by his dreadfully vulnerable circumstances.

Hallom is a slight, well-dressed man, a man with taut, superior posture and an aquiline, arrogant nose, a fiercely worried man with a serious face – on which Peter Woulfe detects, for just a second, a flicker of relief. He wonders if it is connected to his own sudden, stumbling appearance – but it disappears almost at once, to be replaced by a spurious smile of the sort designed to convey pleasure in power and the anticipation of another's pain. The smile does not convince Peter that this gentleman is any more cruel than he is desperate, but he realises it is all one when it comes down to it – which it does so fast that he cannot catch his breath as the man in the brown coat takes two surprisingly delicate steps forwards and swings eagerly at him, his fist connecting with his damaged ear with such force that his brain shifts in his skull.

Peter Woulfe howls, and the room moves around him with a sickening jerk; he finds himself gasping on the sawdust floor while Sealy Hallom turns to Sweetnam and speaks as if Peter and the man in the brown coat were not there at all. 'You can bind books but not send them half a mile? Dear Lord, man – it was not a task of such immense complexity, surely?'

Sweetnam gestures distastefully at Peter Woulfe, who is clasping his head and moaning on the floor. 'The boy, sir – I sent it with him. It seemed wise not to implicate' – he pauses here and gestures in an embarrassed manner at himself and Hallom – 'men of' – he stumbles – 'any standing . . . at all.' He speaks in a rush. 'Those, I mean, whose persons could allow a trail to be traced back to one such as yourself . . . Or, of course . . . any . . .' Here, he is about to say *even more important gentlemen* . . . but catches himself and says instead, 'You impressed upon me the need for absolute anonymity . . . the vital need . . . and a boy with a book, sir . . . who would look twice . . .?'

He looks down at Peter Woulfe with absolute distaste. Peter is breathing slowly, his head ringing, his knees drawn to his chest, his forehead on the floor.

'I was not to know he was a halfwit fornicator who could not be relied upon to put one foot safely in front of the other.' He cannot resist swinging his boot into Peter's side with a grunt. 'He is from' – Sweetnam is slightly breathless as he regains his balance – 'a good family, learned, loyal men of character including' – he nods at Hallom – 'your own associate, the banker Woulfe in Paris. It was surely not too much to expect him to carry the book to the baron?'

Sealy Hallom experiences a moment of hesitation, undetectable to anyone in the room – he is eager to move past these matters of flesh and blood, past the inconsequential Sweetnam, past the cringing young man on the floor, and get straight to the only thing of real importance: the location of the book. But he pauses; things must be done correctly, or there will only be trouble down the road.

'Mr Sweetnam, I am truly charmed by your explanation – truly, I am, but what would become of us, what would become of our noble cause' – here he pauses; he began the sentence with snide indifference, but now remembering just how great the stakes are, he feels an unexpected tightening of his heart – 'the noble enterprise in which we are lucky enough to play these small parts . . . if an inconsequential apothecary who can thread a bookbinder's needle can be allowed to be so incompetent as to have good men hanged?'

He nods at the man the brown coat, who shows his teeth with an eager grin before turning his head towards the back door and emitting a piercing whistle. The door is ajar, and a lemon-bright slice of sunlight cuts into the gloom. Peter Woulfe has been eyeing the door from the floor, wondering if he could make a run for it, knowing it leads to the yard and so out to the alley where he would have a fighting chance of getting away. But before the whistle has stopped ringing in the room, the door bursts open and three squat young men enter, the first with a swagger that is immediately familiar to Peter.

For a foolish moment, he is almost pleased to see Christian. His mud-coloured jacket, the cocky tilt of his head seem almost friendly now in this new terrible world of serious, furious men. But Christian does not acknowledge him; his shoulders convey the vastly superior status of a human who is not wounded and lying on the floor over one who is – of a young man who knows what has been going on all along over one who is nothing but an innocent fool.

One of the boys beside him is carrying Peter bulging satchel, and he puts it carefully on the bench, swinging his arms slightly and clenching his hands to show that they are free now for whatever is required of them.

And what is required? Hallom tenses almost imperceptibly; Sweetnam, after all, has a pistol, which he has been holding down by his side – as if it does not quite belong to him. But he raises it now, looking around desperately, hesitating – for even in this dire moment, he does not dare to point it at Hallom, and so points it at the man in the brown coat.

Armed and desperate he may be, but he is no match at all for the man in the brown coat, and so the shot he fires goes through the ceiling, lodging in a timber beam as the man in the brown coat grabs his arm. To Peter Woulfe, watching from the floor, it seems almost child's play – the ease with which Sweetnam is secured with his arms and legs pinned on the floor, the swift, forceful movement with which the man in the brown coat turns Sweetnam's head and slices off his right ear. It is over just like that. In a flash. Sweetnam lies whimpering and wide-eyed as the man in the brown coat waves the bloody thing across his face.

Hallom says to the man in the brown coat, with equal measures of distaste and approval, 'You like to play with your food before eating it?'

The man in the brown coat tosses the ear on the floor.

Sweetnam desperately turns his head to catch Hallom's eye and speaks in a high, frantic, pain-filled voice: 'Sir, sir, you know I am your loyal servant, loyal to the cause. Do not kill me – I will continue to serve you and the true King in whatever way I can.'

Hallom takes a step closer and looks down at Sweetnam. 'How do I know that any of this is true? How do I know you have not betrayed me? How do I know you have not simply sold the list?'

'No, no, never and surely . . . You can see that . . . Would I be here if I had?'

Hallom nods at the man in the brown coat, who turns Sweetnam's head and, this time with a look of concentration on his face and his tongue peeking out between his lips, applies his knife and removes Sweetnam's left ear before tossing it on the floor.

Sweetnam's shriek splits the room.

Peter Woulfe has gone as still as stone; his heart is barely beating. He can see Sweetnam's left ear lying not six inches away in the sawdust. He never paid much attention to it when it was attached to

Sweetnam, but he now sees there is an unusually dark freckle high up on the rim.

Sweetnam, with his eyes closed, is shouting as loud as he can. 'Stop. Please stop. Do not kill me, I beg you. I will help you – I will help you find the book. I will help you – we must find the book or we are all dead. I am no good to you dead.'

'You have not been much good to me alive either, Mr Sweetnam.'

'Ask the boy, ask the boy – ask the boy what he has done with the book.'

Hallom turns to Peter Woulfe. 'Stand up, boy.'

Despite the pain, Peter stands up. The room spins.

Hallom walks over to Peter's satchel and upends it on the workbench. His precious belongings tumble out. Hallom sweeps them off the bench in disgust – notes, phials, cork-stoppered jars land in a confused clatter on the floor. Hallom spares them barely a glance.

He turns to Peter Woulfe and looks directly into his eyes. 'How can we do this quickly, boy?'

Peter surprises himself by thinking first, *I am not a boy*, and second, of his ears, which his mother often likened to his father's, and how he would like to keep them on his head.

He says, 'Sir . . . if you will let me explain . . . sir.' He is amazed he can speak at all.

'Do not waste my time, boy,' says Hallom.

Peter Woulfe does not wish to waste his time at all. He nods, a movement that causes excruciating pain to reverberate around his skull. He gasps and says through the pain, 'No, sir. No, of course not.'

'The book?'

They are all looking at him. Everyone is listening with utmost attention; there is only the occasional repressed groan from Sweetnam to cut through the silence.

'I lost it. I met a whore down by the docks, and I think she stole it.'

The words land bald-plucked and pitiful in the room.

Hallom pauses – he can almost see it, the tired old whore and the distracted young man, the flash-looking book worth a few pennies more than the quick fuck. But he also sees – in a part of his mind that is almost always these days occupied thus – the face of his exiled King stamped on a coin, sees a world set to rights by the right man on the throne, his own fortunes replaced and the court reclaimed, a prize worth anything.

He turns to Christian. 'Well?'

Christian speaks confidently, his shoulders back. 'There weren't no book. Not in his bag, not wif him. And no whore neither – he didn't meet nobody. And' – he taps his head with one finger while twisting his mouth with derision – 'he ain't the brightest, neither. So, I'll wager he lost it, all right, and some whore has it. But what's a whore down our way gonna do wif a book but flog it? And who's she gonna flog it to? Only a few places she can go . . .' He shrugs, as if to say, *it is a fairly simple matter.*

Hallom, looking at him, thinks a number of things at once, including the surprising thought that, one day, he would like to have a son just like that – but with better teeth.

Chapter Sixteen

Black Boy Alley, off Chick Lane, London

Sukie Bulmer is standing outside The Goat, drinking with Sal and Ma Crofter. It is hot, there are too many people, and the truth is sometimes Sukie does not even like Sal – in fact, there are times when she sees her from a certain distance, in a certain kind of light, when she is repulsed by the very shape of her. And just now, watching her laughing with old Ma Crofter, is one of those times. There is a softness to Sal's shoulders, a slump around her belly that, to thin, sharp Sukie, suggests a kind of unforgivable stupidity. Sukie wonders how Ma Crofter can bear it.

She drains her gin, her lips drawing back in an involuntarily grimace, and shouts out without thinking: 'Oy, Sal, I'm off.'

She imagines sitting in the bed alone, with just one candle lit, the book on her lap and her own thoughts spread out around her.

'Off where?'

'Off home.'

'Hold up.'

And Sal leaves Ma Crofter on the instant and joins Sukie.

'Na, you stay.'

'Na.' Sal slips her arm through Sukie's.

Sukie pinches Sal's forearm viciously.

Sal pulls her arm away sharply. 'Oy! What's that for?'

'Just . . . just nothing.' Sukie hears the slur in her own voice, and having been about to tip into contrition, she instead feels anger surging up inside her. 'Just . . .' She shoves Sal away with all her might. 'Just fuck off.'

Sukie begins to walk away quickly as Sal stumbles; she is quite sure now that Sal has wronged her greatly. She does not look back.

But shortly, her heartbeat begins to steady, her fury starts to settle down, and she is relieved a few moments later to hear footsteps and realise that Sal is following her.

Sal continues to walk behind her, close enough but not too close, and when they arrive at the door, she waits as Sukie opens up. Sukie climbs the rotting steps to her room, wondering if they were so rotten when last she was here or if some fast-moving decay has overrun the place in her absence.

By the third flight, she is breathless, but just as she arrives at the door of their room she turns back and whispers, 'Sorry.'

Sal laughs softly and comes through the murky light to stand close by Sukie as she opens the door.

Sukie is awake long after Sal falls asleep. The room is hot; the air feels thin. She begins to fear that Sal's breathing has sucked up all the sleep in the room, leaving none for her. Her mind is shifting and spinning with the beautiful faces and bodies of flying angels; her body is unsated and unsettled. She would like Sal, or a woman whose face she cannot imagine, to wake now and bite her neck, to bring their body to bear on hers until she is quite exhausted. But she burns at the thought and sleep seems even more impossible.

If she cannot sleep, she wants to look at her book, and it is the roof she thinks of first when she decides she cannot stay in the hot, airless room. She has never been on the roof above this room – has never had call to be – but since she found the book, there has been a pressing lightness inside her that has drawn her to upward places.

She holds the book awkwardly in her right hand and quietly wriggles out the tiny window, feeling lithe and free as her hips clear the frame. She twists up and around, out onto the flat and flimsy roof, moving carefully in case the whole thing gives beneath her. She does not wonder now that the rain seeps through, that there is black mould on the walls below. She thinks of the coins she and Sal give Ma Crofter for their room – their room that is just this skin and bones: half-rotted timbers, a crooked slate covering up a patch of air that Ma Crofter has called her own. And the walls, too – why, they are just a few old sticks of timber pointing across and some plaster thrown over. She wonders why she should not get a few timbers herself and wrap up a bit of her very own air, pay nobody but some men to carry the timbers. For a moment, her head is urgent with these hot, impatient thoughts – and then she laughs at herself; she would not save the money for the timbers, and of course it is not the air alone but the earth beneath she would have to lay claim to.

She lies down on her belly, barely breathing, and lays her cheek upon the book. The heat of the day has gone from the slate, and the dew lies damp and slick. The waning moon is still wide and there is a soft glow all round – a sense of wakefulness. She feels the city thrusting beneath her, and the harsh call of a stray cat splits the silence. But there is a coolness, a spaciousness on this roof that is the same as peace to her tonight, and though she is planning to shift a little and open the book in order to look at it under the moonlight, she falls deeply asleep within seconds. And the angels fly through her dreams – one so close that she can see the soft fair down on her cheek, the shape of her breasts pushing through her thin clothes.

Her next waking thought is that something is pressing urgently upon her eyelids, something bright and insistent, and though she would like to slip back into sleep, she opens her eyes to a narrow slit. The sun is rising bright and glorious over the city, the vast sky filled with colour – it is all so close and so vivid that she feels for a moment as if it is rising for her personally.

She raises herself up on her left arm, her eyes still half shut, and realises with a start that she is not alone – just to her right, barely, tantalisingly within her field of vision, there is a figure. A figure standing in the light of the sun but glowing with its own terrible hue – a figure so fierce and bright, she knows she cannot look directly at it or her eyes will burn out in her head. The sun is firing the sky orange and red in front of her, but this figure is glowing golden, with a searing white light spilling into the space around it. She makes out the shape of a head and naked arms and legs.

She has never seen anything so clearly magnificent. She knows immediately that it is real, because there is nothing she has ever seen – not even the angels in the book, not the beautiful floating images that have come close to her these past few days – that could have prepared her to imagine such a being. It is so beyond her ken that her mind wobbles, and she forgets the roof, the timbers, the slate, the air around her, until she might as well be falling or flying through something or nothing. And she does not move, cannot either close her eyes or dip her head – cannot throw herself flat on the roof as some small and frightened part of her would like. She is caught fast between terror and awe.

And now, a sharp, hot pain spreads through her chest, as if for all the world she has been pierced by a flaming lance. The pain is intolerable, quite the most powerful sensation she has ever felt. She cannot breathe for it. And there is no slipping away, taking her mind off somewhere else as she might with a rough clinker – no, she is quite caught, with no escape. She knows now that this is what dying must feel like, because it is certainly impossible to survive such a feeling.

And then, just as suddenly as it came, the pain is gone, leaving in its wake a soft spreading pleasure that makes her gasp, so that her mouth hangs open and her eyes widen. And then her body slides back down onto the cool slates and, just as she resolves to turn her head and look directly at the golden figure, she falls into a deep sleep.

∽

'What 'appened? Where you bin? What's wrong?' Sal opens her eyes to squint at Sukie's pale, transformed face.

'Nothing, nowhere, nothing.'

'My arse. Where'd you get to? Is it early? It's hot already. Where you bin?' Sal squints again. 'What's in the bag?'

'Nothing. I'm off out to get some grub. Won't be long.'

Sukie, her duffle bag slung over her shoulder, is shutting the door behind her as Sal speaks again: 'What happened to your voice? You sound all funny.'

Sukie runs down the steps – as if on a cushion of air – and then out into the street, which is already thronged with mid-morning bustle. She spots the familiar shape of Rich the pieman over by his stall, finds she is standing there in front of him before she has even decided to cross the street. She is greeting him and he her, but she is not really listening; she is looking at the row of hot golden pies, watching the delicate wisps of steam floating into the warm air. She feels the fierce gaze of an enormous crow perched up on the window ledge behind Rich, sees the forceful plunge of the stony grey beak into the crust of the last pie in the row as if it has already happened. At the edge of her vision, she senses the dip-diving delight of two swallows racing above; looking up she is filled with a glorious sense of expanse, a vast bowl of sky to explore.

Rich calls her back. 'Well, luv?'

And she hears herself asking in response, 'What you got today, Rich?'

He smiles, his eyes crinkling under ginger brows that crackle in the morning light. He is better than the worst; some of what he tells her about his pies will be true. He indicates with his short, stubby finger the first row of pies. 'Well, in this lot, I got your finest rabbit, fresh as fresh.'

And she sees it all, the chop at the back of the neck, the skin peeled off, the knife scraping the pink flesh. She looks at him, wide-eyed. 'Rich, how d'you make the crust?'

'With flour, luv, of course – flour and fat and in my own special way. Lightest crust in London – as well you know.' He holds up his hands proudly, fingers splayed, palms out.

'Oh.'

'And this 'ere lot, your usual' – he points at the second row – 'beef and oysters.'

Her stomach flashes at the word *oyster*. She is sure she can smell them, the putrid tang of the sea, the chewy slime. And then she sees the smooth shoulder-line of a brown bullock jostling in the pen at the market – imagines her teeth sinking into its flesh, tearing like a cat at the tough hide, a spurt of metallic blood filling her mouth.

'All right, Rich,' she whispers and moves off with one glance at the crow, who is watching the pies intently.

Rich's voice trails after her, calling, 'Not 'ungry, luv?'

'Get your hares, fresh hares!'

The boy beside her is young and shrill, his sun-reddened face eager – it is early in the day, early in his life, and he will likely sell all his hares by noon. And to be sure, as she watches, a serious-looking woman stops him, sniffs at the animals, hands him two pennies and takes two sinewy, inert creatures in her fist, holding them by the legs so that their heads barely clear the ground.

It is the coins that Sukie notices; she remembers, with a start, that this is how is it done: dead hares for small silver discs, small silver discs stamped with the head of the King, and the boy is happy to take them, happy to slip them into the purse inside his breeches, which is dangling down there close to his cock, thudding gently against his thigh, where he thinks no one can get the coins, so they will be his until he hands them over by choice – maybe giving some of them to a girl like her so as he can fuck her up against a wall. But, seeing his smooth cheeks, she thinks he may be too young for it just yet. Maybe.

'Wot you looking at?' The boy lights up immediately with anger.

She is too close, paying too much attention to him and his coins and his purse – her wide green eyes unsettle him.

'Fuck off.' His anger makes him leery. His mouth reddens; his lips loosen so that the familiar words come out quite obscene. He would like to chase her off, if he could – he would fuck her away from his coins, away where her eyes couldn't unsettle him anymore.

'Straaawburys, strawburys!' A barrow, a woman with a cracked voice. She wants coins, too, but she is less eager, more weary.

A thin, sweaty young man with a neat beard and coal-dark eyes stands on the corner, shouting in a surprisingly deep, resonant voice, 'He is coming! Our saviour! The time is nigh, and where will you stand? For whom will you stand at Judgement Day?' He directs this last question at Sukie, who has come up close; his voice arches around her. 'Repent, or you will burn.'

He is burning himself, she can see – red-hot embers inside and on this hot, hot day. He does not want coins, not from her or anyone else. He wants, she thinks, to be quenched. A bucket of clean cold water over his head. She would like to perform this small service for him, this man she has never seen before. She would like to stretch up behind him on her toes, lifting the heavy bucket carefully, the water sloshing to the rim, but not spilling, until she could tip it right over him in one go. She smiles at the thought of the steam rising off him.

But she does not have a bucket of water. So she walks on, holding the bag with the book tight in her hot fist.

And all around her, it seems that everyone is burning for something.

Chapter Seventeen

Chick Lane, London

Nico's shop is dark even on this bright day, and when Sukie pushes the door open, she sees that Nico has a candle lit, that he is bending over his counter, peering down at something. And he is not alone; she can see the shape of a young woman there beside him, standing still and companionable as a wife might. Nico's wife.

When Sukie moves across the room and sees Nico's wife lit up by the candle, the first thing she wants to say is, *I know you – for sure and certain, I know you* – but her breath catches in her throat, and she cannot speak at all, for along with the familiarity, there is something else about this woman's face that stills her.

She is dark-eyed and cream-skinned, with high, delicate cheekbones and a large, generous mouth. Of course, Sukie does not know her – she has certainly never seen a face like this before, all the lines of it straight and sure, the eyes clear and bright. She has never seen a living, breathing person so beautiful. And Sukie looks with some confusion at Nico, who continues to peer, bending right down, squinting through a glass – not even looking at his wife. How can he look away so casually? How is it that he can have a shop filled with pretty things and a wife like this hidden away upstairs? Why, it makes no sense at all . . . There he stands beside her as he might stand beside a stone.

Katia Stein, named for her grandmother, looks at the pale, thin girl with the large, light-filled eyes and experiences a quickening of something like fear. A flare of heat rushes up her back. It is not that she recognises Sukie – not at all – but she looks at the girl standing before her and sees a wild animal. She can see the tension running through every sinew, the burning eyes alert and wary – a being so thoroughly alive that everything else dims around her, so alive that it is . . . impossible. Katia's fear is instantly tinged with pity, for this is the wrong place for a wild creature. She would open the doors and windows if a bird had flown in; she would usher it out, flapping her skirts and issuing soft, encouraging cries. And Shapsel Nicodemus would laugh at her – but she would get the creature out, even if she had to cup it in her hands . . . and as it flew off, she would feel both relief and sorrow at its going.

But this girl staring so intently at her is no mere bird to be cupped in her hands and released to the sky. So Katia stands unsure and enrapt, afraid and pitying.

Nico raises his head, says, 'Good morning, Miss Sukie.' His voice is a low-pitched gong booming through the thin, high buzzing that has started in Sukie's ears.

Sukie cannot remember why she has come here. Her thoughts are slipping through the net of her mind; she cannot speak, cannot think – the net itself is slipping . . . and try as she might, she cannot hold it against the tugging fathoms . . . She feels an exquisite relief as her cheek hits the smooth floor.

∽

Nico climbs the narrow stairs with Sukie in his arms. He could not leave her on the floor, there for customers to trip over. He could not, as some part of him would like, simply sweep her out the door. He stands at the top of the stairs, astonished at how light she is.

'It could be the fever.' He turns his mouth away slightly; he is always clean, fastidious, wary of contagion.

'It is not the fever, Shapsel Nicodemus.' Katia lays her hand lightly on Sukie's brow, feels the dry, papery skin. 'See, she is quite cool.'

'Where is she to go?'

They have two rooms above the shop. The bedchamber is furnished with two beds, a small table, and a large dark closet that

Katia brought with her from her mother's house. Furniture for a bigger, taller room.

'You will put her on my bed.'

And so he does.

'She cannot stay,' he ventures to say.

'No,' says Katia, as she places Sukie's bag carefully on the table.

'She cannot. She must awaken, have some small refreshment and be gone.'

She does not reply this time – aware that already his mind has moved downstairs to his shop, his open door, to the many valuable items left unattended.

He turns to go, considers repeating himself, saves his breath and leaves.

Katia Stein looks at the young woman in her bed. Sukie's wiry, red-brown hair springs from her pale, pockmarked forehead. Under the poorly applied powder, she sees light-brown freckles dusting the thin cheeks. Sukie's thin, delicate lips, high, sharp cheekbones and her narrow, pointed jaw make Katia Stein think of knives – and she experiences the same tight twinge in her gut that she feels when looking at a newly sharpened knife.

Quite suddenly, as Katia looks at the delicate veins running through the pale eyelids, Sukie opens her eyes.

Katia starts, recovers herself, puts her hand on Sukie's shoulder and makes a soothing noise.

'Shush. You are quite safe.'

Sukie closes her eyes, opens them again slowly to see Katia's face swim back into her vision.

'You have pain?'

Sukie shakes her head. To be sure, there is still an ache in her chest where the angel lanced her, but that could not be described as pain.

'I will send for someone?'

Sukie shakes her head again.

'Your husband . . . your mother?'

'No.'

'But surely . . .?'

'No. No. No one.'

Katia concludes on the instant that this girl has neither husband nor mother, and without warning, her eyes moisten. All her life, she has been afflicted thus, producing tears at the slightest provocation. She bites her lip. It is foolish, unnecessary, weakening. But though she may bite hard, the evident truth about this girl – her fierce, wild loneliness – swells like a tender fruit in her heart, and the tears spill over onto her cheeks.

Sukie looks at her with blank astonishment. Katia turns her head away. A moment to gather herself – it is surely beyond reason to allow oneself to collapse in sorrow because a strange girl has neither a husband nor a mother, and so, with monumental effort, she steadies her lips, wipes her cheek with one brusque finger and turns back to Sukie.

'Are you hungry?'

'Why are you crying?'

'No, it is nothing. I am not crying . . . Are you hungry?'

'But why are you crying?' Sukie's eyes are as wide as the world as she looks at Katia Stein.

Katia experiences an unsettling feeling of reversal, as if she has set out to sell something and instead found herself about to buy – and she does not know what to say.

She stands abruptly.

Sukie speaks without thinking. 'Don't go. Please stay.'

'You rest. I must . . .' And Katia waves her hand at the door.

As if she is seeing into Katia's mind, Sukie suddenly apprehends a world of things to be attended to: food to be prepared, clothing to be folded . . . fine motes of dust to be wiped on every surface. And it seems unbearable that this woman should leave her now, should enter another room, should set about these matters of her day that do not involve Sukie – and so do not really exist, at least not in the way that the two of them exist together just now, in this room, with the slick tears still damp on Katia Stein's face. And at another time, on any other morning, after any other night, Sukie would not have felt this painful urgency. She would have watched Katia leave, allowed her mind to drift away onto easier, more familiar matters – but now, she is filled with a sense that nothing could be more important, and so she shifts upright in the bed.

'Please stay.'

And Katia pauses. She begins to hum a little tuneless song. '*La la-la la la.*' Abruptly, she sits down on the bed and looks at Sukie's sharp, alert face. She begins to speak with a sigh. 'I am crying because . . . Why should we not cry?' She shrugs her shoulders with a weary gesture that jars with her beauty. 'There are many things to cry about.'

Sukie, sitting upright, with her hair coming out of its bun and her dress askew on her shoulders, looks seriously, silently at Katia.

There is a sudden clamour of seagulls from above, and they listen to them calling through the roof.

'I am crying because . . . though you see I am no longer crying' – she waves her hand in the direction of her face – 'because . . . because you have no mother . . . no husband, and' – she throws in without the certain knowledge – 'no father.'

Sukie has not cried for as long as she can remember, save one time when Sal slipped flat on her arse on the street, and she laughed so much that she ended with tears streaming down her cheeks.

Katia speaks again, hesitantly: 'I do not mean to offend you.'

'No . . .' Sukie is not in fact offended. It is clear to her that the sadness rolling in waves off this beautiful woman has little or nothing to do with her . . . She leans forwards and takes her hand. 'I'm sorry you are so sad.'

'Sad? No, no, I am not sad . . . no.'

Sukie squeezes her hand and smiles a soft gap-toothed smile, her grey eyes misting slightly, turning to green.

And Katia falls silent, stilled by the sensation she is suddenly experiencing in her heart. It is as if she has discovered a small, wounded creature nesting there – a delicate treasure, with a pain and a pulse all of its own. She looks with surprise at Sukie, who looks back at her with such gentle sympathy that it is clear to Katia that Sukie has seen the small, wounded creature, too.

∽

Shapsel Nicodemus Stein stands behind his shop counter. It is a quiet afternoon, too hot for trade.

The usually calm surface of his mind is disturbed. His thoughts are full of his wife, of their marriage. He feels unsettled down to his toes. He knows it is partly to do with Sukie and her book – their invasion of his home – but mostly it is to do with Katia herself.

Shapsel Nicodemus considers himself to be a good husband – they have been married for three years, and they live together in a kindly way, somewhat distant and polite, exchanging little courtesies, small kindnesses that come easily to them both.

She chose him, and though she brought little other than some solid furniture by way of a dowry, he knows she could have made a better match. He does not doubt her value – which is partly to do with her unusual beauty, partly to do with her undoubted efficiency in running their home (she helps, too, with the business, has a good eye, a keen brain) and partly, though he is cloudier on this, to do with a rare tenderness inside her. But in truth, he cannot quite work it out. He often studies her beautiful face when her mind is elsewhere. He sits very quietly, lest any movement might alert her, and runs his careful eye over her complexion, noting the soft purple smudges beneath her eyes, the slight hollows in her cheeks, the light down of hair on her upper lip.

Once a month, at her request, he places his long-fingered brown hands on her marble belly. She trusts these hands – they seem to represent all that is best in her husband: his delicacy, his care, his ability to assess worth. So, while he does not know really what he is doing when he gently presses her soft flesh, they are both sure that he would detect any sign of life within. A single shake of his large, solemn head inevitably follows. Three years now, and nothing, not even the hint of a swelling.

What it comes to is this: even when they are together, he feels alone. And while this is frequently completely acceptable to him – gives him the peace and space he enjoys – today, it is not a comfortable feeling. Today, he feels he is missing something, something very important.

Shapsel Nicodemus locks the shop and goes upstairs to eat.

At first, he is not sure what has changed – he knows only that when he steps into his living room, nothing seems the same.

He pauses and sniffs the air – no, it is not a smell. He glances about the room . . . there is a chair missing; the chair that sits to the left of the fireplace is gone. It has stood there reliably for the three years that they have inhabited these two floors. Katia sits upon it in the evenings. That is what has changed. Quickly, he realises that the pewter candlestick that stands in the middle of the mantle is also missing.

He notes these absences with initial relief – he is far less unsettled now that he has attributed solid physical cause to the air of difference that pervades this usually familiar room. But almost instantly upon the relief falls suspicion – where is the candlestick? It is worth, he estimates, two shillings at least. And the chair, ornate, solid, unusual – a relic from Katia's family – is worth perhaps six shillings. More than double that, were it to be sold with its identical fellow standing on the other side of the fire. He immediately considers the possibility that Sukie has taken both chair and candlestick and disappeared. And equally quickly, he knows that his suspicion is absurd, because she could not have left without him knowing.

All the same, he walks quickly through to the bedchamber to assure himself.

His wife sits on the missing chair by the head of the bed, with Sukie Bulmer's book open on her lap; the pewter candlestick holds a lit candle.

Their bodies lean towards each other with unaccountable familiarity – shoulders touching. As one, they smile at him – he has never
seen his wife look so animated.

'Look here, Nico,' Sukie Bulmer says companionably, indicating
the page in front of them. 'What do you think they're up to here?'

He feels an unfamiliar tightening at the back of his throat.

∽

The small, squat table at which Nico and Katia eat is best for two.
Nico occupies his side of the table fully, his broad shoulders filling the space allotted to him. Katia sits directly across from him.
There is usually a well-balanced inertia – a sense of respite from
the flurry of the day. But now, with Sukie sitting to Katia's right, the
table might as well be floating in the air.

Sukie has never sat like this before, at a table, in a home with
knives and bread and solemnity. It is both alien and somehow
absurd, and there is laughter building in her belly. Nico bows his
head to pray; Katia gazes with doe-eyed seriousness at the surface
of the table. Sukie dips her head, bites her lip. The words are guttural and foreign; Nico's eyes are closed, giving him a foolish, absent
look. She risks a peek at Katia, who catches her eye, but Katia cannot imagine what she is thinking, what there could possibly be to
smile about; she places her hands flat on the table as if to steady it.
Shapsel Nicodemus, opening his eyes, is deeply unsettled by the
unfamiliar expression on his wife's face.

Sukie cannot help it now, and the laughter erupts through her.
Her body begins to shake; her eyes begin to stream. Watching her
with delight, Katia feels as if her chest is filling with something
lighter than air, as if she might any minute begin to float towards
the ceiling away from the table, away from the food and the knives,
away from Shapsel Nicodemus and the shop, to somewhere up
high, to a wide, wide space of flight and light.

Nico, looking at the women with astonishment, decides on the instant that the book must be sold as fast as possible and that Sukie must be given her cut – then she can leave with her pocket full, and he and Katia can go back to normal.

He will make enquiries; he will find a buyer for this strange book.

∽

Nico goes, as he goes five evenings a week, to drink coffee in Bayer's. After he has left, Katia Stein and Sukie Bulmer stand together by the window, watching the steady stream of people moving below – the passers-by seem a hundred miles away, and the two women perched above feel as though they could never be, have never been, part of that distant world. The window is open, and the air rises up from the street, the heat of the day softening just a little.

Sukie's skin glows pale and translucent in the evening light – and she looks to Katia Stein wilder than ever, so intensely alive, so very real that she cannot resist reaching over and touching her cheek. She feels a charge run across the tips of her fingers and finds herself looking at Sukie's thin-lipped mouth with a sharp, unfamiliar hunger.

Sukie, for her part, has traded kisses like cheap coin for as long as she can remember, has felt the touch of a thousand lips, is well accustomed to hungry mouths and grasping hands, but when Katia leans in and kisses her, she feels a delicious plunging sensation she has never felt before. She breathes in the scent of her skin – the powdery sweetness, a muskiness underneath – as if it is the most precious thing in the world.

∽

In Bayer's, Nico, usually cautious when it comes to items of suspect provenance, is telling anyone who will listen about the book, describing it in some detail, emphasising its beauty, what he believes to be its rarity, its value.

Monty Creswell, on hearing about Nico's book, thinks of his cousin in the book trade – and when he meets this cousin at the junction of Saffron Hill, he discovers that he is already on the look-out for a very particular book on behalf of a gentleman who is willing to pay a large reward for one he had filched off him. Straight money, no thief-takers or constables – just the book, quick as you like. So, Monty tells him, with a sense of wonder at the coincidences in the world, about Nico's own very particular book – only thinking afterwards, what with the eagerness of everyone involved, that he should have worked out a cut for himself.

On his return from Bayer's, Shapsel Nicodemus carries the upright chair from the bedroom to the living room and pushes it in beside the other chair to make a makeshift bed for Sukie. Katia gives her a sheet and a heavy brocade cushion, before walking out hurriedly, somewhat unsteady on her feet, leaving Nico to nod goodnight.

It is hot – these long days one after the other with blue skies and no rain have left everything dry and airless. Sukie resolves to stay perfectly still in the one comfortable position she has found, her legs outstretched, her head propped on the cushion – the book tucked in beside her, pulsing away, where no one can get it without waking her.

Chapter Eighteen

Chick Lane, London

Sukie wakes to find birds in the room. That is the first thing – the early dawn has lit up the room, and when she opens her eyes, she can make out the shapes of small bright birds hovering in the far corner by the window. There are five or six of them, moving around each other – she can see no details at this distance, but she can hear their wings cutting delicately through the air, can make out the swirls of flight. She does not bother to squint; she is quite happy to lie awhile and observe the blurred shapes, which seem intimately familiar to her. They are entirely unsurprising in their presence, until it occurs to her to wonder how they have got in and why they are not battering against the window. Still, she does not squint – which despite her short-sightedness, she can do to some effect by narrowing her right eye to the tiniest slit and peering through her bunched-up fist. No, as her thoughts awake, she realises that what she is seeing does not make sense, and so it is better not to see as such, but rather to let it be.

A moment later, she stretches out her hand – an invitation, just to see if one might come – and as she does so, the door opens, and Katia Stein enters the room. She does not appear to notice the birds but walks straight to Sukie. Taking her hand, leaning awkwardly over the high arm of the chair, she whispers, 'How was your sleep?' Morning-voiced, she sounds more foreign than usual to Sukie, who squeezes her hand automatically and smiles.

As Katia leans to kiss her forehead, Sukie sees that the birds are still moving, unperturbed, in the corner of the room.

To Katia, her living room looks all wrong, jarring and alien, now that Sukie is in it, and a question forms, childlike, in her mind:

if this is not home, then where is? She stands up, distracted and unsettled, wanting to be with Sukie but somewhere else.

'Let us go out.'

But the only way out of Nico and Katia's flat is through the shop. And Katia knows that they will have to unlock the heavy front door to go out onto the street and that they will need the large key hanging on the hook by Nico's sleeping head. She remembers, too, that once the door is unlocked, then the shop is as good as open and must be attended. In fact, there is no way of getting out without waking Nico, which gives her a tight, trapped, embarrassed feeling.

All the same, she thinks at least they can go down to the shop, so she leads Sukie quietly down the narrow stairs, and Sukie, not wanting to leave the book behind, pauses to tuck it beneath her arm. The birds do not follow, and as she leaves them behind, it is with a sense that she is going the wrong direction, that she would be far better off to be exiting with them through a window.

The only illumination in Nico's shop is the soft daylight creeping around the locked shutters. Everything is so perfectly still that time itself might have stopped. As they step through the door at the end of the stairs and onto the dark wooden planks, it is as if they have arrived for the first time in a hushed and alien land.

The front door is dark and implacable in front of them.

'How will we get out?' Sukie whispers.

'We can't. Not without the keys.'

In the dim light, Katia can make out the neat rack of men's coats she organised not two days ago, the fox-fur stole draped around the headless dressmaker's doll, the large, locked cabinet with the silver – cups, plates, knives, forks and spoons – the smaller one with the gold. And while she is usually quick to assign value, she cannot decipher these things this morning, cannot quite remember what they stand for and why they are here. She looks at Nico's counter, sure and solid beside her, reaches out to touch it, but it has nothing to offer her this morning. For all its solidity, it leaves her more adrift than before.

And looking sideways at Sukie in the dim light, Katia wonders if she is real at all, if she is not a phantasm that she has conjured herself. Because it does not seem possible that both Sukie and Nico's shop can be real at the same time – she must have imagined one or the other.

With her feet bare on the wooden floor, Sukie suddenly feels sure that there is a stream running deep beneath the boards, imagines they could step down into it and follow the flow, hand in hand, to the sea. She moves her toes on the smooth, well-worn wood and feels there is something misplaced about these planks, lying like this, flat on the ground. She would like to stand them up one by one so they could point to the sky and root themselves in whatever earth this part of London has to offer – a forest of floorboards, and the buried stream that flows through her mind revealed.

She would certainly like to do something, for what seemed like a room of treasures now looks like life caught fast in death's fist – this inert floor, the flat, musty air all around, the beaver-skin hat on the deer-antler hook, the ghostly coats. For a moment, she imagines she has magic so that she can set it all alive again, the kind of magic the old Irish women in the market used to speak of in hushed tones, the kind a flaming ferocious angel might perform with one beat of her massive wings. And the room in her mind fills with foxes and deer, birds and grazing animals, so that she is quite, quite far away.

And Katia, sensing the impossible distance between them, feels terribly alone. Terribly alone and terribly foolish, as if she has believed in all the wrong things all along, and it is too late now – for here she is, alone and in the wrong place. And the ache spreading in her chest is a longing, but for what, she is not sure. For Sukie, who may or may not be real, for the old sense of familiarity she has lost. A sigh escapes her, a deep and forlorn exhalation, but Sukie, so far away, does not connect the sound with the woman standing beside her; it could as well be a soft gust of grief rising up from the earth itself.

Katia feels the tears begin to well, and she tightens up against them – for what could be worse than to be alone and foolish, filled with insatiable longing and crying like a child. But it is no use; her breath catches in her throat and the tears come.

Sukie turns her head and sees that Katia's pale, smooth skin is damp, her dark eyes bright, and she reaches out her long, thin fingers to wipe away the tears. Without thinking, Sukie puts her fingers to her mouth. She has never before tasted someone else's tears – has tasted every other bodily fluid, sometimes accidentally, sometimes for a price, but never tears. And the salty tang shocks her with its intimacy, brings her back from far away into the sparse, light body standing barefoot on the pawnbroker's shop floor. She stretches up to place small delicate kisses on Katia's cheek, both tasting her tears and trying to stem the flow.

Katia turns her head until their lips are touching; her body, tremulous and alert, comes alive, tells her now with absolute certainty that this at least is real.

And Sukie feels a heat welling up within her, up from the floor, like sap rising, spreading out across her shoulder blades – for all the world as if wings were sprouting.

⁓

Sukie has always believed in dragons, in beasts and monsters of all sorts. That there could be enormous creatures who would burn you to a cinder with their breath, or tear you apart with sword-sharp claws, is entirely in keeping with her understanding of life. That she has never yet met one she puts down to luck and the prayers of old Kitty who took her in as a baby and later put her to selling apples with a matter-of-fact kindness that Sukie translated as affection. So, when the man in the brown coat and his friend Jem Mack begin to break down the door of Shapsel Nicodemus's shop with concentrated ferocity, it is such a creature she sees in her mind.

As the door splits open and Sealy Hallom, the two toughs and Peter Woulfe are lit from behind, she experiences a flash of disappointment at their mortal forms – not dragons but merely men. She wastes not even a moment on her disappointment but, ducking low, aims for the daylight behind them.

Sealy Hallom shouts and points – 'There, the girl has the book!' – and dives to grab her.

But Sukie is very good at twisting out of the grasp of taller, stronger men by turning with the full weight of her momentum brought low; she has done it many times before, each time as if it were a matter of life or death. She can kick; she can bite; she can scratch like a wild cat – and she does so now, with a speed and ferocity she has never equalled. In fact, as she breaks away from Sealy Hallom's grasp and runs into the road, she has never felt so swift, so free of the pull of the earth. The men turn to pursue her as if in slow motion.

She ducks under a carter's horse, pivots to the left and slips between a man unloading casks and a slow, fat pony. Sukie is so obviously a thief that Morley Farrell, out for an early morning stroll, thrusts out his walking stick as she races past, cracking her on the shoulder and sending such a shooting pain down her arm that she drops the book. She is moving so fast that by the time she glances back to see where it has landed, she is ten yards ahead. She hesitates for a dangerous moment to gauge the distance between the pursuing men and the book and sees without doubt that she must leave it behind or be caught, and so she turns her head and races on.

Running blindly without her book, away from Nico's shop, away from Katia, Sukie darts into Black Boy Alley and slides into the chill shadow of the wall. Knowing she cannot be seen, she pauses to catch her breath. She looks quickly back, ready to run again if any of the men are close.

She is overcome by a tearing desolation – a feeling so big and so heavy that it threatens to sink her entirely. It is the opposite of her earlier buoyancy, the very opposite. It is dark and heavy and unbearable. She leans her forehead against the wall. Her ears fill with the roar of her agitated body.

She does not see the man in the brown coat pick up the book and pass it to Sealy Hallom; she does not see that none of the men spare her a second glance as they watch Sealy Hallom rip the spine from the book with three forceful, jerking movements. They stand, still breathing hard, as he removes a thin sheet of paper nestled in the pale webbing.

She does not see him dropping the book like a shucked oyster and slipping the sheet of paper into the inner pocket of his blue coat before walking away, without looking back. Nor does she see that Peter Woulfe – who was running after her with the pursuing men, his long legs windmilling him along, some thought in his mind that he would help her, protect her when the men caught her – has stopped to pick up the book, and is standing holding it against his thudding heart.

It takes Peter Woulfe some time to move at all. His legs are wobbling; his hands are shaking. His mind has frozen shut. When he does move, it is to absently open the broken book. He turns the first three pages, and at first, he sees nothing through the blur in his eyes, but after a moment, his mouth falls open. He begins to see that there is a message of the utmost importance encoded within the bright plates. As he turns the pages faster, supporting the broken spine, he sees that the images demonstrate a complex sacred procedure, not evident to the uninitiated – not laid out clear and simple for anyone to understand – but with time, with work, with prayer, he feels sure it is all there to be understood in these bright, intricate pictures. He can see that this book will show him what he needs to understand – how to connect the angels he cannot see or hear with what he does at his workbench, how the processes, the combination of materials, the grinding, the careful combining, the firing, the sparks of bright matter will bring his soul closer to God.

As he flicks eagerly forwards, the pages begin to loosen, so he shuts the book firmly and begins to walk away quickly from Nico's shop, away from anyone who might have a claim on it.

Sukie does not see any of this, but leaning forehead-first against the stinking wall of Black Boy Alley, her body begins to settle. She has lost the book, the beautiful book of angels. But she remembers the birds in Katia's room, the feeling of light and flight, and her body remembers the touch of Katia's lips, the taste of her tears. A surge of desire floods her body.

She thinks of the gaps in the brickwork of Nico's shop, of how she noticed the way the window on the right of Katia's bedroom did not fit quite snug on the inside, and how she suspects it could be jimmied handily enough if you took the time – if you were slow and careful, if you went when there was moon enough to see by, when everyone was sound asleep.

Chapter Nineteen

Many Years Ago

Mount Gabriel, Cork, Ireland

Bridey Leary is young and luminous. Shaped by the twin blessings of beauty and vigour, she is tall, broad-shouldered, broad-hipped, as strong and glossy as a young ox. Her face is alive with youth and curiosity; her blue eyes are as bright as the sky. Her black hair shines with the oily sheen of a raven's wing and her broad, high cheeks are coloured with a deep richness she could surely not have sucked from her worn mother or her thin, brittle father. There is a force in her that cannot be connected to their poor mud cabin or their narrow strip of spuds. She moves barefoot, with an easy grace, murmuring to the cattle, the birds, the snapping dogs, whispering to the trees and the grass, the winds and the clouds. Her father is plainly frightened of her, and her weary mother is frightened for her. She takes no heed of anyone. When the neighbours gather for music and stories, she dances like a wild creature, sings in a deep, mesmerising voice, stays up to greet the dawn.

Every morning, she walks up onto the mountain in her bare feet and feels the force of the earth thrumming kindred beneath her.

Bridey's roots go deep into the past of this mountain; her people settled here first when you could travel the length of Ireland moving from branch to branch and never have need to touch the ground. But this is not how they travelled; they walked, following songlines sung from mother to daughter down the ages, telling stories older than the words used to tell them.

But Bridey's mother, Anna, doesn't know these songs and neither did her mother's mother or her grandmother's mother. They had been lost long ago, even then. Anna Leary has some small scraps of them tucked away in the back of her mind, but she doesn't even know she has them. They are tattered relics – kept because they are old, but mostly forgotten about, because no use can be seen for them.

Every now and again, these remnants creep into Anna's life unbeknownst to her. There is the way she can see the crows rising and falling in the air, as if these very crows have been rising and falling forever in this very place, all day, every day, since before there were days; as if what they are doing is the one real thing and everything around them is a dream, so that it is almost funny to see them land on Woulfe's roof and caw away to each other, as if they have just made up the house and the roof ridge and the men to build it so that they will have somewhere to sit and caw. She has a little laugh to herself about the crows every now and again and feels wider and lighter in her sore-backed, tired-limbed drag of a day.

But, if even she wanted to, she wouldn't know how to explain this to her daughters – her four daughters. Four hungry girls born into a hungry world. Not one son. When she opens her mouth to advise her girls, to instruct them, to explain the world to them, all that ever comes out is her deep conviction that life is hard. No matter what she starts off planning to say, that's what she says – as if by telling them often enough, she can warn them and at least protect them from false hope.

And even while she tells them, she knows she is wasting her breath, because not one of them seems to understand her at all. Bridey, Aggie, Annie and Maura. The three younger ones respond better to a clip on the ear, the threat of the cut of their father's old, cracked belt than to any words their mother might speak. They are joined at the hip, a three-headed creature, always hungry, always noisy; she no sooner silences one of the heads than another starts, mouth wide open, singing the next verse in the endless song they have all been shrieking since they first drew breath: *feed me, soothe me, feed me, she got more than me, where's the dinner, I don't want to, she got more than me.*

And Bridey, head and shoulders over all of them, laughs and won't sweep the floor, won't scrub the spuds, pities her mother – and her mother is hurt in her heart by her big, bright daughter, but she takes this hurt as her due.

Bridey, while she laughs, does not mean to be unkind, to this woman who is clearly not her real mother. This woman who speaks in such tired, old words and offers such scant, irrelevant under-standings, as if she is ceremonially handing her a broken old spade to dig spuds when she, Bridey, has no intention of turning a single sod. This woman who is there pretending to be her mother when she already has a mother – a vast, powerful mother who can feed her and shelter her and teach her the songs and show her the stars.

∾

When the braver local lads try their luck with Bridey, she dismisses them with a regal swat of her paw. Until James Woulfe – the master's nephew, serious and courteous, moonstruck, quite ill with calf-love – comes to her with a sweet, desperate appeal. He comes carrying tribute – a bolt of deep-red cloth such as she has never seen before. He sits before her with his lips gently trembling as he strings word after word on the thread of air between them.

He says *beauty, the most beautiful,* he says *Queen,* he says *High Queen,* he says *the very heart of me, my pulse, my one love, my life.* He says *riches,* he says *land,* he says *fat cattle,* he says *fine stone house.* He gives her the cloth, his head bowed, but he offers her the clothes off his back, offers her his very being – the thick dark hair on his head, the rich blood coursing through his body, his strong young bones.

And when she takes him that night, in the loft on the hay, he weeps with gratitude and awe – knowing well that what he has been gifted is beyond price.

James Woulfe, James Woulfe. After their night together, Bridey Leary says his name in her mind all the time, sometimes softly and tenderly, for when they were naked in the hayloft she looked into his soul and saw all that was bright and good there, and then other times, as the weeks wear on and he never returns to her, she says his name so fierce and furious that it would frighten anyone to hear it. James Woulfe, James Woulfe, *weak, foolish* James Woulfe who took what was precious beyond measure but has given her no fine house, no plump cattle, has given her nothing at all but a little tear in her soul and the small, soft body of her baby buried in the hazel wood.

⟡

On the day her sisters leave for London, Bridey Leary knows one thing for sure: she might be staying behind, but she will not be walking arm in arm with her father back to their damp little house.

It is the worst day of her life. Or the best. She cannot tell. It is a day of great importance, or it doesn't matter a whit. She has lost something – or nothing. They are gone, and she must stay. And staying now means staying forever – this was the only chance; there will be no more money, no more boat fares, no more coins in a small leather purse. *A few shillings to get you started.* Her father has done what he can, and even a blind man could see that he has done his all. There is nothing left in him. That is what it is.

It is not that Bridey, looking at her departing sisters, wants to be with them in the cart; it is not even that she wants to set out for London in a different cart. It is not so simple as that. It is a bigger thing altogether – it is that she must live until she dies like everyone else, and it will be here that she will live and die. This will be her life, and what is she to make of it?

Once the cart is out of sight, she shrugs off her father's arm and climbs over the stile into Murris Collins's lower field. Without looking back, she heads up over the low stone wall at the far side of the field and out onto the boggy, rush-ridden moorland covering the eastern foothills of Mount Gabriel. The sky all around her is blue, but there is a delicate swirl of mist clinging to the top of the mountain. The ancient sandstone rises up in arcs along the foothills, and these folds of stone curve like the ribs of an enormous fossilised creature. In places, the soil is gone altogether, and the bare bone of stone gleams in the sun. There are one or two sculptural hawthorns on the higher ground, but the rest of the land is worn down to a nub by the endless grazing of the sheep and the fires that are set every spring to burn away the unwanted growth.

Bridey Leary knows the mountain as well as she knows her own body, and she thinks of some of the places she could go and sit and sing: the small stand of oak trees hidden round the back, on the dark side of the mountain – twenty or thirty trees not yet felled, because the slope they are growing on is too steep and uneven, and the access is poor. She could go there and sit with the trees, or she could go to the small, bright lake hidden in a dip on the western slope. Or she could go to the mossy cave by the goat path up near the pass. She knows that the morning sun will be hitting the mouth of the cave soon, and the space within will be deep and dark enough for her heart, and so she heads up towards the pass.

As she climbs, she considers – there is the mountain pulsing beneath her with the promise of spring; there is the sky all around; there is the pair of ravens calling above her, their dark wings stark and perfect against the blue; there is the scent on the breeze of the sally trees beginning to bud and bloom; there is the startled thrashing of a pheasant taking to flight ahead of her. There is all this. And more. There is the small body she has buried in the hazel wood below; there is the thrum of magic she feels through her blood and her bones when she goes up on the mountain and sings. There is all this.

But – she will not marry. There is not a man around that she would have for her husband. She does not like digging potato trenches or walking slowly in the rain after cows; she does not like milking; she does not like sweeping or scrubbing dirty clothes. She cannot sew, having refused to learn. But somehow, she must eat. Somehow, she must live before she dies.

She sits at the mouth of the cave, gazing into the mountain with the sun on her back, and begins to sing. She sings a song that is part lullaby, part keen – some of it comes from a tune her mother used to sing to her sisters at night, and other bits come from the cry of shawled women lamenting at funerals. There is something in it, too, of the fiddler's reel, but mostly she makes it up herself as she sings – and it rises and falls and echoes into the cave.

She sings harshly like a raven and softly like a lark. She sings long enough for the sun to cross the mouth of the cave and for shadows to fall. She sings and she sings until she feels the very heart has gone out of her and flown into the mountain. She sings of her baby daughter, gone from her into the ground, of her dead mother, of her sisters gone from her into the world, of weak, foolish James Woulfe. She sings out, asking the mountain not to leave her without comfort. She must live; she must eat; she must not be left entirely alone without human touch.

And so she sings and she sings until she can sing no more.

And, as it always does, the mountain sings back.

⁓

Cornelius Leary's house is poorly built. This is well known. Even by the standards of the underfed, scraggy families on the dark side of the mountain, it is considered a poor show. Wherever Nelius could have done right, he did wrong. The thatch is leaky, and the walls sag. The door is hung wrong, and the rain gets in under it and turns the floor to mud. Whatever the direction of the wind, the chimney smokes. The place is all but a pile of rubble with a cap of straw. Though what does it matter, now that his likely-looking girls are reared and gone to London and their mother is dead?

There are no sons, so now Nelius and his queer eldest daughter simply sleep there and streel out in the morning. Bridey will not marry now – there is nothing for any lad there anymore. There is no land, and she is no catch these days, having gone a bit odd-looking, with eyes that would cut you in two as soon as look at you.

So, what does it matter that Nelius Leary's cabin is a sad pile of leaky stones? It is all the one. All the one, but it keeps out the rain and the worst of the wind – and the land around it is something instead of nothing, until Nelius spends the night of the full moon in March with Dan Cotter and Murris Collins and a big barrel of French brandy that washed up at the cove. And, believing himself to be on a run of luck with his cards, and with nothing substantial to wager, he wagers the cabin itself, knowing as he does so that he is like the butt end of the joke in a story about a foolish man.

Dan Cotter thinks immediately of the stone in the walls, which he knows is good, and how he could knock it down and he and his sons could rebuild it, and how the land is poor but would keep a goat or two or maybe three sheep. A decent man, Dan, so when he wins fair and square, with Murris Collins as witness, he says he will not have them out while Nelius lives. And Nelius laughs and says he went off the notion of living a while ago and Dan will have his winnings soon enough.

The next morning, with his head splitting in two, he tells Bridey that soon enough she will have to get herself a place with a family in the village and learn to scrub for a living. He puts his head down to sleep again and his last waking thought is that he should have sent her off to work a long time ago, even if he is afraid of her.

∾

Nelius Leary's neighbours have grown so used to expecting to find him dead that, when they finally do, on a bleak January morning, three years after his younger daughters left for London, it is something of a letdown. There he is, lying dead in his bed, pale and waxy but not very much paler or waxier than he was yesterday – as if it was only a very small step he needed to take to get to the other side.

Bridey stands like a statue during the burial, and no one can tell if it is grief or relief or nothing at all she is feeling. Only Dan Cotter wonders if she might be frightened, knowing that he is to have the cabin, and he approaches her in a kindly way to say there will be no rushing her out – they can wait 'til spring – and that his wife has said Bridey could come to them and help out around their house in exchange for a roof over her head.

It might be the winter sun behind her, but Dan almost thinks he sees sparks flying off her as he speaks, and so he stumbles a bit with his second offer – which is, if that doesn't suit (no one can call him an unreasonable man), he has spoken to Florry Coughlan in the village, and his missus needs help with her six young children, so she could go to them instead. With the notion of sparks in his head and the image of thatch catching fire, he suddenly imagines his own house in flames and hopes that she will go to Florry. As he remembers it Bridey said nothing at all in response; she didn't even nod – but thinking back he wonders about that, for surely she would have said something. What he remembers for sure is that she turned away from him and their neighbours – not even waiting for the pipe-smoking and eating and drinking that religiously followed every burial – and she went up through the graveyard and away across the fields. He remembers this because it was all wrong to watch her leave with her father barely cold in the ground and no immediate family left to mourn him – and because, from that day on, she was never seen at the Leary house again.

In the years that follow no one knows where she sleeps at night. She is sometimes seen coming down from the mountain in the morning around milking time, and other times she comes along the winding road into the village as if she has been walking awhile and has come a long way. Someone claims to have spotted her once up near the pass on the way to Bantry, but that was ten miles away and it was high-up, wild, inhospitable land, so it is considered unlikely to be true. She is to be seen down by the shore in autumn, taking a bit of seaweed and gathering mussels. There is an unspoken suspicion, when only an egg or two is found under the hens, that Bridey is stealing eggs. And when cattle are scant with their milk, some folk are in the habit of thinking that Bridey has been into the field to have an early morning sup before the milking.

She does not keep herself entirely apart from her old neighbours. She calls in now and then in the evening to be offered a bite of whatever is in the pot before heading out again at nightfall. The local women note that her skin is growing leathery, that she is gone thin as a rake. All the same, it is hard to know how to feel about her at all – it is not that she comes creeping and begging like some of the poor folk who come to their door; it is more than she comes and takes what is offered as her due. And she sits so regally, so straight and certain, with eyes that are still so bright and alive that none of them want their husbands left alone with her. No, you can't feel sorry for her, no matter where she sleeps.

It is rumoured that Nelly Driscoll got a love potion from her that caused her husband to turn overnight from a surly oaf into the most loving, attentive man in the county. And that, when Nelly's cousin Cait set her sights on Dan Cotter's eldest son, Shem, it was Bridey she went to – and whatever it was that Bridey did, Shem was suddenly playing passionate court to her and went around dizzily like a man who had been banged on the head until they were man and wife.

At times, Bridey is to be seen standing still as a stone in the field out the front of the Woulfes' house – as if she is keeping an eye while James Woulfe brings back his new young wife and begins to produce sons with admirable rapidity. At these times, she speaks to no one except James Woulfe, who sometimes approaches her and is seen to wave his arms in an agitated manner before turning and walking away. It is understood locally as an act of great Christian charity when he gives her the use of the cabin he has just had built at the far side of his top field. There are a number of people who are glad to not have to wonder ever again where Bridey Leary goes when it gets cold – even if the cabin is no great shakes and better suited to house a bull or a few pigs than a human.

∽

There was nothing heard of Aggie, Annie and Maura after Nelius died. There had been two letters sent the first year they left – penned by Nelius's cousin Johanna, who was married to a grocer named Almond in Hackney. Johanna wrote that first spring to say that the girls had arrived and were in good health and then, six months later, to say, that by the blessing of God, all three girls had got respectable places: Aggie and Annie were clearing tables in a fashionable inn, and Maura was a kitchen maid in a good house. These letters were read out to Nelius and Bridey by Father Kennedy in his sonorous formal voice.

There was a short letter the following year at Christmas, again read out by Father Kennedy – the girls were well – and then nothing until the following Christmas, when Johanna wrote again to say that they were all in good health. If the scant information left Nelius doubting his daughters' well-being, Father Kennedy could not tell it from his expression. The letters were folded and put in the cubbyhole by the hearth, where they were found by Dan Cotter when he was knocking the place down in the late spring after Nelius's death.

Father Kennedy took it upon himself to write to Johanna and tell her of Nelius Leary's death, and there was no reply. It was the following year before Johanna Almond wrote again – this time to Father Kennedy himself:

It is my sad duty to tell you the worst news. The Leary girls are gone to God. The sweating sickness came to the city, and the fever took them one after the other. They are at peace now. God bless and save them.

Johanna Almond had begun to compose a letter that would have explained how Aggie, falling pregnant, had lost her place at the inn; how all three girls had been put out of their lodgings when her belly began to swell; how the baby girl had been born in something close to a hovel in St Giles where the three sisters shared the one bed; how she, Johanna, had gone with a food parcel that she could ill afford.

But between the guilt and her poor penmanship, it was a struggle too far for Johanna to explain the whole sorry tale that came to the same sorry end anyhow. Aggie was dead and so were Maura and Annie, just as dead – though they had not fallen pregnant and had kept their places. The summer fever had run through the rackety house they were living in, and on her brief visit, Johanna had felt lucky not to catch something herself. It had been a sore trial over the years to watch the girls turn into women who had failed to prosper – Johanna knew well that London was cruel and could eat people up, and in truth, the Leary girls had gone dull and grey-looking and lost their bright sheen very soon after arriving in the city.

And now they were all dead, and the last she heard of the baby was that she was under the shawl of some old tinker woman selling apples at Covent Garden, but there was only one way for that to end – the comfort of the tinker's shawl was just delaying the inevitable – and there was no way of mentioning it without causing more pain and distress and shame to them all. And God knows the news was bad enough without that. So she said nothing at all about the baby – she didn't even have a name for the infant, and if she had thought to make one up, she would never have landed on Sukie.

Father Kennedy did not read this letter out. He sought out Bridey with the envelope already opened and the air of death about him. He said quietly, 'Bridey, the news is not good from London.'

And though he used his kindest voice, he knew only enough to tell her what seemed like the end of the story of the Leary girls in London – and not enough to even imagine a beginning.

Chapter Twenty

June 1744 – *Midsummer*

In the Air Above Chick Lane, London

Sukie drops down from the roof to the window ledge, soft and sure, thinking this is what people do when they want something badly. Because it is not the right night to be out clinging to the brickwork at the back of Nico's shop – it is too bright with the moon and the clear sky. The sun has not long set, and there are still folk on the prowl. Chick Lane feels restless and alert – too bright, too wakeful by half. No, it is not safe at all to be out where you oughtn't to be.

But she could not wait. It is the strangest feeling – her heart is full and hungry all at once, her body light and eager. It has always come easy to her, balancing on the slightest of purchases, moving like a cat, but tonight it is as if there is no weight to her at all as she slips her fingers along the window frame, her bare toes balancing on the ledge. She rarely worries about falling, but tonight it feels altogether impossible. More likely, she will fly.

The wood is always a little forgiving on these old windows; it shifts when she pushes, and a thin gap appears – enough for a fingertip. But there is no rot as there is on some windows, where under the paint you can pick away a little and burrow in with your fingernails and a file and get to the catch. No, this one is sound enough.

She shifts herself to the side until her back is against the bricks framing the window and puts a foot on the other side so that she is quite secure. She is close now – closer to Katia than she has been since this morning. It is brighter outside than in, and the curtains are pulled, so she can see nothing inside the room – but she knows they are in there for sure, Nico by the door and Katia by the window – so close she might even hear Katia breathing. She puts an ear to the cool glass, closes her eyes the better to hear. She wonders, now that she is here: how do you wake one person in a room without waking the other? Could you do it by force of thought alone. *Wake up, wake up?* Will she tap gently and trust to fate? Could anything go wrong on a night like tonight?

She hears the creak of a floorboard, and her eyes spring open – if it is Nico, she is caught, lit up by the moon for anyone to see. But there is no shout, no Nico leaping up; instead, the curtains move, and after a moment, a hand stretches to open the catch and the top sash wheezes quietly open to reveal Katia's pale face. Her eyes are wide – she is caught between delight and horror.

She speaks without making a sound, her lips and expressive hands as clear as any words: *you will fall! Nico will wake!* Sukie grins at her and shakes her head, puts her hands on the top sash and pushes gently until it creaks fully open.

She did not think it through at all, wanting just to get to the window and wake Katia, but now it is obvious – she must go in and join her. Katia cannot climb out, so it is the only way. She puts her head in first; the room smells of a man's sleeping body on a hot summer's night in a room with the windows shut fast – because being too hot is a small price to pay for not being robbed.

Silently, smoothly, Sukie slips in through the window. Katia offers her a hand as she steps carefully to the floor. Seeing Katia's face as her eyes adjust to the dark, Sukie is startled anew by its beauty.

Katia does not let go of her hand, and while it is pure madness with Nico asleep, breathing heavily, not five feet away, Sukie cannot help stepping in closer to her and kissing her softly on the cheek, feeling the warmth of her body against her with a surge of delight. She would, if she could in this moment, stay here forever, but Katia turns gently, silently, and leads her by the hand, out of the room and towards the stairs.

Without the light from the window, it is darker than pitch on the stairs, and they move slowly, Katia touching the wall for balance with one hand, the other still holding Sukie's. There are just eleven steps, smooth and cool on Sukie's bare feet, until they reach the end of the staircase and Katia opens the door into Nico's shop. It seems to Sukie that the shop has been waiting for them all this time.

Katia reaches back to close the door softly, and they stand together in the dark. There is a moment as brief as a quick intake of breath, during which they both begin to wonder: *what will we do?* Until their bodies come together of their own accord, and Katia finds that she is running her mouth along Sukie's hairline, tasting her skin, smelling her hair – astonishing herself by biting Sukie's neck without thinking, so that Sukie winces a little and pushes her taut body against her, reaching up to find Katia's open mouth, kissing her fiercely, running her hands along her back and her hips, feeling the soft, warm shape of her through the thin cotton nightgown.

And Katia puts her hands around Sukie's waist, feels the jut of her hip, the curve of her ribs and thinks, *this is how a bird would feel, this is the shape of flight, wild in my hands,* with such tenderness cutting through her desire that her heart begins to thrash in her chest.

⁓

The next morning, Nico wakes and immediately looks over to see if his wife is asleep in her bed. Every morning, before he is fully awake, without entirely knowing that this is what he is doing, he checks to see that she is still there.

This morning, the bright summer light flooding through the curtains reveals her sleeping form. She is there, of course, just as she always is – deeply asleep this morning, with no covers but one crumpled sheet tangled in her arms. And, just as it does every morning, seeing her there allows a soft intake of breath that begins to awaken his lungs, an inhalation that sets the rhythm of his breathing for the rest of the day. It is a reassurance as essential as the quick unconscious check he does to assure himself that he still has his own body (his legs, his arms, his chest, his feet, his own slightly clammy morning skin), the same body he went to bed with. If you asked him why he was checking and what he feared, he would not know; Katia could not have disappeared in the night – from their room with the fastened windows, from their house with the locked front door – any more than his body could have been spirited away and replaced by another.

It makes so little sense that, as his mind rouses, he forgets, as he always does, that he has ever doubted Katia's presence, doubted that his body is still his own, and he sets about getting up with the sentence in his head that he repeats every morning as his swings his legs out of his bed and prepares to meet the day. *Another day – God be blessed, Shapsel Nicodemus – put your feet on the floor and give thanks.* And this morning feels no different to him than any other; his wife is asleep where she should be, and his body is his own. He is a grateful, lucky man commencing his day on a hot June morning.

He bends to pick up the chamber pot – he habitually takes his first piss in the corridor, having first shut the bedroom door in consideration of his wife – and begins to remember the events of yesterday with detached bemusement. The underlying logic of the events is mystifying to him as he stands in the corridor pissing, and he is not sure that he wants to understand. There was something deeply unsettling about the men who came for the book, the one in the blue coat especially, his evident wealth and standing, the aura of furious determination that was palpable around him – it all jarred uncomfortably with the surrounds of Chick Lane and with the book itself.

The destruction of the book, the piece of paper he saw them remove from the binding – it is a puzzle, and not one that Nico chooses to dwell on over much this morning; he has lost out, certainly, lost out on his cut of the book's value, but he thinks he may be well off without it, well off to have no further dealings with the book. In fact, he begins to forget the images within and the effect they had on him and begins to remember the book as quite ordinary – worth a few shillings but dangerously linked to dangerous men. He would be better off not understanding what is really afoot.

Nor does Nico choose to dwell on what is even more uncomfortable and even more mystifying, which is the change he detected in his wife with the arrival of the book, with the arrival of Sukie. He would not admit it, even to himself, and he certainly could not formulate an explanation, but he suspects that, however dangerous the book might be, Sukie's presence in his home was far more dangerous.

And so it is with no small degree of relief that he opens the door from the corridor into the living room with the intention of opening the windows and airing the room. He hums in a deep, tuneless baritone as he crosses the room, opens the curtains, blinking at the glare of what promises to be another sweltering day, and then opens the windows, before turning to see Sukie stretching and rubbing her eyes in his chair.

Nico moves through his days with the slow, considered pace of a large assured animal; it is rare that his body startles or his heart leaps in his chest, so it is with a particularly unaccustomed jolt that he registers her presence. His feet almost leave the ground; his heart begins to pound and his breath, after the first sharp gasp, turns ragged and uneven.

'All right, Nico.' Sukie smiles at him quite fondly. 'It's hot already, ain't it?'

༄

Katia wakes. The smell of her own body rises sweet and warm; every part of her is alive and echoing with pleasure. She has never before woken to such delight. In the moments before she opens her eyes, she knows the earth to be a glowing magnificent orb, knows she is blessed beyond measure to be alive, to have a body, to have found herself here on Chick Lane, in the city of London, with breasts and a soft belly and the thrum of desire between her legs – knows that she has not been truly alive at all until now.

She remembers the touch of Sukie's skin against hers, how their legs entwined so perfectly, how they fitted hip to hip. She turns on her back, stretches like a cat and smiles, her cheeks widening into a grin so unfamiliar that it almost hurts – so that when the door opens abruptly and Nico appears, he is startled by her appearance, never having seen her like this, and even wondering for a moment if he is in the right room with the right wife.

Katia's grin softens, and she smiles at her husband, feeling a tender appreciation of his shape in his nightshirt, his broad shoulders, his luxurious beard, his beautiful eyes. He is, she thinks, a lovely husband, a kind and beautiful man. Her heart swells with love for him. She would like to do something for him – she will prepare an especially delicious breakfast, do his chops in rosemary and butter as he likes them, let the rinds crisp up just right.

She stretches out a hand to him. 'Come and sit, Shapsel Nicodemus.' And she pats the bed with an unusual gesture of affection, to which he responds awkwardly by moving closer and sitting gingerly beside her. 'I am going to make you a *deee*licious meal of chops with rosemary, just like your grandmother used to make.'

'Thank you, my dear.'

Her eyes narrow; she sees now that he is not quite himself. His usual calm is disturbed.

'She cannot stay.' And lest there be any lack of clarity, he adds, 'Sukie Bulmer. I thought she was gone. She cannot stay.'

'Oh, it will not be for long, Shapsel Nicodemus. The girl has no home, no family. She is back, but it will not be for long.'

'No, my dear, you do not understand.' Nico's heart has still not regained its accustomed rhythm, and he finds it surprisingly hard to speak calmly. 'A girl like that will stay forever if permitted. That is the way of the world.'

Katia thinks, *forever!* Imagine, every night like last night, every morning waking like this, with a day ahead full of unimagined delights. She is suddenly impatient – she must get up and see Sukie and make Nico's chops. Sukie might well like chops in rosemary; Sukie can watch as she cooks. Then Nico will go downstairs to the shop, and there will be a whole morning together.

She pats Nico's arm gently to cover her impatience. 'It will not be for long. And now you must move, and I must rise and dress.'

But he does not move at once. There is an entirely unusual look in his eyes that startles Katia. She tenses a little, feeling more than impatient now, feeling annoyance; this delight she has discovered is too precious to expose to Nico's strange new mood, the mulish reluctance she can tell is brewing in him. She wants to say, *can you not see? It is a beautiful world. Life awaits – Sukie awaits. Do not bother me with this mood of yours.*

But instead, she says, 'I must dress,' and sits up to climb around Nico and out of the bed, leaving him, along with all that is already unsettling him, to wonder at the musky, sweet smell that rises with her.

∽

Katia places four perfectly crisped chops on Nico's plate with a smile. They sit, the three of them, in silence. Sukie is not hungry, eats only a very little of mutton chop Katia has given her, and Katia finds she is not hungry either and eats only a small piece of bread, absently chewed.

Katia looks at Sukie, then, feeling she must ration her gaze, looks to Nico and wants to say, *is she not beautiful, Shapsel Nicodemus? Look at the line of her jaw – and those bright eyes could surely light up any room? And look at the way her hands move when she speaks!*

And though of course he cannot hear his wife's thoughts, Nico looks up from sawing at his chop and – seeing that Sukie's eyes are cast down towards her own plate – takes the opportunity to look at her quickly in a new, considered way. She is certainly not beautiful, he thinks – she is too thin, with no breasts to speak of really, sharp, angular shoulders, and there is nothing of the health that informs true beauty in her cheeks. But there is something in the way she sits, poised for movement yet with a rare stillness, that he finds appealing. She lifts her head – he looks quickly back at his chop, but not before he sees that her eyes are truly striking.

And then there is the fact that she is young and female. She is a young woman here in his home – and so he sits up a little straighter as she looks up at him, bringing his broad shoulders back, lifting his head up a trifle higher than he would if he were alone with Katia, and says kindly, 'You are not hungry?'

She shakes her head with a grin. 'Na, not very.'

And whether it is the grin, which is wide and alive, or the movement of her head, which is almost shy, or even the inconsequential words themselves, this small exchange does something to Nico's already unsettled heart, sending a delicate flutter through his chest, the immediate effect of which is to make him reluctant to leave and go down to the shop. He realises, as he stands up, that he would like to stay near Sukie and look at her some more and make her smile at him again.

But instead, he bids the women good morning and slowly descends the stairs. With each step, he feels as if he is leaving behind something of great value, something that feels real and alive and makes his shop seem tired and dull by comparison. It is only after he opens the shutters, filling the room with daylight, after he unlocks the large chain he used to secure his damaged front door, that he is struck by a realisation – his second painful jolt of the day: he does not know how Sukie entered the house last night. And he is not a superstitious man, but his feeling in the moment is of something deeply uncanny, something beyond locks and chains, something that he does not know how to guard against.

The women have not washed the breakfast plates. It would not occur to Sukie, never having owned plates, but Katia is almost religious in her careful washing of her pewter plates – which were her grandmother's – after every meal. The water – used first for washing faces and hands, then plates and cups, knives, forks and spoons – is carried up the narrow stairs every morning by Nico. Another of his careful courtesies. And each morning Katia washes and dries the cups and plates before putting them carefully away on the dresser that stands between the windows.

But not this morning. This morning, it is obvious that she and Sukie will go to the bedroom as soon as Nico has left, and they will take off each other's clothes with perfectly matched hunger for skin and scent and pleasure.

∽

Katia Stein is a woman transformed. Her back is straighter; her eyes are brighter. She moves around her home as if her very feet have grown lighter.

She washes and dries the plates, sweeps and dusts. Sukie watches her and listens.

She has become as voluble as a rushing stream; she talks and talks, her voice low and rhythmical, speaking with wonderful fluency, from a vast store of words that astounds Sukie. Her speech is coloured by her accent so that her 'th's' are closer to 'z's, her vowels long and languorous. She cries without shame or restraint this morning, tears coursing down her cheeks, a half-smile on her lips, continuing about her tasks while she weeps. Sometimes, her tears end in laughter; sometimes, her laughter ends in tears.

Sukie follows the loops of Katia's thoughts.

'You would like my mother – she is not beautiful, not anymore, but her heart . . . oh, being with her is like sitting by a wonderful fire in winter . . .'

And Sukie listens and listens, loves the very words issuing from her lips, the tilt of her head, the way Katia's fine-boned hands trace a language all of their own.

For a moment, she feels as if she has landed at last in the life she was supposed to have all along, with the smell of beeswax and cabbage, and her heart full of Katia's beauty and tenderness.

'Where'd you get all these . . . all these words?'

Katia pauses to consider, remembers her father's flood of talk filling their flat in Aldgate – his tears, his laughter, the endless turning of his mind, how he leaped between English and Yiddish and Russian, the English words sometimes awkward his mouth, like small, unexpected bones in a mouthful of stew.

She shrugs. 'Where does anybody get their words? My family, I suppose, my . . . life?' She shrugs again.

Sukie does not often feel called to speak, and when she does, it is with a turn of phrase peculiar to the Irish Londoners who trade at Smithfield: slack London vowels and lost consonants, all delivered at seller's speed, dappled with half-understood words from the slower, mistier world of their forebears. She does not really trust words, having long learned the art of feeling one thing and saying another – or better still, feeling nothing at all, saying nothing at all. But now, everything has changed; she is here with this beautiful woman, and she wants to say something real.

So, she takes a breath and speaks seriously, urgently: 'Katia. Listen to me, will you? Listen to me . . .' She moves to touch Katia's cheek softly. She is not sure how to say it, but it must be said. 'You are beautiful.' That is the beginning of what she must say.

Katia shifts uncomfortably. A beautiful woman intimately acquainted with her physical flaws, she knows her lips are overlarge; her head in the mirror is quite massive, and she cannot get her hair to lie flat at the front. So she shakes her head and pulls back a little.

'No, no.' Sukie tries again. 'It's the truth, I'm telling you. Cross my heart.' She touches her chest.

At this, Katia's eyes begin to fill up. She shakes her head with impatience at herself.

'You've got to believe me.'

To Sukie, it is quite the most urgent thing. She must get her meaning across, and she knows that it is not simply that Katia is beautiful – it is more than that; it is something much bigger, which she does not have words for, something to do with Katia's heart.

And she cannot find the words to catch the thought, or indeed the thought to catch the feeling, so she leans in and kisses Katia softly on the mouth.

Chapter Twenty-one

Chick Lane, London

Lying in her bed by the window, Katia waits for Nico's breathing to change. Her heart is beating fast, but everything else has slowed unbearably. Usually, he falls asleep quickly – but tonight, there is a wakeful silence coming from his bed. None of the soft animal sounds of sleep.

Once he is asleep, she will rise quietly and tiptoe in to join Sukie in the living room. She shifts restlessly in her own bed and hears him move in response. It is hot – uncomfortably so. She wants to move and stretch, but she holds herself still for what seems like an eternity. *Stay still*, she says to herself; *stay still and perhaps he will sleep.*

And so she holds herself rigid in the bed, hardly breathing. Surely half the night must have passed. Surely he is asleep. She can hear nothing at all from his bed; he has not moved for an age – and now she is almost tempted to take the silence for sleep. She considers sitting up cautiously. Maybe he has fallen deeply, deeply asleep. She waits a while longer.

She raises herself carefully on one arm.

'Are you awake?'

His voice startles her. She freezes. She considers saying nothing – considers, for one terrible moment, mimicking the sounds of her own sleep. She could make the sort of muffled murmur a sleeping person might make . . . or the quick-in, slow-out sound of a deep sleeper's sigh. But no, that would cross beyond her own private code of loyalty to her husband; she may as well lie outright to him about the housekeeping money.

'Yes.'

'And I.'

'Yes.'

'It is hot.'

'Yes.'

Katia feels the night slipping away. She has never experienced such a desperate sense of urgency about anything before. The only thing that can possibly matter is bringing her body close to Sukie's – Sukie, who is not fifteen feet away in the living room. And yet her husband is awake and eager to send his deep voice out to reach her through the hot night air like an unwelcome embrace. It is impossible. It is absurd. But if she does not hurry, perhaps Sukie will leave through a window, and go and do whatever she usually does at night. Maybe she will not wait much longer.

She hears Nico inhale – he is about to speak again. She could scream. What is it that he needs to say?

'My dear.'

What is she to say to that? What can she say that will help him sleep?

'My dear,' he repeats.

There is unfamiliar hesitancy in his voice. And where once, even last week, this might have evoked some degree of tenderness, now it serves only to stir up her impatience.

'It is . . . a strange thing to have her . . . with us . . . here . . . I find.'

Almost before he has finished the sentence, she cuts across: 'Would you have her out on the streets, Shapsel Nicodemus?' She startles herself with the quick vehemence of her response.

'No, no. I did not mean that. At least, no . . . that is not what I meant.'

He is taken aback by her tone; she does not sound like herself at all. Now, he has lost his tentative hold on what he wanted to say. He goes quiet and considers. No, he would not like to put her out on the streets, and yet yesterday morning, that is exactly what he wanted to do. And so he confuses himself; his usually clear mind misses a step, and he loses the thread of his thoughts.

He knows that there is something he wants to say that he can say only to Katia. The trouble is that he does not know what it is he wants to say, let alone what words he needs to use. And this is unusual for him. He has a careful, precise relationship with speech – uses it when necessary, almost always finds it to be satisfactory.

It is about Sukie, and what it is like to have her in their home. Having her here is . . . deeply unsettling. But it is also good and right, just as it should be. It is both wonderfully *heimish* and deeply uncanny. She is like something lost and forgotten – and then suddenly found . . . something he didn't even know he was missing. Something that belongs. Having her here is . . . all wrong and yet right at the same time.

He thinks of family – and his parents' flat in Aldgate, his father, his mother, his four brothers and two sisters. There is perhaps something of that in it – but this feels somehow better than that.

And he feels . . . it is not exactly that he would like to take her to bed – not that he wouldn't, but no, it is not specifically that . . .

Katia says impatiently, as if his whirring thoughts are keeping her awake, 'I must sleep, Shapsel Nicodemus – it is late.'

'Yes,' he says, feeling very far away from her. 'Yes, it is late.'

And so he settles his head on his pillow, alone with his thoughts, and Katia tightens her body, her eyes wide open, and prepares to wait some more.

∽

The next evening, the church bell rings six, and Nico prepares to close the shop. He waits as he always does for Katia to come down the stairs and join him. It is what they do at the end of every day – they stand together in the shop and review the day's takings, then they price the new items that have come in. Having her there, listening and attending, nodding or gently shaking her head, agreeing with his pricing or gently dissenting, is an essential part of the unfolding of the day. He looks forward to it more than he realises. It puts the day to rest.

But today, everything is different. Katia comes down the stairs with Sukie close behind her, which is not the trouble in and of itself, because Nico is quite pleased to see Sukie – though he is uncomfortable at the prospect of their business, the nuts and bolts of it, the shillings and the pence of it, being revealed to her . . . but that is not quite the problem. The problem is that Katia smiles at him differently, stands differently, speaks differently.

'Good evening.' She touches his arm affectionately, lightly. 'We must attend to business and then eat.' There is a sense of urgency about her that is unfamiliar, as if she is rushing to get to something more important than business or eating.

Nico passes Katia a beaver-skin tricorn hat. In the main, Nico avoids trade in clothing. While profitable, to his mind there is no pleasure in fabric, and the vast and busy clothing trade on Rosemary Lane is distasteful to him. And yet he will take a pledge on a good hat or a well-cut coat – he has a number of good gentlemen's coats on the rail behind him. This is a fine hat, little used and well kept, though with some staining on the band running around the brow line.

Katia glances at it briefly and feels a little flush of disgust. She passes the hat to Sukie to be rid of it, and Sukie squints at it and thinks it must have been nicked – a gentleman's hat, no doubt, hats being easy enough to swipe when drink is taken. She runs her hand along the fine beaver skin, wondering what kind of an animal would need such a pelt, and what a wonderful thing it must be to grow a skin that could keep you dry as well as warm. She puts it on her head, and it is far too large, so she tips it back, cocks her head on one side and grins at Katia.

'Got a lot of things, don't you?' Sukie says to Nico and indicates the room with a wave of her hand.

Nico experiences an impulse to show Sukie some of his most valuable items – there is a solid silver butter knife with a mother-of-pearl handle in the cabinet behind him; he turns to remove it and displays it to her on his open palm. 'This is . . . special.'

She bends briefly, glances at it and looks back at him. 'Very nice. How much?'

He shrugs. 'Too much.'

She laughs and moves away around the room. She feels that she has no need of anything anymore – that she wouldn't buy anything here now, at any price.

Nico and Katia watch her as she moves into the light from the window, and then Nico turns again to his cabinet – he has thought of just the right thing.

'Here is something else. Special.'

This time, he holds a palm-sized leather case in his hand. Katia recognises it but cannot remember what is within.

Nico waits until Sukie is standing by him before pressing the catch, and all three of them watch as the lid pops open.

Katia remembers it now – an octagonal bronze dial with intricate markings and a small glass-covered compass set in the lower half.

'Look.' His fingers move carefully, and he raises a small hinged flap that has been lying flat against the dial. 'See this? This little bird? Here,' he says, holding it out to Sukie, 'you may hold it.'

She takes it, lifts it right up to her face and peers at it. She sees a little bronze bird, its tiny beak pointing out towards the rim of the dial, its wings etched against its body.

'Look,' he says, taking it back, 'it moves.' And he demonstrates, gently bringing the bird around the dial in a semicircle, before handing it to back to her.

'Oh,' says Sukie.

'It is lovely.' Katia speaks, and they both startle slightly, almost as if they had forgotten her.

'But,' says Sukie, 'what is it for?'

'It is a sundial – a dial for telling the time, like any sundial, but for your pocket.'

Sukie thinks of the sundial at Smithfield Market – the small grubby pillar, the rough marks on the stone dial encircling it.

'It catches the sunlight just the same as any other dial,' says Nico, 'but it also does much more. It can tell you the time anywhere on earth. If you move this little bird, and line it up correctly with the markings on the rim, it can tell you the time now in Kyiv or Amsterdam . . . or Paris . . . It is a matter of light and shadow, and correct positioning.'

Light and shadow. Sukie nods slightly. Yes. She knows how the sun falls differently at different times, so that it feels different on her bare head at different times of day. Morning sun and evening sun. And how it feels different again at different times of the year and in different places.

Nico meets her eye before looking back down at the dial and continuing. 'And this,' he says, taping the compass, 'can tell you where north, south, east or west is – no matter where you are. No matter if there is no sun to be seen rising or setting in the sky. No matter where it is, this needle will always point north . . . compelled to do so by an invisible force.' He smiles shyly – 'Magic!' – and moves the compass around so that the needle swings.

Sukie smiles and bends down to peer at it. She sees how the needle is pinned in place, how it moves insistently to point back the same way. Of course. She understands at once. It is trying to get home.

'Now you must imagine that the earth is sliced' – he moves his long hands carefully, as if he were slicing butter – 'into lines, and each line is for a different place – some places far away, some even farther.'

Katia hears her husband inhale and realises that he intends to continue his explanation. She knows that once he is speaking on a topic that interests him, a topic involving ideas like slicing the surface of the earth into lines, he can speak for a considerable time without pause. And she experiences a rush of impatience. Everything will be delayed – checking the day's takings, their evening meal, Nico leaving for Bayer's, and her time alone with Sukie.

Katia cuts across before Nico can continue: 'We must continue our business, Shapsel Nicodemus – it is getting late.' She would like to say, *what does it matter? What does it matter what time it is in*

Paris, or where east is after the sun has risen? What could possibly matter other than the here and now that will happen when you have left and Sukie and I can be alone?

Sukie, looking up at her, senses her agitation and wants to touch her hair and kiss her brow, forgets about Nico and his dial, wants to feel herself come alive in Katia's arms.

And Nico knows that he has lost her and shuts the case with a snap.

Chapter Twenty-two

All at Sea

Peter Woulfe is in the wrong place. Or the wrong time. One or the other. He is in a tiny cabin in the Dover packet, caught in a summer storm of such ferocity that even the captain has begun to pray.

He must cling to his bunk with all his might to avoid being battered against the bunk above him every time the ship plunges head first into the yawning troughs that follow the monstrously tall waves. Each time, it is as if he has left the unsecured parts of his body behind him in the air – his heart, his brain, his guts – while his skin and bones plummet remorselessly ahead. And in the sickening interval before the next wave, his innards crash back into his body for just long enough for him to feel the full horror of his physical being.

It is all wrong. That much is sure. The wrong place to be. He has no idea where he is. Somewhere between Dover and Calais, some nameless patch of seething sea. A place that is not fit for a human. He wonders what sort of creature could survive this. A fish that could swim beneath the surface and be held in the body of the sea like a child in its mother's belly? A bird? No, no bird could survive being tossed like this in such relentless wind.

The roar of the sea and the wind have become one. The ship is shrieking like a dying creature. The wind is tearing through sails that surely cannot hold much longer; the timbers are groaning and gaping under the strain. There is a foot of seawater swirling on the floor of his cabin.

Dover to Calais – a passage that is usually trouble-free. They left with the tide; it was close to midday. He is not sure – is unable to hold the thought as his brain departs his skull again – when that was. Was it yesterday, or is it still today? All he is sure of is that he has travelled at the wrong time. To the wrong place. He had stepped aboard the packet with a sense of bewildered good fortune to be leaving English soil with his body intact. He thought of his ears – of the knives that did not cut him, of the men who did not kill or maim him, of the broken book he held tightly under his arm. It was hot and bright, and the blue sky kissed the calm sea with the generous flourish of a good omen. It seemed like the beginning of something – a reprieve, a release. He knew he would do better from then on. He had a sense in his belly, in his heart, of what was needed of him – discipline, hard work, purification. And of what he was leaving behind – the carnal filth, the confusion, his compulsions. He had a fluttery sense of something within him that had survived for a reason – something that was both bigger than him and small enough to exist inside him.

But now – now, there is nothing. A particularly vicious jolt loosens his grip, and he is thrown up against the bunk above, cracking his back against the slatted base. And while he still does not know where he is, or when he is, he knows he is in pain.

Chapter Twenty-three

Chick Lane, London

It has been three weeks since Sukie first climbed in through Katia and Nico's bedroom window. She comes and goes without warning, without explanation. It is Nico who is outwardly agitated by her absences. It is he who wonders aloud when she will return, paces up and down and looks at his watch as the day wears on – he who seems to settle back into himself when the door opens and she comes into the shop with a grin. And Katia finds herself impatient with him. She cannot really understand what it has to do with him at all.

They have begun to avoid each other's gaze, but now, this morning, as he dresses in their bedroom, Nico looks directly at his wife, and holds her eye. 'Where does she go? Where does she go when she is not with us?'

She cannot reply as part of her would like – *I think she goes out the window, out onto the roof and into another world.* So she says, 'I do not know.'

'What does she do?'

At this, something catches in her throat – all she can think is, *what if she goes to someone else? What if she lies naked in someone else's arms?*

But she shrugs and looks away and says again, 'I do not know.'

Katia thinks of the times when she has gone to greet Sukie in the living room first thing in the morning and caught an outdoor smell lingering on her cheeks, on her clothing. An outdoor smell – she cannot break it down further; it is the smell on the skin and clothing of someone who has been outside, not inside. She tries to quell a sense of rising panic at these moments.

That evening, Nico and Katia sit and eat together. Silently, uneasily. Sukie has gone out. One moment, she was there; the next, she was gone. Nico's head moves towards the door at every little noise. When they have finished eating, he goes to Bayer's. Katia waits alone. It gets darker slowly. She waits in the dimming light.

Nico returns and looks eagerly around. 'Where is Sukie?'

And Katia responds impatiently, 'Why? Your wife is not enough for you anymore, Shapsel Nicodemus?'

Though this is the least of what she is feeling, it is what she can say. What she is actually thinking about is the last thing she said to Sukie that morning, their last touch before they parted. And she cannot remember what it was she said. She remembers touching her elbow lightly – the kind of touch that is meant to mark a pause, a *see you later*, not a *goodbye*.

⌒

Alone on the roof, Sukie looks at the moon. It is almost exactly half full now, butter-bright and tilting like a golden bowl waiting to be filled. Filled with what, she wonders – with the stuff of night that stretches all around in a soft, dark arc over the city. It is peace, perfect peace to be here alone on the cool slate with her heart open wide. It is almost more perfect than being with Katia, this time alone when her body is still alive with pleasure and knows that there will be more to come.

She is perfectly poised between remembering and anticipation. She feels the tug of the vast sky above and the mortal world of Nico and Katia's flat below – feels herself to be perfectly suspended between the two. For now, she is beautifully grateful, and her heart is simply glad.

⌒

It is the middle of the night, and Katia Stein cannot stop laughing – but she must, because even though this nest of blankets on her living-room floor feels like a world apart, in fact her husband is sleeping fourteen feet away, and she must not, she really must not, wake him. She puts her hands to her mouth to stifle the noise.

Sukie giggles beside her. '... Shush ... why are you laughing? Shush!'

Katia buries her head in Sukie's neck and bites down on her own finger. Still, she laughs, and tears stream down her face.

'Shush,' says Sukie, 'Shush ... Stop ... stop!' She shakes her gently. 'What's so funny? What is it?'

Katia shakes her head. 'I don't know, I don't know.'

'Shush! What is it?'

'It is this,' Katia whispers. 'All this' – she gestures at their naked bodies; she doesn't have the words to say what she means – 'all this ... deliciousness ... Why did no one tell me that one could feel like this? Have all *this* for nothing! For free!'

Sukie grins.

'I mean I cannot help wondering' – Katia's laughter rises again and almost swallows her next words – 'why anyone would ever do anything else?'

Sukie giggles. 'Could you do it all day every day? And never get up and get dressed?'

'I think I could!'

'Me too!'

'We might get hungry.'

'We might.' Sukie shrugs as if it is unlikely.

'But no, I am serious! Why is it that people do other things if they could be doing *this*?' She thinks of her neighbours, all the people on Chick Lane who go about doing things like dressing and eating and talking and going to church and synagogue and buying and selling things. 'What could one do? Where could one go? What could one buy or sell that would be as ... what is the word?' She closes her eyes and searches for the right word – her mind fills with a flourish of bright sparks and she smiles and says '... As *golden* as this?'

Sukie shrugs with a grin.

Katia opens her eyes and kisses Sukie's shoulder. 'Maybe no one else knows about it?'

'Oh, they know, all right,' says Sukie.

'What?' says Katia, surprised, suddenly calmer. 'Everyone else knows about this?'

'Well, no . . . not exactly, but a lot of them know that they want it, all right.'

'This?'

'Well, no . . . not this – this is different . . . This is . . . special . . . I don't suppose everyone could have it this good, no matter if they stayed in their beds all day every day . . . unless they was in bed with me, of course . . .' She grins as Katia gently thumps her arm.

'You think maybe it's you then?' Katia says half seriously.

'Or maybe it's you?' Sukie responds.

They fall silent, and Sukie thinks that whatever it is, Katia is right that it is golden, and it is here and now, for as long as this now lasts – which will be until Katia creeps quietly back to her own bed. And then there will be another now. When Katia is gone, Sukie might go out onto the roof awhile, or she might go for a walk in the dark; she might even see if she can get a bit of gin if anywhere is still open . . . or she might just fall asleep here in the blanket nest.

And when she sleeps, she knows she will dream as she has been dreaming every night since she came here.

And in this dream, she will feel the blood in her veins, her feet on the ground, her breath rising and falling. She will dream of a wind that is not the wind sneaking through the timbers of a roof, but a wind that cries through stone and sets a forest full of trees to sigh. She will dream of birds – not the city sparrows chirruping but the jagged call of ravens cutting through the morning. She will dream of walking on earth that her feet remember and of lighting small smouldering fires she knows just how to kindle. She will dream of a song that rises up from the ground and calls her to go walking from one place to the next. A song that she recognises in her very bones.

∽

Katia Stein sits alone in her living room. Sukie is out – somewhere. Nico is downstairs in the shop. The warm summer air is charged with static. It has not rained now for four weeks. There is a storm coming. She is sleepy. She is often sleepy these days. The nights are for Sukie, not for sleeping. So now she sits in her chair, in the mid-morning, when she should be attending to a thousand things, and closes her eyes. She is not asleep, and she is not quite awake. She is aware of the sounds rising up from the lane. It is busy today – there are hawkers crying out, and the busy hum of chatter is split by laughter and a dog barking. Her body is still ringing with the echo of last night's pleasure. Her belly feels soft and warm. Her heart in her chest feels strong and open. She notices first what is missing – the old familiar sadness is absent, along with the flare of unspecific guilt that has long attended her, as if once, long ago, she did some-thing wrong that she cannot remember.

The thrum of her own pulse fills her awareness; she has never before noticed how it can be felt throughout her body – the flutter through her legs and arms, a bee's-wing flicker running all the way down to the tips of her fingers and toes.

As her mind slips closer to sleep, the noise outside the window begins to pulse, too, so that the sounds of the lane seem to beat in time with the beat of her heart. Suddenly, she can hear it all: the clop of horse's hooves, the turning of wheels on the dry, caked road – even the human feet striking the ground as people walk and run and stand about. She hears dogs scratching, pigs rootling, cats skulking, crows landing fierce and certain on hot slate.

And it is not just Chick Lane she can hear – her mind fills with the flood of movement and matter that is the great city of London stretching out around her: the Fleet Ditch moving sluggishly towards the river, the river moving relentlessly towards the sea, the buildings, the windows, the shudder of the glass in the windows – even the delicate tremor of the bricks in all these buildings, the dust rising up from the streets.

And teetering on the brink of sleep, her mind forgets about the skin that distinguishes her from the city around her, so that, for a moment, she is as big as the city; she is flowing in and out of it, and it is flowing in and out of her. She knows that it is good and bad, kind and cruel, that it is full of love and fear, anger and tenderness, grief and hope, that it is all flowing and changing, moment by moment.

She is filled with a mighty sense of her own flow, her own vastness, her own complexity – her tears and her blood and her words and her love. Her own great potency.

The air changes from one instant to the next. Katia smells the dry earth outside rising up to meet rain. She pulls herself back from sleep and opens her eyes.

She stands up and walks to the open window. The first rain for four weeks has begun to fall on London. She stretches out her hand to catch the drops. A scattering for now that will soon turn into a deluge. One falls *plunk* on the palm of her hand. She smiles. It is almost comical – these fat, slow-falling drops of rain after all this drought, falling now as though they have been hiding just out of sight all along. It is wonderful.

Beneath her, a wave of giddiness runs through Chick Lane. There is a rush to bring in rails of clothes; Ned turns his apple cart abruptly and moves towards the alley. Someone calls out, 'Well, that's the summer over so.' A little girl shrieks with delight or frustration.

Katia lowers the sash and puts her head out of the window, turning upwards, hoping to catch a drop in her open mouth. One falls on her forehead.

Turning then, to look down, Katia sees Sukie making her way through the flurry towards Nico's shop, her head jutting forwards, her feet moving quickly and lightly. Katia smiles to see her and calls out, despite the neighbours, 'Sukie! Sukie! Look up!'

And Sukie looks up and waves with a grin before she ducks into the shop.

∽

It is later that day, looking at Sukie across the room as she carries two shallow dishes of cabbage stew to the table, that Katia realises Sukie is going to leave. She realises that she will head out one day as she always does, without explanation, but one day – and it will be one day soon – she will not return.

She will lose Sukie in this city sea; it is inevitable. With the tug of all these tides, it is impossible that they will hold on, and Sukie, anyhow, was not born to hold on to anything. Katia considers for a moment that she could hold on tightly enough for them both, clasp Sukie so tightly that she could not slip away. But she sees in her mind's eye – as clear as day – that Sukie will slip away regardless. Katia will lose her. It is inevitable. It is how she is; it is what she is; it is the very nature of her. Sukie will leave, and what is more, Sukie will forget about her – and forget about their love, as if it were last summer's sun on her skin.

And at the thought of this, Katia's whole body roars in protest. A tearing sensation shoots through her chest; it is impossibly painful. She understands that she will lose Sukie's skin, her mouth, her breath in her ear, the smell of her neck. She will lose the exquisite pleasure of their bodies touching in the night. She will lose it all. There is no other way.

Nico is speaking intently to Sukie across the table – Katia does not know what he is speaking about, only that he is absorbed by whatever it is. She hears him say '. . . and so it would be better like *this* . . .' and he moves his hands carefully through the air to indicate a smooth surface. She sees that he looks so happy, so serious, so sure of himself and the knowledge he is sharing with Sukie – about what? It could be a piece of furniture or a road or the world itself, for all Katia knows. She looks at Sukie's hands propping up her chin as she listens attentively to Nico. Katia thinks she has never looked so beautiful.

She lays the dishes carefully on the table, one in front of Nico, the other in front of Sukie. They are her grandmother's pewter dishes, engraved around the rim. They are deeply familiar. They came all the way from the family's home place in Voronkiv in her mother's trunk – two of a set of eight that she gave to Katia on her wedding day.

Walking slowly back across the room, feeling her feet on the floor with each step, Katia returns for the third dish and turns back towards the table. The dish in her hands has outlasted her grandmother; it will outlast her mother, and it will outlast her. She will give it to a daughter who might never be born, or it will end up in a shop like Nico's.

Standing by the table, Katia remembers her grandmother's yellowing fingers on her deathbed – she understands in this moment that she, too, will lie cold in the ground one day. She understands this now as clearly as she understands that Sukie will leave.

Nico pauses, and Sukie turns to her with a smile. Immediately, Katia's heart leaps like an irrepressible puppy, and her body flares. This feeling she has for Sukie is the very opposite of death. She will die one day. Yes. For sure. But she is not dead yet. She will lose Sukie. Yes. And it will be a loss like death. It will ache dreadfully, and she will weep quietly in the night. She will weep for months, perhaps years.

But for now, Katia sits down. She reaches to touch Sukie's hand lightly. She feels the insistent thrum of the new potent pulse running through her. It is connected to her body's pleasure in Sukie and her heart's eager leap; it is connected to the sense she had that afternoon of the city alive around her and her delight in the raindrops – but it is more than any of that, too. It is all of it – and more than it. It is the very opposite of death. It is alive inside her now – and she realises it belongs to her as surely as if it had been wrapped up and given to her.

And so, on the following Saturday, when Sukie does not return, not that evening, or the following morning, not the following day or the one after, not the following week or the one after that – when it becomes clear that Sukie is not coming back at all, it is Nico who turns pale and cries and Katia who cradles his head.

Chapter Twenty-four

Rue Sainte-Anne, Paris

The sun has set. The July night is silent and still. Peter Woulfe believes himself to be the only person awake in the whole city of Paris. He sits in the flickering pool of light cast by the tallow candle on his desk and opens the book. He is pale and thin, still likely to startle at disturbances, still raw and a little unmoored. If his mother saw him, even in the candlelight, she would remark on the dark shadows beneath his eyes. But the shoes he has just kicked off have new buckles and the coat hanging on the back of his chair has been cleaned. He is in his old bedroom at the top of his uncle Stephen's house on Rue Sainte-Anne. His awareness of the honeyed stone around him, the gracious arches, the wrought iron balconies and the long, latticed shutters serves to calm his mind a little.

His uncle Stephen is irritated with him – that is his primary impression – and his aunt Marie, while concerned, also appears suspicious. He does not know that the night he arrived home she was shocked by his condition and had said privately to her husband, *where on the blessed earth did you send him? To a pack of dogs?* And Stephen replied impatiently, *I sent him to some apothecary fellow – a respectable fellow, I was assured, who knows much about –* he gestured impatiently *– herbs and potions and cures and such like.* And Maire looked suspiciously at her husband and said, *a respectable part of town, you said, an acquaintance of a friend, you said – what sort of a friend?* And Stephen replied, *Oh dear Lord, Maire, please do not start – an acquaintance of a fellow who owes me favour. I am a banker, not a child's nurse, and he is a young man, not a boy. He wanted to go to London to learn about apothecary this summer, so I sent him to London to learn about apothecary. I promised his father* *he would complete his training as a physician here in Paris, and complete it he will. London this summer was a kindness – that he squandered it is not my fault. He must put his head down now.*

A mistake was made somewhere, she could tell, but Marie did not feel like pushing the point that night – the truth is that not everyone who has dealings with a respectable banking house is respectable, and London is known to be a queer, anti-Catholic, immoral place. She knows her husband's network to be extensive and influential, but she worries sometimes that he is too political, too interested in what happens in Ireland and England – when their prosperity and their future will clearly be best served by him rising above all that and concentrating on the reliable management of funds here in France.

That night, she thought wryly, though she did not say it, *you must take your mind off political matters, Stephen, and put your head down now.*

And Stephen Woulfe, grateful that the conversation appeared to be at an end, rubbed his eyes wearily and thought that it was a grave responsibility to have the well-being of your brother's son in your hands.

He never really liked Sealy Hallom, feeling him to be far too fervent in his support for the Jacobite cause, possibly even a little mad – and he reminded himself never again to ask favours of people he did not like. Especially those who were possibly a little mad. Not even small favours as a kindness to one's very odd, and possibly genius, young nephew.

Stephen Woulfe is a banker, yes; he is deeply interested in money. But he is also a Catholic and a proud Irishman. He provides funds to Stuart sympathisers, has met personally with Charles Stuart's purser. He knows that big movements of money always mean something is afoot, and so he keeps his finger on the pulse. And he is drawn to the sinewy, brave men who come to him and talk about funds for secret and magnificent campaigns to right the world, to reclaim what is owed to them. Men who fight and plan and risk everything. Men who wear swords and who are so close to royalty that it cannot help but give him a little shiver of excitement. And of course, if they succeed in their ambitions, if Charles Stuart is put on the British throne – well, then there is no telling what opportunities there might be for a reliable Catholic banker.

And so, he had cultivated Hallom a little, gave him favourable rates and asked him on impulse one day if he knew of a respectable apothecary in London – thinking to do Peter this favour and thinking also that, if Peter were to make a good impression in London, it would strengthen these potentially useful ties with Hallom and his associates.

So much, he had thought cynically on the night of Peter's return, for that notion. He has never managed to arrive comfortably at a conclusion about Peter – his nephew seems both extremely impressive at times and at other times entirely inconsequential, easily dismissed. It could go one way or the other; he could become something or nothing. Only time will tell, Stephen Woulfe thinks, and allows his mind to move to other matters.

And now Peter is alone in his room. He has survived London, survived the dreadful voyage to France, but now that his survival is assured, a dreadful heartache has laid claim to his chest. He feels it as an urgent pain, like an alarm ringing to warn him that some vital part of him has been cut away – as if he has suffered a radical amputation. He cannot let his mind dwell on it – this terrifying sense of incompleteness, of absence, of loss. Every time his thoughts begin to touch on Sukie and the likelihood that he will never see her again, he feels as though he has opened the door into a howling storm that could catch him up and sweep him away altogether. And so, struggling against the wind, he must force the door shut.

He knows he must work, to purify himself, to redeem himself. He feels he must also work for the beauty of the work, for the promise of something brighter and more wonderful than he can fully imagine. He knows he has lost Sukie forever – but he also holds the contradictory thought that, when his alchemical work is successful and he becomes a wealthy and enlightened man, then perhaps he can reclaim her. He could return to London with enough money to search under every stone for her, enough money to pay men to protect him from thugs, enough to buy a beautiful house for her. And while he will offer her all this, it will also be the case that his new enlightened self will be more appealing to her than any number of guineas – so that she will choose of her own free will to be with him, and they will go to bed together and not get up for days and days. He begins to feel the flush of arousal. He must focus his mind.

He begins to carefully leaf through the damaged book. He pulls a sheet of blank paper towards him, takes a pen in his hand. He is ready – more than ready-to begin to understand. He moves slowly, page by page. The first three plates show angels and gods in the frame with ordinary mortals. In plate number four, a man and woman wring out a cloth under the light of the sun and the light of the moon. Turning the pages, he is struck by the overwhelming impression of labour. Most of the plates depict a man and a woman working. Page after page of work. They are sieving, grinding, decanting, weighing, mixing, distilling. And when they are not working, they are waiting. They kneel by furnaces; they pray. The gods and angels come and go; the humans labour.

But he must attend to the detail, not just the impression; he must bring the knowledge he already has to bear. This is not simply a picture book. He is not just a boy. He is man. He has knowledge; he understands what most people don't. He has read extensively; he has studied treatise after treatise. But he has never seen anything quite like this book.

He pauses on the eighth plate. It is divided in two – at the bottom, a man and a woman pray by a furnace. On the top half of the page, a figure he recognises as Mercury stands in a drop of dew suspended between two angels. The sun shines down upon the scene, and he peers closer: there are birds, doves from what he can make out – ten of them, flying beneath the angels. Two of them carry branches, and he recognises the symbols at the end of each branch – one for tartar salt, and one for sal ammoniac. His mind begins to spin. There is a depth and complexity here he could not have imagined. A great mind has compiled this book. It is a guide to the most sacred of undertakings.

He stops breathing. He understands that encoded in these images is a set of processes that will lead to the production of the philosopher's stone. The Great Work. It is here to see. How to reunite the three essential forces from which everything derives. Mercury, sulphur, salt. The soul, the spirit, the body. Energy, mind and matter.

This book demonstrates how to purify and make order out of chaos. How to put things back as they should be.

And he knows what he must do. He must deepen his understanding of the elements – Earth, Water, Air and Fire. He must practise and refine his skill at the core alchemical processes – *Nigredo, Albedo, Rubedo.* The blackening, the whitening, the reddening. He must equip himself and begin to work through the steps illustrated in the book.

He flicks forwards and pauses at plate fourteen. He sees three furnaces, one after the other, across the top of the page. They look exactly alike – brown brick-built furnaces, turreted like medieval castles, with a candle-like flame visible in the grate of each one. They look alike, but he knows enough to know that they represent three different fires – the inner spiritual fire, the secret salt fire and the material fire.

It is not just how to change lead into gold; he knows that the process illustrated in the book before him will also transform his leaden soul into a golden soul – will make all impure things pure. He cannot believe his good fortune, that he should have come into possession of the one book in the world that will guide him to the outcome he desires more than anything.

At the bottom of the page, he sees a man and a woman who appear to know it all. Their lips are pursed, thoughtful; they appear to be invoking a higher power with raised right hands. The words written between them are: *Ora Lege Lege Lege Relege labora et Invenies.*

Pray, read, read, read, read again, work hard, and you will find.

In this instant, he realises that the days are not long enough for all the work he must do, all the reading his must do, all the praying he must do. This time of night is a good time to work; he will work late. And the early mornings also must be reclaimed from the wastelands of sleep. From now on, four hours, sleep a night will be sufficient.

There is a flicker of light under the door, a perfunctory knock, and his aunt enters in her nightgown – Peter startles and looks up guiltily as she says, 'Heavens above, Peter – what are you doing still awake?'

'I'm working, Aunt, just working.' He flushes.

'But it is late, Peter, and you must be up tomorrow early to attend your lectures.' She feels suspicious in a way she cannot quite understand. He is such a sweet boy, and clearly he is just reading.

'I'm not tired, and I have so much to do.'

'Well, you must put out that candle – candles do not buy themselves, you know.' This much is true, though they both know it is of little consequence. 'You must finish your work tomorrow.'

She moves closer; he shuts the book quickly, and as she bends to snuff the candle between practised fingers, he catches sight of the arc of her breasts beneath her pale nightgown and flushes again. Thinking both of breasts and the foolishness of thinking that his work could be finished tomorrow, he bids her goodnight.

'Oh and Peter,' she says, as she walks towards the door, 'you must write to your mother and father – they will be waiting for news of you, of your summer in London . . . you must write something for them.'

'Yes, Aunt.' He nods, but there is simply no way that he will have time for letters with all the work ahead of him – so much work that a whole lifetime may not be enough. 'Goodnight, Aunt.' He will send his mother a gift instead. Something interesting – there are so many wonderful things to buy in Paris.

'Goodnight, Peter. God bless you.'

'God bless.'

Chapter Twenty-five

Mount Gabriel, Cork, Ireland

The first parcel that arrives for Mary Woulfe from Peter comes in a packing case large enough to hold a couple of fat geese, but in fact nestled within are two small stuffed yellow birds. Tucked in between them, attached by a thread to the leg of one of the birds, is a label in her youngest son's handwriting. *Kanarienvögel.*

It is a dull winter's day, and the little birds lie as bright and daft as early daffodils in the straw that Peter has packed tightly around them. Mary lifts one carefully; there is no weight to it at all. She is not sure what to feel. It is beautiful. It is dead. She has never seen a bird so bright before.

She picks up the other bird and stands with one in each hand. Peter has sent them to her; he has chosen them and packed them and sent them all the way from Paris. He has not written. Not even a short note since the summer, and so she has no idea how he is.

What is she to do with them? She cannot put their feathers on her hat – they are far too bright for Sundays in the damp chapel on the side of the hill. What, she wonders, was he thinking? It occurs to her there may be a letter somewhere in the straw – something to explain, but even though she puts the birds down carefully and empties out the case, she finds nothing. She looks again at the birds, and her heart turns – whatever else it was, it was kind of him to think of her, to send her these pretty little creatures. Maybe she can make a brooch with the tail-feathers.

She wishes he would write – even two or three lines, so that she would know how he is.

This is the first of many packages Peter sends his mother. They are always addressed directly to her. There is always an inordinate amount of packing material – shredded foreign-looking paper, the bark of unfamiliar trees, dusty straw, old linen rags, wood chips, torn flour sacks, wool, reeds and dried ferns.

That first year, Peter, delighted by the treasures of the Parisian markets, sends his mother the wing of a silver gyrfalcon, two feathers from an eagle's tail, and a dappled-grey stuffed owl that is so soft and shocked-looking that Mary cannot meet its gaze.

The following summer, he sends her the small, pale skull of a Barbary ape, which she unearths from its crate with horror.

He sends an unlabelled lump of grey rock sprouting thin translucent needles tinged with pink. She keeps it beside her bed and wonders at it.

There is no pattern to the arrivals; they come when they come without rhyme or reason. Sometimes, there are labels; sometimes, there are not. Mary Woulfe is never quite sure how to feel. Sometimes, the contents are beautiful; often, they are uncanny or unwieldy – always, they are somewhat mystifying. She writes each time to thank him, to give him the news from home. But there is never a letter in response.

He sends a leather pouch containing eleven shark's teeth. He sends her a golden crystal the length of her thumb. *Beryl*.

The year after that, he sends her a deep-pink stone labelled *Corinvindum* . . . so small in the middle of the tightly stuffed box it arrives in that she thinks it must be terribly valuable, to have come all on its own such a long way. She has no idea where to put it so that it can be looked at and kept safe. It sits for a month on the top shelf of the dresser in the kitchen. Then she sends for a large glass cabinet from Cork, which she puts in the sitting room.

He sends rocks – oozing green malachite, polished snowflake obsidian, a huge, jagged chunk of iron ore. He sends sheaves of dried lavender; he sends huge pine cones; he sends the carefully wired skeleton of a small mammal with a long, curving tail.

He sends a huge yellow-and-black-striped spider floating in a jar of spirits. She puts it at the back of the cabinet. He sends three long boar tusks that his father and brother wave around and laugh at.

Within three years, the glass cabinet is full, and she must send for another one. Sometimes, every now and again, she pauses and looks at the contents of the cabinets and wonders, what is it he is trying to say to her?

He sends a dull-looking stone, which she turns to reveal a berry-bright splash of red on the underside. *Cinnabar.* The word tastes good on her tongue.

Two years after that, in an enormous wooden crate that stands taller than herself, he sends magnificent reindeer antlers – *Cervus Tarandus* – sixteen-pointed, spreading mightily, velvety soft to the touch. Standing on the kitchen table to pull them up and out of the case, she wonders if he shot the beast himself, wonders where its head is. The antlers are magnificent; they are ridiculous. She is obscurely proud and irritated at the same time. She must get Padeen to hang them on the wall somewhere.

He sends pink salt in a glass tubes; he sends a tray of tiny blue-green birds' eggs. He sends brightly coloured dyes in small jars. He sends nuggets of burnished copper.

Mary Woulfe orders a third glass cabinet and then a fourth.

He does not write, but the web of relatives around him thrums with information: he is with his brother; he is with his cousin; he has travelled to Germany; he has taken to mining; he has rooms in London; he is under the patronage of an earl who pays him well to gather precious minerals. He takes a place as the surgeon on a ship travelling across the globe. She feels him going even farther away.

He sends a long livid-green snake-skin, which she unfurls with a shiver; he sends the spiralled horns of a far-flung desert creature. He sends an achingly beautiful rosebud-pink conch-shell that is almost a foot long. He must be very, very far away, she thinks, to have found such wondrously alien things. He sends her the skin of a small alligator labelled simply *Juvenile Male*. He sends an elephant's foot. She puts the poor, sad thing in the barn beside the reindeer antlers, which had begun to drop grey flakes all over the hall floor.

He sends her six hairy coconuts packed in palm leaves and a giant fluted clam wrapped in llama wool. James Woulfe rubs the wool between his fingers in wonder, thinks of having it spun into yarn – just to see.

Five years later again, he sends a long, shallow crate containing what she thinks at first is an ancient bronze shield, but the label reveals it to be a turtle's shell. *Adult Female, Testudo Mydas.* It is fully five feet long. There is no room for it anywhere. Padeen hangs it in the hayloft, where it rattles ferociously against the wall when the south westerlies blow.

Mary worries he has too much money – if he is spending it in sending these things across the world in packing cases. Or perhaps he does not know how to spend his money, not having a wife or children to spend it on. Has he grown up at all?

He sends her a copy of a paper he has had published in the journal of the Royal Society of London. It is a mark, she understands, of great success.

Philosophical Transactions Giving Some Account of the Present Undertakings, Studies and Labours of the INGENIOUS in Many Considerable Parts of the World.

Ingenious. She reads Peter's section slowly, and with every word she reads, she understands even less about how he is and what he might be doing.

The crooked tube E is fitted to the spout D of the receiver by means of a cork with a hole in its middle, and then well covered with lute; the other end of it goes to the bottom of the vessel F, to the mouth of which it is fitted by a cork, with a semicircular notch in it as at G, but without any lute to fatten it, as there must be a small vent for the escape of the elastic air, and this is the only vent in all the apparatus for that purpose. By this apparatus the fumes are obliged to pass through the water in F, and there deposit all they contain, except their elastic air.

Maurice, leaning over her shoulder, says with a wry grin, 'Well, I hope his elastic air tastes half as good as Padeen's poitín.'

One summer's day, when she is feeling old and tired, a tea-chest arrives, and within it, held in place by crumpled flour sacks, lies a single smaller box. When she opens the box, she finds a stone the size of her fist – an extraordinary-looking thing with delicate white crystals rising up like blossoms. There is a label.

Peter has written *Flos Ferris* and, beneath it, *Flowers of Iron*. Her heart turns just as it did when he came in the kitchen door with a fistful of daisies for her when he was a little boy.

He sends another paper that he has had published. Maurice squints seriously at it, his elbows propped on the kitchen table.

The mercury, which was added only in order to divide the tin, unites with some of the sulphur, and likewise sublimes and forms a cinnabar. The tin which remains, unites with the remaining sulphur, and forms the Aurum mosaicum . . . I have used a glass retort, fixed in a black lead crucible with sand round it; the crucible was put into a proper furnace, and a charcoal fire made around it . . .

Maurice ploughs through in his soft Irish accent, reads almost every word of the seventeen-page paper out to his mother, whose eyesight is now well beyond the task. It seems, in the end, to be about dye – about indigo. About turning indigo, which she knows to be blue, into yellow. There is silence when Maurice finishes, there is nothing to be said. It seems somehow that Peter is further away than ever. She hopes he is well, that he is somehow content, that he is flourishing. Maurice turns towards his bed, Mary walks slowly over to lock the kitchen door, opens it on impulse and looks out into the twilight.

The sky is darkening softly, the ash trees are sighing in the breeze, bats whirr above her – she fancies she can hear a delicate hum rising up from the dewy earth. The night is coming alive. She steps out onto the cobbled yard. She imagines herself walking right out and spending the whole night under the stars. Who or what might she encounter? She thinks of her bed, her pillows, the mattress long moulded to her shape. She turns back to the house – rebukes herself softly for being a silly old woman with a passing fancy. It would be damp, cold, hard, desperately uncomfortable, it could be the death of her at her age – and more than that, the thing she would not like to admit, after all the years spent calling this place her home, is her sense that the vast thrumming night around her is already full of strange, powerful beings whose ways she does not know, whose language she does not speak. For all that she has lived and will die here, for all that she has reared her sons and buried her husband here, for all that she might imagine that this night is calling to her, she knows she does not quite belong.

Chapter Twenty-six

May 1730 – *Bealtaine*

Mount Gabriel, Cork, Ireland

Peter Woulfe is small enough to be under the table. He is looking at the dull planks above him, a world away from the familiar scrubbed surface on the other side. He is small enough to crouch low and be fascinated by the texture of the untrodden earthen floor, young enough to take great pleasure in running his hand along the swirling marks brushed into the surface when it was first laid. He is old enough to listen and to understand most of what is being said.

Why he is under the table rather than hunkered by the fire or sitting on Bridey Leary's lap, he has already forgotten. Perhaps he was frightened; perhaps he was bored. She is telling him a story, one that he thinks he has heard before, but the story sounds different to him now that he is listening to it from under the table. She is speaking straight into the fire, as if he were not here at all, but he knows that the story is especially for him. It is a story about a long-ago time when people knew the way they should be going by the feel of their feet on the ground – a better way altogether than simply looking around and following paths.

Bridey is sitting on the stool by her fire, and from where he squats, he can see her strong, lithe feet, which she wriggles with satisfaction as she speaks. He looks down at his own dirty, pudgy toes.

The story is the one about the woman and her family who came walking here to this very spot in a time that was so long ago there was no time.

As Bridey settles into the telling, her voice rises and falls like the wind that he can hear in the trees outside.

Softly, she says to the fire, 'They were people like us – but better in every way.' He sees her stretch out her left hand to count off the differences on her fingers, one by one. 'They were stronger. They were faster. They were more beautiful, and they were cleverer by far.'

How strong, he wonders, how fast – but he is afraid to ask.

Bridey continues, as if she can hear his thoughts, 'Strong enough to take a small boy in one hand and throw him from here to the village with one flick of the wrist' – she pauses so he can see himself flying through the air – 'and fast enough to run from here to the village to catch him in that same hand before he hits the ground.'

He has been scooped out of the air like a smooth leather ball before she says, 'And that would be without one bead of sweat, even on the hottest day.'

He is not so interested in beauty and cleverness, but all the same she says, 'They were so beautiful it could almost blind you. They were as bright and as light as the midday sun in your eyes. And so clever' – here she laughs to herself in a way that he doesn't understand – 'that they could live rich as royalty here on this very mountain, with no cattle to speak of, no butter, no bread and no spuds.'

And the people in his mind have golden crowns and bright-red cloaks now, but they look hungry, until she says, 'And they never wanted for a bite, they ate like kings four times a day, seven days a week – the sweetest food you could imagine.'

'There was nothing they couldn't reach by climbing, or jumping, or sometimes, when they had a mind to, by flying. They could cross any river with a leap – they could swim like a fish if need be.'

And it is not really necessary to say, but all the same Bridey says, as if she has said it many times before and so must say it the same way.

'And it was all down to the magic they had in them, a powerful old magic running from the crowns of their glowing heads to the very tips of their toes.

'The ones who came here were two women. There was no man' – here she smiles – 'but there were two young lads and a full-grown girl. Now, they had walked from far away, taking their time, enjoying their journey. They walked soft as deer; they sang sweet as birds. They spoke to the trees and the animals and the water chattering in the rivers. And when they got here to this place, one sunny spring day, the mother, who always went first, knew from the feeling in her feet that this was the place for them. She knew that they should settle here for a year or a hundred years, which was all the same to them in those days. So she stood with her head up and her hand on her heart, and she sang out to the mountain, telling her who they were and where they had come from, and asking permission to stay for a while. And then the family waited quietly and patiently, not even doing a thing to set up for the night or to get a fire going. And the wind began to stir in the trees, and the sunlight began to dance all around them, and the mountain sang back that they could stay and welcome.

'It was just here' – she bends forwards and carefully touches the floor by her feet – 'in this blessed spot that they laid their golden heads that first night.'

He looks down again at the pattern on the floor and thinks, *here.*

'And even though they were the only people around, they weren't alone, because back then there were spirits for everything here on this mountain.'

She pauses, and her voice takes on the rhythm of a chant, pulling back Peter's attention, which was beginning to wander to the open door. She taps her bare foot in time.

'There was the spirit of the oak, the spirit of the ash, the spirit of the elm, the spirit of the pine.

'There was the spirit of the primrose, the spirit of the dog rose, the spirit of the bramble, the spirit of the hazel.

'There was a spirit for every leafing thing and every flowering thing.

'A spirit for every feathered thing, and every hoofed thing.

'A spirit for every clawed thing, and every scaly thing.

'A spirit for every hunter, and for every hunted thing.

'There was the spirit of the wind.

'The spirit of the rain.

'The spirit of the sun.

'The spirit of the sea.

'The spirit of the rain on the sea.

'The spirit of the sun on the sea.

'And in those days, spirits moved around as clear as day, and they had their own kind of magic that could do you favours or do you harm. And the family befriended the sprits, knowing just the right offerings to make to them and just the right songs to sing to them. So the spirits did them favours, and they did them no harm. And all went well for the family, and they lived here happier than kings.'

He is old enough, even with his pudgy toes, even with being under the table, to know that this is not a story yet because nothing bad has happened. So he waits.

'And while they were all beautiful, the daughter was the most beautiful of all and the cleverest and the most curious, and it was her who first saw the boat pull up in Canty's Cove. She was up where Connie O'Sullivan's top field is now, lying in the sun, and she sat up and watched the boat come in against the wind. It was long and low in the water, and the men pulling at the oars were tired, so that she almost took one leap down into the water to catch hold of the boat and bring them safely ashore.

'But she didn't. Something stopped her. Instead, she watched them. She lay back against the hill in a way she had that meant they couldn't see her at all. It was a power they all had – this way of sitting back into the grass on a hillside or the bark of a tree or the shingle of a shore, so that no matter how hard you looked, you would see nothing, only the grass or the bark of the tree or the shingle of the shore.'

Peter wriggles flat onto his belly, his chin on his hands, his legs out behind him, and falls completely still. He knows that he is invisible, and that no matter how hard they look, anyone searching under the table would see only a dusty floor.

'She watched long enough to see them ashore, to see that there were no women with them, that they were all grown men except for one skinny young lad, who hurried back and forth through the water from the boat with odd bundles held high over his head. She watched while they gathered wood for a fire; she watched while they sat by the fire and ate hungrily. She watched as they forgot to ask the spirit of the shore if they could stay. And she nearly called down to them to remind them. But she didn't.

'Now, for all that she was clever, she was not good at counting, so when she went back to her family, she could say only that there were more men than you could count on the fingers of both hands and one young lad. And the adults said, *sure, let them off, mind your own business – isn't there enough here for everyone?* And her brothers said, *how big was the lad, do you think he would race us to Kerry and back, for we are sore tired of racing only each other?* And the girl ignored her brothers and thought to herself that she didn't want to mind her own business; she wanted to see what they were at and why they had come at all.

'So she went down the next day to watch, and the day after that again, and she watched and she watched. She would go up a tree, graceful as a cat, and a shiver would come over her, and her skin would look like the bark of the tree, and no one looking up could ever tell she was there at all. And if she wanted to get away, she could run through the trees on the ground as fast as the wind, and she could even swing' – Bridey lifts one arm above her head and holds an invisible branch – 'from tree to tree faster than you could see.

'So she watched and she watched, and she was fed up to the back teeth of watching them waking up and eating, and gathering firewood and fishing and stringing up a bit of shelter for themselves and having their dinner and going to bed, when they began to do some fierce strange things.

'And she would have been a thousand times better off, a thousand, thousand, thousand times better off, to have turned her head away and gone back to her family when these strange things began to happen. But did she? She did not. And was she sorry for it in the end? I tell you, there was never a person so sorry.'

'*Is he here?* Bridey Leary, have you seen Peter?' His mother's voice comes high and urgent into the cabin, his mother following after, blocking the light in the door for a moment, stepping quickly in and saying in the same high tones, 'Have you seen him? He's been gone this hour or more, and the river is very full.'

Bridey does not reply, and Peter, who would like to hear the end of the story and not get the smacking he can hear in his mother's voice, decides he will stay invisible for now. He sees his mother's shoes, her feet moving quickly as she scans the room. He is perfectly still, perfectly invisible. It is the best power of all, better than speed or strength. The shoes come close; Bridey stays silent. They turn and run out the door.

Peter waits, invisible and mute, for the story to continue. Bridey says nothing. He looks at the floor, at his fingers, at his toes; he is sure it has been a very long time since she said anything at all. It feels like hours and hours and hours measured by the impatient beat of his heart. His mother could come back any minute, and then he knows the story will be gone forever.

'Go on, Bridey,' he whispers. 'Go on. Please.' He looks over at Bridey's feet, which are still as stone. 'Please, Bridey. Please.'

She begins to speak. 'Well, she watched the men from the boat, and she watched the boy who was with them, but she watched one man most of all – the boss man. He was a big, tall fella, with shoulders like a giant and big, dirty hands. He had a face as pale as a ghost and crow-black hair. And he had a way with him. He would wash himself in the stream below as if he thought he was blessing the stream with himself.' She snorts. 'And of course, she watched him without a stitch of clothes on him because in those days they didn't bother about things like that.

'She watched and she watched, and she saw them early one morning heading off up the mountain. And when they got right up, right up there by the pass, they lit a fire. And it wasn't just any old fire – they lit the biggest fire you could imagine. A hundred times bigger than any bonfire Padeen ever lit. And the fire burned and burned for days and nights, until they had the whole place burned right down to the bone and everywhere was black as soot and as ugly as sin, and they didn't stop until there were no trees, no gorse, no heather, just bare black rock.

'And then, when it had all cooled down and it was all black and bare, and the rock was fit to crack like a loaf of burned bread, they went hammering at the mountain with big stone mallets – battering away, day in, day out, until they had caves the size of houses dug out, driving every living thing demented with their noise . . . And their own ears were buzzing and their eyes stinging, and their hands were red, and their backs were sore . . . but they didn't mind, because they were mad to get what they were after.'

Bridey pauses. Peter sees her tap her two feet on the floor like a full stop.

'And that's the end of the story.'

Peter's horrified face suddenly appears from under the table. 'Ah, Bridey, it isn't, it isn't!' He wriggles out and pulls himself on his belly, closer to Bridey. He stands up and looks at her indignantly. 'Bridey, it isn't. That makes no sense.'

'Well, no.' She laughs a little and tosses her head. 'I suppose it doesn't.'

'What was it? What was it they were after, Bridey?'

She looks straight at him, considering. He folds his arms across his chest and tilts his chin up.

'What were they after Bridey? Go on!'

She nods slowly, with her lips pursed, as if she might buy him after all.

'Well.' She sighs, resigned; the story will continue. 'Well, what they were after was what the mountain had deep inside her.' She stretches out her right hand and rubs her fingers together right in front of his eyes. 'Bright, shiny stuff.'

'Why?' he asks, with his eyes wide. 'Why?'

'Oh,' she says dismissively, 'just because it was bright and shiny and they could sell it, and they thought it would make them rich.'

'Bright and shiny like gold?'

'I suppose.' She shrugs. 'A bit like gold.'

'And did they get it?'

'They did.'

'And did it make them rich?'

'Oh, it did.'

'How rich?'

'Oh, very rich. But not as rich as they wanted to be.'

'As rich as my daddy?'

'Oh, richer.'

'As rich as Daddy and Uncle Mossie put together?'

'Richer.'

'Mammy says Daddy and Uncle Mossie are the richest men around – and the handsomest.'

'Does she indeed?'

Bridey falls silent.

'Go on, Bridey – go on, tell me more.'

'Sure, what else is there to tell?'

'What about the boy, Bridey? What about the boy?'

'What boy?'

'The boy who came with the men, the one who might race the brothers?'

'Oh, the boy.' She considers for a moment. 'Sure, they treated him like a dog – and not like a good dog but a poor, stupid mutt of a thing that would be no use with cattle or sheep or anything much at all and would get the first kick of everyone's boot and last gnaw of every bone. And they sent him into the mountain every morning before the sun came up to start new fires – deeper and deeper into those black, sooty tunnels every day, until he was half mad with the smoke and the fear and the dark and the roaring in his ears of the wind through the caves.'

Peter's eyes widen. 'So, he wasn't fast?'

'He was not. He was slow and miserable and always snuffling.'

'And was he invisible?'

'He was not. Sure, how would they send him into the mountain and kick him if they couldn't see him?'

'Oh.'

Bridey says nothing, and a delicate wind outside sets the hedgerow to sigh.

'But they couldn't see the girl, because she was invisible and as fast as the wind?'

Bridey says nothing.

Peter takes a bit of Bridey's cloak in his hand and gives a little, urgent tug. 'Bridey, they couldn't see the girl – sure they couldn't?'

'Oh, they could in the end. The fool.'

'And when they saw her, did they kick her?'

'Oh, they did.'

'Hard?'

'Oh, very hard. Sure weren't they big, strong fellas?'

Peter's eyes fill with tears. 'But, Bridey, how? When she was invisible and fast as the wind?'

'Didn't I tell you? It was because she was a fool.'

'A fool?'

'She let the boss fella see her one day, just for the fun of it, because he was handsome and strong, and he walked like a god. She let him see her, right there, down on the lane by the milking parlour and when he saw her, didn't he catch her?'

Bridey's hand shoots out and grabs Peter's arm. Her fingers are sharp, her grip is tight, and his mouth opens in shock before he begins to sob.

'Caught her just like that' – she squeezes more tightly – 'and took her away and tied her with a chain. And then he had his way with her like a tomcat with a cat or the cockerel with his hens.'

Peter's heart fills with horror. He suddenly has a sense of himself being very small in a big, cold world. A shiver runs through him.

Bridey looks down at the top of his head and continues, 'Oh, he was stone mad about her. He couldn't get enough of her at all. But she didn't think much of him – she saw quick enough that he was all swagger on the outside and nothing much underneath, and she missed her family so much she used to howl like a wolf in the night. But it wasn't long before her mother found her and got her back.

'Her mother went right up into the middle of their camp, up there beyond the top field.' She points to the western gable of the cabin. 'She was only a little thing' – here Bridey's hand waves out in front of her to indicate a height about four feet from the ground – 'and they were big, strong men, but she had ferocious magic in her and the spirit of the mountain flowing right through her.'

Bridey pauses and looks down again.

Peter turns his blue eyes up to meet her gaze.

'Are you listening? Are you listening carefully now?'

'I am, Bridey. I am.'

'She stood out there in the clearing, in front of those big men, and she began to tap her foot on the ground.'

Bridey stands up suddenly and moves away from her stool, spins back to face him and begins to tap her left foot rhythmically on the ground.

She starts to sing out loud. Peter cannot make out the words, just the sounds, as if she is using another language altogether. It is not Irish; it is not even English. It sounds like something older and wilder than either.

She sings out a slow, steady beat from deep in her chest. He hunkers down on the floor and sucks his thumb, rapt. Then suddenly, she changes the song, so that every third note is high and fierce, like a fox shriek splitting the day. She begins to move each foot in turn, up and down in the same spot, the fierceness in her gaze mounting. The beat she calls out changes time. The leaves go still in the trees outside. The sunlight coming through the open door falls slow and thick like honey.

Peter understands that this is not just Bridey calling out; this is something much bigger than Bridey. Something bigger than the cabin, bigger even than his house, something as big as the biggest thing he knows, which is the mountain above them.

It could be a minute or a year before Bridey suddenly stops singing, stops moving her feet, claps her hands together and begins to speak again as if she was never singing at all.

'After that, he didn't know which way was up – and it was no bother at all for her to take the girl away from him.'

She sits back down and smiles for the first time. 'Oh, it was a good one, that one. It hit him right between the eyes.' Her own eyes half shut; she nods her approval, as if she is watching the incantation from across three millennia. 'She put that curse right on him and in him and around him and through him . . . and into the blood of his children's children's children. And after it hit him . . . well! . . . After it hit him, he was never the same again . . .'

She ticks the list off on the fingers of her left hand. 'No matter how many trees he cut down, he never had enough wood. No matter how many boatloads of that shiny stuff he sold, he never had enough gold. No matter how many hundreds of sheep he kept on the mountain, he never had enough meat. And' – she pauses and takes a breath – 'no matter how hard he searched, he never again found the girl. And the truth of it is, his heart had gone right out of him and away with her.'

She lays her hand on her chest. 'And without his heart in him, there was nothing for him anywhere. Every bit of food he ever ate went straight to ashes in his mouth. The birds sang flat in his ears. Even the sun looked dull to him, no matter if it was shining like it is today. Oh, it was a good curse all right, that one, and I'll tell you' – she points up at the mountain and then draws one slow, wide circle above her own head with her arm outstretched – 'it was such a good one that it's not finished yet.'

'And the girl, Bridey?' he whispers.

'And the girl, when she got back, had his child in her belly. And that child, when it was born' – she turns now and looks straight at Peter, both eyes boring into his – 'was a good bit like its blessed mother and a good bit like its father, too.'

Mary Woulfe appears suddenly in the door, her pretty face flushed, her hair astray.

'Bridey, any sign of him . . .?' She gasps, puts her hand to her heart and says breathlessly, 'Mother of God, Peter, you had the heart crossways in me!' She runs over to him, lifts him into her arms and squeezes him so tightly that he can hardly breathe.

He wriggles and twists and hits at her breasts and shoulders. 'Mammy, no, Mammy, Mammy, no. Can't you see I'm invisible?'

'Peter, where have you been?'

'Mammy, I'm invisible! Go away!'

She stops squeezing him, sets him on his feet and smacks him on the bottom. 'Peter Woulfe, you are the boldest child I ever met.'

'No, Mammy, no.' He begins to cry. 'I'm invisible!'

Taking him by the wrist, Mary Woulfe pulls Peter towards the door, as he howls with disappointment and fury.

'The whole house has been out looking for him,' she says tightly in Bridey's direction. She pauses at the door to land another smack on Peter's bottom – and this time, Peter feels he has got a smack meant for Bridey, and he howls even louder.

Chapter Twenty-seven

May 1780

Barnard's Inn, Fetter Lane, London

Danby Scott arrives, ashen-faced, at the door of Peter Woulfe's rooms. It is just before four in the morning. He is not accustomed to navigating the streets of London in the dark hours. It is barely two months since he left Hertfordshire; he is still fresh from the arms of his attentive mother and his four older sisters, who have occupied themselves with the task of loving him – attending equally to his mortal body and his immortal soul.

The moon was sailing high in a clear sky when he left his rooms at Gray's Inn, and he began his journey confidently. The delightful tension of anticipation mixed beautifully with a sense of his own bravery. It seemed fitting that there would be something in the nature of a test before he joined the company of Peter Woulfe for breakfast at the ungodly hour of four in the morning. Pickpockets he was prepared for – what coin he has is tucked away against his chest. What he had not expected was that nine different women of the night would solicit his business in the most pressing manner. He will tell himself later that it was twelve, but in truth, he lost count after six – number six having decided to assure herself of his manhood with a firm and unexpected squeeze. He shifts uncomfortably in his breeches at the memory, and some colour returns to his cheeks.

He has carefully practised the secret knock, which is not so much complex as unusual, and he delivers it now, his knuckles striking the oak door with a vigour he does not entirely feel.

Almost instantly, a deep voice answers, 'Yes?'

'Danby Scott, sir, to dine with Peter Woulfe.'

A small hatch in the middle of the door opens, and a hand emerges. Danby grips the hand firmly – notices it is a strong hand and that the skin is rough and dry – before pressing down four times with his thumb on the first knuckle of the third finger. The hand withdraws, and Danby – the very act of knocking and delivering the secret handshake has filled him with the greatest excitement – is left to push the door open fully and step slowly into the room. He removes his hat and gazes expectantly into the gloom.

Ahead of him, he sees Peter Woulfe's tall, thin form moving towards a candle-lit dining table situated at the far end of a vastly cluttered room. In the flicker of light and shadow, he makes out three long workbenches. As he follows his host, there is just enough light to reveal what looks like an Aladdin's cave of apparatus. He sees an elaborate experiment set up: a length of rubber tubing strung between a suspended glass orb, a cork-stoppered jar and a wide basin filled with sand. An enormous pair of scales cast their angular shadows on the book-lined wall. All the available surfaces are covered in bottles, dishes, tongs, pincers, funnels, stained cloths, sheafs of notes, books in precarious piles. There are innumerable glass phials of every shape and size, jars of every colour. He passes three large glass specimen cases, each one crammed full. Not daring to pause, he can only glance at the contents – sees what looks like a stuffed monkey, an enormous whorled shell, the broken tip of narwhal's horn, countless rocks and crystals in a jumble. The room is unusually warm and smells of something entirely unfamiliar – he has never before encountered such a sharp, inhuman scent, as though all manner of things have been burned day and night and never a window opened. It catches him at the back of his throat, singes his nose, and he fears he will sneeze.

Peter Woulfe takes his seat at the head of the table. Danby sees that they are quite alone in the room. He flushes. For a terrible moment, he thinks he is to be the only guest. He looks warily at Woulfe in the candlelight. His host's unruly hair flares out around his head like a greying mane, yet despite this leonine flourish, he looks to Danby like an ancient, eager-eyed bird of prey.

Peter turns his gaze on Danby, but for moment he does not really see the young man at all. It has been such a trying time. He is tired. Bone tired. Robert Perle's nauseating visits, his smoothly executed extortions, are utterly exhausting. He gives Perle the requested money every week, money that they both pretend is an investment in Perle's work, to be repaid when Perle makes his fortune. Peter puts the coins into Perle's soft, expectant hand, and that is bad enough, but he fears Perle wants much more. He thinks mostly of his work when he thinks of his wealth – the vast store of knowledge that he has accumulated, the progress he has made in the spiritual realm. He thinks of the secret, subtle processes he has mastered. Rarely does he think of his actual monetary wealth, which is not insubstantial. Perle, he fears, is after all of it. And he cannot keep him at bay.

And as if that were not bad enough, every morning he wakes to the reproachful face of his dead assistant – and often during the day, when he turns quickly, he is sure he sees him for a moment crouching by the fire, a haunting presence. But that insubstantial apparition cannot light furnaces or grind powders. And the fact is he misses the boy's help. He cannot bear the thought of finding another young fellow, of explaining everything – the equipment, the furnaces, the need for extreme care. The great urgency of it all. Because time is moving ever faster. He can feel it. And today, he fears he is no closer than he has ever been to completing the Great Work. He has begun to think that he is an outdated relic, a failure – that all the prayer, all the work, all the expense, has amounted to nothing.

Worse again, though, worse even than failure, is the creeping suspicion that he is a filthy mortal sinner – because what else could you call it? There is his terrible temper, leading to the unfortunate death of Mal, and this vile association with Perle . . . There is the indisputable fact that he shouts at the unfortunate slattern who clatters in every week to mop his floor and moves things of the greatest importance . . . and then – he hates to remember it, but she comes right into his mind as if the image of the grey old thing with her mop bucket has evoked its very opposite – there is the copper-haired young woman at the White Horse and his quite disgusting delight in her thighs and her buttocks and her pillowy stomach.

He might pray – and God Himself knows the hours Peter spends daily in prayer, the care he takes with his work – inscribing precise invocations, messages to the blessed angels, attaching them with clear intent onto key elements of his apparatus before each procedure. He might do all that, and with excellent penmanship to boot, but he fears his scrubby, dirty soul will forever see him held at arm's length. Denied. Barred. Kept out.

He shakes his head a little, remembers the young man standing uncertainly before him, speaks abruptly.

'Mr Scott, please sit here – just here.' And he indicates the chair immediately to his right.

Danby hesitates. He would be much happier further down the table, and ideally at a table filled with so many guests that he could simply sit and listen.

Blinking in the candlelight, coming slowly back to the present, Peter Woulfe considers the young man, who smiles uncertainly at him, and in an instant, it becomes clear to him that what he has suspected since their meeting at the Temple Coffee House is true – Danby Scott is a man of unusual purity of soul. It is not just that he stands there, young and strong, as if on the brink of a high dive into deep blue sea; not alone his fresh, healthy cheeks or the bright clarity of his green eyes – Peter Woulfe believes he has caught a glimpse of something delicate and rare within Danby Scott, something akin to a precious stone turning slowly in the light.

He experiences a movement in his heart like a clenched fist loosening for a moment. 'Please sit,' he repeats.

Danby Scott sits. He brings his bright-green eyes to meet Woulfe's gaze and finds the older man is looking at him as if he were a long-awaited package suddenly delivered.

Peter is experiencing a giddy, almost dizzying, sensation of possibility. This young man is bright and alive and full of promise; what is more, he is evidently good. Maybe not all is lost. He beams. He sits back. Out of nowhere, he suddenly has the fluttery feeling he sometimes gets when he is about embark on work of great significance.

Without preamble, he says, 'Mr Scott, are you familiar with the process of nitration? Of adding *aqua fortis* to substances in carefully controlled amounts?'

'Not entirely familiar, sir, though I have read some accounts of the subject.'

Peter Woulfe nods. 'Not every substance is receptive. Some resist. It is a delicate balance – with the possibility of either dire or wonderful results.' He smiles somewhat sheepishly.

'Dire, sir?'

'Well, in the case of indigo – enormous explosions.'

'And wonderful?'

'Oh, vast wealth!'

They both laugh. Peter cannot remember the last time he laughed.

Danby says, 'One is certainly preferable to the other!'

'Yes. Indeed.' Peter is still laughing; he is surprised to feel tears forming in his eyes. He sits forwards eagerly. 'There is much to discuss . . . You are interested in the natural sciences, yes?'

Danby nods and begins to reply when a knock on the door interrupts him.

Peter stands, says, 'Wait just a moment, please,' and walks briskly to the door.

Danby watches as Peter Woulfe listens carefully before opening the hatch and putting his hand through the gap. There is a brief pause before he turns and makes his way back to the table.

Behind him, sleek and eager, his head bent forwards like a wet dog emerging from the water, Robert Perle steps into the room.

'Woulfe – dear cousin! Good morning!' Perle crosses the room with brisk steps and smiles at Danby.

Danby notices a particular brightness in Perle's damp brown eyes and thinks that his cousin must also have encountered some pressing women of the night, though he realises that Perle may not have been entirely displeased by the opportunities afforded to him on his walk to Barnard's Inn. The thought unsettles Danby, makes him feel not only young but also slightly foolish and even somewhat unmanly. Perle, his senior by ten years, was a frequent visitor when he was a child, always seeming to occupy a different sphere – a smarter, more worldly sphere – his clothes carrying an exotic scent – lilies, coal smoke, coffee – into the familiar must of his mother's entrance hall. Danby came to think of it as the smell of London, and he catches the slightest hint of it as Perle passes him to take his seat on Peter Woulfe's left.

Danby wonders at the unpleasant feeling in his belly, thinks perhaps that he does not like his cousin.

Peter Woulfe speaks. 'I must thank you, Perle, for bringing young Mr Scott into our company.'

Perle smiles openly, looks generous and alive and says, 'Oh, he is a young man of prodigious' – he taps his head – 'brain, Woulfe. He has been educating away this past decade or more, nose-deep in the natural sciences. My cousin, Marianne, married a man of great learning, and it seems that inclination has descended to his son.'

Danby feels as though his hair has been ruffled by a passing adult and flushes again. Perle, for his part, knows what he has said to be true, while finding it hard to believe that Danby, so recently a snot-nosed youngster – and even today looking the very picture of youth and innocence – could quite have the capacities attributed to him by his mother.

Peter swivels his head, gives all of his considerable attention to Danby again. 'Your father has an interest in natural philosophy?'

'He had a very great interest, sir, and gathered a considerable library, but I regret to say he departed this life when I was but six years of age.'

'But you have occupied yourself in this library?'

'I have, sir.'

Peter nods, as if to say, of course, it is just as he suspected.

Perle suddenly stands up. Gesturing around the room – urbane and yet somehow uncouth at the same time – he says, 'What a collection, Woulfe. What a marvellous collection.'

Peter Woulfe looks around as if he is seeing it all for the first time. This large room, where he has lived and worked for the past twenty years, contains at least five times as much material as it could reasonably be expected to hold. There are seven furnaces in the room, which ought to be impossible, but he has contrived an elaborate flue system, has learned to work in the heat. There are the three long workbenches overflowing with apparatus. And all around him, shelved and in piles on every available surface, there are books, books and more books.

Perle moves towards the nearest workbench, lifts a blue glass jar, replaces it, picks up a shallow dish, sniffs at the contents and puts it back down on the bench. Peter watches with a creeping horror crawling through his belly. He is aghast as Perle surveys his bench, touches his belongings, moves closer to the slim book lying open on the bench.

'Wonderful, Woulfe – wonderful.' Perle picks up the book. '*Mutus Liber.*' He leafs through the book. 'I have heard of it, of course, but this is an unusual edition, I think?'

'Yes,' says Peter Woulfe, and then, thinking the better of it, 'No. In fact, it is quite a common edition, of no great worth.'

Perle brings the book right up to his face, peers at one of the plates.

In the silence that falls, the possibility that Perle will ask to borrow the book floods Peter with panic. He rises and moves to join Perle, taking the book out of his hands and saying, his voice as steady and neutral as he can make it, 'But it is of some senti-mental value to me.' He pauses. 'My uncle gave it to me. When I was a young man.'

'The plates in your edition are well coloured. I have heard there are variations in the editions – some of significant importance.'

Peter Woulfe closes the book.

There is another knock on the door. Peter tucks the book under his arm and crosses the room again. He returns this time with two men. Perle greets George Dunblaine and Timothy Patten cordially and comes to sit at the table. Woulfe slips the book beneath his chair and performs the most perfunctory of introductions, waving his hands vaguely in the direction of his guests – leaving Danby unsure as to which is Dunblaine and which is Patten, and Patten and Dunblaine unsure as to how Danby Scott has come to be here at all.

Danby is suddenly terribly hungry. There are four large covered dishes on the table, but Peter Woulfe has not mentioned them, has not lifted the lids, has not said, *help yourselves, gentlemen.* Danby believes he can detect the smell of kidneys, also fried fish, perhaps lamb chops. He is conscious of a low grumbling in his stomach that will soon build to an audible growl. He thinks he might well die of starvation on the spot.

Now that his eyes have adjusted to the light, he sees that the cloak Peter Woulfe is wearing is ancient-looking and dirty. The fellow he thinks is Dunblaine is shifting restlessly in his chair, his fingers noticeably twitching, and Patten across the table is dark-browed, impatient-looking and distinctly shabby. They have come all the way across London at the crack of dawn, to perform a secret hand-shake, to gain admittance to Peter Woulfe's closely guarded rooms in order to talk about important alchemical matters with Woulfe – and now they find their host distracted and two unfamiliar men in situ. Patten glowers; Dunblaine folds his arms.

Danby considers that, Robert Perle aside, he has rarely seen a more motley gathering of men. What are they about? He knows that they are clever men who have set about important, interesting work. That they have equipment and skills he can only imagine. That there is something ancient and powerful about what they do. He knows it has to do with precious metals and fire and wealth and magic. That these men might be mages – they might be frauds.

But now, whatever they are at, this morning it all looks shabby and shadowy, and he is terribly, terribly hungry.

He suddenly wonders what his mother would make of Peter Woulfe, thinks perhaps he should make enquiries as to Woulfe's family and origins. There is a burr to his voice that suggests some kind of misty foreignness.

Dunblaine removes the lid from the serving dish nearest him; the men begin to help themselves. Danby takes a mouthful of greyish kidney. As he works the food around his mouth, his mood abruptly changes. He begins to enjoy the very fact of being in this unfamiliar place with these unusual men – wishes to explore the room, examine the apparatus on view. Thinks that Dunblaine, who has just passed him the salt, may well be a decent fellow after all. He remembers that Woulfe has received the Copley Medal, is a great friend of General Rainsford.

Abruptly, Peter leans over to him and whispers fiercely, 'You must come again, alone, early on Tuesday – I will demonstrate to you then some of the processes I have devised . . .' His voice falls lower again, so that Danby is not entirely sure that he has heard correctly. '. . . though you must swear on your mother's life not to tell a living soul.'

Chapter Twenty-eight

Barnard's Inn, Fetter Lane, London

Peter Woulfe creeps to the window, anxiety alive in his belly. He stands to the side and peers with his eyes almost closed into the shadows. And sure enough, there he is. Robert Perle standing half obscured by the wall of the court. He is a day early to collect his three guineas. Jagoe, the porter, instructed to let no one past without an appointment, mounted the stairs to tell him he has a visitor with a matter of some importance to discuss. These past two months, Perle has come as agreed on Saturday afternoon. That is bad enough – God knows that is bad enough – but this, whatever this is, it is bound to be worse. He cannot but feel it is to do with the book. The book that Perle sniffed out from a room filled with hundreds of valuable items as the thing he would like to take from Peter Woulfe.

He leans a little forwards, as if a glimpse of the man's face might provide a clue as to how best to proceed. But between the shadows and the distance, and his desire not to be seen peering out the window, Peter cannot make out much more than the fact that Perle still has a face. There is certainly a pale smudge beneath his hat. The fellow is standing quite still, not leaning or slouching or gazing about. And for a moment, the pale smudge of face notwithstanding, he wonders if the figure is quite real. He could be a straw man in Perle's coat, left there in order to distract him from his work.

But a slight shift, from left leg to right, confirms that the figure is flesh and blood. He considers that, if he himself were a different kind of man, he could get his pistol and shoot Perle quite cleanly from window – Peter is a good shot, always has been. It would be quite the easiest thing in one way, but he dismisses the idea as soon as it forms. No, he is not quite mad – no, though the thought did offer some small relief for a moment.

How long will the fellow wait?

Does he intend to besiege him, for heaven's sake? Rainsford's dinner is due to begin in one hour, a select gathering prior to the talk at the Royal Society. Having accepted the invitation, he would not like to miss it. But he cannot very well walk past Perle without acknowledging him. He cannot avoid him if he is to leave Barnard's Inn by any means other than the bedroom window.

A long sigh escapes Peter Woulfe. There is much – *much* – that requires his attention. And he is weary, deeply weary. He is plagued every morning by the boy's face; he is haunted all day long by the flicker of his presence. He regrets – yes, there is no other word for it – he regrets his rage that terrible day, regrets the outcome, which, though he could not have been expected to foresee it, was so very unfortunate. And at this his eyes begin to water. How very different everything ould have been if he had not lost his temper on that foggy day in March. Perle would not be standing outside, for one thing. And the boy himself would be here, quietly helping him with his work.

He has invited young Scott to visit again. That Perle is Scott's cousin is yet another irritant. Why should it always be that what is good and beautiful and true must suffer contagion from the gross and impure?

But Peter Woulfe straightens his spine, sets his jaw. It must be separated out – that is the work of his life, the very essence of the work. And so, on the instant, he decides to admit Perle. He must be dealt with. Peter cannot skulk here in his rooms indefinitely – cannot be distracted from his work, cannot be made to feel like a common criminal. He will summon him up, find out what the fellow wants. He hastens to his door and shouts for Jagoe.

Almost as if he has run up the stairs, Perle appears within moments. 'Good day, Woulfe.'

'Perle.'

Peter Woulfe has seated himself at the head of the empty table. He does not ask Perle to sit down.

'I fear I am not at leisure today. My work aside' – he waves a hand at his workbenches – 'I have an appointment shortly in Cadogan Square.'

'I will not detain you.'

'I understand you have a matter of some urgency you wish to discuss?'

'Yes, a matter that need not delay you for more than a few minutes.'

Perle pulls out a chair and sits down. It is clear now to Woulfe that this is his suffering come to greet him.

He sits quite impassive as Perle leans forwards, elbows on the table. 'It is a simple matter, a small thing.'

Peter knows now that his worst fears are correct.

'There is a book I wish to borrow. With some urgency. To help me with my work.'

Peter holds his voice steady. 'I do not generally lend my books, Mr Perle, but if you wish to consult my library, you are of course welcome.'

Perle nods. 'You have an extensive collection of books – a true scholar's collection. But there is just one book I would like: that slight volume you were kind enough to show me the other day. The *Mutus Liber*.'

Peter thinks again of his pistol – how it could make a nice, neat hole in Robert Perle. It would be the simplest way out, but he cannot bring himself to truly consider it.

Instead, he inclines his head, turn his palms to the ceiling and says, 'You would be more than welcome to it, of course, but unfortunately, I have mislaid it.' He sits back in his chair and gestures helplessly around the vastly cluttered room. 'I'm afraid I have simply no idea where it is.'

Chapter Twenty-nine

27 Craven Street, London

What is it about his cousin's house that Danby Scott so dislikes? He wonders as he sets his foot on the first of the three steps leading to Robert Perle's front door. Perle's house is a substantial, four-storied terraced house on Craven Street. There is a pleasing symmetry of well-built sameness stretching on either side, the hint of rich curtains behind the windows, a bright cleanliness to all the glass. Danby, as yet unfamiliar with the fashionable and not so fashionable parts of London, sees enough to know that Craven Street is more fashionable than not. But the house itself feels somehow wrong to Danby – he cannot put his finger on why, could not put his finger on it during either of his two previous visits. Gorridge admits him, and as he steps into the hall, he wonders if it is that the hall is slightly narrower than it should be for its height, or that the two doors to the left are not exactly evenly spaced? Or it is the smell? He detects something almost metallic underlying the familiar scent of floor wax as he hands over his coat to Gorridge.

Just as he did on both of Danby's earlier visits, Robert Perle emerges abruptly from the basement door behind the stairs. Perle straightens his cuffs and smiles absently at his cousin. Danby notices that he is flushed and slightly breathless as he walks briskly towards the bottom of the stairs and beckons him to join him.

'Come, we will sit upstairs.'

Danby experiences a twinge of disappointment – he has never yet been invited to view Perle's laboratory in the basement, imagines a treasure trove of equipment and all matter of fascinating experiments under way. Though he has never quite understood the nature of Perle's work, he has always understood that it is immensely important and special.

He follows his cousin, and as is his habit every time he climbs any stairs anywhere, he counts the steps as he goes up: ten to the return, two quick steps on the landing and then another nine. Twenty-one – uneven, not a pleasing number to Danby's orderly mind. Robert Perle flings open his drawing-room door.

Accustomed as Danby is to the shabby comfort of his family home, to a house that has had the same excellent furniture for three generations, he is struck by the newness of everything in Perle's drawing room; it is all so bright and clean. Sitting in an overstuffed chair across from his cousin, he has the sense that something is being said, loudly and clearly, by the room and its contents – wonders if he might be going slightly mad to think such a thing, blinks once or twice. It is something to do with the purchase of items, with accumulation, to do with pounds, shillings and pence. No one talks about money at home – not his mother, nor his sisters, and certainly not the rooms or their contents. There is enough of it, and that is all that has ever needed to be said.

'Well!' Perle claps his hands. 'You are well?'

'Yes, thank you. I am.' He forgets about the room and what it might be trying to say. He is well – it is all so enlivening, this new life in London. Everything is to be savoured: plays, coffee-houses, lectures, his new friends, Campbell's sister Diana . . . and he has the appetite for it all. Everything is extraordinary, and he has the immense good luck to be himself, Danby Scott, in the midst of it all.

He almost forgets his manners, but just in time continues, 'And I trust you are well, too?'

'Yes. But busy. Busy with my work, of course, and a number of other matters.'

In the slight pause that follows, Danby realises that his presence must be an interruption to this busy work, wonders if he should offer to leave before he remembers that he has been summoned, so he simply nods and waits.

Perle dives straight in. 'Peter Woulfe is quite the character, isn't he? What do you make of him?'

'Oh, he is a most interesting man. I am to go to his rooms on Tuesday and observe a demonstration.'

Perle's eyes widen; he sits forwards. Like a man suddenly presented with the perfect tools for a difficult job, he feels a flush of excitement. First, the boy's death, and now, his cousin – a subtle extraction device that could be inserted into Peter Woulfe's rooms . . . and perhaps even into his mind.

'Well, you must be sure to remember everything he shows you. I would be most eager to hear all about it. Please pay most careful attention. Take careful notes. Woulfe is . . . exceptional . . . and he has some magnificent possessions, rare items – and a particularly interesting collection of books. You could learn a lot . . . under his wing . . . as it were.'

Danby had almost forgotten about the invitation – it has been a busy whirl of week – but he has a vivid recollection of the extraordinarily cluttered rooms, and an unsettling image of the slow-witted young man pops into his mind.

'It is said . . .' Perle pauses. 'It is said that he knows things that other men do not – has ploughed through the ancients and uncovered great wisdom. Most valuable wisdom . . . though he is shockingly secretive about it all.'

Danby raises his eyebrows and nods slightly.

'You know, don't you,' Perle says patronisingly, 'what it's all about really? All that work, all that time, all that money spent on equipment?'

Danby shrugs – he knows that he doesn't know . . . he doesn't entirely care but is too polite to say so.

Perle's eyes glint. 'Nothing less than eternal youth and endless riches. And by riches, I mean solid, gold riches.' He taps his finger on his thigh to emphasise the last three words.

Danby looks blankly back at his cousin – it is not that he doesn't understand the words Perle is using; it is that he feels so young, so strong and healthy that he cannot imagine ever being anything other than young and strong and healthy. And gold . . . well, gold is good to have, but it does not seem as appealing to him in this moment as Campbell's sister Diana, with her rosebud lips and her big soft eyes . . . unless more gold would help him in his efforts to woo her . . . which he doubts, because she is not that kind of girl . . . at least, he hopes not . . . No, if he is interested in anything, it is in the whiff of magic around Woulfe, the fascinating glimmer of something arcane and mysterious.

Perle says severely, 'You must attend very carefully on Tuesday, observe every detail, take copious notes. Nothing is irrelevant . . . Note every single detail. This is an extraordinary opportunity.'

Looking at Danby's open young face, Perle casts around in his mind. He knows that everyone has a price . . . knows that there is way into every soul . . . . if not through greed, then through fear . . . . . or shame . . . . what, he wonders, is the way into Danby's shiny little soul ? Something to do with his mother? Or his sisters? Some embarrassment? Just what has young Danby been up to, he wonders, with all the temptations of London?

Perle's eyes narrow as he looks at Danby. He considers greed and fear and shame. His cousin sits there, looking offensively innocent. Of course, there is always simple physical pain. It occurs to him with surge of annoyance that, without strapping Danby to a chair in his basement and applying a pincer to his fingernails, he may not be able to make his cousin do what he wants.

Chapter Thirty

Smithfield, London

It has not occurred to Mal Burkiss to feel apprehensive. He feels content and somewhat sleepy. He has just eaten three plum duffs. He has a splinter in the tip of the first finger of his left hand, and he is picking at it with his thumbnail while he waits. It is when Sukie Bulmer enters, leading a broad-shouldered man he has never seen before, that he feels the first prickings of anxiety.

Mal sits at the far side of a small, scrubbed table that is usually lodged against the back wall but has now been pulled into the middle of the room in the manner of a desk. The one-roomed shack is lit by a lamp, and Mal can just make out the man's florid face, can see that he is embarrassed, restless and somewhat suspicious. He is wearing a shiny black coat that has seen better days, strong boots and a soft black hat.

There is one chair and a stool in the room. Mal is occupying the chair, and Sukie ushers the unfamiliar man towards the stool. He steps neatly over it and sits down so that he is facing Mal.

Sukie nods with barely suppressed pride in Mal's direction. 'This is 'im.'

The man grunts, as if he is not yet sure that speech is warranted, as if he will decide for himself rather than take Sukie's word for it.

Mal looks to Sukie, and the certainty in her small, tight face reassures him. She has folded her arms across her chest, and her chin has raised itself somewhat defiantly.

Sukie has told him to keep his mouth shut unless he has something to say, so he nods at the man in greeting.

The man narrows his eyes, looks carefully at Mal and then back at Sukie. 'You stayin'?'

Sukie nods.

He turns back to Mal and appears to reach a decision. He stands up and begins to undo his breeches.

Straight-backed, his eyes on Mal, he lifts his shirt a little to reveal a pale taut belly, pauses a moment and lowers his breeches until the dark hair of his groin appears.

Mal leans towards the man with a blank expression on his face. He is not two inches away when he manages to bring his good eye properly to bear on the goose-egg protuberance extending from the man's lower belly.

'Does it 'urt?' he asks.

'Na.'

'You 'ad it long?'

'Last summer but one.'

Mal raises his head and looks at the man. 'I'm gonna put my 'and on it now.'

The man nods once.

Mal sits back and puts his hand gently on the wen. He closes his eyes and waits for a moment.

When his world has narrowed to the contents of his own head and his awareness of his hand on the wen, he begins to whisper quietly – so quietly that even the man beside him cannot make out a word.

His lips are barely moving, but the sentence is loud and clear in his mind. *Good day, wen – this is Mal here.* He is keen to be polite – as respectful as a gentleman might be to another gentleman. He pauses as if the wen must acknowledge him before they can proceed. In the pause, he feels a heavy sadness coming from the wen – a deep, dispirited sag, as heavy as a sack of coal. He nods gently in response.

Before he can think what to say next, his heart fills with a feeling of strain and exhaustion, and a sigh escapes him. The weariness of the world pulses up his arm and threatens to overcome him. He thinks he might cry. He is torn for a moment between sympathy and fear. He doubts whether it is quite fair to banish this wen, wonders where the sadness will go.

But as he feels the weight begin to lodge in his own stomach, he remembers his task, what he has been asked to do.

He straightens his back and pushes firmly on the wen, says clearly in his mind, no longer with the tone a gentleman might use to another, but as one might speak to a dog awaiting instructions, *No. Not here. No. You must go away.*

His brow has furrowed into a frown; he looks quite fierce. He is determined to wait, if need be, until there can be no mistaking his decision, no skulking return. *You cannot stay here.*

And the sadness lifts from his chest, retreats down his arm as he pushes his hand firmly against the wen.

He waits a moment, with his eyes still closed, until he feels nothing, then opens his eyes and looks up at the man.

The man's florid face is wet with tears. He looks down at Mal, his eyes bright and shocked.

Mal moves his hand, and they look together at the man's belly.

The wen is still there, exactly as it was before; the man touches it himself and then looks to Mal, says in shaky voice, 'It's still there.'

Mal nods. 'It don't work just like that. Sudden. It'll take some time.'

'Oh.' The man is wide-eyed and damp, like a new-washed babe.

Mal says kindly, setting his hand on the man's shoulder, 'You can come back, come back 'ere, if it ain't gone in time.'

Sukie steps forwards, and the man begins to gather his breeches, shakily tying them closed, tucking in his shirt.

She says firmly, not unkindly, 'There'll be a charge for a second visit, though, mind you.'

The man nods and fumbles for his coin purse.

'And come along . . . there's others waiting to see 'im.'

$\backsim$

The next morning, Sukie waits while Mal sleeps. He is flat out – inert, like something that has fallen a from a height. His head is on her pillow – her soft grey pillow, which he bled all over that first morning in March, the blood seeping right through into the stuffing, leaving a dark-brown stain on the cover. She has turned it around so that she cannot see it, but she knows it's there.

Sukie does not like sharing anymore; she has had a lifetime of it – sharing cramped rooms, beds, mattresses, blankets, pisspots, crumbling pies torn in half, mugs of small beer passed back and forth, getting flatter and flatter until the last mouthful is as warm as spit. It is her feeling around sharing that has led her to live alone in Dan Rutter's shack off Smithfield. It is shelter in so far as it keeps out some of the rain. The wind blows through almost unabated, nearly lifting the roof at times, pressing up with a swell that Sukie fears could set the whole place to flight.

It is not much warmer than the street. True, she can light a fire, and the walls hold in a bit of heat along with the smoke – but more than that, the thin timber walls enclose a space she can call her own. It has been hers for a decade now, and if there was comfort to be made in such a place, Sukie has made it. She has stuffed rugs into the walls in certain places – and not just any old rags but colours she likes, stuffed neatly with care so that the blues and greens are around her head when she sleeps and the reds and browns are behind the chair. The chair itself she bought from a bleary lost-looking Irish man two summers ago, and it was only afterwards that she wondered if he had brought it all the way from wherever he was from only to sell it for thruppence? It is light-framed, with a rush woven seat, moulded by now to support Sukie's arse in perfect comfort.

There's the one pot, the stand for it, the poker hanging neatly on its hook. One cup, one dish and a sack on a nail by the end of the bed that holds her clothes.

And it is as she sits in her chair and looks at the boy asleep in her bed that she runs her mind over herself, trying to identify the unfamiliar feeling that is colouring her morning.

Mal is covered by her grey blanket and her brown shawl – and without the shawl around her shoulders, she is colder than normal. But it is not coldness – no, not a matter of the temperature. It is this proximity to another person, a proximity that does not feel like something taken away. In fact, it feels like fullness, like having had just enough to eat. And she breathes very gently while she approaches this feeling, links it to food, savours it – does not move even an inch for fear of disturbing it.

⁓

They are coming every morning now – enough of them to block the way, so that yesterday, crab-faced Eliza shouted in at Sukie that it wasn't fucking Bartholomew Fair as she pushed past, swinging her stick. Sukie puts her head out and counts twenty-eight folk waiting, making a fierce racket with their chat, five of the women carrying babies. One of them at the front of the queue holds a red-cheeked creature emitting a ceaseless howl, her face blank and distant as if she cannot hear at all anymore. There's an old woman half bent over her crutch, a man with two sticks, and a younger woman, her face almost yellow, sitting on a stool with an anxious-looking girl hovering beside her. Twenty-eight times half a shilling – fourteen shillings – and for the most part handed over so willingly that she wonders if they shouldn't make it more.

Sukie sees the man with the sticks begin to wobble, until a woman behind pulls him upright with a yank at his coat. But by consensus, the woman with the roaring baby enters first – Sukie sees that she is neatly dressed, her brown gown old but clean, her hair pulled back – the width of her pale, flat cheeks belying the thinness of her arms and waist.

She thrusts the infant at Mal and whispers desperately, 'I think there's something wrong with him – something bad in him.'

Mal takes the child in his two hands, holding it out in front of him, and the crying stops on the instant. The mother lets out an *oooh* of relief, and her eyes begin to glisten.

Mal echoes the sound *oooh*, does not take his eyes from the child, its blotched red face, swollen and puffy, eyes lost under furrowed brows, its thin dark hair starting up from its head. He feels the body between his hands, as tight as drum, his two thumbs almost meeting across the chest. Without thinking, he repeats *oooh*, and the two women watch, entranced.

The infant squirms and releases a fart like a cannon's roar; its eyes open in surprise. In the following moments, the sounds of an enormous, wind-filled, explosive bowel movement fill the room. A fetid smell follows.

Sukie covers her mouth with her hand, looks at the mother and begins to laugh.

The mother speaks quietly, in a tight, tearful voice. 'Well, you may laugh – well, you may – and I with my wits almost gone after a week of it, and five others at home and my husband at sea . . .' And her voice catches on a sob. 'What if he starts again?'

Mal raises his gaze to her and turns the infant carefully to show the drooping head, the chest heaving, his breath catching between slow, relieved sighs. Mal smiles wide and crooked, his right eye looking at the door, his left straight at the mother. 'He's let it all out now, ain't he?'

And he begins to laugh quietly, his shoulders hunching, his eyes narrowing, the sound *oooh oooh oooh* now rising and falling between silent spasms of laughter. His chest hurts, tight and sharp like knives digging in, and tears spring to his eyes. He cannot remember the last time he laughed like this.

The next day, there are more than Sukie can count, the narrow alley thronged and the babble of voices filling the air. This time,

Sukie sees that there are more of the truly stricken – a girl with twisted limbs slumped in a barrow, making loud animal sounds, and three young women around her attending to her drool – laughing amongst themselves in between times, seeming, despite it all, to be glad to be standing about together on this bright day.

Mal, for his part, waits inside for them as he has done every morning this past week – and as each person walks in, he tries to let the last person go completely, so that there will be room inside him, in a space that he imagines as a small, sunny room, for the next person and their woes.

He is inordinately hungry these days. He would eat his weight every day if Sukie could supply him fast enough. Eels, beef and oyster pies, apples – though he prefers apples cooked and grimaces just a little if they are bitter – Williams pears, baked spuds.

She watches as he stuffs one plum duff after another into his mouth, and while it is surely greed of the first order, he eats with the simple relish of a small child, a smile of pleasure shaping his chewing lips, so that Sukie cannot mind it at all, though she wonders how she will buy enough for him, worries that he will simply eat every penny he brings in, and then they will be back where they started.

⌒

Sukie notes the shift as sure as if the weather itself has changed. How she tells, she couldn't say right off – Don Stander doesn't smile quickly as usual when she passes him, but it isn't that alone. Old Eliza does smile, but not quite in the right way . . . All the same, it is nothing that you could catch as clear as day – just a feeling. An old, unsafe feeling that creeps up her bones and tells her that not a soul in this warren by Smithfield would stand by her if she had need of them. Not one of them, though she has lived peaceful and clean in her shack now for ten years, argued with no one, kept her own counsel.

This knowledge does not land with a sadness – for she has an ancient view on these things, a view extending as far as the stars and back, somehow tied up with the implacable movement of the river tides and the way the seasons follow in turn, so that matters of the everyday, such as death and hunger, violence and injustice, seem all of a size.

But it is not quite the same now that Mal has come – while she has long been accustomed to seeing her own frail-boned life as an autumn leaf in the wind, she has an altogether different feeling about him. She loves his body as if it were a precious thing. It is no one bit of him as such – though it is his soft, wide shoulders and his round, cheerful face, the nutty colour of his hair. It is not simply the look in his eyes, nor indeed the cast in his eye, but it is something to do with the light that catches there when he smiles. And then there is the way he has about him, how he moves so softly and quietly, how he is ready at all times to be pleased with whatever bit of food she gives him, how they sit together so peacefully – no, it is not the same now, with him about. She would not like to see him hurt or fooled – broken down into less than he is.

So, she is frightened, frightened by this feeling that they are no longer safe. She has long known there is danger in not having enough: you can be summed up to the price of the nothing you own – you can weigh so light on the scales as to be brushed off like dust – but she knows, too, that there is danger in having. Folk don't like to see it. Especially not when they have you marked down for nothing.

So, what she sees is that Don Stander, old Eliza, Tom the Ducks and probably Pat High Beecham, too, have all started to sum up the custom standing in a rowdy line outside her door – started to count the coins flowing in. And while they do not know that she has them in a jar under the third board beneath her bed, it would not take much for anyone to find it if they had a mind to – to simply come and take it for themselves if they so decided.

The solution to that is to pay a burly fellow, to have it known they are under protection. She has avoided such matters for many years, needed no protection but that which she had by virtue of having so little that no one would bother to rob her.

Then again, if someone were to take her coins, they could always get more. No, she realises it is not the coins as such that she is worried about. It is Mal – their little life, their quiet evenings eating and sitting.

Chapter Thirty-one

Barnard's Inn, Fetter Lane, London

Peter Woulfe sits by the light of one candle and opens the *Mutus Liber*.

Leafing back and forth through the book, he gazes again at the images he has decoded over more than three decades of careful study. He has followed the secret instructions lurking beneath the images in each individual plate; he has devised endlessly ingenious experiments to fulfil these instructions.

He has had success: he has isolated the extraordinarily volatile salt of the dew, a tremendous achievement. But the lapis evades him – the stone that will turn lead into gold, death into life, the substance that will render the imperfect perfect, the impure pure.

He has read so many books – bigger, thicker more complicated books full of arcane and immensely important text – and yet he still returns to this slim, cardboard-covered volume. It is almost childish – a book of pictures, with no text. A stubbornly mute book. How many times can he return to it and expect to find something new? How many chances can he possibly have before time runs out altogether and death comes, as surely it must?

He sighs and puts his hand to his brow. The air in the room is thick; his brow is clammy. It has been so long since he has even had the time to take a walk – the last time he considered it, he could not find his hat.

For a rare and fleeting moment, Peter Woulfe sees himself as another person might see him: crouched intently by his candle in this hot, smelly room with his worn, stained book. As perhaps Mal might see him if he were to look just now. And a shocked little tremor runs through him – because he looks old – old and alone. Very alone, here in the night with the curtains drawn and his one flickering candle – because, though it embarrasses him to admit it, even to himself, he does not want to take his book out in the daylight in case Perle somehow appears and takes it from him. Yes, Mal, looking from above or glancing over from his place by the fire, would see him as old and alone and foolish – but then of course, the lad couldn't possibly understand. No one he has yet met truly understands.

And suddenly he doesn't even understand it himself. A chill wind stirs around his heart. What if none of it makes sense at all? What if he has wasted his life on a foolish, expensive endeavour that has left him old, alone and barely able to breathe in this impossibly stuffy room? What if it is not just his own scrubby soul, his own lack of good works, that has prevented his success? What if . . . the terrible thought creeps in . . . what if the entire enterprise is simply impossible and therefore foolish in and of itself? Gold from lead, the pure from the impure – what if this thing that he is trying to do, this endless, careful, skilled work bringing material substances back to their purest state, is simply a fool's game? A charlatan's own unwitting self-deception?

He stands up abruptly. It is unbearable – he must find his hat; he must take a walk. He can see himself striding through the dark London streets with the cool slap of wind on his cheeks, striding along and arriving at an altogether fresher, less odious conclusion.

He begins to search for his hat – moving papers, books, bottles and jars, soiled cloths and dusty rocks – and as he searches, his fingers remember the exact feeling of the felted brim, so that everything else he touches feels quite wrong. He searches and searches, but no matter how he searches, he cannot find it, and if he cannot find his hat, he might well be a fool, and if he is a fool . . . well, then he could be a self-deceiving charlatan engaged in a ludicrous undertaking. Oh, he groans, it is impossible to work it all out alone. Someone else should know where his hat is – the dead boy would probably know; he would simply hand him his hat, and then he could take a walk in the dark and arrive at a much better conclusion.

In fact, if Mal were here now, he might try to explain it all to him – explain it to him as he never did when he was alive, tell him that this work to bring substances back to their perfect, golden state is nothing less than the sacred endeavour to purify Soul and Spirit. His own Soul, yes, and his poor tired Spirit . . . yes . . . but not just *his* Soul, not just *his* Spirit. *All* Soul. *All* Spirit. And so he has worked and worked here in this room, for decades and decades, in order to redeem the entire imperfect world. That is what he would say to the boy – he would say, *spiritus mundi, anima mundi!* And even as he imagines explaining it, as he imagines Mal's face turned to him with an open, interested expression, he begins to remember. Something spreads through him from his heart, pulsing like an insistent, reassuring whisper: truth and beauty, spirit and soul, angels on earth, men in heaven – it is all promised; it is all possible.

Surely, there is something true and beautiful underneath all this chaos . . . something golden and good that can emerge when things are put in the right order, when the right method is applied, when divine energy is channelled? There must be. This is the promise of the ancients – concealed and encoded for the worthy to uncover through their labours. This is the promise, and it must be true.

⁓

He crosses the room back to where he started, to where the book lies open. He has always particularly loved the way the images look in candlelight, the animation of shadow and flame across the page. Sometimes in this half-light, it is as if the figures are looking right at him, willing him to understand. He considers the book anew as he stands there without his hat. It strikes him for the first time that none of the people in the book labour alone.

What he needs is the presence of a person with a pure, bright aura to act as a conduit for the cosmic energy so necessary for success in this enterprise – someone who could also provide an antidote to his own feelings of despair and doubt. He forgets about his hat, forgets about the walk – if he were to start from a different beginning, with young Scott here in the room, perhaps then the outcome might be different.

∽

'You may observe, but I beg of you not to speak. Stand please.' Peter Woulfe takes Danby Scott gently by the shoulders and steers him two paces to the right. 'Here in the east. Yes, excellent. The reddish-gold hair' – he gestures – 'your youth – yes, here in the east.' He moves him another two inches to the right. 'Excellent . . . Now, don't move' – he pauses with his fingers to his lips and considers – '. . . unless the sun goes down. Yes, in that eventuality, you may move, I suppose.'

By Danby's reckoning, the sun is not due to go down for at least ten hours, but he says nothing.

Peter turns back suddenly and says fiercely, 'You do understand, don't you? What this is all about? *Spiritus mundi! Anima mundi!*'

Danby nods, his eyes wide. 'Of course.'

Peter stands with his palms open to the heavens and closes his eyes. The room is vibrating around him. He feels ballooning within him a sense of hope that he has not felt for a very long time. He allows his mind to settle, thinks clean and blank thoughts.

He must harness the secret salt fire and begin the purification. He must find his way back to the red earth of Adam before the fall. He must create order from disorder, starting here and now in this very room with Danby Scott standing in the east.

He prays to God, to all the angels. *Come now; help me now.*

And then it comes to him – comes to him as a shape. A shape he does not have a name for – he has never seen precisely this shape before, but it feels immediately familiar to him. A wonderfully complex shape that will contain the whole process in space and time.

Instantly, he knows the materials he will require to make this shape manifest – the crucibles and glass bottles he will use . . . he can see the angle and length of the tubes that will connect the bottles. He sees the flame of his burner, the heat of his furnaces. He sees the shape in time, the darkness and the light that will divide the days – days that cannot be rushed – the days it will take for the distillation, for the firing, for the digestion. In one instant, he intuits a perfect circularity from aim to goal, and the beauty of it causes his breath to fall still, as if undue movement might disturb the balance.

He inhales; he forgets to breath out. He selects a tall glass bottle from the shelf above his bench. He begins. Time disappears.

It is forty-five minutes in mortal time before Danby Scott moves very, very quietly to sit on the arm of the chair behind him; it is another fifty-six minutes before he leans back a little and knocks over the tower of books and papers that had been precariously stacked on the seat of the chair.

He jumps up guiltily. 'I beg your pardon, Mr Woulfe. I beg your pardon – my fault entirely. Let me . . . I will just put it all back . . . the way it was.' He begins to gather the books, the papers that have spread across the floor.

Peter looks over at him from a long way away. He had forgotten all about him; he has, in this moment, forgotten even his name, but all the same, as he watches the young man scrambling to gather the books, the skittish pages sliding across the floor, something in him softens. He sees Danby's youth, his flushed, embarrassed face, remembers suddenly the impatience of youth, the endless embarrassments, and thinks sadly, *oh, he should be out chasing girls and drinking too much beer with his friends; he should not be standing here watching something he cannot possibly understand.*

And so he dismisses him.

'So good of you to come, Mr Scott, but perhaps you would be happier returning another day – when I am less distracted by my work.'

There is no way around it. He must continue alone. No one can help him now.

Chapter Thirty-two

27 Craven Street, London

'Well?' Perle says. 'Well?'

Back in Perle's drawing room, beholding his cousin's smooth, eager face, sitting on the same overstuffed chair he sat on last time, Danby thinks, *never again. I am never coming here again, cousin or no.*

'Well? What did you see, boy? What did you learn? What is he up to?'

'Oh, I'm afraid I could not make head nor tail of it, cousin. It is all very' – Danby waves his hands – 'obscure.'

'It is, and it isn't. You must focus on the details. It is all in the detail. What exactly did he do? What materials did he use? What equipment?'

'Oh, I'm afraid I can't remember.'

'You remember nothing? Surely that is not possible?'

Danby shrugs.

'Did you take notes?'

'No, I did not.'

A vein begins to throb in Perle's temple. 'I told you to take notes.'

Danby shrugs again.

'You must go again next week, and this time you must take notes.'

'I might.'

'You must.' Perle thinks of all the beautifully sharp implements in his basement. Tempting but impractical. Instead, he will put out some feelers, some delicate, nuanced feelers and see what tender spots his young cousin might have that he can probe. He simply cannot be as incorruptible as he looks.

Danby looks away towards the window, indicates the sky beyond with a vague nod and stands up.

'Forgive me – I have another appointment shortly.'

Eighty-two seconds and twenty-one quick steps down the stairs later, Danby looks out onto Craven Street and inhales the dungy air with relief – no, he will not visit Robert Perle again, and now that he has had time to consider it, he will not visit Peter Woulfe again either. It is all a bit odd and unseemly, and he has other much more pleasing things to attend to. All this talk of Soul and Spirit is better suited to church on a Sunday – and that leaves the rest of the week for study and play.

A little shiver comes over him. He is better off out of it all. Magic or no.

Chapter Thirty-three

Smithfield, London

It is approaching midnight, and the sun has not long fallen after a day of fierce, stifling heat. Mal Burkiss, slumped in Sukie Bulmer's chair, feels the pull of sleep as though the contents of his mind are a sea yielding to the moon. Sukie has wedged the door tight – there is trouble stirring in the city; the apprentices are out with flaming torches.

Mal, too, has heard the low, angry hum of a small, distant mob, but he is unperturbed. It is far away and going in the other direction, and with the door closed, he feels as safe as a creature curled in its shell.

An urgent fist bangs on the flimsy door.

The gentleman who fills the doorway is all cloak and coins, his voice like a hammer on an anvil, his money clinking in the purse he swings before them. A sheen of sweat coats his pale face. He dips his head under the low beam, flicking his cloak to reveal a girl clasped tightly under his arm. At first, it seems his arm is bound tight lest she might fall – Mal then realises it is lest she might run. The lantern Sukie raises casts a wavering light on her, and he sees she is long-nosed and angular, foal-like, her head swinging, her feet alive on the floor. Mal is flooded with fear as they enter. Oh, the terror these two creatures have brought with them. For a moment, he can hardly breathe.

'Well, boy? Well? I have heard great things of you. If you can help my daughter, I will reward you handsomely.' He thrusts a handful of coins towards Sukie, who swiftly pockets them in a purse around her neck.

Up close, Mal can see the whites of her eyes flashing as they spin like marbles, the corners of her mouth burbling with foam. Her head, her eyes, her feet-all appear to operate independently of one another. There is no rhythm; instead, a chaotic fluidity pulls her first one way and then the other – the only line he can follow is her father's arm curving like a steel band around her shoulder, riveted by his fierce white fingers on her arm. Without it, Mal imagines she would break into pieces and go spinning off in every which way.

The gentleman's eyes are dark and bright, his voice fast and sure. 'What is it you must do? Can you do it now? It is a matter of the greatest urgency. I will hold her still.'

Mal puts his hand out slowly – not to touch her, just to close the gap a little – and casts himself out, more tentatively than usual, to see if he can find her. But he finds only waters running frantically in and out, soft, slipping sand sucking him down, a fierce wind shrieking and howling from all sides. There is no one there, no one he can meet tonight, in this furious elemental storm.

When he has reeled himself in, coming back with relief to the safe shores of his own body and mind, Mal Burkiss turns to the man in the cloak, speaks to him with uncharacteristic firmness as if he were an equal. 'I can't help her this night.'

As the words come out and the man's face comes into focus, he remembers this is a gentleman, remembers the fury and half ducks his head, as if expecting a blow.

And sure enough, the man raises his free hand, clenched to a fist. 'You have not tried. You must try harder.'

'I can't. Not now.' He would like to say how it pains him to fail this girl in her distress, but that would require more words than he has ever spoken together, so he simply shakes his head.

'I will not pay you to simply stand there and shake your head, boy.'

And Mal sees that the man is almost equally divided between the great, fear-filled force he is applying to his right arm and the fury animating his left.

Sukie moves closer, reclaims the man's coins from her purse hanging around her neck and offers them back.

Into the silence comes the girl's voice, high and childish, words all akimbo, one sentence tripping on the other. 'Oh, is it you? Is it *you?*

Well, I declare.' Her head swivels to Mal Burkiss; she catches one of his eyes firmly with hers. She continues, 'I tell you, madam. And when we arrive at my aunt's, there will be pudding. God so wills it. And his angels. Do you like my gown? Whip you so whippen, until your mother wills it, like a soft, soft flower. Flowery flowerery ow-ee ...' The words lose themselves in a stream of animal sound: *eeee ooooow eee oooooow.*

She begins to buck and twist under her father's grip, and Mal looks to meet his gaze – he is preparing to say that he will try again soon, perhaps even on the morrow, when he sees how the angry mouth has gone slack with horror and helplessness. Mal sees fat, incongruous drops of tears shining on the pale cheeks.

The gentleman speaks now in a tight, desperate voice. 'You must help her, as God is my witness, or we will not survive another night.'

The girl's feet slide; her body twists, and with a crash that shakes the cabin, father and daughter are suddenly on their knees.

He shouts to be heard above the girl's howling. 'I tell you, her mother will be at the bottom of the river by sunrise, and we two will not be far behind her.'

He is now holding his daughter with both arms as she wrestles and writhes. He looks up helplessly at Sukie and Mal, and for a moment Mal sees the boy he must have been, before his mouth tightens again, and with an angry gesture, he opens his arms and releases his daughter.

The girl takes off in a crazed whirling motion, flying around, circling the shack like a dervish. The table and chair are over-turned. She plucks frantically at the rags stuffed in the walls – her hands seeming to operate independently of her swinging torso – all the time issuing a high, inhuman howl. As she flings herself and their few belongings around, Sukie Bulmer fears for the very walls. She finds, to her surprise, that she would like to kick the gentleman kneeling on her floor, would like to send her foot swinging into his well-clad gut and punish him for bringing this horror to her door.

The noise and the motion of the girl fill the room, changing the beat of time, the sense of space, until it seems as if the floor itself is moving, and it is as if Sukie and Mal and the gentlemen in the cloak are the crew on a storm-struck ship.

Mal Burkiss's gaze follows the girl's movement, a fraction behind, as if his habitual slowness cannot keep pace. In fact, his attention is on what he sees as the swirling trails of colour unfurling behind her, twirling in and out like so many airborne snakes – as alive and livid in their movement as the girl herself. He sees deep sorrow sliding over red-hot rage, the unrestrained force of puckish play, livid fear and a fierce energy that is the lust for life itself – all these battling and twisting round the room, open-mouthed, feeding on each other, voraciously mating and spawning, filling the room with new versions of themselves.

He knows that, if he does not stay very still, he will risk a bite, but as still as he stands, something latches on. He is conscious at first of feeling hungry – a fierce, specific hunger for a food he cannot recall. And fast, too fast on the heels of this hunger, comes a rush of paralysing sorrow, and now Mal – swinging so fast between these extremes fears for his very soul – says out loud with quiet fierceness, 'No. No, get off – get off me. Go away!'

He turns to the gentleman, who has got to his feet, who stands with his arms half raised as if to protect himself, and he sees at once that this is a weak and foolish man – for all his cloak and coin, for all his fatherly concern.

Into Mal Burkiss's clean, soft mind comes the memory of a boy in the foundling home who screamed in his sleep, fought with demons all night long, a boy who was so shattered in his waking hours that he could heed no instruction, shook like a frightened animal, fought with everyone and was beaten like a dog.

Mal addresses the man. 'What's happened to her?'

He turns to Mal with a sudden flash of fury. 'You will not question me, boy. Can you fix her? That is all I need to know from you. Can you fix her?'

The girl falls silent, pauses in her frantic motion and drops to the floor like a stone.

Mal's stomach plunges in horror; a cold, hopeless terror fills his veins. For a moment, it threatens to sink him entirely – but instead he steps forwards.

She lies there, curled up on her side, breathing fast, her eyes open.

He crouches down, turns her head gently towards him, looks into her eyes and says what he knows to be true. 'Dear . . . girl . . . dear,' he whispers – the words do not come easy to him. 'It is not your fault, dear girl.'

He moves slowly to lay his hand on her shoulder. She receives his touch, meets his eye as if she has just seen him for the first time and smiles.

'Dear . . . girl . . .' he repeats. His hand stays on her shoulder. 'I know it is not your fault.'

The room fills with a thin, high silence. Nobody moves.

The girl looks around at the shack, her gaze resting for a moment on Sukie and then on her father.

Recognising him, she speaks quite clearly: 'Papa?'

'Sophie?' He leans forwards, his eyes wide.

She looks around again with a smile. 'Papa?'

'Sophie? . . . Sophie? How do you feel, Sophie?'

'I feel quite well all of a sudden, Papa.' She moves to sit up and gazes at him with a calm smile.

Her father stands frozen.

She repeats, 'I feel quite well, Papa.'

He steps forwards, blinking. 'You feel . . . quite well?'

'Yes, Papa.'

'That is . . . very good, Sophie. Very good.'

'Yes, Papa.' She looks around at the shack. 'And I know now what to do about all our troubles. It is simple. I must stay here.'

He runs his hand across his eyes. 'It is very good, Sophie, very good.'

'Yes, and now I will stay here and always be well.' She indicates Mal and Sukie with a nod of her head. 'With them.'

'It is very good, Sophie, very good. But of course, you cannot stay here. I will bring you home now, in a moment – and we can come again.'

'No, I don't want to go home. I want to stay here.'

'Sophie, child, of course we must go home. You cannot stay here.'

'No, Papa, I will not go home – I must stay here.'

'We will go home, Sophie, but we can return.'

'No, I will stay here.' She turns her head to look at Mal. 'With him.' She looks down at his hand on her shoulder and smiles.

Her father says roughly to Mal, 'Get your hand off her at once.'

'I don't want to go, Papa. I want to stay here.'

'I said, get your hand off her.'

Mal slowly withdraws his hand. The girl begins to shriek. The shack fills again with intolerable, inhuman noise.

The father covers his ears with his hands, turns furiously to Mal and roars above the noise, 'What have you done to her? What did you say to her? What trick have you played?'

Mal says slowly, 'You must bring her back tomorrow.'

'I must, must I?' His dark eyes narrow. He looks around him, at the shack, at Sukie. 'Oh! Oh, I see! I see what you're about . . . I see what you are at. I see it now.'

He steps forwards and scoops his daughter up forcefully. Sophie's shriek has become a howl.

His eyes glistening, his voice shaking with fury, the father turns to Mal. 'You, boy, are a trickster. You are nothing more than a scrubby little thief. I will have you hanged.'

He barrels his way out, almost breaking the door and leaving it swinging behind them. He strides down the lane with his daughter in his arms, and the last they hear is her voice rising into the warm night.

There are many ways for people like Mal Burkiss to end up in gaol – all told, in fact, it is more likely than not. One way is to try to cure the daughter of an angry, wealthy gentleman.

It is mid-morning on the following day – a day of fierce, bright heat – when the thief-catchers arrive. They are fast and sure in their movements – strong-armed, precise and relentless in their grasp – and even if the thought had come fast enough, there is no chance to run.

Abruptly, Mal plunges into his own private sea and is thus cushioned from the noise and violence of his arrest. He sees what is happening, all right; he hears it, too, feels the rough hands on him – but what he sees and hears is dulled, and the hands that reach for him come towards him as if through soft green water.

Sukie Bulmer, however, is fully present and feels with painful clarity the fingers clamped on her thin, old arms, feels her utter helplessness with a crashing sense of horror. As she watches Mal being shackled not two feet away from her, his hair standing up, his soft, wandering eyes gone dull and confused, the ache in her old chest makes her fear that her heart will break apart right on the spot.

Chapter Thirty-four

Newgate Gaol, London

The cold, dark walls are slick with the condensing breath of two hundred men – walls that have been untouched by sunlight since the dark-beamed roof first went on four centuries ago. It is as well to call this gaol cell a cave, for the stones that form it and the men who inhabit it know no difference. The stink of men and shit and piss is such that the gaolers cover their faces with cloth before opening the door. The thick oak door has long forgotten it ever grew, has turned black and shiny, sits snug and remorseless in its deep recess.

Mal Burkiss, crouching by the door, touches the wood as if it were a friend, traces the ridges of old growth rings with his fingers. When he sleeps, which is most of time, he hears the sweet chatter of birds, the rustle of small creatures he has never seen in his waking hours and so cannot name – though he is sure they have small, bright eyes and soft, inquisitive noses.

He is both there in the damp, stinking cave and not there at all. It is as if, for the past three days since the thief-takers came, he has been holding his breath. His heartbeat has slowed; his skin has gone cool and clammy. It is not the stench that poses the greatest risk to him, noisome as it is, not the wailing and shrieking that assaults his ears – no, there is something far more dangerous to him in the foul ether of Newgate. Should he surface, Mal Burkiss, enclosed in a cave with the anguish of a hundred broken men, risks nothing less than the complete annihilation of his soul.

∾

Sukie Bulmer makes her way to Newgate Gaol. Head down, her cloak over her head, fleet-footed as though she were twenty years younger, she hugs the walls, stays in the shadows, moves silently – wills herself invisible. She knows well it is too late to visit Mal, and already today, early in the morning, she brought him an oyster pie that she fears was eaten by the pock-faced guard – but her every instinct is to be near him this night. The world is breaking apart. She has seen many strange things in her life, many terrifying things, but nothing to match this.

The mob has been gathering itself over four days – reproducing and expanding, getting louder and more reckless, and now on this bright, hot night, it is building to a consuming crescendo. The air is filled with the shriek and crackle of a hundred buildings aflame. The voice of the mob is a terrifying roar, threatening to devour all who cross its path, and underneath this roar – a tone deeper, terrifyingly audible to Sukie but not to everyone – is a guttural howl that rises and falls with an ancient, animal force.

Every person she has seen this night looks transformed – some by fear and some by fury. Men racing along, their breath fast and urgent, the ground shaking with the force of their feet. Women striding and shrieking, their arms waving, their skirts tucked up, as if a wildness has spread like a contagion through the populace.

Anyone with wealth to lose stays shut up inside, praying to their God that this fever will pass them by. Everywhere, doors are barred, windows shuttered. Many have hung out blue flags to support the mob, to mark themselves as fit for deliverance.

'Go home, old woman, and shut your door if you have one,' pants a plump, red-faced man who scurries past her. 'All hell has broken loose.'

And to be sure, it seems as if some long-shut gate has indeed burst open, allowing the straining fury of the damned to escape and rampage amongst the citizenry. Hungry flames lick up towards the sky, and a strange pinkish glow, quite independent of the fires, appears to come from the stones beneath the city – and what could that be if not the fires of hell stoked up?

As Sukie Bulmer makes her way through the city, it becomes clear that she is heading towards the very heart of the chaos. As she nears the gaol, there is something different in the eyes of the men and women – a furious intent, a concentrated, righteous rage. The guttural howl gets louder; the rhythm speeds up. Self-preservation should send Sukie straight back to the shack by Smithfield if she had a whit of sense, but yet she pushes forwards.

Newgate Gaol looms before her. The night sky behind it is on fire; a great heaving mass of people is gathered outside.

She blinks her old eyes. It looks as if there are flames issuing from the very windows. Roaring, whooping, screeching like demons, the mob has torn into the gaol itself.

The men and women forming the thick throng outside the gaol – the ones who have not breached the fortress – are voluble and delirious. They stand perched on the very edge of something, willing their braver, stronger fellows forwards – they are more excited, more aroused by what they are witnessing than the men bent to the physical work of tearing the place asunder. Crying out and swaying, a collective pulse running through them, they are urging the head of the beast forwards with a ravenous desire. No fire could be big enough, no destruction satisfying enough, to sate this vast and furious hunger.

Sukie Bulmer dips her head, lowers her shoulders and plunges into the crowd. Her body is rendered younger, more fluid than it has been for many a year as she begins to force her way forwards. It is not that she thinks her proximity will save Mal from the cataclysm unfolding before her. No, she is not thinking at all, simply following the thread that runs from her heart to his.

She pushes and dips, sidles and shoves, uses her elbows, aims a kick here and there at an unmoving shin – takes tiny sips of air, goes head first for the most part and allows her body to squeeze through after.

But all of a sudden, she cannot breathe. She is held fast between a large man's lower back and a rigid chest behind her. She tries to dip, tries to edge sideways, tries to straighten up, tries to catch a breath of air – but there is no movement vouchsafed to her, not one fraction of an inch to allow her ribcage to expand. She cannot breathe; her heart has not enough room to beat. And she is held like this for longer than she can bear.

With a final great effort, she pushes back with all her strength – but nothing happens; she has no more room, and her strength is fading. Suddenly, she feels old and weak and foolish. She can feel her mind beginning to mist over.

And she prepares to yield, to allow the life to flow right out of her, to die here, half upright, wedged between this shiny grey coat stinking of tobacco and the iron-fast ribcage pushing against her ear. She thinks she will not even hit the ground for many an hour, will only topple over quite stiff when the crowd begins to disperse in some unimaginably distant future.

But the man in the grey coat moves his arm, and a space opens up, bringing a gust of what feels like fresh air and enough room to inhale it. And then, what seemed impossible is possible again – she propels herself forwards, under his arm, into a softer place, a more open place, where the heat of the crowd around her seems a warm fog compared to the fierce glow emitting from the fortress in front of her.

And what she sees now is not the familiar building of Newgate Gaol but rather a primitive, rugged shape appearing to have emerged out of the earth. This is the source of the guttural howl – a tearing, shrieking animal roar, as if the earth is birthing herself.

There are bright figures, the force of their shoulders turned bull-like, barrelling through the great arched opening. Flame-thrown shadows cast high into the night sky give the figures vast, angular wings. One immense man, shouting instructions, waving his arms, seems to have flames issuing from his very hands.

Sukie Bulmer, her mouth hanging open with the shock of recognition, knows she has been here before, has witnessed this very scene.

She recognises the bright figures, almost calls out to them by name, with ancient syllables just on the tip of her tongue. These are no mere mortal men but avenging angels. And she knows for certain now that this is not hell at all; it is the other place. Heaven in all its dreadful, righteous glory.

Out through the flame-blackened stone comes a stream of blinking prisoners – some shuffling in irons, others walking unsteadily with an air of wonderment. Men from one side, women from the other, converging in a confused huddle. The crowd begins to roar its approval, makes a path for them, and so they come, hundreds and hundreds of them, some bewildered, some lit up by the same wild ecstasy of the liberators. One young man walks along between the surging crowd, waving his fist in the air, as if accepting tribute.

She does not see Mal until he is nigh upon her, but he has seen her, has picked her out in the darkness from amongst the gathered hundreds.

He comes up to her and touches her arm gently. 'Here I am.'

And Sukie Bulmer reaches out, pushes his hair out of his face, flicks her hand as if to dust the shoulder of his grimy coat, nods in confirmation and says in a voice that wavers more than he remembers, 'There you are.'

Chapter Thirty-five

Barnard's Inn, Fetter Lane, London

Like a fly buzzing in the far corner of a large room, in the part of his mind reserved for detecting danger to his physical person, Peter Woulfe has been dimly aware all day that something unsettling is afoot in the city.

He woke earlier with a start, his heart thundering in his chest, to a particularly clear vision of the dead lad's face gazing at him. A bad start. He rose and dressed. He prayed. He threw himself into his work. He would brook no distraction. Not from the living, not from the dead.

All day, the city around him has grown louder and more chaotic. Fires roaring, windows breaking, guns firing and people screaming. He has shut his mind to it. Shops and homes being torn asunder. Churches burning. The army summoned. Dead bodies in the streets.

He has a vague sense of what it is all about, gleaned from the porter to whom he half listened as he collected his morning post. It is that all the problems of the world are down to the Catholics in the city of London, ungodly heathens, papists, and that is the root of all that is wrong. He remembers for the first time in a long time that he is a Catholic. Not to himself – no, he is far beyond that now, but certainly to the anti-Catholic mob currently roaming the city.

An unaccustomed sensation of fear scurries through his chest. He moves across the room and checks the large bolts on the door, casts his eye around at the delicate experiments he must protect at all costs.

Even now, he must feed the fires or everything will be ruined, and so he crosses and stoops to the wood basket, feeling a tightness his in lower back that dismays him. He is getting too old to be bending for fuel every day without a boy to help, and it is just as this thought strikes him that the sound of an explosion thunders against his windows.

The air swells and circles. His heart leaps; his ears begin to ring. The unmistakable pattern of flames dancing sets the glass in the windows a-swim. Langdale's distillery next door has exploded.

He turns with horror to look at his room.

His books, his furnaces, his equipment, his notes, his life's work. Dear Lord, it will all go up in smoke. Everything.

He will stay. He will burn alive with it all . . . It is the simplest, purest solution. He stands still in the middle of the room and turns his palms to heaven. Smoke creeps through the floorboards. The flames begin to lick at the window; he can feel the heat rising up from the floor beneath him – feels it on his feet, and on his face as it presses in against the glass.

He looks around again. Perhaps something can be salvaged. He begins to scrabble frantically. He gathers an armful of notes, rushes to his workbench, picks up a sealed glass vessel, attempts to tuck two small jars under his arm . . . before dropping everything on the bench in resignation and racing to the hearth, where he loosens the third stone on the left. It is a large, flat stone, and it conceals a surprisingly deep crevice from which he removes the *Mutus Liber* and a large, weighty black purse. He tucks the book under his arm and ties the purse hastily around his waist, before running to the door.

⁓

Peter Woulfe emerges into Fetter Lane, into a world transformed. The flames from Langdale's distillery soar into the sky. He experiences the sound of thousand men and women shrieking like a hot and furious smack across the face.

He turns back to see Barnard's Inn succumbing to the fire. Everything he once owned will soon be smoke and flame and ash.

He breathes, as breathe he must, and all at once, his head begins to float. The air is no longer merely air – the volatile compounds of Langdale's distillate have been reanimated and diffused through the atmosphere, there to intoxicate any soul who takes a breath. Not that inhalation has been deemed sufficient by the horde of frenzied people crowding Fetter Lane. No, in the midst of the flames, he sees that six or seven large casks have been opened and their contents distributed amongst the crowd.

An incongruous order is prevailing when it comes to the distribution; every single member of the vast crowd appears to have access to the spirits – a sup, a gulp, and the cups are passed along, safe in the knowledge than another will be coming soon, and sure enough, despite the flames, a team is working in the bowels of Langdale's to liberate cask after cask so that there is a steady supply.

He has never seen such red faces – the flames, the excitement, the spirits racing through their veins, bleary-eyed, scarlet-cheeked, demonic – why, some of them are dancing and singing. He can see giddy bedraggled urchins bouncing on their toes, can make out the shape of infants bound to their drunken mother's backs – they are all far too close to the flames.

And just as he opens his mouth to cry out, *take care, that liquid is most flammable!*, a fresh explosion rips through the night. The crowd pauses as if they were one entity, and in the silence that follows, Peter Woulfe hears only his own heart.

Up from the ground spurts a stream of liquid fire, shooting into the air before cascading down to earth and beginning to flow down the street towards him. It is quite extraordinarily beautiful. There is something that has always moved him deeply about the transition from liquid to ether to flame, and here it is made manifest on a scale he could never replicate at his workbench, a vast and magnificent demonstration of volatility, of energy shifting form.

'Oh,' he whispers. 'Oh.'

He steps back slowly against the wall of the Inn, as if he has all the time in the world, and the river of fire flows past him not two feet away.

He sees now that this is how things ought really to be, that this is what God had in mind when he created ether and liquid and fire – this glorious conflagration, this flow of matter and spirit.

As if he is recollecting something he used to know, he sees that this is how things must have been before . . . a long, long time ago, before everything changed, before everything became confined to itself alone, ether to ether, liquid to liquid, flame to flame.

And just as he reaches this point in his thoughts, a flaming figure detaches from the crowd and comes shrieking, swirling down Fetter Lane, dancing in and out of the fiery stream. The figure is magnificent. Peter believes that this flaming, swirling creature has something to say to him – something about the place of the human soul in the flow of energy and matter.

It is a man, or it is a woman – which, he cannot be certain – but surely it is singing a song that holds an ancient truth, if only he can listen closely, if only he can hear what it is saying. And so Peter Woulfe leans in, focuses all of his being on the flaming figure that is approaching him with frenzied speed.

What he sees is a person catastrophically alight. He sees terror-filled eyes, hears not an ancient song but a howl of agony, sees the furious intent of a creature who wants to live. Without thinking, he unfastens his cloak, his long, heavy, unfashionable cloak, and opens his long arms like a crazed matador about to embrace the bull.

He gathers the fiery woman (for he sees now that it is a woman) into the folds of his cloak.

He can feel the heat pushing through the thick fabric; the smell of smouldering cloth fills his nose. He bundles the thrashing woman backwards through the gateway of the Inn, away from the still flowing river of fire. He wrestles her to the ground, the weight of his body pressing her to the cobbles, his long arms engulfing her, his chest compressing her, willing the flames out with all his might, until she ceases to struggle and he feels her fall still, and a sigh of relief escapes him. Surely, the fire beneath the cloak has been extinguished. The once flaming figure lies now inanimate, swathed in black, quite, quite still.

For a dreadful moment, he fears it is the woman herself he has extinguished. So he kneels hurriedly and uncovers her blackened face. He slaps her cheek lightly, and she murmurs. No, not dead. Oh, she is not dead, and she is no longer on fire. It is now that Peter Woulfe feels the first pricklings of pride. He has quite heroically saved this woman. It was quite a selfless act. At personal risk to himself. A good act.

But then, with a sinking heart, he realises he must tend to her burns, or she may die in screeching agony in a day or two. He knows well the care that must be taken in the tending of burns, the time involved – it is quite the last thing he would like to be doing. But do it he will. His jaw stiffens. He will complete this good act, save this woman . . .

And now he begins to worry that she may have been so badly burned that saving her was merely a cruelty. So he gently unwraps the cloak, feels a rush of heat rise up from the body and begins to pat frantically at the charred clothing, lest the introduction of air rekindle the flames.

'Oy, what you doin to 'er? Oy, you leave 'er alone!'

A red-faced man comes rushing towards him, waving his arms, and two more stout fellows follow swiftly behind him.

'Geddoffer! Geddoffer!' shouts the first man as he pushes Peter away from the unconscious woman, so that he falls back on the cobbles. 'What d'you do to her? 'What d'you do?'

He turns to the woman. 'All right, luv?' He shakes her, pinches at her cheek. 'You all right, luv?'

And her eyes open before Peter Woulfe can begin his protest.

'Did he hurt you, did he?'

'I assure you I did not . . .'

'Shut your gob, you – we're having no more of it, can't you see?' The man raises his fierce, bleary eyes, and his gaze burrows into

Peter – he waves his arm to indicate the newly transformed world, the fires, the mob, the spirits freely on tap . . . 'Having no more of it, don't you see?' And the two men with him fold their arms and stare down at Peter, too.

The woman on the ground moans, and in the flurry that follows, the men gather her up, pushing and shoving at Peter Woulfe, who has half risen from the ground. Before he can utter another word, the men have gone back out through the gateway, carrying the woman between them, and he can only shout, 'You must tend to her burns – you must apply salve to her burns, or she might well die!'

He follows them in order to shout this again, louder, clearer, more authoritatively, to make sure that they will heed him – rushes through the gate, pauses by the edge of the fiery river still plunging down Fetter Lane and calls out to their backs, 'You, fellow – you must tend to her burns, or she will die!'

But he may as well, he realises bitterly, be pissing straight into the wind. They have disappeared.

And suddenly cold, he wraps his arms around his chest and shivers despite the hot night. He leans against the rough stone and looks back at the scene at Langdale's. If anything, there are more people, more flames, more crazed dancing in dangerous proximity to the fires. His soul fills with weariness. What can it matter? Good acts or not – surely we are all damned.

Damned and oddly cold – it is now that Peter Woulfe realises his cloak has disappeared with the woman. It is still wrapped around her, and now it has gone God knows where. He looks down at his pale hands clasping his arms across his chest, and everything stops for one terrible moment. The book. He no longer has the book. He was holding it before he saved the woman, but he is not holding it now.

He jumps away from the wall in horror and looks at the ground around him. There is no book there. He races back through the gate way to where he lay the woman on the ground. A human chain of men has begun to pass buckets of water across the courtyard to save what can be saved of the Inn. In the light of the flames, he can see the dreadful truth: there is no book lying on the cobbles. He drops to the ground, onto his hands and knees and looks furiously around. But no matter whether he is standing or kneeling, it is clear – there is no book to be seen.

Peter Woulfe stands and puts a hand to his brow. He hesitates for a moment, then runs back through the gate. The crowd has grown even more chaotic; the fiery river is still flowing – there is barely room to stand. He drops to his knees again and searches frantically on the ground. Within seconds, he finds a rotting head of turnip, three apple cores and an oyster shell – but no book. Someone stands on his left hand; a knee cracks against his ribcage. He stands up with the intention of following the men who carried the woman away. Of course, that is where it must be, in the folds of his cloak, which is wrapped around the wounded woman. He will follow them and reclaim it at any cost.

The crowd surges around him, lifting him right off the ground for a moment. He pushes his way through and retreats to the gateway again to catch his breath. Leaning against the wall, he realises it is no use – he cannot possibly follow them in this crush. He has lost it. He has lost the book. Dear Lord, after all these years. He has lost it.

A wave of horror floods him. His rooms are on fire, and he has lost the book. He stands frozen and looks out at the crazed throng. He cannot think – he cannot move, for now he can only stand and stare. He must be the most unworthy man alive, to be such a careless fool.

Across the street, at the edge of the crowd, two figures pull his attention: an old woman and a young man. They are not crazed – indeed, something in the way they stand together, watching the scene before them speaks of an ease and contentment that is entirely at odds with the chaos around them. There is something oddly familiar about the young man – a stillness in the way he stands, the width of his shoulders, the angle of his head, the way in which he is watching the drama before him with a strangely absent air.

The young man's head turns; his face is caught in the flickering light, and with a shock that goes straight to his knees, Peter Woulfe recognises Mal Burkiss.

In the same moment, Mal Burkiss recognises Peter Woulfe – and before he has time to worry about the consequences of being seen by his former employer, a smile spreads across his face. A fondness he did not know existed surfaces, makes him altogether pleased to see the old fellow.

He raises his hand in greeting.

Peter Woulfe raises his in automatic response.

Mal nods in acknowledgement.

Peter is struck by the unmistakable difference between a ghost and a living person – here, before him, is a living, breathing person. He is not a ghost. He is not twenty yards away. He is manifestly not dead.

Peter stands with his mouth open and his hand still in the air while Mal Burkiss turns and begins to walk slowly away with the old woman at his side.

But he cannot let them go like this, simply walking out of his sight, and so he hurries after them, arms flapping, calling, 'Boy! Boy!'

He sees their curious glance back at him, the two faces turning as one, and knows that their instinct is to take to flight. They begin to walk faster. What should he call out that will not frighten them away altogether?

'Wait, wait!' He thinks about running – he would not catch the boy if he ran, but he would surely be faster than the old woman. But her arm is threaded through Mal's, and they shuffle faster together.

'Wait!'

He sprints as he has not done for years and catches up with them.

'It is that . . .' He pauses to catch his breath . . . He finds he is not at all sure what to say. 'It is that . . . you are quite well?' His hand goes slowly to his own temple. 'Quite . . . well?'

Mal nods slowly; the old woman glares suspiciously. In the silence that follows, Peter finds he has nothing to say. What could he have to say, after all, to this slow-witted boy and his old mother?

'Good. Yes. Good.' His head begins to droop. He has nothing more – nothing more he can say or do.

They turn away, and he feels, for no reason that he can understand, as though his heart might break, as though a sadness that is not his own has come rushing over him as he watches them walk away.

Seeing Mal's slow, deliberate gait, Peter Woulfe remembers how he always placed his feet with such hesitant care when he moved around the room, remembers with a pang how he found it both soothing and irritating by turns.

The old woman beside him is strikingly tiny, shorter than Mal and terribly slight, even in her cloak. She walks along lightly, as if she is barely touching the surface of the ground. For a moment, he imagines that she is a miniature human from a different land altogether – someone who has just come to visit a while and might fly away at any moment. There is something about the way she moves, the way she carries her head, the shape of her back that startles him. It feels both familiar and alien. And deep in the recesses of his mind, a memory of something fragile and precious flickers.

One more moment, he thinks; *wait just one more moment*. He cannot simply let them walk away; he knows there is something more that must be done or said, something to be remembered. But he has no idea what it is.

Quite desperately, he calls again, 'Wait.'

They turn back.

'Here,' says Peter Woulfe. Suddenly inspired, he runs forwards, fumbling with the cord around his waist, and removes the big black purse. 'Here, boy. Take this.' Too heavy to hold with one hand, he proffers it with both outstretched. 'Take it.'

Mal is wide-eyed, uncertain, too slow to respond, and it is the old woman who reaches out and takes the purse, sagging for a moment under the unexpected weight.

He says again, more forcefully, 'Yes, take it.'

And the old woman, letting not one whit of her bewilderment show, nods her thanks, as if it were the most usual thing in the world, and begins to move away, pulling Mal along with her.

Peter, watching them recede into the dark, feels a surge of relief rushing through him.

༄

Peter Woulfe takes a room in the Staple Inn where, despite the noise that continues to rage around Holbourn, he sleeps deep and dreams. He dreams he is naked in a woodland. He does not know if he has recently shed his clothes or has never been clothed, only that the chill kiss of air is welcome on his skin and his unshod feet recognise the earth beneath him.

He awakes plagued by all the important things he has forgotten. He has so much accumulated knowledge – more than any man he knows. And yet he cannot banish this sense that he has forgotten something of the utmost importance. He has an astonishing memory for detail. He remembers so much – the specifics of innumerable classifications, of flora, of fauna and of minerals. Procedures for the most lengthy and complex experiments. The geology, rocks, rivers and soil of the seventeen countries he has visited and explored. The marine life of the two vast oceans he has crossed.

But he has failed to remember something. It could be a face or a story or a particular feeling he once had. His mind falls on his long-dead mother, on his home. He has not thought of his home for many years. He remembers a feeling of homesickness in the distant past and his sense of shrugging it off like an unwelcome hand around his ankle. A thing to hold him back. Something to be free of.

Now, he thinks of the prosperous square house tucked into the foothills of Mount Gabriel on the south-west tip of Ireland, of his childhood bedroom, of his rock collection occupying the three shelves over the bed.

And that is when he decides to go home.

Chapter Thirty-six

Cable Street, London

Sukie and Mal cannot go back to Dan Rutter's shack. Who is to say that the thief-takers will not return? And so, they are starting anew. With a fat bag of coins.

Neither of them knows how to spend it. Mal thinks of plum duffs; Sukie thinks of a place where they could be the right temperature and safe. They take two shabby, overpriced rooms off Cable Street.

Before they have spent even a hundredth of Peter Woulfe's money, Sukie gets a pain in her chest. It is the kind of pain that insists on being yielded to. There is no pushing through, pretending nothing is wrong. It is too big for that, and so she lies in the bed, propped up by pillows. Mal moves about quietly, tending the fire. He is an easy companion to the pain. Just once, she wonders if he will heal her. Should she ask? But she doesn't ask, and anyway, just having him there helps.

After two days the pain subsides, and she is left blank, washed out, light as a feather. Into the new empty space inside her comes a sense that there is something very important she must understand. Yet she has neither the energy nor the focus to pursue any line of thought at all. She is aware most of all of her left hand – her thin, old hand lying on the bed-cover. She finds it astonishing that she should have a hand. That she has lived all these years with this very hand – fingers, nails, wrinkled skin, the bones beneath. She feels a surge of such love and gratitude for it that her eyes begin to water, and her chest begins to ache.

She drifts into sleep and dreams that she is flying, kept aloft by her grip on the smooth glass elbow of an angel.

When she wakes, she tries to tell Mal.

'An angel,' he repeats.

'An angel's elbow,' she corrects him gently, her hand waving gently in the air above the bed-cover. 'A beautiful glass elbow.'

'An elbow?' he says, touching his own elbow slowly.

She is not sure if he has understood, not sure if it matters. She closes her eyes again so that she can see the flame-coloured glass – all bright and alive, delicate but strong, blown from the lips of a god.

He goes to lay a stick on the fire, his mind full of angels and elbows, and when he returns to the bed, he sees for certain what he had begun to suspect – that she is on her way. He takes her hand to wait with her and knows that it will not be long.

Chapter Thirty-seven

Mount Gabriel, Cork, Ireland

It has been thirteen years since Peter Woulfe last made the journey home. By coach to Bristol, by boat across the Irish Sea to the port of Cork and then by horseback over two nights and three days to the square, grey house on the foothills of Mount Gabriel.

That last time, it was to arrive too late to see his mother die or even to help his brothers carry her to her grave. It was to arrive at the strange in-between time after a death, to find his place in something that he had not been part of – to feel at a distance from everyone and everything, even from himself. It was as if he could have been closer to it all, felt it to be more real, if it had been described in one of her letters – if he had been reading about it on his own in his rooms in London. Even standing by her grave, a surprisingly small scar in the graveyard overlooking the sea, the earth not settled enough to take a gravestone yet, he felt no sense of reality. At home, the house was hushed and draughty, and outside the barns and the fields were already Maurice's territory – their father was a full five years' dead by then and Maurice was well used to the reins. Peter Woulfe could see enough to know that he had everything in hand – the glossy cattle, the bustle in the dairy, the whitewashed barns, the air of calm, competence that prevailed. There was no place for him. He could not remember if there had ever really been.

This time, as he rides across the bridge over the estuary, the tide is rising and the midday sun gleams on the shallow water. The soft hump of Mount Gabriel came into his view as he steered left along the curve of Roaringwater Bay an hour ago, but now that he is closer, he cannot see it so clearly. The one winding street of the village rises up ahead of him. He can ride slowly through the village – risk the greetings and meetings and reintroductions that are almost inevitable – or he can take the small, twisting road to his right and cut across the bog path to home. He turns right.

The house is smaller than he remembers – though not in fact small at all. A square, unlovely three-storey house – grey and implacable in the afternoon sun. It is still tucked into the foothills of the mountain, but up close, the mountain, too, is smaller than it has been in his mind all these years. It is all startlingly unfamiliar.

He stands uncertainly at the front door – a door he has used perhaps once or twice in his lifetime – the back door, opening straight into the kitchen, being the usual entry point for family and friends. But he cannot quite bring himself to go round into the cobbled yard, to walk in through the undoubtedly open door and to introduce himself to the unknown women who are undoubtedly in the kitchen – and so he turns the handle, puts his shoulder to the door, which is so stiff he worries for a moment that it is locked, and enters into the front hall.

Inside, the house itself is colder and quieter than he ever remembers it being. The afternoon light behind him catches fine motes of dust drifting up the wide, white stairs. There is an expensive-looking rug on the floor than he does not remember. He instinctively bends to take off his filthy boots. A dog begins to bark, belatedly alerted to his presence, and within moments, he is greeted by Maurice, by Johanna, his thin, formal wife, and by their one pale, quiet son, James.

He is shocked almost to the point of saying it out loud to see that Maurice, who is only seven years older than him, is now an old man, that he has shrunk in height, that he is now inhabiting his skin as if it were a piece of old clothing beginning to sag. He looks around at his relatives, at his old home and thinks, *is this it? Is this all?*

⌒

Later that evening, he resolves to take a walk – so he goes out the back door, up past the pasture and up onto the moor. Once he is out on the moor, he remembers the feel of the place, the particular softness of the air, the bright clarity of the sky, the mountain pulsing beneath his feet as the summer sun awakens the earth.

He is pushing his way through the heather on a gentle rise when he sees the girls crouched low to sup from the stream. As they squat there with their backs rounded under russet shawls, their legs and faces pale in the sunlight, they appear to have emerged out of the earth, mushrooming from their broad feet and stocky calves. They are like nothing so much as the small herd of reddish-brown cattle drinking twenty yards downstream. He remembers in a flash that these lands, wild and lonely in the winter, are populated in summer by the young women and their cattle, up from the lowland pastures to booley for the soft months, to save the winter pastures.

They raise their heads slowly to observe him, and he is not sure now how to greet them; he has been too long in the city, but being clearly within sight on the broad expanse of moorland, it is evident that he must make some acknowledgement, so he raises his hand and nods in a civil manner as he continues along the slight impression in the heather that he has taken for a path. And as the path takes him closer, curving down towards the stream and the girls, he sees their faces more clearly, sees that they are observing him with a collective smirk that has nothing bovine about it.

It is as surprising to him as if the gorse-covered rock behind them were to look him squarely in the eye and wink. And his first thought is that they are mocking him. He wonders if it is his manner of walking, his dress, something about the expression on his face. And so he straightens his shoulders and tilts his chin up, prepares to greet the girls in Irish, so they will know at least that he is not English. He has excellent Spanish, excellent French; he is confident he can dig in his memory for sufficient Irish.

'*Dia dhaoibh*,' he says, finding that his mouth remembers the shape of the words, pleased with his guttural pronunciation.

The girls – ten of them, all certainly of marriageable age – laugh at him unabashedly.

It is not right at all that they should be laughing at him. Peter Woulfe resolves to pay them no more heed and pass them by.

But his path takes him right into their midst, where they begin to stir slowly, their bright faces much closer than is comfortable.

They are sisters or perhaps cousins, all alike in the way of these close-knit rural populations – the one closest to him with red-gold hair glinting in the sun, sky-blue eyes and plump, bright lips moist from the stream. The others have variations on the same tones, as though some have received a drop more or less of the essential colouring. They are all unsettlingly familiar to him.

They laugh again.

He turns to shoo them away . . . 'Wwssshhh, away with you,' he says, reminding himself of his mother, years ago, with the geese.

But they simply laugh at him, pause when he pauses, move forwards when he does, and step nimbly back as one when he takes a frustrated step towards them.

It must be that they do not know who he is. Not only is he much older than them, and a man – he is also a Woulfe. If he met them in the village or down by the house, they would surely not treat him like this. There would be head-bowing and respectful murmurs. But now he remembers how, as a boy, he stayed away from these slopes during the summer – his family with their large expanse of pasture having no need to booley, his father accepting the commoner's ancestral right to graze this wild and rocky land – so that, when the girls and their cattle arrived in May, there was no place for him on this part of the mountain.

But it is too late now; he is on his way, and he cannot turn back. No, what he does instead is alter his course, one, two long strides, and he is now heading up a steep slope away from the girls and towards the Dane works. And checking quickly behind him he sees they have not followed.

The Dane works. He has not thought of them for years. The old mines. Places he remembers as gaps in the earth you could fall into, holes that would swallow you up.

As a child, he was scared away by the fairies who were said to live there, by his mother's stories of what the fairies had done to people who disturbed them. The good people who had retreated underground in ancient times, where they lived in splendour, danced and sang surrounded by vast quantities of gold. You might meet them and speak to them, but it was generally agreed that the risks of dealing with them were too great – they might promise you riches but take away your very soul. Time was different with them, too, so they could steal you away and send you back as an old man when everyone you loved was dead. He had believed it absolutely then.

But now, coming up to the dank hole in the earth, the primitive copper mine with the spoil heaps of shattered stone in front, he lays his hand on the wet wall, aghast – how could this have been here all along, not half a mile from his house? A mine with ore to yield. While he has been wandering so far away, gathering specimens in other countries, blasting foreign rock. A copper mine here on this very mountain.

His mind begins to whirr – surely now, with new techniques, he could blast deeper into this mine, support the shaft more effectively, extract much more ore.

He crouches and enters the cave. He can see where the last fire to have been lit here was set. There are sodden ancient sticks lying in a heap – so black, so soft, as if they are trying to return to soil as soon as possible.

Picking up a stick, he thinks of the hand that spliced this oak – so very long ago that he feels a plunging sensation in his belly. Who lit this fire? And it is pale, boyish hands he sees in his mind's eye – delicate, long-fingered hands laying a fire with care, bringing it to life with loving intent. A shiver runs through him. It is cold in the cave, even this evening with the sun shining, and he feels it must have been colder then – here in this cave with the slick damp and the grey drear. And the poor boy lighting the fire one morning, kindling sparks in the belly of a sodden hill. Perhaps he was from a far-away, hot place – and so felt the cold more keenly.

And he shakes his head to free it from the image of the boy. It was probably not a boy at all. It was long ago; it is not his fault, not his business.

He can hear his father's herdsman, Padeen, saying, with his head jerking back over his shoulder, 'That all happened in auld God's time. In auld God's time.' And as a boy he had wondered at the way Padeen said it – as if it were well known that there was a time before this god, when another god held sway, a time so long ago there is no point in Peter Woulfe trying to understand it. That was what he took it to mean: *leave it alone; there's no sense in bothering with it.*

But now, a man, fully grown, standing here alone, he wonders about Padeen's auld God and whether it was auld God or new God who looked down when this fire was set, when these stones were crushed. And if there was a god looking over that god's shoulder and one before that one, too.

It strikes him like a blow between the eyes that Padeen must indeed have seen it like that, and believed it to be true. And Bridey Leary – he hasn't thought about Bridey for forty years – is that what she saw, too, a long line of gods peering over each other's shoulders? The thought makes him dizzy, and a light wind stirs outside the cave. He closes his eyes and sees not gods but a lengthy line of Brideys stretching back into the past, each one brighter and younger than the one ahead of her, until, God forgive him, he sees that she is almost naked and so luminous it hurts his mind.

And again, he shakes his head – it is not only blasphemy but madness that threatens him now.

He steps out onto the open mountainside to take a breath and is shocked to discover that the sun has begun to dip below the hills. He must have lost an hour; he was sure he had time for a good stretch before nightfall on this long summer day.

He would not like to admit it to himself, but he does not want to be out here alone as the day darkens. He is unsettled; his heart is low and confused, and he makes his way as quickly as he dares down the awkward slope. He hears the fire before he sees it, a vast, great crackling bonfire, and as he comes cautiously over the rise, it flares below him. It is attended by the booley girls – why, they must have been gathering firing for weeks to get this blaze going. They are excited, their high voices rising with the sparks into the darkening sky.

One of the girls flings a large branch of pine on the fire, and the great resulting *whoosh* causes them all to laugh. Out of the laughter comes song, a song that to Peter Woulfe, standing on the hill behind them, sounds wild and discordant and dangerous. They sing loud and unabashed, and a rhythm emerges from their feet; they begin to stamp in time and raise their arms, until one of the girls – with a whoop and a wriggle – discards her shawl and her blouse and presents her pale breasts to the flame-lit air. The others swiftly follow her lead, and Peter Woulfe, both dismayed and aroused, can tell from the casual ease with which they shed their clothes that this is not the first time they have done so – no, indeed, they must do it all the time when they are up here alone and free on these soft, summer nights.

And he does not know what to do. They are in his way; he could go round, but it would be a fierce scramble through the gorse and the thick brambles along the uneven ground – and he can barely see his feet now. He resolves to wait – he won't watch; he turns his head away – he can just wait. But the singing builds in volume and the pull of the fire proves too much for him; his eyes return in time to see the girls begin to slip off their skirts, so that within minutes, they are all buck naked and whooping like savages.

And they do not look stocky at all now; they are much taller in the firelight – tall and curved and luscious, their hair flowing free and bright, their skin glowing like pears, like peaches – soft, ripe fruit whose juice would drip down your face after the first bite.

Dear God, dear God, it is altogether too much for him. If he had a gun, he would be inclined to shout out and let off a few shots. It is too much for him, this wildness, this nakedness, this crazed world of female wickedness – for that is what it looks

like to him, watching from above: sheer unrestrained wickedness. There is nothing to keep them in check – to be sure, he
felt powerless enough during the earlier encounter, and that was
when they had their clothes on. Now, there is no telling what
they might do – there are ten of them and one of him – could
they tear him apart with their bare, frenzied hands?

And as he watches, two of the girls come closer together, their
bodies touching, their dance slowing, moving together in perfect
unison, their bodies merging until he cannot tell one from the other.
A weakness comes over him, and he sits down, despite the gorse
pricking through his heavy breeches. He sits with his arms wrapped
around his knees and discovers that he can barely keep his eyes open.
His heavy eyelids begin to close. But even with his eyes closed, he
sees the girls dancing, singing, moving together in slow, deliberate
passion. He sees the fire burning – the gorse, the heather, the peaty
soil, the air round them, all seeming to undulate with them.

∽

Shortly after sunrise the next morning, he walks unsteadily into
the kitchen, where a young woman whose name he has forgotten
is cooking breakfast for the farmhands. He is deeply relieved to see
that she is fully clothed and that her hair is neatly back in a bun.

After he wishes her good morning, he says to her, as if it is a
matter of nothing much at all, 'Those girls at the booleying above –
now, what townlands would they be from at all?'

And she says, with a quick, keen glance at him, 'At the booley,
Mr Woulfe? Why, there has been no booleying up above this past
twenty years since your father claimed it for the sheep.'

∽

Peter Woulfe lies exhausted and wakeful in his bed and thinks of
Bridey Leary asleep over the hill, a thin blanket of soil over her and

no headstone. And what of it? He could find her yet. He knows well that there is a place for every dead person here and someone to remember that place. He could surely find her. And when he finds her, what will he do? He will ask her the questions he should have her asked a long time ago.

What, he should have asked, *is your power? And how can it be learned?*

He imagines himself bent towards the earth, asking these questions in a whisper. He imagines himself getting the answers. Stranger things have happened. It appeals to him now, in this moment, the idea of this wisdom rising softly from the damp earth of his homeland, from the old bones beneath.

Aggie Connors. That is her name, the girl in the kitchen. He will ask her.

He goes down into the reek of spices and pig blood, where they are stirring up the black pudding, and he asks Aggie, 'Where is old Bridey Leary from the cabin up above buried?'

But Aggie, for the second time that day, has the better of Mr Woulfe and tries not to show it. 'Buried, Mr Woulfe? They couldn't bury her yet, what with her living still.'

And Peter Woulfe says impatiently, 'No Bridey *Leary*,' realising he has been too long away to put the correct accent on the first syllable. '*Lair*-eey . . . *Lair*-eey. The old woman from up above in the little cabin . . . beneath the top field. She died' – he pauses; it was after his father died, all right, for he remembers her alive then, but perhaps before his mother – 'fifteen or twenty years ago.'

Aggie's lip juts out. 'Beg your pardon, sir, but she did not. What with her being alive this very day.' He shakes his head and opens his mouth to speak, but Aggie takes her chance and points at a can drying by the sink. 'Didn't I bring her that very can full of porridge this very morning?' She adds for good measure, 'Myself.'

Chapter Thirty-eight

August 1780 – *Lughnasa*

Mount Gabriel, Cork, Ireland

Someone has whitewashed the walls of the cabin, and Peter Woulfe can see as he approaches that the thatch on the roof has been patched recently. But there is grass right up to the door, dandelions sprouting bright and ragged, and a vigorous clump of nettles growing under the window. There are no hens scratching, no cat to be seen, and the place has an air of being both tended and desolate.

Peter pauses at the door – it has been painted green, but not this year or last year, and it is beginning to flake. It is pulled shut, both top and bottom, no half swing of welcome, shut against whatever draft there may be, even on this sunny August morning. His stomach flares with anxiety. She is so old she must be cold all the time. He considers turning away. A kindly visit to this old tenant of his father's. It is the right thing to do, no doubt. But is it necessary?

He could tell himself she is asleep, that it is better not to disturb her. Indeed, she must be so immensely old that it is hard to imagine she ever fully wakes – so old that he finds it embarrassing to contemplate. What could be left of her? He thinks of bones in an old sack. She may not know him at all – she may be blind, deaf, her wits gone astray, and then what would be the point of calling in? He would only disturb her, agitate her, cause unnecessary distress, and for what? She has gone this long without a visit from him – what difference could it make now? To her, or to him? This notion he had in the early morning that she might have something to say that he needed to hear seems foolish now. There could be nothing for him here. Nothing but embarrassment at human frailty. So, it would be simply a kindness. Simply that.

He would never come to her door without something for her, and so in his pocket he has put a small phial of lavender oil from his toiletry case. A trip to the kitchen to ask for food, to have it wrapped, to carry it away, felt beyond him. The oil is high quality; it is of significant value. He distilled himself – it would be costly to buy even in London, impossible to purchase here. It is an outrageous gift to bring a dying peasant woman in the middle of nowhere. But it is what he thought of bringing, and so he has brought it. Hand in his pocket, he rubs the phial between his fingers as he hesitates at the door. He would like to turn away, but instead he pulls the door open and ducks his head.

It is dark within; very little of the daylight penetrates the deep-set windows. He must keep his head bent slightly to avoid the beams. There is a fire glowing in the hearth, but there is no other movement that he can make out.

In his agitation he forgot to call out before he came in, to say, *good morning*, to call, *Bridey?* He didn't even give a knock. So now he is here, half blinded in the dim room, unannounced, afraid to shout lest he wake her.

So, he whispers, 'Bridey?' as he steps further into the room. There is no reply. He is far too big for the room. His head brushes the beams; his wide shoulders, his feet, even his hands are out of scale.

There is a red settle he does not remember standing against the wall by the fire. As his eyes begin to adjust, he can just make out blankets on the settle and a shape beneath them, a shape so slight and insignificant that it could be nothing or it could be a very old woman gone slight as a bird in her deathbed. The air smells of must and turf, and there is a metallic tang that catches the back of his throat.

He stands still, and the thought strikes him that he could be the one to find her dead – why not this morning rather than any other morning? It is as likely as not. He steps closer to the settle, stretches out a tentative hand towards the blankets. His fingers brush against the rough wool; his heart is pounding in his chest.

'Ce ata ann?'

The voice comes from behind him; he straightens up, like a thief caught, and cracks his head on the beam above. Bright sparks fill his vision; both hands fly to his skull. It is impossibly painful. He has surely broken his head.

The voice behind him speaks again. 'Ce ata ann?'

He cannot think. His eyes are streaming; his ears are ringing. The sound behind him could be a question or the call of a startled crow.

He turns carefully, head in hands, to see the shape of a woman standing just inside the door with the daylight at her back.

She makes another sound. It is a question. 'Ce thusa?'

His brain has surely been dislodged in his skull. It takes an eternity for him to remember. 'Peter, Peter Woulfe.'

The woman says nothing; he cannot see her face.

So, he repeats slowly, 'Peter, Peter Woulfe.' He feels the words unfamiliar in his mouth, is unsure that he has used the right language, the right sounds.

He is opening his mouth to try again when the woman speaks. 'Now, which Peter, Peter Woulfe, would that be?'

And the full sentence, the rhythm of the speech, the tone, which could equally be mocking or curious, knowing or unknowing, reveals her. There is no one else who speaks just like – so that the same handful of words could be caress or a slap, an answer or a question.

'Bridey.' He hesitates – should he clarify that he is not his brother's son or his father's nephew? – before saying, 'It's me, Petey, come home from London to visit awhile.' And then he says, 'Is mise.'

She steps closer. She is more hunched about the shoulders, to be sure, but she is light and steady on her feet. Another step brings her closer again, and she looks up at him. His eyes begin to clear. It is the same face, with the same bright eyes, the same strong nose, the same sure jut of chin. The lines around her eyes and mouth are so

deep that you could slip a penny in them; the skin has darkened to a
deep, leathery tan, the forehead now creviced with three horizontal
slashes.

'Well now, isn't that fine.'

He looks down at her face with the naturalist's sense of wonder. Indeed, for a moment, with his head aching and his heart
pounding, with his words and thoughts unmoored, he forgets
that it is a face at all, and he looks at her as he would look at a
dried-out riverbed, or at the layers of ancient sediment in a seam
of sandstone. There is history here to be read. There is a process
to be understood – the patterning of water moving, the upsurge
of bedrock twisting and buckling an impossibly long time ago. It
is all there, if only he could study it long enough.

She speaks again. 'Back awhile.' And this time the words are
clearer to him. 'And you gone so long.'

He understands the words – but it cannot have been that long
ago since they were here together before, in this same cabin, with
the same fire lit, and it is surely the same cloak she is wearing.

'Sit yourself down. Sit down, sit down, and we'll have a sup.'

He backs towards the settle and puts his hand down to test the
blankets – there is nothing underneath, nothing at all, only the
blankets hunched up. He shifts them aside and sits cautiously as if
the settle might break beneath him, and indeed it creaks as it takes
his weight. His knees ride up higher than the bench; his large feet
splay out in front of him.

Bridey moves slowly but surely, steady on her feet but more careful than he remembers. She goes towards the hearth, bends to take
the poker, stokes up the fire and swings the pot in over the flame.
As he watches, he has a dizzying sense of inevitability – her movements are so certain, so deliberate. Watching her, he understands
that this particular fire must be stoked, with this poker, that this
is the moment in which to stoke it and no other. This pot is to be
swung, in just this manner, over this fire and no other – as if Bridey
and the fire and the poker and the pot were all inevitable, laid out

to unfold like this from the time of the first fire and the first pot and the first woman tending a fire.

Bridey looks over at him on the settle. He has his right hand pressed to the crown of his head, and even with his grown-man skin, weathered by fifty-four years of life and the sun of three continents, he looks as pale as a little boy.

She says, 'You hit your head a right crack there.' And then she laughs as though she has told a joke.

He smiles at her joke, then winces, and repeats carefully, as if he is learning the words for the first time, 'A right crack.'

Bridey comes close and peers down. 'Bend over, and let me see what you've done.'

Obediently, he dips his head and leans forwards.

'Tut tut tut tut tut.' She clicks her tongue against her teeth, a sound that is all at once soft and sharp, disapproving and soothing. 'You're bleeding like a pig.'

And he looks at his hands and understands that they are wet and sticky and that what he can feel running down his neck and dribbling from his right ear is his own blood.

Her head jerks up to indicate the beams above. 'You must have hit the hanging nail.' She looks back at him severely.

He looks up – he can just make out the shape of a stubby nail jutting out from the beam. Should he have known, he wonders, that that is where her hanging nail is, where it has probably always been? On the beam between the wall and the fireplace, just where she might hang herbs to dry or a lantern at night. Was that his mistake?

'Mind now – mind you don't bleed on the good blanket.'

And he shifts along immediately, away from the blankets.

She moves away from him, and he closes his eyes. When he opens them again, she is standing with large tin bowl in the crook of her arm and a bit of sacking in her hand.

'Throw this around your shoulders. Bend your head.'

He pulls the sacking around his shoulders, holds the two ends tight in one fist, and bends his head. He feels her fingers carefully parting his hair and the soft wet swirl of a cloth running over his scalp, cold water joining with the blood to drip past his ear. She is gentle and rhythmical; the cloth swirls and is dipped in the bowl, swirls and is dipped in the bowl. He hears the water running out of the cloth. In his mind's eye, he sees her old hand squeezing the cloth tight, sees the blood colouring the water. The cloth comes down around his neck, behind his ears, in a swift, firm motion – once, twice, three times – and is squeezed and returned, this time more firmly to the crown of his head.

'Put your hand up now, and press down on that.'

She moves away, and he presses down hard, conscious that he must keep whatever blood remains to him in his head. She is gone out the door; he is alone in the room, with his heartbeat, and the pain building in his head. He closes his eyes and leans back against the settle. He can hear the fire and wonders when the pot will boil.

He is not sure how long she has been gone; he can feel the blood soaking into the cloth. Will she be back in time with her bowl and her water so that it can be wrung dry and applied again, or must he sit here and let it drip down?

It is a minor wound, he knows. The cut will heal; the head will ache. He will have forgotten it in a week, but all the same, he can feel something slipping away with the blood, some part of his life force that could just slip away and not come back. And he feels he could sit here by this fire, let his hand drop down, and just let it go.

The pot boils. She is still gone. He stands awkwardly, swings the pot away from the flame, then sits back on the settle. Despite the pressure he is applying, the cloth is quite soaked through. How long has she been gone? The length of a pot boiling, the length of time it takes half the blood in his head to soak into a small, damp cloth.

And then she is back, slow and deliberate, moving across the room towards him, to stand in front of him with her hands cupped before her, holding an earthy mass of damp moss. She squeezes it, her two hands working together rhythmically, making a soft squelching sound, and the smell of earth rises into the air. He understands before she says it that he must dip his head again, but this time he doesn't want to.

'Bend your head.'

He looks up, but her hood is up, and he can't see her eyes. He can see the outline of her in the light from the window behind her – the fall of her cloak, the crags and folds. He is suddenly frightened, not by his wound, not by the earth in her hands, but by the shape of the old woman before him. It is her stance more than anything that strikes fear into him – her wide, angular shoulders, her two feet planted firm on the floor, her hands moving in front of her. It is so unlikely that she should be standing here like this, alive and not dead. It is far more likely that she is really dead under the blanket and that he is dreaming.

'Bend your head,' she repeats, less patiently, and he realises it is all one to her whether he bends it or not. If he does not, she will turn away and drop what is in her hands into the scrap bucket by the table. Within seconds, she will turn away and he will hear the soft plop of damp moss hitting tin. He could stand and walk back to the house with his hand on his head to find some padding and a better cloth. For a moment, he thinks he has already stood up, bid her good day and started walking.

It is up to him, he realises. He can bend his head or not as he wishes; it matters not a whit to anyone else.

He bends, lets his hand holding the bloody cloth fall away from his head. Her hands move upwards; he feels the moss, cool and soft on his scalp. Moments ago, she could have turned away, but now that she has not turned away and is pressing the moss onto his wound, he feels the full force of her presence. She is nowhere else. Her old hands move purposefully and carefully. The moss is cooling and immediately soothing.

She produces a strip of cloth from within her cloak and brings it across the top of his head and down under his chin and then around again, before tucking the loose end in over his left ear. Then she pauses with her hands in mid-air to look at her work.

'Hmmm . . . you'll do well enough. Well enough.'

His head aches less already; he no longer feels that part of him is slipping away. He understands that she has sealed the wound, has held him together so that he will last intact another day. And that is enough for now. He feels a surge of gratitude. It is more than enough; it is more than anyone could ever ask for, and she has done it for him. He thinks of the lavender oil in his pocket, an extravagant gift, but no longer enough.

'Thank you,' he whispers.

But there is more; she places both hands gently on the top of his head and lets them rest there. There is no need for it, the bandage is secure; the wound is sealed. Her hands are just the right weight, resting delicately – as if something airborne has landed to visit awhile.

'Thank you,' he says again. His throat has tightened; he realises there are tears in his eyes.

She says nothing, but her hands remain where they are. It is not necessary. It is more than he deserves. He is aware of his heart in his chest.

And now he understands. This is her gift to him. It is love. It is freely given, and nothing is expected in return.

The Mountain's Song

I too was once molten with passion
surging up on a bed of fire
my mouth open wide
the fierce thud of my veins leaping out of my skin
the glistening salts of my body forming again and again
for the tongue of the wind to lick

and anything at all was possible

I took in the wind and the rain
the sea and the soil
the hot kiss of the sun
gathered it all in upon myself
rising and writhing
the force of my fire forging

There was nothing I could not encompass

Time was different then
it was slow
and it was fast
form was different then
there was nothing I could not become

But I settled on this shape
curving up from the lap of the sea
a fine, fat arse of plenty
lush thighs reclining
my fire tucked away in my depths

I brought forth trees and insects and animals
there was sheer bliss for me in the burst of leaf
the slow plunge of roots, the sharp snap of jaws

I lived and loved like this for aeons – forever and for one flash
of star-time

I bred fairy folk and dreamers
formed their bones, their teeth, the rich red blood pulsing in their veins
I shaped them from myself
folk who knew how to be sung by me
folk who ate and loved, laughed and wept, birthed and grieved with me
and I took them back into myself when they died
folded my arms around them
fierce and tender like a mother welcoming a lost child

I knew them all
and I know you

I know you

The taste of your blood
the heft of your bone
the cut of your teeth

Every hair on your head

And you know me

You know I was wronged by the theft of my trees
wounded by the slashes on my flank where man after man took my ore
to make himself feel big
but their lust was for the wrong thing
they stole the wrong treasure altogether

I'd have shared my wealth with them freely
I'd have made them as big as the night sky
if only they had asked the right questions in the right way
but they were looking for the wrong secrets
so they made themselves nothing but small and soul-broken

And they left me worn down, bone tired, drier than chaff
a fire scalded old hag, robbed blind
a balding, bristle-chinned scold with her pockets turned out

I am still healing
and I will heal in one short flash of star-time
Because I am ancient and I am new

I am seed rich, womb warm, blood red, ready to pulse again
I am future and past, I am here and I am now

So what then, has been lost?

What has been lost?

It is you

You have been lost

It is you

It is your feet on my earth – your heart beating like a bird
resting in my cupped palms
it is the kiss of your breath rising
into the morning mist

That is what has been lost

It is you

you can choose to forget
but if you don't remember
you will always be poor and lost
and full of fear

So listen
because when this song is sung and sung and sung
again
it will lose its anger and its sorrow

the kernel unfurled is so simple
the secret so easily available
that it will become as light as a child's game of feathers and
leaves
intricate on the ground
traced and retraced throughout the long summer evening
and left for the wind to take away before morning.

Author's Note

What is the perfect amount of information to have about a real-life historical figure around whom you want to weave a fictional story?

In the case of Peter Woulfe, real-life chemist, inventor of the Woulfe bottle and Fellow of the Royal Society, I started off knowing very little – which was ideal for my purposes of letting my imagination run riot. I had read that he was gifted and eccentric, that he sometimes invited a select group of people to breakfast at 4am in his rooms in Barnard's Inn to which admittance was granted by means of secret handshake. One visitor reported that Woulfe's rooms were so chaotically cluttered that when he visited, he put down his hat for a moment and never found it again. Peter Woulfe's cure for ill health was to take a bone-jolting coach ride from London to Edinburgh and back. The gem of information that really got me interested was in the account of the items auctioned after Woulfe's death – amongst the paraphernalia for sale it was reported that some of the apparatus had little notes attached, they were handwritten messages and prayers – 'invocations' – to the angels. It was this piece of information more than anything that made me want to invent a story around Peter Woulfe. I loved the image of a highly intelligent, educated scientist secretly invoking the help of unseen spirits. He is described in one source as 'The last true alchemist.' And living as he did in the middle of the Enlightenment, it seemed to me that he was particularly well placed to dance between the arcane wisdom of the ancients and the new scientific thinking that was spreading throughout Europe. He was also an Irishman living in England, someone from the periphery with all the additional, angular perspective that that can bring. I have cherry picked some of the facts available about Peter Woulfe's life as a framework for this novel and invented almost all of what happened within that.

The biggest liberty I have taken with his biography is that I have caused my fictional Peter to be born in West Cork, not Co. Clare like his historical counterpart. That is because I wanted to write about the unseen spirits of the landscape that I was living in – and the central impulse to research Irish alchemists in the first place came from a desire to understand more about the ancient copper mines on Mount Gabriel here in West Cork and the efforts of people over thousands of years to extract precious minerals from the earth. On a bright day here with the sun hitting the mountain and the sea stretching off into the horizon it is hard to imagine that any precious mineral, or any experimental alchemical process, could be as wonderful as the alchemy of the living landscape right under our feet. I allowed my fictional Peter Woulfe to be born here so that I could explore the relationship between the people, the landscape, the precious minerals and the unseen spirits of this place – it allowed me to give him the magical heritage of an eccentric and extremely clever scientist who also believed in angels.

Sukie, Katia and Nico, Bridie, Mal, Danby Scott and Robert Perle are all products of my imagination with no counterparts in the historical record.

Emmanuel Swedenborg is very much in the historical record – another fascinating example of a man who was at the cutting edge of scientific progress in his field (metallurgy and mining) while secretly plunging deeply into mysticism and writing extensively about his communications with the angelic orders. I was delighted to realise that I could let Peter Woulfe and Swedenborg meet in London in 1744. Swedenborg was in fact in London that summer and is recorded as having taken off all his clothes and run into the streets talking to the angels in the midst of what could variously be described as a psychotic break or perhaps a spiritual emergency.

During the Gordon riots of 1780 part of Barnard's Inn was destroyed when the distillery next door exploded – a fact that provided the inspiration for the final section of the book.

The *Mutus Liber* or *Mute Book* is a real book. First printed in 1677, it has long been famous in alchemical circles for its mysterious authorship and its even more mysterious contents. It has meant a lot of different things to a lot of people over the centuries – including Carl Jung who owned a copy – and so I very much enjoyed using it as a catalyst in my plot and allowing it to mean very different things to my fictional characters.

Acknowledgements

It took an embarrassing length of time to write this book, and during that embarrassing length of time I tested the patience of my nearest and dearest in many, many ways. First of all, I talked about it all the time – thinking that everything that happened anywhere in the world to anyone at all was somehow linked to something in my book, if only I could have five more minutes to explain how. I am hoping that this kind of trying behaviour is at its worst with the first novel and will improve from here on in.

Not only did I bore my friends and family rigid, I also put a shocking amount of time and effort into writing this book that could, and arguably should, have been spent making money to help support my young family or cleaning the house or growing vegetables or making dinner or being a good sister, daughter, friend, and neighbour . . . even sorting socks would have been more tangibly useful than many of the hours I spent staring at my laptop 'writing' and God knows the socks never did get sorted . . . this is slightly funny but also slightly serious – almost every writer, and certainly every first time novelist is writing from a time/money/patience overdraft that is usually drawn on the account of loved ones who are in one way or another facilitating the diversion of this precious time, money and patience into a nebulous creative enterprise that may or may not bear as much as a bite of fruit in the end. My loving and patient wife Iseult has borne the brunt of this in my case and provided gargantuan amounts of support, without which there is no way I could have seen this book through to the end. In fact, without her encouragement, I would never even have started it.

I would like to acknowledge the unfailing support of my sister, Eve O'Donnell, who has shown up time and time again to support me and my family with so much love and patience.

Thank you to Helen Ennis and Eithne Ní Mhurchú, who have been stalwart friends and family of choice, offering support and unflagging kindness through thick and thin.

Thank you to Mary Doorley for a serendipitous and lovely, literary friendship that has come down the generations, a full 60 years from reading Chekov in Rathmines with Mum, to reading *Sparks of Bright Matter* in Dunmanway.

Thanks to Jamie McCarthy Fisher who read the very earliest draft with great patience and has offered encouragement throughout. Much gratitude to Christine Breen who provided skilled editorial input and faith in the book at a critical juncture, and to Niall Williams, whose support and belief in my writing has been a beacon on hopeless days.

Thank you to Riann Coulter, early reader, true friend and unflagging cheerleader for my writing, who has offered endless encouragement and steadfast belief in me when I most doubted myself.

Thank you to my old friends Kevin Murphy, Claire Ewing and Lynn Scarff who read alternative beginnings and then all responded with completely conflicting advice – which turned out to be extremely helpful in the end.

Thanks to all at Blake Friedman – Samuel Hodder, who found *Sparks* in his submissions pile, helped me bash it into shape and get a publisher before handing me over to the wonderful Sian Ellis-Martin who has been an invaluable champion throughout this process. Thank you too to Isobel Dixon, whose warmth and energy makes me even more grateful to have landed with Blake Friedman.

Thank you to my editor Deirdre Nolan at Eriu who spotted the magic in *Sparks* and has done so much to get it out into the world. And to all at Bonnier Books UK who are working hard to get *Sparks* onto bookshelves. Thanks to my copy editor, Katie Lumsden, who possesses a particular genius for times, dates, places and general narrative coherence.

Loveday and Robin, I don't think I have to thank you for anything in relation to this book – I'm sure we can all agree that if you didn't exist it would have been done and dusted years ago, but luckily you have both turned out to be absolutely awesome (phew!) so the delay was more than worth it.

∽

Thank you finally to the spirits of the landscape here, the human and non-human beings whose stories can be heard if you listen closely. And most especially, thank you to the spirit of Mount Gabriel for allowing me to live and write here.